Message from God:
"Be nice, or I can mess up your wonderful life."

Lani tried to pull me up, and I jerked my arm away

"Stop it. Stop touching me." My own bitchiness drove me to my feet in shock. "God...this is so backward. I'm supposed to be...being nice to *you*."

"Really? Why is that?"

"Because of God."

"Because of *what*?" He could have pushed me down in the gutter and walked away, but he caught me as I swayed into him, and something in my gut spoke loudly. *This guy has heard it all; you cannot weird him out.*

He laughed incredulously, despite that I leaned on him to where I think most people would have been panicking. He asked, "Do I look like some sort of a charity case?"

I groped through my dizzy head for something not weird or rude. "You just look new around here."

He didn't say anything else, but every few seconds he would chuckle, like I had said something so funny he could hardly stand it. I paid him no mind, just managed to glance over my shoulder once or twice to make sure my friends weren't coming to see Lani Garver half carrying me into the sunset.

Praise for *What Happened to Lani Garver*

"Carol Plum-Ucci writes like an angel. Smart, funny, irreverent, yet masterful. I liked this book even better than *The Body of Christopher Creed,* which I loved."

> —Terry Trueman, author of *Stuck in Neutral,*
> a Michael L. Printz Award Honor Book

"Intense and riveting; I sat down to read *What Happened to Lani Garver* and didn't stop until I'd read the very last word. An important and honest story, worth a second and even a third read."

> —Han Nolan, author of *Dancing on the Edge,*
> winner of the National Book Award

"This novel should cement [Plum-Ucci's] reputation as a writer whose stories keep readers turning pages and whose books contain a mystery that lingers long after the last page."

> —*VOYA*

What Happened to Lani Garver

CAROL PLUM-UCCI

Harcourt, Inc.

Orlando   Austin   New York
San Diego   Toronto   London

www.HarcourtBooks.com

First Harcourt paperback edition 2004

The Library of Congress has cataloged the hardcover edition as follows:
Plum-Ucci, Carol.
What happened to Lani Garver/Carol Plum-Ucci.
p. cm.
Summary: Sixteen-year-old Claire is unable to face her fears about a
recurrence of her leukemia, her eating disorder, her need to fit in with the
popular crowd on Hackett Island, and her mother's alcoholism until the
enigmatic Lani Garver helps her get control of her life at the risk of his own.
[1. Emotional problems—Fiction.   2. Homosexuality—Fiction.
3. Cancer—Patients—Fiction.   4. Prejudices—Fiction.
5. Alcoholism—Fiction.   6. Islands—Fiction.]   I. Title.
PZ7.P7323Wh   2002
[Fic]—dc21   2002000051
ISBN 0-15-216813-3
ISBN 0-15-205088-4 pb

Text set in Sabon
Display set in Belucian
Designed by Cathy Riggs

A C E G H F D B
Printed in the United States of America

To Harriet, C. S., Corrie,
Sarah Ellen, and Rick.
Thank you.

Acknowledgments

My thanks go to many people who took time from life's incessant business to lay some information on me:

Thanks, Steve Hodsdon, flight paramedic of Virtual Health of South Jersey, for information (disgusting) on head wounds and emergency room procedures. (I've no stomach for the stuff, Steve; your stomach was appreciated.)

Dr. Nina Stolzenberg, thanks much for giving me gritty, up-to-date research on post-traumatic stress disorder among juvenile cancer patients and their families. You gave me a lot to work with. Julie Still, Rutgers Camden librarian, thanks for guiding me through labyrinths of info on group hysteria, defense mechanisms, and convenient recollection as specifically pertains to preconceived prejudice. You guys are good friends and search-engine gurus extraordinaire.

Thank you, Dr. Bill Whitlow, psychologist, Rutgers State University, for helping me understand your very intriguing research on the unreliable state of memory when faced with the unexpected. Thanks also for your helpful insights concerning convenient recollection and group hysteria. And you are, as the faculty warned, a truly nice guy!

Thanks, Stephanie Ucci, my favorite high school "consultant," for accuracy in current high school buzz words (I would never have described a boy as a "hottie," and still don't like it, but...*vhat*-ever you say, dahling). Thanks, Ellen Zolkos, for giving me your years from the Creative and Performing Arts High School of Philly in such grand, open-book format. You are a way-trusting daughter; I owe you many lunches. Thanks, Rodd Zolkos; you are a walking encyclopedia of rock 'n' roll trivia, and I hope you write the book someday.

Thanks to my editor at Harcourt, Karen Grove, for driving a hard bargain and not letting my laziness get in the way of your perfection. I want to be you when I grow up.

And finally, to my suspected angel, who wishes to remain unnamed...thanks for opening the doors so I could hear the cries of anguish of so many people like Lani. I have enjoyed marveling with you how Lani turned out to be nothing like you. Maybe we can call ourselves Dr. Frankenstein and Igor, giggling over a subject who arose with a little more grace in his/her countenance.

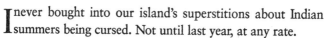

I never bought into our island's superstitions about Indian summers being cursed. Not until last year, at any rate.

Indian summer is a period from three to five days in the late fall when the weather turns hot like summer again. According to island legend, if an Indian summer falls in October, it brings good luck. If one falls in November, it brings a curse. I'm a Hackett native (meaning "born and raised here," as opposed to meaning "savage") and most of us natives have no use for legends or curses or stories requiring big imaginations. These stories get stirred up among the summer tourists, who think the island and all its fog are very romantic.

Our parents cluck about the summer people having too much money and too much downtime, and how they need an excuse to close up their summer homes and stop doing weekends after mid-October. If they didn't find a good curse or legend, they would just stay, and then they couldn't make all their rich-people money back in Philadelphia.

It is true that almost every year, during October or November, there comes a time when we can wear our shorts and Reefs and lay out in the front yards with a bunch of friends and get one final tan. And it's true that out of nowhere the wind will kick up, and everyone on the island will scramble for winter parkas. If ever we bought into the curse legend at all, it was because Indian summer days in November are followed by an outrageous ice storm lots of times, which is a pain in the ass because ice is a winter problem and all Hackett's money goes to fix summer problems, like beach erosion.

I have heard a few islanders muttering about curses, though—when frozen pipes burst and sewers back up and the drawbridges to the mainland mall are closed on a Saturday. But it's what happened when Lani Garver showed up that made me look at the curse theory again. It was during an Indian summer spell in early November that Lani Garver first came to Hackett. And in the frosty, windy, fogless hours between Indian summer and an impending ice storm, I watched a bunch of guys try to drown him. I watched Lani sink in the murky waters of the harbor, and I never saw him resurface.

Even after Indian summer passes, some nights are warm, and the fog rolls in thick. If it looks dense enough to hide me, I sneak my rusting pink bike off the porch and ride up the three-mile stretch of meadow grass to Fisherman's Wharf.

At least five hundred tides have rolled in and out of Hackett since the night they tortured Lani, and any physical evidence of a drowning would be long gone. Yet I feel drawn to the place...to search the surface of the water, the thick night fog rolling onto Hackett, and to wait. For what, I wish I knew.

Some thirty feet past the last commercial trawler, the pier ends and there's a piling that stands higher than the rest. On foggy nights I lay my bike in the shadows between spotlights, hug on that piling, and stare through the deep blue haze.

It plays tricks on your eyes. At first the fog seems motionless...like a silk screen over an empty stage, lit in deep blue. You can see the silk screen starting to move...up and down, or side to side. You can't tell which. The motion blurs what's forming beyond it...but you strain your gaze, squinting until you're breathing through your eyeballs.

A few times I've seen that fog swirl into a pattern, like a human body. Head, then shoulders appear with hazy white ribbons dancing around them. One time, the body floated in close and hovered almost, until the ribbons around the shoulders took on more shape...like wings folded neatly.

I swayed away from the piling, watching the wings float so near I could almost see them plainly. I could make out the color of bone without density around the arms.

"Lani, it's me...It's Claire..."

One arm reached through a mist of white ribbons toward me. *If I reach for him, I'll fall...* As if timed with my decision to freeze, the form dissolved slowly to mere mist again.

I kept staring and waiting, and finally knocked my head against the piling once or twice. I'm not a lunatic. At least, I try hard to stay grounded. I gave myself a hundred reasons why it's understandable that I could go through bouts of hallucinations. Fishermen have this saying that the deep doesn't bother swallowing just anybody. "The sea takes the extraordinary and leaves the rest be." Any fisherman lost at sea earns that saying on his memorial stone. I believe it about Lani, despite that he will never have a stone.

We don't talk about the drowning around the island. We don't really talk about what led up to it, either. If I hear Lani's name, it's usually in mentions of him having gone to our high school for only two days, and isn't that weird, as if the greater mysteries never existed. Maybe that's the way people need to remember it.

Lani pronounced his name *Lonny,* and someone told me it had been spelled that way at one time. Sometime in the years before he came to Hackett Island, he had started to change or hide everything about himself that could somehow define him. *Lonny* is a boy's name. Who knows what *Lani* is? I had guessed his age to be around my own, sixteen, but the fact is, we never really knew. We never knew his birthplace. No one knew where he'd been in the years before his arrival on Hackett last fall. Truth be told, we were never completely sure *he* wasn't a *she.*

We hadn't known any of the things that you normally find out when you're deciding whether someone is going to fit in or not. He was determined to be like that. No one really gets why. I know it turned a lot of normal high school kids into potential killers. No one can say why that is, either.

I used to say my curiosity about him, my being drawn to him, cost me my friends. But I think it's more truthful to say it cost me my popularity. I hear stupidness floating around the bathroom at school, girls being all "pa-arty ha-ardy" and "tooooooooo studly" and "soooooooo sloshed," and I'm all thinking, *Claire, you were that shallow once.* My biggest shudder comes from the fact that at one time I considered cheerleading the most important thing under the sun. School seems like the home of the walking dead these days.

I'm spending my weekends with new musician friends in Philly, but Monday through Friday I'm stuck here. And the wharf feels kind of alive at night. It's not restful, in spite of the deadness in the air. It's one of the few places on Hackett that gives off any sort of energy. If that's not supernatural or mystical, it's still something. It probably has little to do with ghosts, because ghosts have to do with people who died. I think my problem is a part of me has never been able to accept that Lani Garver actually *did* die.

I stare at the water and get a flash of his eyes, the last time I saw them, twenty feet under. . . . Neon whites blaring, circling black dots. *Claire, you're leaving me down here, you're turning your back, where are you going, why . . .*

Lani, I can't save you and me, too, because I'm selfish, because I see air . . . I can never decide if I could still see his eyes below as I finally gulped in air, or if they had branded themselves in my brain so that even the sudden screams from above could never erase them. . . .

"—*do something, this got way screwed up, we goddamn killed somebody, Jesus Christ, we goddamn killed somebody*—"

I've had days, weeks, to remember his flashing eyes, over and over. I've wondered if their wideness was not horror at all but, rather, laughter.

The mind is like the fog. It's like the dark water...sometimes it shows you what you want or need to see. I tell myself that.

While I'm dissecting the fog, I'm searching what I know of his entire life for the answers to what happened, not just those last few minutes. *Why did he really come to Hackett? Why was I drawn to him, and nobody else was? What was Lani Garver? Was he one of those super-kind gay boys that certain girls love to bare their souls to? Is his body caught under some sunken boat wreck that will prevent it from ever being found? Or did he escape? Are there other Claires out there, and is he busy making another basket case into a rational, useful member of the human race? Was Lani Garver an angel?* If I knew the answers to *who* Lani was and *what* he was, I would have more peace accepting where he is.

There are answers that I would love to have, but not so badly that I have ever asked the questions aloud—to anyone. There are certain types of wrong answers that could mess you up bad, make you doubt everything that gives you hope—especially about the big truths, like the realness of a supernatural and the existence of angels.

What keeps me feeling most alive is not getting bonfire-induced, imagination-infested, beer-breath theology and spouting back, "*Doyee,* if that's what you believe, well, then, it *must* be the *truth.*"

As Lani used to say, "Truth and belief are a stallion and a mule." That still cracks me up sometimes.

I get my biggest power rush not by searching for answers. The power comes, weirdly, from simply asking myself the questions....

What Happened to Lani Garver

1

How can some people's lives look so good when they're so foul underneath? That's the question I ask when I leaf through this photo album Macy gave me for my sixteenth birthday. I got it at my surprise party in October of sophomore year, three weeks to the day before Lani Garver showed up on Hackett.

It's full of pictures of me and Macy and our other friends, and we've got some wild and happy parade of the teeth going on. And it's not like we were faking happiness for pictures. That's what terrifies me most. If anyone had asked, my friends and I would have said in a heartbeat, "We rule the cule," and would have believed ourselves.

Macy scrawled titles by each picture in her pretty handwriting that slants backwards. The one most likely to rip our sides was "Uh-Oh, The Umbrella Ride," because of the disgusting story behind it, but like all "true brew stories," you find a place for it in your heart.

The summer after freshman year, Macy's big sister, Mary Beth, decided it was time to introduce us to Oleander's whiskey, better known by Hackett's fishermen as Old Sweat Sock. She felt we were getting too cocky about our alcohol imbibement tales. Mary Beth was eighteen but had a fake ID. She bought a good-sized bottle of Old Sweat Sock at the Rod 'N' Reel.

The six of us passed this bottle around in her car as she gunned it down Mariner Road to Fisherman's Wharf for some general goofing around.

Myra Whitehall, who sat in the passenger seat, announced that she suddenly wasn't feeling so great. Mary Beth didn't want to slow down, because this Jeep full of Hackett's finest studs was bumper smooching her Mustang, and she didn't want them to see hurl flying out of her passenger window. She kept saying, "Deal with it, Myra!"

Myra couldn't help rolling down the window, and to our disgust from the backseat, the ocean breeze was blowing *in*—way hard. Macy rooted through Mary Beth's stuff and came up with an umbrella. She snapped it open and shoved it up in front of the four of us in back. When Myra's stomach said, "No more," we screamed some combo victory chant/barnyard noises, completely protected from impending doom. The Jeep passed us with all-too-embarrassing curses and loud requests for car wash reimbursement. Geneva Graham snapped this picture on the wharf right after we got there.

I was smiling so completely. Except for Myra—who had just been ruined socially for at least a week—we all were.

Right next to that photo there's "Lesbian Hayride," which happened around Halloween of freshman year. I don't even remember how we lucked out so well, but Macy and I ended up in a hay wagon with about a dozen guys from the fish frat—that's the sons of Hackett's commercial fishermen, who are sometimes lifeguards and usually very hunky. We were trying not to act stupid, but also to act like we could care less about these breathtaking studs. As Mary Beth had lectured us, the only way to catch a guy in the fish frat is to pretend you don't care.

Macy and I were standing in the middle of this cart, baying at the moon, or something acceptably retarded, when the wagon jerked and I fell on my back. Macy fell on top of me—

with my spider legs all sprawled and her in the middle of them. I tried to tell her to get off, but I was like a jellyfish—major embarrassment laughing fit in process. And I could hear her laughing just as hard in my ear. I didn't know this at the time, but supposedly watching lesbians is some hot thing for upper-classmen. And these hunks were joking, all "Go, ladies! Be ladies!" Macy loved the attention. I was paralyzed with shock, like I was every time my naiveness caught up with me.

It wasn't exactly a big secret—just something we rarely talked about—but I had missed a year and a half of junior high school. My knowledge of sex was full of holes—everything you'd learn in seventh grade and the first half of eighth.

In this bonfire picture, we're surrounded by upperclassmen fish frat, and my smile is plastered on due to information overload about lesbians. Two of these guys actually asked for our phone numbers, and I wasn't even upset when they never called. The fact that they even asked was, like, too amazing. I figured they probably heard we were a couple of freshmen convent queens in disguise. The picture was good enough for me.

"March," "April," "June," "September" are four pictures on the same page. The first three were taken by my mom, of Macy teaching me a back handspring, each getting a little more graceful. "September" is my junior varsity cheerleading photo.

Great stuff. "Not a cloud on the horizon," an outsider might say. I can see a few clouds in some pictures, but only because I know my own life.

My mom, the former Coast Regional Homecoming Queen who never grew out of it, took a picture of me after my first day at Coast, all excited. She thought I was on my way to becoming her—I only had to add the cheerleading pom-poms and studly boyfriends. Macy called this picture "Claire Still Has No Friends But She's Getting There."

I was sprawled out in a chair in our living room, with my head on my hand. My hair, miraculously, had grown past my shoulders in the six months since I went back to eighth grade. I no longer had "chemotherapy cheeks," as my dad called them, which are the color of half-dried rubber cement. I see my hair, my complexion, and I can read some sort of magic determination in them: *Get rid of the past.* And my eyes caught the flash so they seemed to shine with hope.

Coast Regional High School was a huge place, where girls with problems could remake their lives. New faces poured in from four other barrier islands, which meant that to four-fifths of these kids, you did not have a past. There was a kind of hope whizzing around the corridors. Joe Hunk could ask you out tomorrow, even if you had been a dork-breath yesterday. You could work your way into a seat in the cafeteria at that fourth table from the door—which around here is known as the Queen's Table—even if you were shoveled off to the corner with the invisible unknowns during the first week. Some eighth-grade science nerd could save up for a foil job, come into school a raving blond, and totally believe her life would change.

I tried to tell myself just to forget about anything like becoming outrageously popular. I felt at a serious disadvantage even to a science nerd, having heard my last dirty joke at a sixth-grade pajama party, and then dropping into Homeschool Hell for the Sick for a year and a half. If you start eighth grade in January, completely naive, looking like something the cat dragged in, you can only hope for a huge high school like Coast to help you disappear a little better.

But even *my* brain couldn't help figuring out which crowds were going to have all the fun. A group of girls sat at the fourth lunch table from the door in the cafeteria, and they were so cute, and so not shy, and just mean enough that nobody would dare pick on them. Despite that cheerleading tryouts had not been held yet, they were starting to be called the Freshmen Cheerleaders, and their table was nicknamed—in mumbles from girls who didn't sit there—the Queen's Table.

I didn't doubt that these girls would be cool around here. In fact, they were all from Hackett, so I knew them from grade school, and they had been popular since about fifth grade, or whenever it is you start to think about stuff like that. Most had swapped jokes with me at a bunch of sixth-grade slumber parties.

The second week of high school, I was going past them into the girls' bathroom, and Eli Spellings didn't keep her voice low enough.

"Look, there goes that leukemia girl. Her hair grew back way nice, at least. Remember her from January? She looked like she'd been nuked in a microwave. Was that sickening, or what?"

I went into a stall and leaned against the side, with my hand over my mouth. I totally forgot to sit down and go to the bathroom. I had been suspicious that these kinds of remarks flew. It's just that people were polite enough not to say them where I could hear.

Macy Matlock was standing in the middle of them, as usual, and happened to take a different view of the thing. I heard her mouth go off, because you can't miss that.

"You pig, Eli. What the hell is wrong with you?" I heard something like a slap, like she smacked a book to the floor, or cracked a notebook on the sink ledge. "That girl is one of the sweetest people you'd ever want to meet, and not only that, but she just heard you."

Footsteps clomped my way, and I prayed to wake up from this nightmare. But there she was, gazing in the stall door, because I'd been too stupid to lock it. I glanced back, thinking the veins in my face would crack open.

She grabbed my wrist, and before I knew it, we were

moving back toward this bathroom meeting of the Queen's Table, which amounted to about seven glares, all mowing me down to nothing.

"I know you heard that, Claire. Eli has something to say."

Macy folded her arms across her chest, giving Eli the death look, and I waited for them to jerk past me and run, or get meaner. What I didn't understand had a lot more to do with Macy than anyone else.

She has a big mouth, but her heart is bigger over certain matters of principle. Second, if she believes something and glares into your eyes, you believe it, too, no questions asked. For whatever reason, she totally believed Eli owed me an apology. Eli spit out what would have made the Pope happy.

"Claire. Oh my god. I didn't know you could hear me, I mean...not that I should be saying shit like that, anyway. I just...last year? I didn't know what to say to you, that's all. I'm just really stupid...Okay?"

I glanced at Macy in stunned awe, then at the floor, realizing some response was expected. Nurses forever warned me that people wouldn't know what to say. It was completely forgivable.

But it came out something like, "Forget it...please...I don't think...anyone should have to know...what to say...," and my voice box pizzled out because I couldn't smile and think of words at the same time.

Macy kicked her in the ankle. "See! Did I tell you she was sweet?"

Her loudness made me jump, and for whatever reason, they thought that was funny. Myra Whitehall grabbed my arm and pulled me along with them. "Come on, hang with us? I was at Kim Norris's sixth-grade slumber party with you. Remember?"

I felt sure they were just feeling sorry for Claire with the Novelty Sickness in Her Past, and I didn't want that. We were going into fourth period, which meant the cafeteria, which meant they were thinking I would sit at the so-called Queen's Table. I only got swept along with it because I was in shock.

There's a photo of all of us at the Queen's Table, taken three days later by Myra. My arms are crossed, and I'm biting my lip over my smile. I don't belong at this table, or in this picture with Eli Spellings, Geneva Graham, and Macy Matlock. And if I smiled too big, they would see the evidence in the photo later. Macy called that one "Claire the Humble, Macy the Horrible. Every Bitch Needs a Claire."

She was referring to her darker side, which everyone knew she had, because of her big mouth. For Macy's good part, she would never tolerate evil treatment toward somebody who had done nothing to deserve it. For example, I had not done anything to deserve Eli's bathroom ignorance, because you can't help having been sick. Macy would shove people for remarks on girls with huge chests, kids with bad skin, people with disabilities.

But those people were few and far between compared to people who *could* help what was wrong with them. Other people were obnoxious, dorky, phony, smelly, fat-yet-overeating, whiny, wimpy, stingy, clumsy, overly horny, or butt smooches. She had managed to perfect herself and could not see why it was so hard for anybody else. And she would rip on these people and not care who heard.

"Lyda Barone Bombs Out Macy" is a funny photo in a sick way, because I have this look of horror on my face as a glowing Lyda Barone clings to my arm. Lyda had all but wrapped herself around me for about a week, probably because I was the only person who had ever been nice to her. Everyone said she smelled. She looked like she would because she didn't wash her hair a whole lot, but I never actually smelled anything.

My look of horror came because of a trick Macy had started to pull in pictures. She would plan out ways she could "enhance" the picture, all the way back to when she was posing. She knew she wanted to pen in "air stink" squiggles going from Lyda's armpits to her own nose, so she posed all wide-eyed with her eyes going in that direction. I knew what she was up to, because she'd done it before, but it was hard to lecture her when you're cracking up.

When I say a foulness lay under the surface of these pictures, I can't say exactly what breed of garbage was ready to squirt from behind each person's eyeballs. But I can talk about myself, and it would only be fair to do that. Other people's foulness had to be there, and it had to be as big, or bigger, than my own. I say that because of what happened when Lani Garver showed up. A new kid walks into school, and you can't tell by staring whether it's a girl or a guy. A stink the size of Kansas doesn't get raised out of people's sweetness and kindness. I ended up being a victim, and everyone else wound up on the let's-obliterate-the-gay-kid squad. What does that say about whose garbage is bigger? And here's some dirt on me:

While all my daytime fun was going on, I had started having nightmares that were gory and disgusting. I would wake up all *Claire, you are nuthouse material.* In these dreams, girls I had never seen before would cut swirly designs in their legs with knives, or swallow forks, or part their hair with razor blades, stuff like that. I hadn't had a single nightmare I could remember while on chemo, and yet here I was in the greatest time period of my life having these dreams like something out of a horror flick.

And what's worse is I was not entirely scared of them. Some totally sick part of me was obsessed with them. I would make them into songs that I would play on my electric guitar, down in the basement. I had a notebook full of lyrics that would have choked the devil. Sometimes I was all ashamed of this thing, and yet these lyrics rhymed and rhythmed out so well that I couldn't bring myself to burn them. Nobody knew about this. Who could I tell? Macy was tone-deaf. My mom would tell the whole island, and my dad had just gotten remarried.

When I started my job at Sydney's Café, at the beginning of sophomore year, Macy took a picture and called it "Claire Decides to Ruin Every Saturday Night for Two Hours Over 25 Bucks." It's me with my acoustic guitar, singing cheery old folk songs into the mike. You would think my brain was a flower shop.

We actually had that photo album in the cafeteria during lunch on the day Lani Garver first showed up. Macy was cursing a blue streak because none of the pictures from my surprise party had turned out.

"We finally get you a boyfriend in the fish frat, and there's no evidence of 'Macy Performs a Miracle.' *Shit...*" A photo landed in front of me that was supposed to be me and Scott, but above our noses was only white and flash.

"Smiles are good." I handed it back, and she glared at my usual calm like a cat in the dark.

"That *was* a miracle"—she started smacking overexposures down on the table, and I couldn't argue—"being that you couldn't seduce a tree trunk."

I laced my fingers across my stomach, stretching out in the chair and pondering on that. "Seduce somebody. Like, how do you *seduce* somebody? Like, why should I have to *seduce* somebody? Can't we just be chilling and some guy likes me for that?"

Eli raised her head from copying Geneva Graham's Spanish homework, and they both giggled.

Macy threw her head down on the table in a shock fest. "Help this woman before she loses what I just helped her catch. She's deeply disturbed."

"Watch this, Claire." Eli nudged Geneva, who could catch

just about anybody, at least for a night or two. "Do your peanut-butter thing."

I watched, mildly amused, as Geneva upset half the cafeteria, sucking peanut-butter glops off her pinky, her eyes burning a hole into one dying bastard after another.

"You try." She pushed her mutilated PB&J at me.

I blinked at it long enough to make them think I might. "I don't eat peanut butter."

"Claire, Little Miss Chronic Diet," Geneva groaned. "Use your salad dressing!"

"It's watery, low-fat Italian. I'll end up feeding my shirt." My grin slid a little wider, because they knew there was no chance of this thing happening.

"Hey, she already caught herself a hottie, without any peanut butter, cigarette lighter, Vaseline lip, dangly earring, tongue piercing, pedicure wiggling, sassy butt, helpless routine." Myra stopped for air and her collie-dog eyes glowed. She was sweet. Always on my side. "You know, maybe you should be asking *her* for lessons. Claire, how'd you catch Scott Dern?"

I looked down at my laced fingers, sniffing to break the silence. "I don't know. I don't think he likes me very much. He's not exactly...talkative."

"He's fish frat! They're too cool to be motormouths." Eli waved me down. "You have to get him *alone.*"

"She's had him *alone.* At least, she had him *alone with me and Phil,*" Macy snapped, and started tossing ruined photos over her back into the aisle in frustration. "I don't have any evidence of that night at Phil's house, or the party night. Four rolls down the toilet! What gives with this goddamn camera—"

Eli, Myra, and Geneva were still stuck on the *alone* business, boring holes through me like three Cheshire cats. I just let my grin wander higher, so they could think what they wanted, because this conversation was moving dangerously close to some garbage I didn't want to spew about Scott.

Albert Fein saved me by picking up one of the overexposed pictures as he came past with his tray. "Somebody's pictures are on the floor."

"It's a picture of Claire McKenzie in her underwear. If you want, she'll autograph it." Macy glared dead into his eyes, and Albert Fein was just dorky enough to try to stare through the overexposure.

The girls cracked up until Albert's ears turned red, and I held out my hand for it. "I'm not in my underwear, Albert. Give it here."

"You can still autograph it." He pulled it away, and I flopped my arm back down in frustration because I knew what was coming, and I knew it would start a fight with my friends.

Macy said it for him in this nasty, screechy twang. *"Aren't you that famous guitar player from Sydney's?* Don't you know anything, Albert? 'Famous' and 'Sydney's' do not go in the same sentence. This is an island. The only famous people are tourists."

I nodded hard in agreement, hoping that would end it, but it didn't.

"She's breaking up our Saturday nights! For what, Albert?"

He grinned from ear to ear just because she was talking to him; the fact that she was telling him off didn't seem to matter. "Well, *I* think it's cool—"

"Good, then you can go chuck money at her with all the fishwives while we're waiting to go party. Now, give me that picture and get out of here..." She trailed off from her dork attack, staring over my shoulder, down the aisle. Her hawk eye was working itself big-time on somebody, which was not unusual. But I was facing Myra, Geneva, and Eli, and their eyebrows were lowering, too.

I tilted my head backward over my chair, and that was how I recognized Lani Garver from homeroom. Upside down. He had just stood up from a table over in the corner and was putting trash on a lunch tray. I brought my head back up and yawned. I probably could have ignored this whole thing nicely, if it wasn't for Albert.

"Is that *thing* a boy or a girl?"

My head snapped up to his braces smile, and thank god I was yawning, because I might have actually hollered at him. I could never forget what eighth grade felt like. And I didn't get how some overweight, underbuilt bucktoothed kid finds room to goof on somebody else who looks funny. *Is it because we're talking to you? Get your power somewhere else, hypocrite...*

"It's a boy." I kept yawning to keep from snapping the news. "The teacher asked how to spell his name. It's L-A-N-I, but he said you pronounce it *Lonny.*"

"Looks like a damn girl." Albert kept up. "Except that would be one very tall girl. Jesus, maybe it's one of those... those...*hermaphrodisiacs*—"

I rubbed my eyes in annoyance, knowing Macy would handle it, which she did. "Who asked you! The only thing I remember anyone asking you is to leave, mean face. Can the kid help it if he has long eyelashes and pink cheeks? What are you—jealous? Roll on out of here before somebody starts in on *your* looks."

I gave her the time-out sign because Albert was moving away from us, grinning to hide the redness on his ear tips.

She turned her gaze to Myra and Eli and Geneva. "Cut it out! No stare fests. Claire said it was a boy."

I sat there blinking as she kept rolling her neck to get the kinks out. Every roll gave her another opportunity to check out Lani Garver over my shoulder.

And she didn't lecture again when Geneva piped up.

"Claire, I think that *guy* is wearing blush and eyeliner. The teacher actually asked, '*Are you a guy?*'"

Eli and Myra turned to watch me suspiciously. I had noticed only two things in homeroom—his height and the drumsticks shoved into his jeans' back pocket. I'm five ten but would have only come up to this kid's cheekbones. I had seen the sticks and thought, *Hmm, a drummer. Way cool.*

"You know what? I don't think the teacher ever did ask—"

"Claire, you are so dense." Macy surrendered and stared. This boy-girl was now coming up the aisle, which gave me a chance to look without being too obvious.

The first challenge was the combination of shoulders and face. I wouldn't say there were muscles, just larger bones that made the shoulders broad. And yet, you would look at this face and think, *Girl. No question.* Geneva had a point, because the face looked to be done over with really subtle makeup—until it got within about six feet of you. Then you realize, *That's not makeup.* It's just really peachy skin, overly thick eyelashes, natural pipeline lips. The dark hair was to Lani Garver's shoulders—with the top layers kind of bobbed under and going behind the ears. Guys don't plan their hair. *Girl,* I thought.

Lani passed by us, and I looked at the back view. Most girls had hips. *Guy?*

I tried to look at this person as a butch girl, which would have worked, except for the big shoulder bones. I decided it looked slightly more like a gay guy. I waited as this Lani Garver turned left at the front and gave us a profile. Macy could always see into my head along with everybody else's.

"You're waiting to see if there are bumps in the front. Nope, no triangles." Her tone was curious and not mean, because if this turned out to be a girl, the haircut was cute, and no one can fault a girl for being over six foot and flat-chested. "God almighty. I *hope* it's a girl."

Without her head moving, her eyes wandered sideways until they caught the table where the fish frat were sitting. I let my own eyes wander past the cluster of big muscles, anchor tattoos, and sunburnt noses even in chilly November. Fortunately, they were just talking among themselves and eating. The fish frat didn't notice people easily. They waited for everyone to notice them.

Lani Garver's dark-chocolate brown eyes caught on this and that thing on the tray, like there was no real thought, and all the staring didn't register.

My eyes couldn't help falling to you-know-where. I'm not saying it was a huge bump. But girls' jeans zippers tend to lean almost backward, when they're skinny and their jeans are tight. This zipper came out—at least more than it went in. *Guy.*

Lani placed a tray in the holder above the trash can, then the hands smacked together in a dainty way, like to get the garbage-can dirt off them. *Girl?* Then the eyes met mine. With a couple hundred kids in the cafeteria, there were a lot of different directions those eyes could have gone. It felt a little eerie. I met the gaze as evenly as I could, feeling weirdly challenged by it, like I had to prove I wasn't intimidated.

I ended up breaking this brief looking-match because Macy nudged me hard in the arm. A picture landed in front of me.

"The only one. In four rolls. What is *up* with that?"

Lani Garver's stare was forgotten for the moment. I gazed at the picture and tried not to move at all. That was my trick when I became completely nervous. *If I don't move, nobody will notice me; nobody will see me freaking on the inside. I'll be invisible.*

My internal freaking had to do with two things in this picture: the great smile on my face and the horrible thoughts that had been running through my brain at that time.

"Must have something to do with your flash," I managed to mutter, because Macy was six inches away, looking right at my face.

"If you'd get rid of your Barbie camera and buy something decent—" Geneva giggled.

Macy turned to her. "It's just pink; it's not Barbie. Shut up."

I could not get over my smile in the picture. Macy snapped it about fifteen seconds after I came out of my house yesterday morning. I had not seen her at first. I was counting the number of days I had been extremely tired, and the number of times I'd gotten dizzy. I was trying to decide whether I was having a cancer relapse. I remember deciding that it had surely returned. Then I looked up and saw Macy with the camera to her face. Without even thinking, I made peace signs with both hands and smiled.

In this picture I was smiling the most peaceful smile I had ever seen in my life.

"Claire, Jesus Christ!" Macy snatched a plastic salad fork from my hand. I realized I had picked it up and raked my thumb over it. It had snapped. I glanced at the few drops of blood on the blank page of the photo album and stuck my thumb in my mouth and sucked.

"You got blood all over the page!"

I mumbled around my thumb, "Three drops. Chill out."

"Are you all right?"

"Fine."

"You're a klutz!"

"Part of my charm."

"You stuck your thumb right down on that! What is wrong with you? Let me see." I let her pull my thumb out of my mouth, before she raised a loud enough stink that everyone would be looking. It was a deep cut, but small.

She sighed in relief, casting a final look at the three drops on the page. "Don't be giving me heart attacks. I *hate* blood."

I sat stock-still after putting my thumb back up to my teeth. I didn't know which thought was making me freeze worse—that I might have a blood disease, or that my Lisa-cuts-herself-with-razor-blades nightmares might be invading my real life.

Macy hawkeyed my face, and I knew I hadn't managed to completely wipe off my horrified look. She followed my eyes, which happened to be laying into Lani Garver, who had retreated to the semidarkness of the alcove between the cafeteria and the B corridor. Macy never misses a trick, but her imagination was only as big as her world.

"Are we about to have another Lyda Barone adventure? Are you going to have ants in your pants until you can be nice to that new kid? I guess...you remember what it felt like to be the new, huh?"

I let out an absent laugh. Talking about my return to eighth grade was the closest we usually came to talking about my leukemia. It's not that I didn't trust my friends to be nice and sympathetic. It's just that fun-loving kids don't hear that sort of stuff very well. I never wanted to think about junior high, let alone talk about it, and it's probably one of the reasons I adored my friends so much. I loved their carefree outlooks on life more than anything under the sun.

Macy groaned. "Fine. If you really must go say hello and sing, like, 'The Happy Welcome Song,' I'll come along for the ride. Just...please don't bring any more strange people over to our table. I end up being the one doing the that-seat's-taken routine after a week of dork overload, and I've got a heart, too, Claire."

I laughed, removing my thumb. "Don't make me out to be some saint. That's so not true—"

"Girl Scout, then."

"Fuck you."

"Don't curse. It makes you blush. Look. Perfect chance.

See where he-perhaps-she is?" She sized up Lani. A paperback book was open in the long, graceful fingers. "It's a girl. Guys don't read books. At least, not in public."

"I swear, Macy. I have less than zero interest in going over there."

"Don't ruin my image of you, Claire. Maybe I admire your heart. Now's your chance to be nice. I know you're feeling sorry for that new kid."

She was telling the truth. She just wasn't telling all of it.

"Yeah? And I'll bet right now, Macy, your biggest problem is, you won't be able to stand yourself until you find out if that's a girl or a boy."

She raised her eyebrows shamelessly. "Hey, I'm not the one blowing my hair under while putting a tight shirt over zero tits. That person is just begging for someone to come up and hint around for some answers. I'm just a victim here."

"You're a victim, and I'm a white whale."

She laid the peace-sign-and-smile photo into the album and scrawled beside it, "Claire as Usual." I flinched but didn't have a whole lot of time for backlash thoughts.

"Come on. Let's go find out." She pulled me to my feet, and I let myself be dragged along by the wrist.

2

Macy leaned against the wall, about four feet from this oddly put together person. I leaned up behind her. "Are you new?" Her voice sounded overly innocent.

"Yeah. I'm Lani."

"Lani?" After Macy got a spelling, she asked, "What kind of a name is that?"

I almost smiled, thinking, *It can't be this easy.* But instead of "boy's name" or "girl's name," the answer came back, "I think it's Hawaiian."

"Wow, you're Hawaiian?" Macy asked.

"Well..." Lani was chewing gum, and it rolled pensively around behind juicy-looking lips, which made me think, *Girl,* though the voice sounded slightly low for a girl. "I think I'm a little bit of everything, like...a mutt. You know? One of those stray dogs you buy at the pound?"

"Too funny..." Macy made one of her plastic laughs, though I hoped it didn't sound fake to Lani. She groped for something else.

"Uh...what are you reading?"

"*The Essential Jung.*" The jacket of the book flashed in our faces. I guess she was hoping for *Makeovers for Girls* or *Football Digest.*

"Yuck, psych class," Macy babbled. "I'm so glad I don't have to take that college-prep boring garbage."

Lani Garver's chocolate brown eyes looked amused. "You don't like psych? Let me tell you, I hate chemistry. There was never a stupider chemistry person."

We laughed easily, because you almost have to when someone is cutting on themselves. But then the silence got a little awkward. Macy never misses a detail, but she's not careful enough with her eyes. They started wandering up and down Lani Garver, stopping at this or that very obvious spot, and she didn't bother to cover up her overly curious hawk eye, which was showing her impatience. Lani watched her take everything in until I couldn't help clearing my throat.

It came out too loud and brought Lani's eyes to me. Since Macy was being rude, the line that followed seemed extremely humane and merciful. "Hey, you know what? I saw you on Saturday night. You were playing guitar at that little café that stays open all winter. Sydney's? You're Claire McKenzie."

I had to smile over the idea that a stranger would remember my first and last name. I felt Macy's gaze pouring on me, hoping I would help her out here.

"And ... you're a drummer?"

The nod was hearty. "But nobody's going to pay me for it. I'm not that good. And I never knew anyone who could play the whole 'Dust in the Wind.' How'd you learn to play so well?"

No girl/guy hints there. "I can't really remember *not* playing, but I guess I got way better in ... junior high."

My friends had instinctively figured out that when "junior high" came out of my mouth, they should look for a new subject. Macy burst into some talking jag, like she usually does. I just stood by and watched. Cheerleading this, and buying clothes that. She got this kid laughing over why it might be called *Shore* Mall, if it's on the mainland, and why we have a *Forest* Inn on Ocean Drive, since Hackett never saw a tree bigger than a bayberry or a twisted pine. I thought Lani might say, "Daw, doesn't the Forest Inn sign say OWNERS, ED AND

JOANNE FOREST?" But polite laughter came in all the right places.

Finally Macy's curiosity got to be too much. I came out of my stupor with a jolt of adrenaline as she let fly.

"...take offense or anything, but can I ask you a personal question?"

"Yeah, go ahead."

"Are you...a girl?" Macy asked.

I was turning all shades of red, but Lani didn't flinch. "Oh! No. Not a girl. Sorry."

We waited, I guess because we were expecting to hear the natural next line, *I'm a boy*. The smile on his face left me feeling he enjoyed the awkward pause and the notion that our heads might be slightly confused.

"Okay," Macy finally stumbled. "You're a guy."

After that I forever thought of and referred to Lani as a he. The truth is, he never actually answered. I was vaguely aware he might have been intentionally playing some game, so I held my breath, hoping it wouldn't ignite Macy into some blunt attack, some *Are you gay?* Fortunately, she saw where the line was.

"I'm really sorry. I just, you know. I couldn't make you out. I mean, you seem really *cool* and everything."

Lani didn't seem to care. "I get accused of being a girl sometimes. I guess there's worse things to be accused of. If people were confusing me with a bull rhino, I would be upset."

He giggled along with Macy. It was one of those high-pitched giggles that hits the same note, like, seven times in a row. It made me giggle, too.

"I guess it has its good points, being confused with a girl," he went on. "People don't always treat girls fairly, and now I can sympathize with them. Like, did you know that if a girl takes a shirt to the dry cleaner, she'll pay a dollar fifty more to have that shirt cleaned than a guy would? And a girl pays, like, seven dollars more for a haircut?"

"You're kidding." Macy had her feet spread apart, and she was swaying from side to side. She always did that when she got nervous. I guessed, now that she had her answer, she was looking for a way to move on.

"So, being that I'm not a girl, does that mean you can't show me around this drab-looking island?" he asked with the same ease. "Show me what stays open in the winter."

Macy laughed, shaking her head, but didn't say anything. I could sense her close-down routine. She hadn't made up her mind about him yet.

"Or you?" His eyes turned to me again. "Are all your friends girls?"

I started to shake my head no, because that seemed dumb. But come to think of it, I didn't have any close guy friends. I had Scott, and Macy had Phil, but it was hard for girls to "buddy up" to the guys we hung with. Sometimes I watched a rare girl who could get with them and crack jokes and act perfectly natural. I wished I could be like that. I always felt like I would say something dumb at any second.

I probably felt that way because it was true. Like, here's what I said back to Lani: "Well, I'll be your friend, if Macy will be your friend."

I tried to cover my dumbness with another throat-clearing session, but it wasn't really working. *Is that how you pick your friends, Claire? By how much nerve Macy has?*

Macy turned her back to Lani and laughed loudly in my face. Macy liked it when I screwed up sometimes. It left her sure that she was the star of our show.

Like an apology for my brain flake, I made it worse. "Yeah, I'll be your friend."

Macy still had her back to Lani, and she gave me the wide-eyed, evil glare that means *If you get any stupider, I'll kill you.*

Embarrassed, I tore my eyes from her, and I noticed that Lani was staring intently at the back of her head—almost like he had X-ray eyes and could see the look on her face. His grin sagged but didn't go away completely. Macy spun, and in the second it took to face him, she got her charm back.

"Don't mind her," she giggled. "Claire is always contradicting herself. It's because she lives and breathes music. Those artistic kids—they can't think and talk at the same time. We have to go now, but we'll see you around."

Macy took hold of my sweater and jerked me toward the corridor. We walked toward her locker, and she said, "Don't get any ideas about being his friend. God, I can't believe you said that."

I sighed, rolling my eyes. "I thought he was nice. Is that a crime?"

"No! I thought he was nice, too. And it's not that he's gay. Okay? I mean, my cousin Ron is gay. I love my cousin Ron. He just had the good sense not to let it show until he got out of here and went to New York City."

I knew what she was saying but couldn't figure out how that was fair. Like, if some guy grows up kind of swishy like that, he's supposed to go out for football? And learn to scratch and clomp around like the fish frat? Just to keep his big secret?

"Don't give me that you're-being-unfair look," she snapped. Nothing got past Macy's vision, especially concerning me and my thoughts. But she kept walking for a few moments before adding more. I gathered this was a gray area in the let's-pass-judgment file, and she was usually pretty clear about where her lines were.

"I'm saying, if you beg for trouble, you're going to get it. No, a guy can't help being a *femme*. But does he have to, like, *blow* his hair under like that? And that little wiggle walk? Oh my god. Tell me he didn't practice. He's trying to make a statement. He's going to get his ass kicked. Do you want to be right in the middle of it?"

I crossed over some line from being slightly annoyed to feeling very twitchy. I wondered if I was annoyed because I was tired lately. Or I was annoyed because Macy makes this shit up, half the time. *Little wiggle . . .*

"He's got a skinny butt. I swear . . . I didn't notice any hula going on."

Sure enough, she looked at me like I was out of my mind. "Are you *blind*? God, you're dense. How could you not see that, Claire?"

"I don't know."

I had never seen Jenna Dawes's underwear, despite how Macy went on and on about how Jenna shouldn't wear skirts to school if she couldn't keep her thighs together. I had never smelled Lyda Barone's onion-ring underarm, never seen Larry Boogers's boogers, which Macy swore on her life were all over his book-bag strap. Not that I was up for any close examinations, but what difference would it make? There was a certain way things always happened. Macy spotted somebody's big-time flaw. I often secretly thought she was seeing/hearing/smelling things. Then, within two weeks, everyone else had noticed it, too, and I felt like a blind person.

I decided it wasn't worth it to get in an argument that I would surely lose. I yawned, instead, and it made me feel dizzy. Then I got so dizzy, the world started to spin.

3

I hauled it into history class without saying much more than bye to Macy. I didn't want to tell her I felt like fainting so soon after I had grossed her out with my bloody thumb. After sitting for a while, I felt better. But I had given myself such a jolt that I couldn't stop waiting for it to come back. I started seriously thinking that I should see a doctor. I didn't know how I could do that, not without spewing to my mom, who uses every serious problem lately as an excuse to load up on vodka and whatever. Or my dad, whose brilliant idea last time was that I live with him in Philadelphia to be close to the better research hospitals.

I'm not giving up my life. This can't be happening. The thought stuck with me all afternoon, even though the dizziness had not shown up again by the time cheerleading practice started. By then I had something else to focus on—the fact that Ms. D'Angelo and I were mortal enemies.

Ms. D'Angelo thought I was a huge cow interrupting her petite little cheerleading squad. She would gaze at me in practice sometimes while she was yelling at us.

I hadn't given a thought to being at least half a head taller than everyone else on the squad until I sprained my ankle at summer practice and had to go for an X ray. I overheard Ms. D'Angelo telling the doctor out in the corridor, "I hate having big girls on my squad. They're just all wrong for cheerleading. They always get hurt."

I tried to pretend I never heard it, but every time I got in her presence, I felt like a heifer in need of milking. I couldn't change my height, but I decided I could compensate by going from somewhat thin to thin-thin. I lost five pounds, which wasn't the perfect solution, but Macy had this funny saying: You can't be too rich or too thin. I lost five more pounds, hoping Ms. D'Angelo would think, *Wow, McKenzie must have heard me call her a cow. Maybe I shouldn't shoot my fat mouth off.* Unfortunately, she still looked at me like she thought I was a cow. But I was afraid to lose any more weight and fool with my health.

Normally I could fight my "cow" paranoia with good thoughts, like that I worked my butt off to get on cheerleading, and I deserved to be here. But we were standing in formation that day, and I got zapped with the realization of how Ms. D'Angelo viewed me, because from my spot in the back, I could see the part in everyone's hair. *You look like Shaquille O'Neal. Cave dweller, meaty-beef drumstick-chomping Viking...Boom! Boom!...High school topples as mammoth cheerleader attempts back handspring...*

I did my invisible-cheerleader act, which is going through as much of practice as possible behind somebody else, on the far side of somebody else, or moving around as little as possible. Ms. D'Angelo called me up front afterward to demonstrate some routine I had picked up pretty fast, but I knew she was just doing it so everyone could get a load of my cowness. It took everything I had not to bite her head off.

Since I was looking for symptoms of cancer relapse, I couldn't help adding that to the list. Tiredness, dizziness, *irritability.* After we finished practice, I checked my legs in the locker room for any suspiciously ugly bruises, which had been one of my first symptoms last time. I didn't see even a small bruise, but I was so abnormally tired, the lack of bruises didn't make me feel much better.

"Claire! You coming tonight?"

Macy's voice echoed over from the next row of lockers, among slamming doors and talking. I straddled a bench, hugging my backpack, waiting for everyone else.

"What's tonight?"

"Study group, fool!"

Geneva cackled, and I forced a smile. All I wanted to do was crash out on my bed for a hundred hours. But I had noticed I could almost count on one of my charming nightmares when I felt this exhausted. Macy's "study group" was more appealing.

"What are we studying tonight? Sydney's or Fisherman's Wharf?" I asked, because Macy's study groups were just a lame excuse for us all to party on a weeknight.

"Phil said Scott's dad is back from sea. We can use the boat," Macy hollered over the lockers.

Scott, Scott, Scott. My sigh must have been louder than I thought, because Geneva piped up.

"Claire, he's a complete hunk, and you are acting really strange. If you don't like him, give him up so somebody else can snag him." She laughed right away, so no one would think she was boyfriend snatching.

But I had to wonder. About her potential snagging talents, *and* about me. Geneva would probably not be bugged by the stupid things that bugged me about Scott. It would be enough for her that he looked like something that just jumped out of *Baywatch.* Me? I had been hoping for a boyfriend who could hear me out about music, being that all of my friends couldn't care less about it. I needed a guy who would listen to rhythm and blues, hash out the history of rock 'n' roll with me, and argue about great stuff like The Who versus the Stones. Scott was just as tone-deaf as all my other friends. He even refused to dance at dances.

I figured this next thing was legit enough to spew. "He calls me on the phone every night, and the whole time, he talks to the guys hanging out at his house. He says about two words to me, and then I listen to him chronically bust on them. Are we having fun yet?"

"Well, maybe you should talk about things that *he's* interested in," Geneva advised in this highly instructional tone, like maybe her mother had said it to her once.

"Like?"

"Like his pickup truck! Him and Vince are almost done fixing it. He *loves* that pickup truck. Are you deaf and blind?"

Problem...I don't like pickup trucks. "Yeah, thanks, you're right."

"And not only that, Claire, but once he gets done fixing his truck? You will have a boyfriend with an actual, real-live *car*. You can turn that sun mouth into a kissing machine."

I grinned while everyone hooted. What Geneva called "sun mouth" was a trait of lots of guys in the fish frat. Because they fished for their dads already, and because some were lifeguards, they were always in the sun. Their lips got all sunburned, and it looked way good. Even in the winter you can tell who's had sun mouth, because this sandy color stays on the surface of the lips. It drives girls crazy. The problem is that sun mouth does not necessarily mean someone kisses good. My biggest secret was that Scott was the *worst*. He had sent me home with an actual fat lip the Friday night before, and I stared at the swelling in the bathroom mirror, thinking, *Am I a dog bone?*

I watched Geneva pound on her locker for me about my future sex life, and I remembered that one time at a party last year, she ended up in a bedroom with Scott, though he never followed through in the weeks following. Before she decided she didn't care, she went on and on about him being some hot-lips Romeo. I wondered if it was me, or *my* kissing—if I could turn some Romeo into a bulldog lolling over a soup bone.

Maybe I was a lesbian. Or a secret science nerd, and I should be going out with William Hymen, who was doomed to pick his boogers and look at them, and to love chemistry, what with a last name like Hymen.

Stop, Claire. Take a goddamn nap and the nightmares that come with, because it beats stooping to mean fests, hypocrite. Don't forget eighth grade. I stood up too fast or something. It came over me again, like out in the corridor at lunchtime— this airy feeling, like I was on a ship. The room leaned to one side. Automatically, I moved toward the door.

To get Geneva's eyes off me, I groped my brain for an answer. "I'm sure that truck will...start us off with a bang."

I walked calmly past their hooting, into the corridor, trying to put some distance between myself and my own bad kissing. And I didn't want an audience if I fainted.

The warm, salty wind flowed around my head as I walked cautiously onto Hackett Boulevard—a too-awesome name for our two-lane main drag. It was warm enough that I wondered if Indian summer was coming. The thought ran through me that Indian summers in November could bring a curse to my health, and then I tried to put those stupid tourist thoughts out of my head. I breathed deeply and regularly, and the dizziness started to die down as I passed Bunny's Market. I waved to Bunny, who was bagging groceries—he stooped to bagging in the off-season. Then I passed the gas station and saw Macy's dad half under a pickup truck. I recognized Mr. Matlock's legs, but I didn't have to. He doesn't hire help at the Hackett Pump after Labor Day.

I came up to Sydney's Café and decided to go in, because Sydney gave me free lemonade as part of the Saturday-night deal.

Sydney wasn't behind the counter, and between me and the

lemonade maker stood Lani Garver. I stared, in awe of my bad luck, as he searched through the fattening stuff. He was alone, no friends, probably feeling incredibly freaky in this new place.

Message from God: "Be nice, or I can mess up your wonderful life."

My family was not into any religion known for jamming people full of guilt trips, yet occasionally a thought like this would strike me like a bolt of lightning. I figured maybe God was not very smart, because the threats made me more tired and didn't give me any energy to do the good deeds I was supposed to be thinking about. My head started reeling bad this time—enough that I was afraid to even go up the single step into Sydney's and lose my balance before God and Lani Garver.

Mrs. DeGrossa had the first duplex after the café. She was a nosy old person, but her decrepit Nova wasn't at the curb. I plopped down on her step, laid my head on top of my backpack, closed my eyes, and surrendered. My thought was *Okay...if I fall onto the concrete, someone will tell Sydney, and she'll call my mom. I give up...*

Next thing I knew, the sounds of breathing and chewing were above my head. I opened one eye and saw a set of drumsticks in a back pocket. The butt sat, and the drumsticks disappeared.

"Claire. Are you sick?" Lani's arm went around me, like, shaking me a little.

"I'm fine."

"Are you fainting?"

I didn't answer. I thought I might have already fainted and was coming out of it.

"Eat something." One of Sydney's sticky buns appeared in my face. I shut my eyes at the sight of it.

"...don't eat junk food, thanks."

"I know. You're too skinny. Claire..." He forced my shoulders up.

"Macy says you can't be too rich or too skinny." I stared at this sticky bun in my face again. "Uhm...you're making me sick."

The sticky bun retreated, but he kept up the argument. "Did you eat today?"

He was way off base. "I ate right before I met you."

"That was, what? Eleven o'clock? It's six now. Do you do this every day?"

My head started to clear a little. Since my politeness was asleep, I spewed the truth. "You're probably skinnier than I am. You've got room to talk."

"What*ever*," he replied in a way that sounded totally girlish.

Now that I'd heard him say he was not a girl, I would think of him always as *boy-boy-boy*. But I had to admit he was one of the prettiest boys I had ever seen. Perfect features. If it weren't for that girly hairstyle, he might have been a cute boy. From the neck up. No muscles, just aircraft-carrier bones, or something.

"It's not a hunger thing. I started feeling this way right after I saw you. And that was right after I ate."

"I live up the street. Come to my house, and we'll call somebody to come get you."

He was pointing to a duplex across Tenth Street, behind Bunny's. It looked just like my house, and every other house near the business district, except for the paint job.

"My mom's a seamstress...got a Thanksgiving wedding...she's working until nine tonight."

"You got a dad?" he asked.

"Divorced."

"Sisters or brothers with driver's licenses?"

"Only child, but...I only live six blocks from here..."

"There is no way you are walking six blocks. Just make it over to my house."

"You don't have to be so nice."

"Nice. Who, what, hell, nice? Is it demented to cut you a break?"

Yeah, I realized in my weary head. *People don't cut me breaks. I cut them all the breaks. I don't know how to act when—*

He tried to pull me up, and I jerked my arm away.

"Stop it. Stop touching me." My own bitchiness drove me to my feet in shock. "God...this is so backward. I'm supposed to be...being nice to *you.*"

"Really? Why is that?"

"Because of God."

"Because of *what*?" He could have pushed me down in the gutter and walked away. Crazy person...drug addict...He caught me as I swayed into him, and something in my gut spoke loudly. *This guy has heard it all; you cannot weird him out. Go screw, Macy.*

He laughed incredulously, despite that I leaned on him to where I think most people would have been panicking. He asked, "Do I look like some sort of a charity case?"

I groped through my dizzy head for something not weird or rude. "You just look new around here."

He didn't say anything else, but every few seconds he would chuckle, like I had said something so funny he could hardly stand it. I paid him no mind, just managed to glance over my shoulder once or twice to make sure my friends weren't coming to see Lani Garver half carrying me into the sunset.

It was a typical duplex like thousands on Hackett—three rooms downstairs and two bedrooms upstairs, and a balcony over the front porch. The furniture was nothing out of *House Beautiful,* but vacuum lines showed on the tan carpeting, and not a thing was out of place. I gathered there weren't several little kids living here.

A lady came through the kitchen doorway, smiling, but I hadn't thought about conversations with parents when I agreed to come here. Fortunately, Lani just pushed me in the back, toward the stairs.

"Mom, Claire. Claire, Mom," he said when we were already climbing. She said after us, "How do you do?" Most people on Hackett met you and said, "Hey."

"Hey...hope you like it here...it's pretty nice...if you can stand winter fog," I rambled over my shoulder, swaying like an idiot and bouncing off the wall once. I'm sure I came across like a crack queen, despite my effort. My own mom lived for my friends walking through our door. If someone didn't stop to blather with her, she would have to remember she wasn't a popular teenager anymore and her life was over. Then she would drink.

Mrs. Garver's footsteps retreated to the kitchen again as Lani steered me into the bedroom on the right. He didn't have a bed, just a box spring and mattress on the floor. It was covered with a cushy gold quilt and five bed pillows. I fell on them gratefully.

"Your mom said, 'How do you do,'" I muttered. "What are you, rich Philadelphia people? What are you doing here in the winter? You didn't let me talk to her. She'll think I'm some sleaze and we're up here doing the nasty..."

I could hear him moving about as I rubbed my eyes.

"Is this normal for you? That you're fainting, and you're worried about a complete stranger's opinion of you?" he asked.

I didn't laugh, though some of the tension ran out of my spine. "Call it...my job in life. None of my friends know how to be nice enough to the moms. My mom? She thinks she used to be me. She wishes she *was* me. She needs a husband, which she's not going to get..." There wasn't any point in saying, "Not unless she quits slurring and staggering at the Rod 'N' Reel." This guy might ask if I'd done anything to turn her into a drunk, and I didn't want to get on that sore subject.

He mumbled, "You're saying...if she had a husband maybe she wouldn't have to live vicariously through her child?" Then he giggled easily.

I didn't know what *vicariously* meant. I just let out a polite giggle, but it sounded trembly. He lit three different candles over by his disc player. *Gay thing,* my weary brain decided, making me edgy again.

"So, you used to be summer people?" I asked.

He blew out a match, watching the flame die down to an ember. "Yeah. My dad just passed away, and my mom's sister lives here year-round. She wanted to be near her sister again permanently."

"Wow. Sorry."

Lani shrugged. "My dad was a good guy, but we weren't really close."

I thought that sounded a little odd. If they weren't close, why did he think his dad was a good guy?

"You like Hackett?" I tried to sound casual.

"I think I might." He just tossed the matches on top of his stereo with an easy shrug, like he was oblivious to the stare fests he'd been causing. "Moving isn't anything unusual for me. I've moved almost every year since fifth grade."

I guessed that was why he'd talked to Macy and me so easily today—experience. "Why'd you move so much?"

He plopped down on the mattress. "First it was my dad's job in the military. Then I ran away. I lived as a runaway for two years. This is my first year back."

"You 'ran away,'" I repeated, watching him meet my gaze, though he didn't look comfortable. I'd never met a kid who ran away before. At least, not for more than a couple nights. *A couple years?* I was shocked he looked so healthy.

"Why did you run away?"

"We were living in a small town at the time." He squirmed a little. "People like me do better in big cities. But I don't like to talk about my life much. What's up with you? If it's not a starvation diet?"

Macy would come drag me out by the ear if she had any clue I was with a guy who ran away and wouldn't talk about it. I wasn't about to be completely stupid.

"Well...I don't really like talking about me, either."

He just looked away to the corner. "Do you have friends you can talk to?"

"I have friends."

He looked back again, like I hadn't answered his question. I rolled my eyes. "What I've got is a pretty serious problem. They wouldn't know what to do about it. They're just... *normal.*"

"There's this charming thing called 'getting a load off,' even if they couldn't help."

"I suppose I could get a load off." I shrugged, uneasy. "I guess I'm afraid of freaking them out. Maybe they'd back off from me. Not to be mean or anything, but...they're just not used to big problems."

I thought maybe he'd give me a lecture on picking less shallow friends, at which point I would have left no matter how bad I felt. But his eyebrows hooked together like he had some sort of a challenge.

"And you can't talk to your mom."

I shook my head. "She topples pretty easily. Last time I had a serious problem...she let me go stay with my dad in Philadelphia until...it was over. Not that she's a bad person or anything. She's just real emotional, and we all decided I needed, you know, someone who wouldn't pace the floor all night and make me all crazy, too."

I was leaving big holes in this story, like *She was a happy, weekend partyer before I got sick.* I was trying to get this kid backed off, not sucked in.

But he wasn't staring, like, to get all the missing details. He just blinked into the darkening corner. "What about your dad?"

"He's a little more together than my mom." Hazy echoes wandered through my head of my dad laying all the cards out a few times: *Your mom is an overgrown child. She drinks because she doesn't cope well with reality. You didn't cause that; it's not your fault.* "He can read my mind sometimes. But it's hard to take seriously people's advice when they never talk unless *you* call *them.* Not that I blame him. He waited until after...my problem ended...to get remarried. He's only been remarried a year. He's a musician, so he has to work constantly to keep him and Suhar out of debt. I can't lay anything else on him."

"So, you can't talk to your mom, your dad, or your friends."

I hadn't really thought of myself as being in any sort of a

corner until he put it that way. I laughed a little but rolled onto my side, which I knew from experience helps you to not puke. I felt like puking, probably from feeling dizzy.

"There're also counselors, rabbis, pastors," he said with a tiny note of sarcasm, like that was a brilliant idea. It was just a small thing, but I couldn't remember hearing too many kids tell another *kid* to go to a *grown-up* for help. Maybe a dork would. But there was something very not-dorky about him. Dorks are usually very sheltered. He seemed streetwise, older....I couldn't put my finger on it yet.

I went on. "My dad thought I should get counseling, but...I just wanted to get back to the island, back to my life. My mom doesn't see the need for stuff like that. She's the type who'll spew anything to anyone and can't see why I'm not like that. She brought the island pastor over a couple times, but it was more like 'Try and find out for me if anything's up with her,' rather than 'See if there isn't something she wants to talk about.' You know."

"So...even the very religious guy seems like a spy for the enemy."

"Yeah." I let go of a weak giggle. "But I don't really, you know, enjoy talking about it to anyone. I don't need ol' Pastor Stedman. I can talk to God, direct, if I want."

He laughed. "Well, I don't think that's gonna help in this case."

"Why not? You some sort of atheist?"

"No. I talk to God. A lot. But I don't have the type of God in my head who would tell me to be nice to the new kid while I'm trying not to faint."

I thought on that—me staggering into Sydney's on a mission of sainthood. I cracked up weakly. "I'm dumb sometimes. My friends will tell you."

"What else does this God tell you? Not to eat doughnuts?"

"Very funny, ha-ha. But sometimes I feel like..." I tried to figure how to say my thought without sounding even more stupid. "I feel like God has entire, whole control over whether my illness stays away or comes back. And my only bargaining power is to be, like, *super* nice. Only problem is, I've probably got some killer-bitch tendencies."

I realized I'd just said "illness," and yet he hadn't turned to stare. I watched him study the corner, his dark eyebrows knit together like he enjoyed the challenge. The question he asked next didn't make much sense, had nothing to do with illness.

"Do you ever get mad?"

"What do you mean?" I asked, confused. "Mad at who?"

"At anyone. Your friends. Your mom."

"I get mad at my mom pretty regularly," I admitted, though I couldn't figure what this had to do with anything. "If I don't remind her to pay the bills, the electric will go out or something. Yet if I show that I'm mad and remind her too loudly? She doesn't respond well to that." *She's shot in the ass all night, and I'm stuck with my guilt.*

"And your friends? You get mad at them?"

"I get... annoyed sometimes because—" I stopped, Macy's lecture ringing in my head. *You're not only trusting a strange kid who ran away, but you're talking about us?*

I heard a moan and realized it was mine. I felt worse than when I came here, when I thought there was a chance I could walk home. I started swallowing spit and decided I'd better prepare him for a bedroom version of "The Umbrella Ride."

"You ran away, right?"

"Right."

"You've seen a lot, then?"

"Sure."

"Sick people?"

"Tons."

I didn't expect the easiness in his answers but was relieved. "Good. Cuz I'm scared I'm going to puke. Sorry." I shut my eyes, then I snapped them open. Last thing I wanted to do besides puke was have a nightmare in a strange bed. "How'd we get on the subject of my friends? What were we talking about? God or something..."

"Don't really think we were talking about God"—he whizzed a wastepaper basket over by the side of the bed but looked more distracted by his thought than grossed out by me—"...think we were talking about *control.*"

I didn't know what he meant, but I noticed how his fingers dangled loosely between his knees, like he was not the least bit rattled by me. It was hard to believe I could threaten to hurl, and any kid would be taking this whole scenario so well. "You're not going to call nine-one-one on me, are you?"

"Not unless you want me to."

"No way. I just want—" My gut whirled until I thought my stomach was in my brains. I thought, *I just want some goddamn control.* Probably because he had just babbled that word. "I want to...to sleep."

"Go ahead."

I watched his hands flip, like he had shrugged. *Yeah, so I can meet some...Sally who swallows forks and knives right in front of you.* "I can't sleep here."

"I don't bite."

"You're too nice," I said.

"*I'm* too nice."

I didn't catch the sarcasm in his voice until he started giggling again. *He thinks I'm nice, ha. I'm really selfish...If I bother people I'll lose them, and I want to keep them, which is not the same as being nice. It would feel pretty great...to bother just one person...somebody I didn't care about so much...*

"I had cancer in junior high." I gripped the corner of the pillowcase—watching for a twitch, a squirm, a something.

His eyes merely missed a blink as they widened for a second. He said, "Okay..."

I waited, but he had nothing to add. "So...you ever know anybody with cancer?"

He nodded. "I've had friends with AIDS. There's a certain type of brain cancer associated with that. Couple of friends..."

AIDS. *Gayness, drug abuse, runaways...the terms* should *put me on edge,* I thought hazily. But talking to someone my own age who knew about anything this serious...it gave me a rush. I reached out, grabbed hold of his fingers, and squeezed them. I waited for him to pull away, but he kept staring absently at the corner.

He finally asked, "So, you've never had a support group? A counselor? Friends who had the same thing?"

I tried to remember what happened in eighth grade. "My mom kept saying the chances of a recurrence were slim, like, less than one in five. She needed to forget the whole thing—"

"Jesus." He pinched the bridge of his nose with the hand I wasn't turning to sludge and kept his eyes clamped shut. When he opened them, they were full of something—anger, maybe. I guessed he thought I should have been in a support group.

"Yeah, well. I could have talked myself blue in the face to someone, and it wouldn't have helped my *real* problem."

"What's your *real* problem?"

"That I'm afraid it's come back." I just started spewing again—how tiredness had turned to dizzy spells and how I had not felt like fainting since chemo. He looked concerned but not horrified. I had just told him some stuff that would make most of my friends politely freeze in horror.

"How old are you?" I asked suddenly. The feeling rushed through me like maybe he was, somehow, a lot older. Maybe he was really college age but his running away set him back. He listened like a grown-up—like he was expected to do something constructive and not just join in my pity fest.

His mind seemed to stop concentrating, but his eyes looked weary. He rolled them. "How old am I? I'm *ancient.*" His laugh sounded tired.

"What do you mean?" I figured he probably meant something like *It's not the years; it's the mileage.* But he didn't answer. He trudged around the mattress and flopped down on the other side. He blinked at the ceiling a bunch of times.

His hair fell back on the pillow, giving me a chance to look at him more closely than I had dared in school. He had one of those baby noses that blended into his cheeks without a single flaw. His dark brown eyelashes, impossibly long, made me think of a toddler who hadn't grown into his face yet. So much maturity coming through such innocent features—that froze me, reminding me of some sci-fi story I had read of an old man stuck in a child's body.

"'Ancient'...That's a funny comment." I finally ran a finger down his peachy cheek and came back with equal sarcasm. "Do you even shave yet?"

"No."

"Well, then?"

He took my hand off his face, plopped it down on my own chest, then patted it with too much patience. "Go to sleep, why don't you? Let me think..."

"I'm not asking you to solve my problems." He looked too stirred up. I felt uncomfortable, like I was a pain. "Don't fret. If I'm not in remission anymore, there's nothing we can do."

His hand came down on my head in a "dad" sort of way that gave me another weird twitch. He rubbed my hair and stared off at the ceiling, either like I was three or he was sixty. It left me half annoyed, half hypnotized.

"Claire, I'm not saying you're still in remission or not in remission. I'm saying you've got so many issues, I don't see how you could tell one thing from the other."

"'Issues'...What do you mean?"

He kept thumping his head lightly against the wall, staring at the ceiling. But his hand came down over my forehead and then my eyes, so I had to shut them.

"I'm not going to sleep on your bed," I informed him.

"Then try to relax so I can think."

I didn't exactly have a choice. I could imagine myself trying to walk home and heaving in the gutter with ten drivers catching the view.

"Sometimes I have nightmares." I tried to warn him.

"Go figure."

I caught more sarcasm but couldn't figure how he would know about my nightmares. "They're bloody. I don't wake up well."

"Do you scream? I can turn up the radio."

My eyes filled up, to my shock. I wanted to think of something awful to say so he would stop being so nice. But I couldn't think of anything. "I don't scream. I'm just not...in a great mood when I wake up."

"You're in a worse mood than *this*?"

I laughed, sniffing up tears, feeling completely stupid. "Sorry if...I upset you."

He laced his fingers on his stomach and stared at me with a look of shock that I would have expected when I said I'd had cancer, but I couldn't make sense of it now.

"You're an odd one..." I yawned. "Are you going to tell me how old you are?"

That's the last thing I remember until I was dreaming. It wasn't a bloody nightmare, though it had that same deranged feel to it. I dreamed about Lani's arrival on Hackett. It wasn't by bus or car. I saw him walking toward me out of the mist with something heavy on his back, like a shiny pack or a roll of fluorescent blankets...coming off the water at the end of Fisherman's Wharf.

5

I stared into a radio alarm that said 8:10, and I couldn't decide whether it was morning or night. The room was dark... *night*. My surroundings made sense when I saw the three pinheads of candlelight.

Lani lay flat on his back, on the far side of the bed, fingers laced across his stomach. He didn't use a pillow. I hazily remembered having a dream about him that hadn't upset me too badly. But without any pillow, he looked almost laid out, like a vampire, or a corpse in a funeral home. I flicked at his arm, hoping he would roll over, because I had some tingly, power-nap high I didn't want to lose via freaky thoughts.

His lips were a little opened, but I was surprised when they moved so easily. "You're feeling better."

I couldn't argue.

He inhaled deeply. "Mom made meat loaf. Smell?"

I could smell beef wafting up. It made my mouth water as I stood up.

"Wanna eat before you leave?"

"I hardly ever eat red meat, thanks."

He sat up. After a long exhale he asked, "Now, how did I know you were going to say that? No red meat, no sticky buns..." He stood up and stretched. "No fun..."

"I have plenty of fun. Just not with sugar and dead cows."

I tied my cheerleading jacket around my waist because Indian summer had definitely hit and the air had grown thick with wet heat. I hiked up my backpack with a jerk to help me ignore my stomach's begging. Since I lost weight for cheerleading, I had stuck pretty well to a regimented plan—fruit for breakfast, salad for lunch. Dinner, I ate whatever I wanted, so long as it didn't include anything fried, too much red meat, or any desserts. My stomach was telling me this gravy could definitely be on my diet, but I'd already eaten red meat once this week. "I look like I just woke up from a hundred-year sleep. Your mom's going to think we did the nasty up here."

"And that would be the end of the universe?"

I giggled, traipsing after him and his sarcasm. When we got to the foot of the stairs, his mom came through the kitchen door.

"Would you like to invite your friend for dinner, Lani? I've kept it warm."

My eyes felt all swollen from sleep. I was afraid to say no, because moms take that sort of thing like personal rejection. But Lani piped up.

"She already said no thanks. She needs to get on home."

His mom walked right up to me and stuck her hand out. "It was very nice having you. I hope you come back soon."

Having me. I had hardly said a thing to her. I looked into her eyes as I shook hands, and I saw something there. Almost an urgency. She *was* hoping we did the nasty up there. As if my presence made her son not gay.

"You have a really nice house...and your cooking smells really great...Some other time, okay? My mom is waiting for me—"

Lani pulled me out the door almost before I finished blathering. He let out an uninterested half giggle, which seemed more directed at me than his mother.

"You know what she's thinking, don't you?" I started.

"Yes."

"And you're not embarrassed? She's your *mom*. Moms create guilt."

"Yeah, you're right." He nodded genuinely. "Except she's not really and truly my mom. I'm adopted. Which means I can always tell myself, *She's just a lady who is nice to me when the mood strikes her,* and I can believe myself. I don't have as much guilt."

"Wow, you're adopted ..." I didn't know what I wanted to say about that. I still had starch in my head from sleep. "You've had a very unusual life."

"Yeah, it's an epic classic."

"Can I hear some of it?"

"Maybe sometime." Before I could ask what was wrong with *now,* he cleared his throat and jumped back on my life. "So you're scared you're sick again. Your friends are helpless, your mom is hysterical, God is a jerk, and your father has a do-not-disturb sign plastered to his forehead."

I cracked up. "You're making it sound horrible."

"So ... how would you feel about getting tested without anybody knowing? If it turns out to be something else, then you won't freak your mom out, and your friends wouldn't know, either. And you wouldn't have to bother your dad."

The concept almost stopped me in my tracks. But I was very familiar, by this point in my life, with the arrival of a thousand insurance forms in the mail every time I had a check-up. "There's no way for me to get tested without my parents knowing."

"There might be. We could take a bus. It's a long ride. Do you know how you get a test done at your doctor's office and you have to wait, like, ten days for results?"

I had to nod. "Story of my life."

"That's because they send those samples up to research labs. If you go right to a big city clinic at a research hospital, you can get your results in a couple hours. And some of those clinics also treat kids without parental permission."

"Why?"

"Because a lot of them are runaways, and everyone knows it."

I stopped and stared. He was streetwise beyond my wildest dreams. Getting on a bus and going far away seemed way radical. But I wanted to make sense out of his mixed-up personality. The only gay people I had ever met were summer tourists. They were usually businessmen from Philadelphia, who would rent duplexes for a couple of weeks and have all their friends down. You could tell who they were because they used beach chairs instead of towels, and smelled like expensive sunblock, and they smiled a lot, and some of them giggled, and they wore those awful, plastic flip-flops instead of Reefs. I tried to fit Lani in with this picture and it didn't work out very well. He seemed more "raw" and stripped down. A guy who seemed happy with a mattress and didn't use a pillow would go to the beach with a towel like us natives, and get all sandy and sunburned, and not care. "You don't . . . fit any of the usual categories."

His grin looked irritated. "You're trying to stereotype me. Don't do that. I hate it."

"I am not." I'd had a public-school education. I knew better. "There's a difference between stereotyping and deciding where somebody fits in."

"What's the difference? It's all for the purpose of passing judgment."

"I wouldn't say that. It just helps you get to know somebody better." I thought of his weird wording in school that day. *Not a girl.* "It's easier to say what you're *not* like than what you're like. You're not like a lot of the guys around here, but you're not like a girl, either. You don't look like a grownup. You don't act like a kid. You're definitely not a dork. But

I couldn't see you running for class president somehow—" I stopped because I could sense annoyance rolling off him.

"I don't like being put in boxes. Boy, girl, dork, popular—those are boxes."

"Sorry. But..." I wanted to know *something*. "How old are you?"

"Age is a box."

I watched him, stumped. "Age is kind of important. If you were, like, twenty...I don't know how I'd feel about being your friend."

"What difference does it make?"

I sighed as an annoying thought dawned on me. "Let me guess. You're one of those super geniuses who's got everything figured out all differently than the rest of us."

"Genius is a box."

"Okay..." I felt caught in some game—one I was losing. I thought of a question having to do with actions rather than labels, or his "boxes." "If you read Albert Einstein, would you understand him?"

"I've read Einstein. I understand him."

I didn't want to call him a liar, though I figured he had to be one. "What's a kid doing living on the streets and reading Einstein?"

"It happens." He shrugged easily. "There's no correlation between homelessness and stupidity."

I supposed he was trying to tell me that I was using boxes again. I kept quiet.

"As for me and the library, that started in about fifth grade...whenever it is that boys need to look like boys, and girls like girls. I had to find hideouts where I could be in peace for a while. The school playgrounds, the street corners, the places most people hang, are not really safe if you're too different from everybody else. The library was good. The dangerous kids won't show up there. Librarians are nice. They'll talk to you ... and one librarian told me once, 'If you can understand human behavior, it can't hurt you nearly as much.' That just always stuck with me. Besides, if you're a runaway, the seats are comfortable. I've spent days and days reading in libraries."

"Interesting." I would never have put together runaway kids and libraries before. But hearing him put it that way, it made a lot of sense. "So ... what all did you read?"

He sighed uncomfortably and mumbled out a bunch of mishmash, which I started to realize were last names. The only ones I recognized were Marx, Darwin, Freud, and Hegel.

"Jesus Christ," I breathed.

"Yeah, him, too. But listen. This is very important." He stopped and turned a finger in my face. "You cannot tell anybody that I know a lot of stuff. I'm trusting you with secrets that I don't usually tell people, and only because you're such a pro at keeping your own secrets. I need for people to think I'm less sharp than I am."

"But why?" I figured he deserved some kudos. He wasn't going to get any kudos on his looks—not around here, where muscles "rule the cule."

"Because seeing through human behavior is, like, a blessing and a curse." He started talking fast, like his mouth had to keep up with his thoughts. His graceful hands moved to emphasize his thoughts. "I *had* to understand why kids bullied, or I would have been completely ... helpless. Knowing bullies were once bullied, knowing they depend on your fear, knowing that they hate their own feelings of victimization and not really you and that none of this has changed one speck since Moses managed to walk out of Egypt ... all that stuff makes you react differently than if you're just using your gut."

"Like how?"

"Because ..." His hands kept moving in that graceful way. "... your gut would tell you to be afraid. Fear is what bullies feed off, and it paralyzes you, too. If you're thinking *pity* instead of *fear*, they don't get such a charge. And sometimes you can think on your feet and figure out how to get away. You can't if your mind is paralyzed."

"Oh." I watched him with a little more respect. He had hinted that he wasn't a very good fighter, but maybe in a way he was. He might not land hard punches—not with those hands—but it sounded like he had a pocketful of tricks.

"At the same time"—he shuddered—"when people realize you can see past their eyes and into their heads? They don't take kindly to that. In the city, you could get mugged. Around here? Forget mugged. You could get lynched. So, you can't tell."

"Okay." I wanted to be polite but felt kind of insulted by his statements about Hackett. "I don't think you have to be worried about getting lynched around here, Lani. People just want to have fun—"

"You're laughing."

I realized I was. "I just think you're overreacting."

"Yeah? Believe me, you wouldn't like it much if I started looking inside your head at *your* hidden garbage. I won't. But just put yourself in the shoes of somebody whose hidden garbage is over the top—"

"Wait...What about me and my 'garbage'?" I slowed down to stare at him.

"See? You're defensive already—"

"That's because I'm fine. I don't have 'garbage.'" I forced a laugh, which sounded half strangled. I had told him about cancer. Not that cancer qualifies as "garbage." But I sensed he thought it could bring on some psycho-weirdness after-affect in my case. I stopped and put my fingers up to my forehead, covering my face, remembering what a jerk I'd been in his bedroom. *"I have nightmares. They're bloody..."*

"That's called the 'defensive stance.'" He pulled on my

arms, grinning. "Did you know the people most afraid of their own thoughts spend half their lives with their arms crossed? Put your arms down, here." He flopped them down. "Now. Look me in the eye and tell me you don't have any hidden garbage in your life."

I wanted to say it. But I'm a bad liar and had a strong sense it would come out all muddled. I settled on "I can see why people would totally hate you."

"If you're going to hate me, you might as well hear all my thoughts about you."

"I don't want to." But I felt suddenly scared that maybe he could see into my basement. See my "bloody lyrics." See my electric guitar that only Macy knew about—and only because I was cranking it so loud one day I couldn't hear her come in upstairs. I had just been ripping on some blues runs, thank god. No razor-blade lyrics. "Go ahead...say what you were going to say." I curled my toes to brace myself.

"I think you would do yourself a favor to go see a shrink."

I did my standing-stock-still routine, but he was right in my face. It was not a situation where you can become invisible. My insides started exploding. "I think you have nerve. It's not your business, telling me a thing like that."

"Claire, simmer. A shrink is a status symbol. It's like having a masseuse."

" 'A masseuse'?" I let myself boil over. "The only masseuse on the island goes back to Philly in the winter. Cuz the only people that come to her are rich lady tourists and faggots—"

I threw a hand over my mouth, and he raised a hand to his. I got the impression his was to keep from laughing. I sunk down onto the lawn beside the sidewalk. I could not believe I had just spewed that word in his face.

"That's another version of the defensive stance," his voice went off, muffled, behind his fingers. "You just lowered yourself out of my gaze and turned away."

"Up yours."

"Honestly, I understand. This is part of the reason why I could never become a shrink. I'm too blunt."

"You're a bloody nightmare." Since I knew nothing about psychology, or any of the stuff he had read, I got paranoid. "What is it... that you know about me?"

He sat down cross-legged on the sidewalk, facing me. "Only that you've been through a trauma, you've never talked it out, and you're having nightmares."

"That's it? That's all you think you know?" *Doyee.* I had just implied that there was something else.

"I'm not a shrink, Claire. But it's probably not as bad as you're thinking it is."

And I am not going to see one. "You could *make* people nuts."

"I guess that's it."

"Don't be sarcastic. Tell me. I want to hear what you think you know about my hidden garbage."

"I—" He stopped for a minute. Then he got that cranking-mind look again, and things started spilling out in half sentences. Like his mind was working so fast, only parts could break the sound barrier. "You're not a criminal, for pete's sake... had illness and trauma... no one to talk to... but the shit always comes out somewhere. Mutilation dreams, you said... Gone beyond dreaming, or you wouldn't be so crazed... Music. You've got artistic tendencies so probably... don't know if you're old enough to be writing music yet... Sixteen-year-olds dump in poetry... same part of the brain as dreams... You're writing bloody poetry."

It was close enough to make my jaw hang. It was like being naked while he decided if my headlights were pink or brown. The only reason I didn't slap him is that he could have predicted it. "You're a regular nightmare."

"I could get myself lynched. So, you won't tell your friends I'm like this."

"I'm going home now." I stood up. He picked up my backpack and handed it to me. I swiped it and started on my merry way. I could feel him staring after me.

I stopped, because I didn't want him to think he had totally gotten the better of me. "Where is this place you want to take me?"

"Philly. Franklin Hospital. Come to the bus station at eight tomorrow morning."

I decided I would just not show up. Somehow it felt like getting even. "Okay."

"And if I don't see you, I'll just go on to school."

I turned, slowly. *Mind reader.* "Uh...what makes you think I wouldn't come?"

"You didn't turn around until after you asked. We're not connecting. I've been a pain. I'm sorry, I'm just too blunt." Then he turned and started walking back toward his house.

He is obnoxious and weird, I decided. I wasn't going anywhere with him. *I don't care if I'm half dead.* I turned and hurried toward my house, where I knew I'd find a ton of great phone messages.

6

I threw my coat and backpack into the hall closet and headed for the kitchen to check the answering machine. I found five messages from Macy and one from Scott. Two for Mom. I listened to them while eating a drumstick from the chicken Mom had left in the microwave.

The first two from Macy were along the lines of "Where *are* you, dork? We're waiting for you!" then the click as she hung up.

The one from Scott went, "Hey! Yo! Claire woman! Where's the Claire woman? *Yo, Vince, get your hands off me, fish breath. What does it look like I'm doing! I'm talking to the Claire woman! Her answering machine at any rate, yo!* Claire! Are you home, Claire?"

My grin rose and fell in all of about ten seconds. The *what ifs* of the future buzzed around my head, making the chicken tough to swallow.... *could lose all of this if I got sick again...*

The last three were Macy's. "*Claire, we're heading out in Vince's car in ten minutes.*" "*We're heading out in five minutes...*" "*We're heading out in two minutes...*"

I tossed a drumstick bone into the sink, eyeing some salad I'd put up on the counter. I grabbed a handful of lettuce and shoved it in my mouth as I erased all evidence of the phone messages, whipped a pen out of the drawer, and started scribbling my mom a note saying I went to Macy's for study group. The front door slammed, and I heard my mother's keys drop inside her handbag. The pencil flopped on the counter, and I drummed my fingers in frustration.

"Claire? How was your day? Did you get dinner?" She came around the corner into the kitchen and kissed my cheek. "Did I get any phone messages?"

"Two from Aunt Phyllis. She wants you to call her. I think you're about to be roped into making Tina's homecoming dress."

"Tina made Mainland Homecoming Court?" She clapped her hands together and spun twirls in the kitchen. "Go, Tina! Go, Tina! Go, Tina!"

"Go, Tina!" I threw in, despite my eyes wanting to roll to China. Mom's sizeable butt flew this way and that. A few of her cheerleading pictures still sat on the dining room breakfront, along with her homecoming queen photos. She had been cute, not heavy then. Just...perfect. More like Macy than me. No one would guess we were mother and daughter these days—not with my height and slenderness. I looked just like my dad. "Besides, you know you'll end up making the dress—"

"And it will be the most beautiful dress from here to Philadelphia! Your own father would drool—"

I put a smile on my face, to take some of the harshness out of my thought. "Speaking of Dad, can you make sure Aunt Phyllis pays you back for the fabric this time? Being that she's got a husband and you've got none?"

"Did you eat? Where's the mail?"

"I didn't exactly eat," I said, trying to get a strategy together in a flash. "I lay down after cheerleading, and it turned into a two-hour crash-out nap. I just woke up."

I didn't have to say *where* this happened.

Her perked-up eyebrows dropped for a moment, and she

looked me up and down. "Oh. You just...got tired after cheerleading and lay down for a bit."

Nap...why did I say that? I never take naps unless I'm sick.

"Oh. Yeah, tough practice, that's all. I'm fine. Great."

Fortunately her mind was rolling too quickly to doubt me. "Good, because it's Ginny DeGrossa's birthday this weekend. Party-party, party-hardy." She pinched my cheek. "You have to make one of your famous health salads. I'm making my lasagna and fried chicken, and if I don't have something for all the health nuts—"

"You're having a party *here*? For Mrs. DeGrossa?" I stuck my head in the refrigerator to get some air. "Mom. She calls the cops on me with a noise complaint if I don't stop playing at Sydney's right at ten every Saturday night. I can't stand her."

"Well...pretend you can."

"Since when is Mrs. DeGrossa in *Les Girls*?"

"She's not. But there's no birthdays in *Les Girls* until after Thanksgiving, and we've done the Rod 'N' Reel for four weekends in a row now. It's our excuse to do something exotic."

Les Girls is my mom's clique of divorced and single ladies who wear too much perfume and too much makeup just to go to the local bar. I don't think any of them could get as sloshed as my mom, but they never seemed to mind her slurring and swaying. They kept asking her out with them—though no man ever did.

"How about *the movies*? Wouldn't kill you guys to go to the mainland."

"Drive over those drawbridges at night? You can feel them shift when the wind blows."

"You cannot. That's ridiculous."

"Can, too." Her way of saying, *No one wants to be the designated driver.*

I sighed. "Does this party mean I have to mow the grass, too?"

"Yes."

I started sorting through the mail, flinging junk coupons and credit card applications in the trash.

"Come on, Claire. Don't I always cook and clean for the parties with your friends?"

I plastered my smile back on, which meant the conversation was about to get dangerous. "I would rather you pay the electric bill than spend money on parties you conjure up with Macy before you even ask me."

"I'm the world's worst ogre! That's why your friends love me. Get over yourself."

"Mom..." I held up an electric bill with a pink notice in it, my grin rising higher. "Do we know what pink means?"

"Pink means we have thirty whole days before blue."

"And how much is our little party going to cost?"

"I'll catch up. If your father would pay his support on time—"

"How much, Mom?"

"Get over yourself. How much does it cost to bake a lasagna and a few bins of fried chicken?"

"Does this party mean I'll have to use my Sydney's money to pay the electric bill again?"

She went to the refrigerator and stuck her head in—her turn to get away from my gaze. "I never asked you to do that, Claire. I was going down to pay it in person."

That one was a lie. I managed to keep the grin as I bubbled over. "We sat in the dark for two days, Mom."

She slammed the fridge, deciding she hadn't heard me. "And eat something before you make me crazy. You look like your father—irresponsible, musician, scarecrow...and as for Ginny DeGrossa, if I throw her this party, she'll stop calling the police on you. I promise. She's got an anxiety disorder, okay? Not everyone is as young and as spry as you are, my dear."

Spry...*a mom word for "healthy."* I grabbed my jacket. "I'm outta here."

"Where? It's a school night."

"To...the Pirate's Den for a burger. I've got those deadly red-meat cravings."

"Uh-huh. I'm sure you're *not* meeting Macy and Myra and Geneva and Eli. I'm sure I was *never* your age." She held out a five-dollar bill from her handbag, which I started at. "Order yourself a milk shake. They use real milk at the Pirate's Den—"

I took the five, shoved it back in her wallet, my plaster grin starting to hurt. "Mom, take your cash and pay that bill. Before it gets pissed away."

"And you stay out of Vince Clementi's car! You hear? He's trouble. You know what his father was."

"Maybe...a *drunk*?" I hinted.

"Maybe...a clammer!"

"A clammer is an alcoholic who can't get work on a fishing boat."

"And be back by ten. It's a school night."

I could see her hands shaking a little. She was waiting for me to leave before she went for the vodka bottle. *Thinks I'm blind and stupid.* I rarely said anything about her drinking beyond these types of stupid hints. One Saturday night I got mad and called her a drunk, and she spouted off quickly, "I was fine before you got sick!" It had been a way ugly thing to say, and she apologized when she got sober, saying it had come out all wrong. But she had spoken the whole truth. Before I got sick she had been pretty much like other moms—loved her crowd, loved a party, but knew when to switch to Pepsi or call it a night.

"I will stay out of Vince's car, I will be home soon...and I love you, Mom."

That first thing was a lie, but the last was what she lived for. She hugged me tight. I could remember a time when her hugs were overwhelming and she felt like the biggest, funnest person in the world. This year she felt short and almost breakable, despite the pillows on her hips and thighs. I left.

I started walking down Hackett Boulevard, knowing my friends would come by quickly. That's what we did if we were going somewhere and didn't want our parents to see us get in Vince Clementi's Impala.

Vince was the only sophomore to have a driver's license, probably because he flunked at least one grade. He was kind of a scary guy, but we tolerated him after he got a car—being that he drove us all around.

I had only walked about three blocks toward the business district when brakes screeched beside me. Vince's Impala was twelve years old, and the back end sank way down from having carried too many bodies. The passenger-side door flew open, and I looked through the sea of grins and laughs, wondering if I'd have to sit in the trunk again.

"Just get in!" Vince hollered. "I ain't paid off my last ticket for hauling you fag hags around—"

Mike Mayer's huge hand reached out from the backseat, and next thing I knew, my forehead was sliding across the ceiling as a thousand hands tried to wedge me in.

Mike said, "Claire, pull your feet in. Jesus Christ, do you have to be so *long*?"

My head knocked into the driver's-side back window, and I fought to curl my legs while a fit of giggles spazzed me. My eyelashes caught in Phil's eyebrow, and we giggled as Vince gunned it.

I tried to decide who was where. Scott's voice came from beside Vince. Geneva was singing with the radio, sort of behind my back, which meant she was sitting in Scott's lap. I couldn't hate her for that, I decided. Vince was avoiding Officer Dan, Hackett's dreaded teenage-driving hawk, and there had been no time to rearrange when I arrived. Phil, Macy, Eli, Myra, and Mike were under me in the back somehow.

Geneva sang loudly with the end of a Felicia Almonara song. "Ahh, I love Jennifer Martinez," she said.

I would have let it go. But I think Macy's hawk eye works even when it's buried under bodies. She jabbed me in the side. "Claire, was that Jennifer Martinez?"

"You think I don't know my tunes?" Geneva barked back.

I wondered if I should have complained about Scott to Geneva. She wasn't exactly known for breaking up couples, but she was one of those girls who either had a boyfriend or was seriously scoping for one.

"Claire knows every tune that ever buzzed," Phil shouted, jostling me around. "And you don't know shit. Claire, who's singing?" Phil and Geneva didn't get along so great. They used to go out. He shook me again, trying to squirt information, I guess.

He only stopped after I said, "It's Felicia."

I could feel Geneva seething as Macy poked me victoriously. She hadn't missed where Geneva was sitting.

Geneva defended herself. "Claire only knows, like, The Doors, and shit. Hey, Claire! When are you going to bring your *elec*tric guitar down to Sydney's?"

I jerked up until I found Macy's face in the crowd and froze. *Ratted me out...*

Her mouth formed the O shape, and I tried to dig through my panicked head about what she had heard that day. *Blues runs. That's it, I* think...

"I'm sorry...I'm sorry," she murmured loud enough for me to hear. "Remember that week that Lyda Barone wouldn't leave us alone? And I was so mad at you?"

"What did you tell them?"

"That you had an electric guitar in your basement, and you sound like a dying cow. Claire, I'm sorry, I'm sorry."

I sighed. You always knew where you stood with Macy, because she always told the truth. If she'd heard any girls-butchering-their-brains-out stuff, she would have let me know that, too. Still, I couldn't relax, what with the responses coming down.

"Neerr…neerrrr…neeeeeerrrrrr! Claire's gonna be the next Jimi Hendrix!" Phil bounced me as he ground his butt around the seat.

All the guys were making a chorus of *neeeeeer-neeeeeer*s, all calling me Pearl Jam and Judas Priest and fifteen other totally guy groups. All except for my own boyfriend, who was singing along with the radio like this whole thing wasn't happening.

Geneva kicked in right on cue. "That's pretty cool, Claire. But don't you feel like a *guy* doing that?"

Any thought of feeling butch had never crossed my mind, and I could hear the echo of Lani rambling on about his "boxes" until I realized how obnoxious it is when it's happening to you.

I said, "*No…*," and lay there seething, despite how Macy kept poking me, mumbling, "I'm sorry. I'm sorry. I'll get her off Scott. I promise."

Fortunately, their abuse turned to whooping from the guys as gravel crunched under the tires, because Vince liked to gun it down Mariner Road. There were no houses along this five-mile stretch to the wharf, so the cops didn't patrol it. They didn't think anyone would be stupid enough to lead foot it down a gravel road chocked with flood-tide debris and sand holes. They didn't understand the extent of Vince Clementi's insanity.

Vince's speed sent my cheek smashing into Phil's forehead, who said, "Hang tight, babe. I'll make you comfy."

My body shifted, and suddenly I was in a wind machine, staring up at the stars. Like I needed more attention. But the summerlike air on my blushing face felt good, and having my head out the window put some distance between me and my embarrassment. Part of me wanted to shove myself back into the car, waiting for Vince to hit a pothole and separate my neck from my body. Yet, I could feel the security of everyone's hands on my legs and arms. Vince really cooked it, up to probably sixty. I kept trying to turn my neck to see where we were going, but the wind kept forcing my eyes shut.

Scott squeezed my ankle, shouting something to Vince about don't be lame and go over any potholes. Vince swerved on purpose—probably to get even with Scott for telling him his business. At this speed my body jerked out the window from the waist up and only stopped because of Scott's death grip.

I screamed. I tried to look ahead by making a wind block with squinted eyelashes. It couldn't last more than a couple of minutes.

The road curved, then sped us down this giant sand dune toward the spotlights on the wharf parking lot. I caught a glimpse of Tony Clementi's truck there, and this combo of good and bad feelings whipped up more. Tony was Vince's big brother and a fisherman, about five years older than us. He was known to be such a great partyer that he made me uncomfortable at a party. He was nuts before he even had anything to drink. Some people said it had to do with his size, five five, which meant he constantly felt the need to prove himself. Others said his size was the "side problem," and the "real problem" was Vince and Tony's dad, who had been in the habit of hurling beer bottles at smart-mouthed sons instead of getting up off the couch to take care of it. When Tony was four years old, a hurled Rolling Rock fractured his skull and supposedly affected that part of his brain in charge of growth.

Vince, at seventeen, was six-foot-one and at about age twelve had hit the size where he could hurl something back at

Mr. Clementi without fearing revenge. Tony never reached nearly that size. He took abuse until he was seventeen. On a Saturday night in August that year, Mr. Clementi decided to take a left instead of a right coming out of the Rod 'N' Reel in a drunken stupor.

Kids wondered with cackles if Mr. Clementi's death meant he had defined the phrase *taking a long walk off a short pier*, but no one wondered with Vince and Tony in hearing distance. If you said anything in front of them other than "He drowned trying to save a night fisherman," they'd beat you to tomato juice. Go figure how kids could defend a dad like that. It's funny what we accepted from somebody who owned a car.

The bigger weirdness was how Tony managed to be twice everything Vince was when he was only half the size. He was twice as surly, twice as daring, twice as nuts. Vince drove crazily. Tony did crazy things in the paths of cars.

And there I was, out Vince's window to my waist, when I thought I saw Tony standing in the middle of the road. I strained my eyes through my eyelash windscreen, but already my heart was banging.

"Vince, don't swerve!" I shouted, but my shouting was drowned in everyone else's... *"Swerve! Don't hit him this time! Swerve!"*

Vince wasn't slowing down. This was one of their psycho-brother games. When it started four months ago, Vince would refuse to slow down, and Tony would dive out of the headlights at the last minute. When that version got to be no fun anymore, Tony started waiting until Vince hit the brakes, and he would splatter onto the windshield. He'd suffer a few serious bruises and feel it was worth it to see if he could make a girl wet herself. I felt close to wetting myself. A lot of girl's voices screamed, *"Swerve!,"* which meant, if Vince swerved right, Tony's body would take my head off on this narrow stretch of road.

Vince jammed on the brakes and didn't swerve, which gave me a second of relief before realizing Tony was adding a new dimension to the psycho show. Instead of splattering onto the windshield, he kept rolling or kicking, then he was on the roof of the car. He spilled over the side and came down on top of me, never realizing I was halfway out the window. He hit like a freight train, and my neck nearly did a one eighty before Tony and I spilled onto Mariner Road. Vince hadn't completely stopped yet.

7

Tony had never gotten anyone killed, because his brain hatched intelligence only when people were about to die. He wrapped his arms and legs around me tight, so ninety percent of the hitting-rolling impact was on him. He's got fisherman skin, like bricks. I thought we rolled about ten miles in the meadow grass alongside the parking lot, but when I untangled myself from his laughing convulsion and stood up, the car was only about fifteen feet in front. Doors flew open. My neck was bouncing like my head was on a spring, and my head hurt kind of all over, but I figured it came from the goose egg under my bangs, where my palm already pressed down instinctively. I wanted to panic but didn't need to hear a lot of screams.

Tony's face danced in front of me, and he was sucking his knuckles. In the redness of the taillight, his whole face looked evenly red, so I gathered he wasn't bleeding—not that I cared.

He hollered, "Vince, what the hell are you doing, hanging a girl out the window!"

Probably his version of an apology. I searched my tangled brain for words from my aunt Phyllis, an emergency room nurse. ...*face bleeds worse than any other body part...need pressure*...Not panicking was like holding back a dam explosion, especially when nobody was doing anything constructive.

Macy was all "Scott! Scott! She's holding her head!"

She and Tony were trying to pull my hand down, and I didn't think they knew how face injuries could gush. I started shoving arms off me.

"Someone go down to the boat and bring up the first-aid kit!" My even voice got lost in their clatter.

"She's okay. Just give her some breathing room." Scott's arms went around me.

I didn't want to get blood all over his football jacket, so I pushed off him and ducked under his arm. *Solve it myself.* My shaking legs carried me toward the dock. Tony fell in beside me. The smell of beer blew up my nostrils.

"Babe, slow down and let me look! I'm a fisherman! I seen injuries you ain't even heard of!"

I shook away, thinking, *Yeah, I'll trust you—who flings himself in front of a moving Impala.*

"Broken shell, something..." My voice shook. "Get some ice. By the bait shop."

"Ice, ice, ain't I nice?" He ran off.

Scott gripped my arms. "Claire, if it's really bloody under there, you could get blood all over my dad's boat! You'll get my ass kicked. Don't do it!"

When he wrapped his arms around me again, I realized no one comprehended the size of this problem. It was like the Sophomore Show. Macy's part was to get my boyfriend focused on me and not Geneva, and his role was to be Mr. Comforting.

"Everybody shut *up*!" I finally yelled at the bedlam. "Stop giggling, stop screaming, just shut up and act your fuckin' ages."

You could have heard a fish jump. *Sincerely un-Claire,* but I felt like I had been trying to walk up a wall. I lifted my hand so my palm full of warm blood was perfectly visible to Scott and felt the wound explode with warmth. "Well, then... we've got a problem. Because I can either fix this with your dad's

64

first-aid kit, or we can all go to the emergency room and get in a lot of trouble."

Before I finished the sentence, blood ran through my eyelashes, and I sniffed it up my nostrils. I leaned forward so when it dripped off my chin it would hit the ground and not the sleeves of my cheerleading jacket, still tied around my waist. Blood on my sacred cheerleading jacket would give my mom a drama fest.

Scott steered me forward, and I could hear Mike telling everyone to shut up again.

"We'll just clean it up. Your old man'll think it was crew if—"

Tony, holding a bait bucket full of crushed ice, caught up with us on the dock as we reached the bow. I dug my free hand into it. Ice helps bleeding stop, but the freezing cold ate into the raw wound. I actually let Scott carry most of my weight as I focused on not hurling the ice a couple of miles.

He let me down easy until I was sitting on the dock, staring into an audience of sneakers, none of which was moving.

"I'm gonna puke." It was Macy's voice, and I remembered her tantrum during lunch when I cut my thumb. *My night life's invading my day life . . .*

"Just take your girlfriend on the boat," I told Phil, just to put something in the air.

Tony took ice chips and started washing my face off. As he dropped little fistfuls of bloody ice into the harbor, he started laughing. Howling, actually. Who knew why, except that it's probably a Tony Clementi way to relieve stress. I allowed myself to join in because laughter might keep all these frozen feet from snapping off at the ankles.

I grabbed a fresh fistful of ice and switched hands again, which were shaking bad. Scott sat down behind me, and I leaned back on him, thinking his body heat might stop my all-over body trembles.

After a few minutes he asked, "Think it stopped bleeding?"

"Dunno. You tell me."

He leaned around the side, and he and Tony stared just above my eyes as I slowly drew my hand away.

Tony shook his head. "Damn. Your scalp is, like, standing up. It's pulled up from your skull right below where your hair starts. Like, all the little hairs are still in place—" He laughed like that was awesome. I could have done without the description.

I slammed the ice onto the wound again, which probably made him add his version of comfort. "But the part that's standing up is only about an inch long! And the blood, it's just…running. It ain't gushing now."

"Tony, chill down," Scott interrupted. "It's still bleeding but probably not so bad that you couldn't get to my dad's bathroom without leaving a trail of blood. Can you get up?"

I nodded, yet didn't complain when Scott hauled me up like he was some hoist. A deluge of *whew!*s hit the air, and Tony started directing traffic onto the bow.

"She's never been so okay! Little head gash—bleeds like hell, but hey. Did you know a concussion can add ten points to your IQ?"

So, why aren't you Einstein? I forced a weak grin because I liked how his stupidness was actually making people laugh in relief and move on. I could clean the thing out without the helpless stares. Even before Scott got the light on in the bathroom, I could hear them giggling and sparking a doobie on the stern, kind of a subdued version of the usual. Sets of eyes kept looking in at us, but I could not get over the feeling that everyone's biggest wish was to pretend the whole thing never happened. Except Macy, who kept shouting, "Just shut *up*, you psycho queen!" Obviously at Tony, who would be denying that he caused all of this.

"You sure you're okay?" Scott pulled the first-aid kit from a little overhead cabinet.

"No ... not sure."

"God. You handle shit good, woman."

"Too good," I mumbled, studying the rest of my face in the mirror under my palm. No other marks, just a blood streak Tony had missed with the ice. "I should have wigged out or cried or something. Listen to them now ..."

But even Scott wasn't hearing me. He was looking out the door and shouting behavior lectures because of the squeaking we were hearing. Commercial fishing boats are not like yachts. Fishing captains keep them regulation clean, but there are no frills, and nothing really looks and sounds new. The squeaking meant the guys were climbing on the salt-infested hoist for Mr. Dern's giant fishing net, and probably pushing it out, suspending each other over the cold water.

"Too good, too good," I moaned under my breath.

I let my hand go, determined not to scream, no matter what I saw in the mirror. It was pretty much like Tony described. A little flap of my forehead stood straight up about a quarter inch below my hairline, and you could almost see my skull, all caked with beach sand. Tissue jutted around the edge that filled up with blood again after a couple seconds. I let the wound stay open and snatched a wet paper towel from Scott.

"Got peroxide?"

He stuck a bottle in my hand. I kept dousing the wound, and injuries of lesser value started making themselves known. My knuckles stung, and I noticed that they were skinned. My hip and knee felt skinned, too, but when I glanced at my jeans, they were not torn, just muddy. No mom-nervous-breakdown sights visible.

I squirted my bangs with a bottle of squirt soap and stuck my whole forehead under the faucet. The numbness from the ice took the edge off the pain.

"Found a big butterfly." Scott pulled a bandage out of the kit and tossed me a clean towel. "I watched my dad butterfly crew a couple times. Let me do it."

I nodded, and satisfied that it was dry enough, I let the towel down.

Scott stared. "Claire. That's fuckin' disgusting."

I snatched the little packet out of his hand and tore it.

"No...I can do it," he said. "I seen worse. Just...you being a girl and all—"

"What does that have to do with it?" My voice was shaking with impatience, so I yelled to keep from sounding whiny. "Don't all people bleed!"

I dropped the open bandage into his giant paw, and now that more blood had run down my forehead, I caught it in a wet paper towel.

"How'd you learn first aid? You one of them new lifeguards I don't know about?"

I didn't answer.

Truth was, I had spent a lot of time during chemo listening to my aunt Phyllis describing this or that first-aid technique. She saw that it interested me and spouted all sorts of emergency-room stuff to pass some boring hours. I don't know why it interested me, except that it gave me a feeling of control over the universe, which seemed so out of control, at least from a medical standpoint.

But this was not the place to say that. Scott had just told me a contusion was disgusting. *What if he knew I was scared I might need more chemo?*

After a minute, I couldn't resist temptation any longer and looked at my blood on the paper towels. When I had been sick, one doctor had cheerily explained that healthy blood was a darker red, while mine had an orange tinge to it. The spots on the paper towels looked dark red now, like healthy blood, but it was dark in here, and I was practically seeing double. The universe was being sucked into this place I sometimes called the Claire Zone of Bad Luck.

Bad luck that Scott Dern looks like he does. Despite that I was tall, here was a blond, green-eyed version of Superman, who looked down on my forehead, despite his feet being spread out to get himself eye level. If someone took a picture of us from behind me, it would show Scott Dern on three sides. He eyed the wound, and the slightly cross-eyed effect made him look focused and serious. Laying the butterfly on, he scrunched his nose in disgust—a freckled, permanently sun-scorched nose that spelled *To hell with what I look like. So I'm lucky, so what.* From that sun mouth I smelled Wrigley's Spearmint, and I watched a piece flatten in perfect teeth as he grimaced and pressed on the bandage.

Bad luck. You could lose him. The thought tried to back up on me, but I jammed it down.

I knew he'd hit my hairline on the top, and my own aim would have stopped the bleeding better. But I wanted to be this smaller person whose worst problem was that my butterfly was tangled in my hair, and who could be saved by someone big and strong and so much the hunk you could hardly stand it.

I grabbed on to the sleeves of his jacket, almost feeling myself shrink in size as his arms curled around me. He kissed my forehead below the bandage, then started kissing me big-time. Kissing him had never been this easy—so not strewn with teeth and spit. After a minute I realized, *That's it. That's the secret. It's what Geneva does to make guys kiss great. She acts...small. Nothing like a big dude saving a helpless girl to bring on the gallant routine.*

I tried to ignore an overwhelming sense of doom by gripping his neck harder. But the noises from the deck wafted in— the growing sounds of laughter and hollers, and either Vince or Tony Clementi was already daring the guys into a round of chicken. Like we hadn't already had one accident. Yeah, I was too good.

This doom feeling grew. I could almost hear the problem

out loud. *You're not Geneva. You're not small. You're not helpless. You've been through more stuff in your life than these people have. Their crap is naive—you're not naive. You didn't realize it before because there hadn't been any accidents.*

It wasn't the type of thought that I wanted to have right then. I gripped Scott's neck like it was the only thing in the world that mattered. If he'd kicked the bathroom door closed and got a big, bad idea in his head, who knows, I might have done the old "back flop" as Macy called it. I might have done anything to hang on to the people I loved and everything that was familiar.

One great redeeming value about these guys I learned from Mary Beth—they lie. They don't screw girls half as much as they'd like you to think, and if a girl isn't half raping them, they're usually pretty cool. Scott finally ended this kissing, and I could see he was still shook up, not thinking at all about finding a crew bunk. "If you want to go home or anything, I'll get Vince. That was—*whew*—way nasty."

Part of me wanted to go home. But my hair was wet. I wanted my bangs to dry before I went running in to Mom, all "Hi, did you pay your bills," with a butterfly bandage plastered in plain view. Why give her another reason to knock off a late-night vodka...?

"I'll be okay, thanks. Just...let's destroy the evidence."

I got stuck with most of the cleanup, because it was Scott's dad's boat, and this game of chicken sounded like it might actually happen. I stayed in there alone, cleaning stray drops of blood. I found a Bunny's Market plastic bag under the sink and shoved everything in. I went out into the warm wind and tossed it over the side. The wind meant the current would carry it far out to sea by sunrise.

Scott had been sitting cross-armed on the stern, shaking his head. He pulled me up to him and said, "Hey, Claire needs to go home!"

Since we just had this conversation about how I didn't want to go home yet, I took it he was trying to keep them from playing chicken.

Tony's laughter rang out from above, where he straddled the hoist, swinging a beer up to the moon. "How long does a chicken round take, Dern? Don't be a flake. Krilley, we're doing *sea* chicken...no girl's game."

Tony jumped down off the hoist in front of Phil, sloshing beer. Scott flew up to them. "Uh-uh, nobody goes in the water. Warm air don't mean warm water. Look." He pointed at his dad's large, night-glow digital barometer. "Water temperature, fifty-two degrees. He'll go into fuckin' shock—"

"He'll be toasty! Took those people on the *Titanic* twenty minutes to die, and the water was thirty-four degrees. We're talking about a couple minutes. Fine seaman you're going to make, Dern."

I sympathized as Scott cracked a smile he couldn't control. It was hard to think of these people having two accidents in one night. *Good luck. That's what these people have. They can dive off flybridges at low tide and not break their necks, and I can just be minding my own business and end up way sick.* I shook off my pity party, despite a headache that made it hard to laugh with them. Then I heard what this chicken involved.

"You jump in the fishing net, Krilley. We submerge you for three minutes. So you got three minutes to either get out of the net or hold your breath." Tony moved to the crank of one of the two huge fishing nets. "If you come up in the net, you're still chicken. You gotta come up first. And I don't need to tell you. The more you fight the net, the more tangled up you can get. You ready?"

"Make it two minutes," Mike shouted. "Three is for those Olympic guys' lungs—"

"We did three minutes at sea. None of us was chicken. Almost got fired, but—" He let out a high-pitched laugh at the moon, then turned to Phil. "You in, Krilley?"

Phil grabbed Tony's beer can, downed the rest, squashed the can in one hand, and tossed it over the side. Then he took off his jacket and tossed it into Tony's gut. But you could hear hesitation in his nervous laugh.

I looked at this dangling net and some feeling of doom shot through me...the same feeling of doom as when a nurse came toward me with an IV. I stood frozen until I had to twist my shoulders to start breathing again. The net hung like an open jaw of a shark. *Somebody could die in that net...*

I tried telling myself I was still in shock from cutting my head. We had yet to see somebody get hurt diving off a bridge or any of the other chickens these guys carried out. Yet I backed up and grabbed hold of the ladder as if there would be some need to run.

"How are you gonna know if I'm drowning?" Phil asked.

"We watch your bubbles." Tony shrugged. "If we don't see any, we know we gotta haul you up fast."

"That sucks! I gotta, like, *die* before you see I'm in real trouble? This ain't no chicken. It's suicide. *Three minutes?*"

They talked it over, hushing Macy every thirty seconds, because she hates these games of chicken. They got the time down to two-and-a-half minutes, but my stomach still felt uneasy. Two-and-a-half minutes, in the freezing water, in a tangled net...I kept waiting for Tony to say he was joking, but he looked deadly serious.

I turned my head as Phil finally dived into the net. His bulk brought the net down to only about two inches above the deck. I could still see the spotlit shadows of Vince and Tony, all distorted on the bridge, as they took turns getting underneath him and tossing his body, head over heels. When they finally stopped, he must have been three feet off the ground.

He kept begging, "Don't go so crazy!"

"I don't have to watch this." Macy spun on her heel and burst past me, climbing onto the dock. "G'night, Phil! Come on, Claire!"

Myra, Eli, and Geneva were doing the screaming-and-covering-their-eyes routine that made these guys feel magnanimous, and they ignored Macy. *It's not any boyfriend of theirs.* Macy jammed her hands on her hips, watching me, and I climbed onto the dock.

"They only do this stuff to hear the girls get off on it," she told me, pushing me in front of her. "If we wouldn't get all panicked, then they wouldn't have any fun! And *this* one is for *my* benefit. It's got nothing to do with Phil. It has to do with *me*. Except Phil agrees to be an asshole—"

"What'd you do? Something while I was in the bathroom?"

"Couldn't you hear me? I called Tony a psycho queen. You could hear me at the toll bridges."

"Oh, well..." I stumbled, looking over my shoulder. They were about to drop her boyfriend into water so cold it made cramps in your feet if you stepped in it. "Sticks and stones, you know? So what?"

"Stop looking at them!" She jerked me around, and at that point I realized she was basically running her mouth so she wouldn't give the guys any attention. "Do you know what Tony said back to me? He says, 'Maybe I'm a psycho, and maybe I'm proud of it. I ain't no queen. People could get killed for saying less.'"

Despite her jabbering, my mind flashed to Lani. I felt glad I didn't get some giant brain flake to bring him along, try to make people like him. She pushed at me because I wasn't on her wavelength. "So, next thing you know, he's pulling a chicken on my boyfriend. He's getting even with *me* by using *Phil*."

I said the only thing that came to mind that made total sense. It even made my feelings of doom go away. "These guys have been hanging out together since they were born. They're not going to drown each other. Phil would not have jumped in a fishing net if he thought they wouldn't pull him up in time."

They have good luck. I have bad luck. We heard a slight splash, and I jumped around to see they had lowered the net enough so that Phil's shoulders and back hit the water. His cursing screeched through the air. Despite what Tony had said about Phil being "toasty," the truth is you'd rather walk naked into twenty-degree air than land fully clothed in fifty-two-degree water.

She grabbed hold of both my arms, like she could squash them. "Tony's gotta pull this? Just because someone called him a queen? What's wrong with him?"

"I don't know, Macy." I just listened as she kept babbling, knowing her two worst problems had backed into each other. She hated times when she wasn't in charge, and these chicken games were some honor thing with the guys that had nothing to do with her. Second, if she couldn't figure out somebody's behavior, then she couldn't control that, either. Not that Tony could ever be figured out. I didn't think he needed motives.

"Macy, they're acting like a bunch of retards. But your boyfriend will not drown. You see those people down there? Their lives are perfect. You guys just don't have bad luck."

I heard a much bigger splash over my shoulder. Macy started reciting curse after curse as I turned and saw the net had gone under. In the spotlight, the normally green surface of the water was a mass of white bubbles. I watched, trying to decide how they would tell which were Phil's air bubbles and which came from the net. One of Mrs. Whitehall's lectures backed up on me. She was the only mom of our crowd that gave lectures worth hearing...*You kids, you get hurt because you never think of the details!* Eli, Myra, and Geneva were missing the details, screaming and throwing themselves on shoulders of guys who acted like they couldn't care less, but you knew differently.

Macy ran for the boat. She couldn't take the suspense anymore, and this was a scary enough chicken to let Tony watch her scream. I walked toward Vince's car because I didn't need to watch their good luck. Phil would surface, while I, on the other hand...

I slammed the back door of the Impala and threw my aching head back, thinking the silence would have been great. But I hated my own pity party so much that I wished I had stayed down there. The types of questions I most hated started backing up on me.

Can a trauma like falling out of a moving car bring on a relapse? If a relapse is already happening, can head trauma speed it up?

I sat there with my eyes shut. *Bad luck.* I couldn't ignore how things had actually gone that night. Any girl in that car would have loved to be the one with her head out the window, getting all that attention. It just so happens, it's me. *I* end up with my scalp hanging open. *They* end up partying and laughing. Phil could get thrown into a tangled fishing net and not drown, then I'd be minding my own business and wind up sick.

I searched my head for something not so self-pitying. The only thing to surface was a recent nightmare, and lyrics that started to form, almost out of nowhere.

> *Tracy's staring at the mirror...*
> *Parts her hair with Daddy's razor...*

I thrashed forward, reaching for Vince's MP3 player, which sat on the dash. *Empty.* After feeling for the glove box and finding it locked, I flopped back again and thought to amuse myself by counting stars out the window. But the Hackett night fog had come on Indian-summer thick, and I couldn't see much of anything except twirling ghosts. I shut my eyes again. As much as I was horrified by the stuff I dreamed about and wrote about, I was also drawn to it...

drawn to the shock of what would fly through my head if I just let go.

> *Parts her hair with Daddy's razor.*
> *Opens up a dark red river.*
> *Combing blond and blood together*
> *Never ceases to amaze her.*

"Claire, you are out to fucking lunch," I said. I laughed and wished I hadn't, because it sounded evil. "You deserve your bad luck."

I heard shouting from the dock. Then footsteps with louder screams and shouts. I couldn't see them at first because of the fog. Nine people started coming clear almost all at once, about thirty feet from the car. I lurched up as I saw Macy being carried in somebody's arms. Her blond hair hung down, and drops of water were falling off of it.

Message from God: Don't wish for good luck.

I froze in terror, and some thought shot up to the heavens that I hadn't meant anyone should have bad luck just so I could have good luck.

Before I could scream, the fog opened more and I saw only the top of the head on the person carrying Macy. It was even more wet and dripping drops down through her hair. I realized she was kissing the face underneath it.

Tony Clementi was swatting her foot and saying, "Told ya nothin' would happen."

8

I trudged up to the bus terminal the next morning, trying not to limp from my bruised hipbone, but the pain made my eyes water. I was still very sure I would not go with Lani. But the bruise where I rolled with Tony was huge. My heart had fallen through the floor when I saw it that morning. *Leukemia bruise.* It scared me enough to make me go to the bus station, hoping for something to overcome my fears about going.

It would have to be miraculous, because the whole concept of this trip was freaking me out. I was getting on my first bus *and* cutting school. My mom had gotten stuck next to a drunken horn-toad on a bus trip to the casinos once. She forbid me to ever get on a bus. If we got caught, I'd hear from all four of my mother's sisters, who would want to know what drugs I was on. Beyond that, Lani had talked about being able to get answers right away at a research clinic, and I was freaked by how fast my life could come crashing down.

I saw him first thing when I came up to the Hackett bus terminal. It's just a huge tin roof on steel legs, with four benches underneath. He sat on a bench, staring off to the side at a Greyhound pulling out. Its sign read, NEW YORK CITY/ ATLANTIC CITY.

He looked funny to me again—hair of a girl; shoulders of a guy; hands of a girl, folded across the chest of a guy; crossed, skinny legs dangling army boots. It seemed strange

77

that all these mismatched parts could be topped off with rosy, Indian-like skin and deep chocolate eyes. The sight stopped me cold, but I trudged on after a minute.

Lani finally looked at me, and I could see his eyebrows shoot up. He shook his head, giving me a "dad" look, despite his dimples showing up.

"Don't pass judgment." I eased myself down beside him.

"Okay. But, uhm, your bangs are standing straight up in three spots. Looks like a crown."

I could read amusement on his face as I tried to flatten them for the tenth time since last night. "It's a butterfly bandage that's caught in my bangs," I said, feeling humiliated.

"Have some fun last night?"

"I...*yeah*. It was fun. Nothing happened. To anyone except me. I'm the bad-luck queen. I...uhm..."

I looked for the words to tell him I was too freaked out—I wanted to go home and crash out on my bed as soon as my mom left for work. He was staring at that Atlantic City bus for all he was worth. It pulled onto Hackett Boulevard. He let out a sigh, like he was relieved.

"A few people on that bus just got off to use the soda machine, take a potty break. I saw some guy I hadn't seen in... a lot of years."

There was an urgency in his voice that made me stare. "Old friend?"

"Not exactly. It was some guy from one of the schools I used to go to. He was, like, three years older than me. Can I ask you something? Did you know what *oral sex* was in eighth grade?"

He leaned over and almost whispered the *oral sex* part. I could feel my eyebrows shooting up, scrunching my butterfly. His face turned kind of red, like he was embarrassed by the terminology.

"Yeah. Didn't you?"

He shook his head.

I had to laugh in spite of myself. "Everyone knows that by eighth grade."

Then I remembered him telling me how he avoided the street corners and locker rooms and spent more time in the library. I looked him up and down, thinking, *How in hell could somebody understand the theory of relativity but not know about oral sex?*

"Anyway, the guy who told me what oral sex was just got off that bus for a minute. I really, really wish I hadn't seen him. He used to flip out on me in the school yard, you know, '*You're gay, you stupid faggot,*' and then if he saw me alone, he'd try to get me to do stuff with him."

"You mean like..." I wanted to say *sex,* but the story had me kind of rooted to the spot. I didn't have to say it.

"Like *yeah,* like *stuff.*" Lani took in the ceiling for a moment. "And he had all these words for it that I'd never heard of. I had never even heard of oral sex."

"So...the same guy who called you a faggot in public came on to you in private?" I tried not to sound too interested, but this was far juicier than anything Macy had ever come up with.

Lani stood up, but I just froze in my seat, not wanting him to change the subject. He was filling in my junior high knowledge holes big-time.

He nodded. "And, one day, all of a sudden, I heard a voice behind me. I never even turned around. But I knew his voice. And right there in the library he gives me this, this endless blow-by-blow description...Sorry about the pun."

I might have laughed, but this hypnotized me. "He *did* come on to you."

"For sure. I was so ready to puke." He crossed his arms, rubbing them.

"Did you say anything to him just now?"

"He got off the bus with some girl. Our eyes locked, and you could tell he remembered me and was, like, ready to die.

He was all scared I would do something in front of this girl to let on about his dirty little secrets. I just looked away again. I mean, I could have winked or smiled or something just to be a jerk—but what's the point? People create their own little hells. They don't need my help."

He leaned back against the side of the bench, staring wide-eyed at the floor. "I walked out of the library, and two months later, I walked out of Shinoquin."

"Shinoquin?"

"The little town we were living in. Stuff like that happened all too often in Shinoquin. It's a lot like Hackett, only replace fishermen with coal miners. I'm really glad we're going to Philly today, Claire. I had forgotten how little towns can make me feel so ... *out there,* and freakish and lonely. I need a break already. We're killing two birds with one stone here. Funny how things can work out, you know?"

Lani started trudging toward the bus pulling in, without waiting for me to answer. I opened my mouth, but a muttered curse rolled out instead of an argument. *What kind of a bitch would I be to back out now?*

He half turned to wait for me but looked lost in his own thought. "So, my looks make strange people feel like they want to proposition me. So what? If it gets on my nerves, too bad. I can always move on."

"Yeah, but what is up with people who proposition you one minute and gay bash on you the next? That's too weird."

"Yeah." He meandered slowly toward the bus and I fell in. He said, "But that's one thing I love about the cities. It's becoming almost taboo in the cities to gay bash. Because if some guy gay bashes, people there get suspicious that he is ... how can I say it ... a closet gay? Or ... a person who has those tendencies subconsciously? Something like that."

The whole scenario was pretty juicy. So juicy that I missed the fact that he'd just hinted he could run away again. It went right over my head. I asked, "You've been propositioned more than once?"

He snorted a laugh. "I forget how naive most people are. Stay that way, Claire. It's cool."

"No, it's not cool. It's getting old. My friends always laugh at me." I shook my head, embarrassed by my curiosity but more embarrassed by how none of this made sense to me. "We're talking about a guy with a girl, who propositioned *you* once, and then called you a faggot. What *is* a person like that?"

"Do you mean, is there a clinical name for someone like that?"

"Well... yeah."

"Dunno. I think they call it 'hypocritical.'"

He got on the bus, leaving me at the foot of the steps, entranced... *homophobic homo... gay gay basher*... It didn't bother him there was nothing to call a person like that. Yet, the way he told it, this thing happened to him more than once. I thought maybe I could get wonderfully caught up on my education if I got on this bus.

Yet, I was still freaked. I put one foot on the step, and it felt like walking into the gas chamber. My supposed leukemia bruise screamed. I think the fire that shot up to my head scared me just enough to make me do the right thing. It gets hard playing the denial role when your body keeps kicking you in the brains. I took a deep breath and forced myself up the steps.

I plopped down beside Lani in silence, watching, wide-eyed, as the bus pulled out. I needed to think about something other than me. So I drove the conversation around quickly to where we'd been outside. "So... did you ever... like anyone?"

"Romantically?"

"Yeah." I was careful not to say girl or boy. I know that sounds funny. I mean, it was all but a no-brainer. But he hadn't actually ever said he was gay. He said other people had called him that.

He kind of laughed. "I like being alone."

"Well...that's not normal," I argued. I'd heard people say, all haughty, "I don't want to be with anyone right now," but that always changed the first time somebody halfway decent showed any interest. I wanted to tell him that, but it occurred to me that maybe he'd been grabbed or molested a few times, what with all this propositioning going on. Maybe it left him kind of messed up about romance.

The best I could come up with at the moment was "D'you ever think of another haircut? Not to be mean, or anything, but—"

"—but don't I bring a lot of my problems on myself?"

"Well..."

He shook his head, then nodded, then shook his head again. "I don't know. How do you *not* be yourself? One of my earliest memories is having a Barbie in my hand. I think a haircut would be like...I don't know...like using a Band-Aid on someone who'd been gored by a rhino."

I laughed, mostly because he was laughing, but there was a sadness in his face. I took up one of his hands and squeezed it, as much for him as for the fact that I could use some comfort myself.

He turned sideways in the seat, leaning his cheek against the backrest, and grinned at me sleepily. "I don't like to talk about my life very much. It's so...rad. If you don't mind, I'm done."

I nodded, feeling like a pry queen all of a sudden. "You brought it up."

"I know. But you need to go to the clinic and face the music. I just wanted to make sure you got on the bus."

I watched him smile at me victoriously. I didn't want to smile back, because I was too busy thinking, *Smart, smart bugger...* But his smile beamed so easily. It looked strong, yet in an innocent way. I wasn't used to being with people who seemed strong.

"I hate you," I said, but we ended up grinning together.

9

I dropped off to sleep to escape my bruises. I dreamed that I was arguing with my dad, that he was trying to get me to stay with him while doing chemo again.

His new wife, Suhar, stood beside him, twirling her wedding ring without meeting my eyes. Her blond hair flowed down her back, and her eyes glowed with their usual sweetness. But when I looked down at her wedding ring, it was cutting into her skin like it had a razor edge. Blood ran over her palm, her wrist...

I woke up with a jolt. Lani had fallen asleep in a strange position—with his back almost completely to me, and his forehead pushed into the glass. It looked so...symbolic—people wanting to be helpful, yet turning their backs.

I tried to ignore his position and think through the spiderweb of my own problems. My stomach sank low, as if a relapse was already confirmed and I was having to make impossible choices, based on impossible memories.

Starting a new school while I was on chemo last time had seemed crazy. It seemed crazier now. Last time, I had been put on the homeschooling network, and my dad had hired a tutor who came every day, but only between noon and two. There were no kids in my dad's building. I only stayed in the hospital once, for a week. A head cold had turned into pneumonia, so I had to stay in an isolation ward. In other words, I had not been exposed to many kids with my illness—very few kids at all during that whole time.

The guitar was what kept me sane. My dad had kept a game going when I felt good enough. Before he would go to his teaching job at University of the Arts, he would record some acoustic stuff for me. I was sure I could never learn anything that difficult. He would say, "Come on, it's easier than it looks." It was never easy, but it wasn't impossible, and the stuff was so pretty you couldn't stay away from it.

All day long, I would sit there trying to get my fingers working like his had. When I got tired, I would fall asleep with that guitar under my arm, then wake up and try some more.

I would complain to my dad about finding new definitions to *lonely* and *feeling like crap.* He would tell me, "There are times in life to grow, and there are times in life to shine. One can't grow and shine at the same time; it just doesn't work that way. Now you're growing. Tomorrow you'll shine."

I was always *Aw, bull,* and it was kind of comforting to get back with my mom at the end, who understood the importance of having fun *now,* before you get too old or too socially retarded.

I supposed I "shined" from learning all that guitar playing, if you can call a gig in a glorified island bakery during the off-season months "shining." Definitely, it was not worth losing most of junior high. And since I wasn't about to go through another year of staring at walls and a guitar . . . the other option was I could stay with my mom—and probably send her into cardiac arrest this time.

Her life had revolved around me and my friends and my parties, even before she and my dad split up, when I was four. My friends said she was the most fun of all the moms. Grown-ups agreed. In her senior yearbook from Coast, she was voted Person Most Likely to Party, and islanders kept feeding off her energy even after some of them got married and had kids, after she and my dad split up. I saw her "get happy" many Saturday nights when I was a kid. But she always made other people happy, too—and me happy. It was a trip being with her at a party. I was real proud that my laughing, popular mom was all mine.

If it's possible, I think, she started drinking too much because she cared too much. She would get all looped when I was sick, saying a couple of drinks helped her to sleep. Fine. But she'd be crashed out by nine o'clock, then wide awake at two. I would jump awake in the night, realizing she was standing right over top of me, like, breathing Old Sweat Sock right in my face. I would ask her what was wrong, and she'd say, "I just love you, that's all," and leave the room again. One time I heard her on the phone right after, and my dad was yelling at her. I couldn't hear what he was saying, but I could overhear her sniffing, all "...sorry, Chad, I just have this overwhelming fear she's going to stop breathing..."

I felt like her stupor drinking was all my fault, though I still kept going home some weekends, for a while, because I missed her and the island. But it got to be too hard to watch, and my big hope was that she didn't drink so much while I was at my dad's. I stayed away entirely the last few months. It didn't help. She never went back to her old self. If I was sick again now, she might take an even bigger fall—turn from a night drunk into an all-day drunk. There didn't seem to be any way I could stay with her.

I could have elbowed Lani in the back and woken him up, but instead I sat there muttering curse after curse under my breath, because there was not much else to say about my choices.

I quit cursing when I fell hypnotized under the sky blue girders as we came onto the Ben Franklin Bridge. Those steel girders always had that mood-boosting effect on me. They reached so high that a few white, silky clouds wandered through the suspensions and touched the tips, which looked like steeples. It was such a contrast to Hackett's little drawbridges, which had to rise and back cars up for half a mile when any decent-sized boat passed into the bay.

All the islanders hated waiting in their cars when the Philadelphia people's beautiful yachts passed. The fish frat and their parents called huge yachts "fag hacks," and the wait for a toll bridge to go down "faggots on parade."

The water under the Ben Franklin was so far down that an enormous navy ship could pass underneath. And I looked ahead at the six lanes of traffic dotted with all sorts of blinking signs and lights.

It made me feel like the city was a bigger and better sort of "island"...a magical place full of skyscrapers and other proof of how people thought harder and bigger here. I started feeling relieved that I was coming back. Maybe a cure for cancer had been discovered in Philadelphia just last week.

The waiting room of this real-life, no-pay clinic changed my mind about that. It was nothing like Children's Hospital, where I had done chemo, and I was freaked by the hullabaloo of people who looked like they had very big problems. Sick babies cried, methadone addicts twitched, pregnant teenagers sat stone-faced with toddlers running around their feet. There was an AIDS clinic within this clinic, and so beyond the serious-faced people, there was a silent majority of pale, unhealthy-looking adults, some so thin that their sad eyes took over their faces.

I stared at my feet most of the time, playing invisible patient.

And Lani, who had seemed like such a freak show in Hackett, kept running into people in there that he actually knew by name. Before I went off to get my blood taken, he had talked to a guy, then a pregnant girl who yackety-yacked in his ear like they had months to catch up on. Both conversations were long and made me feel more isolated.

He just kind of left me sitting there stewing for almost the whole hour. When they finally called me for blood testing, I felt so snubbed that I didn't even holler to him to go with me. Big comfort he was turning out to be.

I sat there in a stupor while they took my blood, trying to answer their questions with the least amount of words and not get all upset by them. I had already accepted the worst. Some Dr. Lowenstein came in, a woman, who looked busy and barely smiled at me. Last, a triage nurse appeared, because the first nurse had seen my butterfly and wanted to know about it.

"Could all this dizziness be caused from hitting your head?" she asked, pushing at the wound.

"No. I did that last night, and I've been dizzy for three weeks."

She kept playing with the butterfly and didn't look happy. "Butterflies work best when they're applied properly. Look ... you've got hair in it, and— Who did this to you? A blind person?"

Scott, the neurosurgeon. "My boyfriend. I fell out of a moving car. We were trying to solve too many problems at once. It's not his fault."

"Whose fault is it?"

Mine. All I'd wanted to think about was kissing Scott. "Don't lecture me, okay?"

"Kids ..." She shook her head. "Did you bother cleaning it out? Butterflies don't work at all when they're covering an infection—"

"Excuse me. I know how to clean a wound," I busted in, but I could feel my bangs sticking up again, making me look like a horned toad. It was too much. I yanked the butterfly hard, thinking, *So long, hairs.* But it had been catching hairs all night and morning, and I ended up ripping the wound wide open again trying to twist and pull.

I was uttering curses as fresh blood dripped down my face, and the nurse's attitude eased up finally when I started to cry. "I just wanted to show you how clean it was! It was really, really clean!"

"I'm sure it was." She sounded serious and not sarcastic as she tried to squeeze the wound together with her fingers. "We would have probably ended up doing that anyway. You can't be walking around with a butterfly that's half in your hair. Now that you've reopened it, we'd better stitch it. Or you'll end up with a charming scar."

I sputtered and spit blood off my lips as she handed me a cold pack, saying, "I'll find a medic. Just try to stay calm."

She left me alone again with my on-fire wound and half my bangs hanging off a butterfly gripped in my bloody palm. *Lani's out there in the waiting room busy talking to everybody else... This day cannot get worse,* I decided. I thought you could wait forever to get treated in a clinic this size, but a medic showed up fast. Less than five minutes after the nurse ran out, a huge African American medic yanked back the drape, asking, "You the dingle-wop that jumped out of a moving car last night?"

"That's me." I was too stressed to argue with him.

"You trying out for Deep Thinker of the Universe?"

"Don't beat me up. I'm kind of...way tired."

"Then why don't you kids stay home some nights? You got a home?"

"Yes."

"You got a bed to sleep in?"

"Yes."

"Then you got more than most around here. What are you doin', bein' way tired?"

I told him the head wound was a sidebar and what the real problem was.

"Oooo, damn. Okay. You can be way tired."

I could see a syringe on the tray he carried in, and I shut my eyes until he'd shot my forehead full of some numbing agent. I hardly blinked, used to being stuck. He'd stayed quiet through that part, but then started in again. "You need to go out in the waiting room and find yourself a floating angel."

"A what?"

"They come with you on visits like these. They hold your hand and they tell you good stuff and make sense of this world so you realize it's not so bad—"

"Oh, I came with a friend. He's out there." I jerked my thumb toward the waiting room. "Thinks he's at a family reunion. Not much help."

"That's cuz he's a *friend*. Floating angels aren't friends; they're real angels. They're *real*. Didn't you see any of 'em out there?" His beaming smile flashed, and I gathered he was pulling my leg, the other option being that he was nuts. I decided to be polite and not hate myself more.

"Uh, no. What do they look like?"

"Like faggots."

My eyebrows shot up. I waited for him to laugh, but he was slick. He kept banging stuff around on his cart and whistling until I cracked up, and then he looked all surprised.

"What're you laughing at? There's nothing funny about that. Not if you got your common sense working. Angels don't have a gender. Remember that from church school?"

"I'm Protestant," I responded. "We've got the no-frills religion. No angels, no art, no saints, no Mary—"

"That's not Protestant. That's just white-people trash," he informed me. "Angels don't have a gender. So what they gonna look like?"

He kept staring like I was supposed to answer. Being that I hate examining tables, I switched to the stool that was supposed to be for him, thinking that would distract him. But he kept staring.

I finally said, "My mom watches *Oprah*. She says angels are people who do good deeds."

He slammed the needle and thread down on the tray.

"You *are* trying for Deep Thinker of the Universe. 'My mom watches *Oprah*,' therefore angels are people? Where do you go to school, so's they teach you logic like that?"

"Uh, the islands." I giggled.

"That explains a lot. Don't see too many floating angels down at the shore. Likely to get themselves killed, something. Too many rednecks."

I tried to will my grin off my face, but it wasn't working. So, I was a dingle-wop, white-trash Protestant, retard, redneck. Somehow it was worth it, to run into someone who could make my grin work. I decided to play back.

"So, if an angel is not a person, how do they get themselves killed by rednecks? I thought angels aren't supposed to die."

"Well, they're like the Good Lord, you know? They killed him, but he just jumped back up again when nobody was looking, see? Faked 'em all out."

I guessed I appreciated this medic's dedication to screwing up my pity party.

"So these angels look like...*f-faggots*." I shot a glance into the corridor, and he seemed to enjoy watching me smile over my own nerve.

"Yes. Floating angels, that is. There's all kinds of angels. You got your cherubs, what look like fat babies. Then there's big ones, fighter angels; they look like...water towers or something. *Big*. You don't want to mess with them. Floating angels look like humans."

"Except they float."

He cleaned out the wound again, pressing on my forehead to see if it was numb. When I flinched, he glanced at his watch and sighed.

"They could float in the air if they wanted to, I suppose. But they're more modest than that. And they're way smarter than humans, so they'd rather outsmart them. They're called floaters because they float from person to person, you know? This one's in trouble, so they float here. They fix up that person's life, so they move over there. They float *around,* not up and down."

"Like a...vagabond?"

"Yeah, 'cept they ain't dirty. Floating angels like to be in the shower."

I totally cracked up, but he just turned his back and started cleaning his scissors with an alcohol wipe. I felt my eyebrows shooting up and got an awful thought. *What if he's nuts? Should I let this guy sew up my face?*

The curtain pulled back and Lani stared at me. "Couldn't find you."

"I've only been back here for half an hour," I couldn't resist saying. "Where have *you* been?"

"For the past fifteen minutes, I've been over at the research lab, making sure they can finish your blood work today, like they promised."

"Thanks, Dad. And before that?"

"Don't be jealous." He giggled like I was oh-so-touching, circled around behind me, and put his arms around my neck so we were cheek to cheek. "I've got other friends besides you."

Out flew: "I'm in a foul mood, so I might as well tell you. They look creepy."

"Maybe. But then, you sound bitchy."

"Gawd."

He giggled in my ear, and this enormous black guy giggled in my face. I was being taken apart. The medic started laying sutures in, but my forehead was pretty numb, and if I shut my eyes, all I could feel was pricks and tugs.

"Lani Garver. I'm trying to tell this good woman that she

needs to find herself a floating angel. She won't believe me that they're real."

My eyes flashed open as I realized these two knew each other. I turned my eyes sideways to take in Lani's nose without moving my head. "Is there anybody here you *don't* know?"

"Yeah, lots of people. This is a luck-out job. I know Marcus, and you lucked out, Claire. Marcus has won Medic of the Year three years in a row. He won't even leave a scar." I felt better on hearing that news.

But I told Lani, "He's trying to get me to believe in that TV show *Touched by an Angel*."

"That's not about any floating angel," Marcus said, reaching for the scissors. "I don't know *what* that is. Actors, or something. For one thing, there's two angels with catowees. Explain to me what angels are doing with catowees?" He laid down the scissors, spread his fingers like he was holding two invisible melons out from his chest. "What're they supposed to use them for? Angels don't make babies. They *like* babies, they just don't care about *making* them. If angels don't nurse babies, what're they doing with catowees? Dig?"

"They're like boys *and* girls." I sighed, thinking about my blood work.

"And I'm telling you . . . there's a few out there in the waiting room any time, day or night. You ought to go find you one. Take the edge off you, missus. You're a sourpuss."

"Yeah, I know." I sighed again as Lani unwrapped his arms from my neck and started massaging my shoulders. It felt good. Not only was I worried about stuff way over my head, I was worried about little stuff, like Marcus covering the stitches with a small enough Band-Aid that I could make up something believable, in case my mother saw it. I knew I could pick the sutures out myself, later.

I eyed Marcus as he pressed a normal-sized Band-Aid to my forehead. He was wearing a surgical cap, but his hair swung out of it easily. He had hair like Michael Jackson. But he was muscular, reminding me of some of the earlier Motown singers. Between that hair and that kind of more-sensitive musician look, this nicely stacked Marcus resembled the creature he was talking about.

"Are you a floating angel?" I asked, to get his goat.

He picked up the clipboard with my papers and started writing on them. He didn't even look at me. "Now, if you were listening to even the first thing I told you, you would know that couldn't be the case."

"Why not?"

"What're you staring at right now?"

"Uh, your hands." I was watching him write on the clipboard.

"What do you see on them?"

I realized he was wearing a wedding ring. "Are you married?"

He looked at me like I was a loony tune, and Lani cracked up. "Don't try to argue with him, Claire. He truly believes this thing, and a lot of other people around here do, too."

"You're kidding."

"No."

"How come I've never heard of a floating angel before?"

Lani bit his lip, like, digging for his thought. "People generally have to be in a *lot* of trouble before their orderly little versions of reality crack open. People around here? They're in a *lot* of trouble. So, they can believe in lots of stuff."

I swung around to look at him as he stopped rubbing my shoulders. "Well, I'm in a lot of trouble. I just can't believe in stuff like angels that get in the shower."

I thought he would laugh, but his grin was kind of peaceful. "You are not in trouble, girlfriend. You just think you are."

To argue the point would sound like a pity party. I just let go of a sigh.

"There's actually a book on the subject," he said. "And I

own it, somewhere in my stuff. There probably aren't many copies floating around. It's a very, very old book."

"About floating angels?"

"About all different sorts of angels. But they're in there. It's not some concept dreamed up by an AIDS patient, like, yesterday. The book I have is a translation of a translation of a translation originally written by some philosopher who lived in the first century A.D., Andovenes. I'll let you see it. It's very cool."

I groaned, thinking of *The Essential Jung,* another of his favorites. "I'll read it if you let me copy your Jung homework that's due Monday."

His laugh sounded affectionate and yet sarcastic. "You're just...an intellectual giant in the making, Claire."

"Thanks a lot. But you've got room. You believe in Einstein, and you believe in angels."

As Marcus cleaned up, Lani tried to pass off on me some story about it being a myth that intelligent people don't believe in God. "Brilliant people seem generally repelled from any box, like Catholic or Protestant."

"Whatever." I looked him up and down. He resembled one of these creatures even more than Marcus had. And he was laughing at me in a way that was all too condescending.

"Are you a floating angel? You sure look like one."

Marcus had stepped out, but I could see him standing by a cart in the hallway, filling out more papers. "Marcus, is Lani a floating angel?"

I kind of regretted the joke as soon as I said it. He looked at Lani in a serious way that made me realize he probably did believe this stuff, and even if you don't agree with someone, you should be polite about what they believe. Fortunately, Marcus could hold his own in a match of sarcasm.

"Ahhhh...I don't know. Looks like a gay kid to me. Lani, you a gay kid?"

I flinched at the ease in which he spouted the question. I had dwelled on it all day yesterday before deciding not to go there.

Lani hadn't stopped laughing at me yet and responded easily between chuckles. "Gay is a box."

"Don't get him started," I begged, but Marcus came through the doorway, eyeing Lani dangerously. "He wiggles out of every label you try to put on him."

He took Lani's face in his hand, turning it side to side, squeezing his cheeks. And he jumped gracefully into this game of asking "action" questions that had stumped me last night.

"You like boys?"

Lani's face was all scrunched in Marcus's hand, but he laughed. "Yes. I love boys."

"Girls?"

"I love girls."

"You bi?"

"Bisexual is a pretty sizable box."

Marcus let go and nodded at me. "He's a flamer. Take my word on that one."

I wiped a tear from my eye, but my grin kept spreading like I had a hanger in my cheeks. "But how can you tell?"

He turned and his massive size took up most of the entranceway. He draped the curtain over his shoulder so he looked like a black Paul Bunyan, and I fell into the drama, leaning up to hear his big secret.

"One thing I didn't tell you about floating angels that makes them different from most of the other angels." He cast a glance over his shoulder, both ways, and then pierced my eyes again. "They got a streak of mean that seeps way low. They're like Johnny Good-Deed-Doer; just don't push them. God informs them, you know, 'Look, there's some evil person at work down there,' and then God turns his back, cuz he can't take the violence, you know? Floaters come down, do the dirty work. You ever hear of some wicked parent, all drunk and whipping on their kids, who meets a violent ending?"

I thought of Mr. Clementi and shuddered, even though I was laughing.

"You can be sure there was a floater behind that. This boy here?" He dropped the drape, came back over to a grinning Lani. "Doesn't have that streak of mean in him. He's a fussy-wussy. You know? Ol' run-of-the-mill, whisker-suckin' faggot."

He slapped Lani's cheek playfully and turned on his heel. I had stopped laughing, though my eyes still bulged and my mouth formed the O shape. That list of adjectives was way over the top. At least *I* thought it was. Lani was chuckling, same as he chuckled at his mother the night before, like it didn't matter.

"God, you're so...sure of yourself." It was the only phrase I could conjure up.

"Around here? It's a term of affection. You hear the word *faggot* as often as you hear *penicillin,* in case you didn't notice."

"I'm not deaf."

His grin faded as he took my hand.

"Hey. I didn't come in here to get accosted by your boxes. I came to tell you the doctor wants to see you, across the street. Her office is over there." My heart lit up like a blowtorch. *Her office.* Why not here, where she'd seen me?

"Did they tell you anything?" I asked. "They're not allowed to tell you anything."

"She did not tell me anything."

He knew something. I could tell by how he had trouble looking at me after he implied that there was news. I had come to recognize that expression on nurses who were not very experienced yet, and from my parents when they had news for me that wasn't great. It was a casual voice that was out of place under the circumstances. *People shouldn't try to be casual in situations like this. It's all wrong, and it always gives them away.* All the jollies were forgotten, and I didn't want to move.

He raised my hand to his lips and kissed it, one of his older-guy gestures of comfort, I guessed, and then he put his other hand on my back and started pushing me toward the door. It was like being pushed over a cliff. I wondered what in hell kind of troubled friends he had, that he would be so rock steady in a situation like this.

10

This Dr. Lowenstein stood rooting through papers on her desk, looking only slightly less busy and distracted than she had across the street. She beckoned us in, because her mouth was full. She was gripping half an egg salad sandwich.

She swallowed, then said, "Sorry to make you walk over here. But a body has to eat. I eat in my office every day, and if a patient is up and walking, I see them here."

I thought, *Yeah, sure.* Snickering orderlies over at Children's used to refer to Dr. Haverford's office as the drop-dead zone, a place for getting only bad news. Good news you got in the examining room. I dropped into a chair on the other side of Dr. Lowenstein's desk, and Lani just leaned against the door frame.

The doctor cast Lani a glance, and he raised his eyebrows up and down quickly before finding something on the floor to gaze at. It made me more sure they had been talking.

When I tore my eyes from him, the doctor was holding out the other half of her sandwich to me.

"Here, eat this. It's past lunchtime. You must be starved."

"Thanks, I'm not hungry."

She laid a napkin on the desk in front of me and dropped the half sandwich on top. "Come on. It's great stuff. From the Jewish deli across the street. I can't eat in front of kids."

I wanted that sandwich about as much as I wanted five more stitches. "Thanks, I don't do mayonnaise."

"Oh really? Why not?"

She sounded annoyingly casual, and I wanted to scream, *Just get it over with.*

"Because it's fattening. I'm a cheerleader, and I'm already, you know, a gargantuan."

She took another bite, studying me. "You think you're fat?"

I shook my head, then nodded, then shook my head. "I don't think I'm fat. I just think...I'm a cow." My nervous laugh rang out as I watched Lani sniff and glare at the floor.

"'A cow,'" the doctor repeated, like that was way interesting. "Been on a diet recently?"

"About...three months ago, I lost ten pounds. But I did it really healthy. I would never skip meals, do anything to jeopardize my health... *What is up?*"

She had a chart in front of her, which I assumed was mine, and she started shaking her head slowly as she chewed a mouthful of sandwich. I thought five years passed before she swallowed. I figured at that point, she'd get on with it.

But she said, "What do you think would happen to you if you ate mayonnaise? Do you think it would make you sick to your stomach?"

"I...no." My impatience created short, blasting sentences. "I ate mayonnaise accidentally last week. It didn't make me sick. *What is up?*"

"Nothing is *up.* No bad cell counts. You've got the red cells, white cells of your average human being, so you should be happy about that. Some things are *down,* which disturbs me. I had them looked into after you weighed in this morning at a hundred and twenty."

"What does my weight have to do with it?"

"You're five foot ten."

"So?" I was trying to figure out if she was saying I'd had a relapse or not, but she seemed more interested in staring.

She leaned over the desk at me. "You're five foot ten and weigh a hundred and twenty pounds," she repeated, like I was missing something. "Sure, some people are naturally that thin. But certain people who care about you say that you've got a list of things you won't eat. And that list is as long as your arm."

Lani's eyes came slowly off the floor and gazed into mine, like he had nothing to be ashamed of. *So, he actually had come over here to spew this at her. That's how they talked.* It wasn't exactly like ratting somebody out, but it felt strange, like I was being ganged up on, and I still couldn't figure out what all this had to do with a relapse.

"Am I sick, or not?"

"You are still in remission."

It was so *not* what I expected to hear that I sat there in dumbfounded silence. I was too shocked to jump up and down. Even if I'd found my legs, what she said next would have wiped away a big part of my glee.

"Your eating habits are dangerous. They might jeopardize your remission in roundabout ways. Which isn't to say you completely surprise me. I've seen people a lot sicker than you who decide an eating disorder is going to solve the problems of the universe."

I let my jaw drop down, so I could hurl out, *You're crazy,* but it just kind of hung there until I laughed.

"That list of symptoms you gave us this morning, they're not just indicative of a relapse. Did you know dizziness could come from your body substituting adrenaline for nutrition? I see things like this every day in kids your age. You're getting older; you're independent—at least independent enough to get yourself to a place like this. And yet, you can't control Mom. You can't control Dad. Can't control the things your friends do...but you sure can control how big around your thighs are—"

"Lady, I've had cancer! Will you hear yourself? I eat more healthy than anybody I know!" I flopped back in the chair in frustration. "Not only that, my parents are just your average people...perfectly average *divorced* people, but they don't fight much. Except when I'm sick—"

I shifted around, because her eyebrows shot up like she was making a big deal out of nothing.

"I know Dr. Haverford very well," she said to my amazement. My doctor over at Children's.

"Oh, great! So are you going to tell my mom that I was here?"

I didn't like how she grinned at Lani and he grinned back, like they understood something I was missing.

"Dr. Haverford said to tell you he will not tell your mom. He said he got a little tired of prescribing Valium to her last time you were sick." She watched me, like we shared some big bad secret.

"He said he would have been more happy about prescribing sleeping pills if she had done as he asked and took you to a support group, too."

"But that was *me*. I didn't want to go to a support group."

"Why not?"

I sighed, my head reeling as I tried to remember. "My dad was getting married. The support group was up here. I didn't want to stay with him longer—"

"There are cancer support groups all over the place. There are also Web sites and chat rooms and—"

"My mom didn't push it, and I...It was *my* choice," I said again.

"Lot of weight on your shoulders."

"Whatever."

Lani's eyebrows were all cocked up, all *I told you so,* and his superior attitude about so many things finally boiled over the top. The doctor was trying to shove some flyer in my hand, and I balled it up and hurled it at Lani. I flopped back down and slid low in the chair, completely embarrassed.

But he just cracked up as it whizzed past him into the corridor, and said, "Nice."

"That is...*was*...a list of therapists, support groups, and Web sites—"

"Look." I put my hand up, like *stop*. "Sorry if...I'm uptight right now. But I don't see what all good it's going to do me to talk to a bunch of people who are down on their luck. Like my mom said, what if their luck runs out? Do I need friends who could die?"

"That's not the point," she said. "We're all going to have our ticket punched. That's a fact of life. The point is to have people in your life who can relate to you, listen to you. If you had that, you wouldn't be sneaking around at a charity clinic. And I highly doubt you'd be eating like you were trying to disappear."

I shook my head, standing my ground. "I eat three meals a day, every day!"

"Consisting of?"

I might have believed her a little better about needing counseling if she wasn't bringing my eating into it. I recited my diet of fruit for breakfast, salad for lunch.

"But I eat plenty of dinner—anything I want! Noodles, gravy, potatoes..."

Lani had retrieved the flyer and tossed it back at me. I caught it as he said, "She eats a salad at eleven o'clock and then goes to cheerleading after school—"

I hurled it back, and this time his ducking mechanism worked, but he kept talking. "And she doesn't get done until six o'clock."

"And I suppose you use no-fat dressing," the doctor added.

"You guys, you don't understand," I heard myself saying. "Do you know how hard it is for a girl who's five ten to get on cheerleading? I had to do everything twice as good... *Stop!*" I held my hands up defensively before they could start in on *Did I have to be a cheerleader? Did I have some sort of starlet complex?* Fortunately, they kept their huge mouths shut while I dropped my head onto my hands on the desk, trying to find words for this very important thought making my gut explode.

"I know...who I am. I am Myra's friend. Eli's and Geneva's friend. I am Macy Matlock's *best* friend. They are not perfect people, but nothing in my life has made me feel so good as...knowing who loves me. I want my life to stay as much like it is as possible. I don't want it cluttered with a bunch of talk about bad memories or family problems I can't help. Especially if I'm healthy, I don't want to make changes. Except...okay. I'll eat more. I'll gain ten pounds back, okay?"

Dr. Lowenstein rubbed her eyes, like she was tired. I wondered how many people she'd seen that day.

"No, Claire, don't 'gain ten pounds back.' Just eat more. Eat some junk food. Eat French fries with your salad. Forget about what you eat, and just eat it. Stay off the scales, okay? If your pants don't fit, just go out and buy a bigger pair. Think you can do that? Because I'm doubtful."

"Why?"

She started to say something and stopped, glancing at Lani, who raised his eyebrows again.

"I trust this kid," she said to me, jerking her thumb. "He reminds me of one of our floating angels."

I felt surprised that even a doctor would take that concept seriously. Sounded like the type of legend that would float around the janitors and LPNs.

"I get the feeling he really cares about you. So, if he can report back to me that you passed this little test I'm going to give you, then I won't call your parents and lecture them about making you get some therapy. Who knows what can of worms a phone call home might open in some cases. Is that a deal? Because from my end, that's a supreme compromise."

"What do I have to do?"

"I want the two of you to go to a diner or an ice-cream parlor or something of that nature. And Claire, I want you to order a hot fudge sundae. I want you to eat the whole thing. If you can't eat it, or you don't want to, or you feel an urge to vomit afterward, I want one of you to be honest with me. We've got a big problem if you can't do that. We can't ignore it, not given your history. All right?"

I nodded, forced a grin on my face, and said, "Piece of cake."

She rolled her eyes at my bad pun, taking a big bite out of her sandwich, and I turned my eyes up to Lani and let my panic roll out of them. I had not eaten ice cream since July. The very thought was making my stomach ball up like a metal crusher eating a tin can. Yet, I couldn't say that. To say it would sound like an eating disorder. Which it wasn't. *Was it?*

I shook my head the slightest bit, so he would see, but not her. As much as I shook my head, he nodded his. He smiled and winked in a way that was supposed to be reassuring, and I decided he would definitely sit there and not get upset, even if it took me four fucking hours to eat a thing like that. But as usual, I felt like I was surrounded by people who cared . . . and yet I still had to do impossible things myself.

11

The Indian-summer sun shone hot on my face as we wandered onto Pine Street. I inhaled a huge breath of warm air, trying to clear my head. For lack of any other way to express utter relief and complete humiliation, I cracked up laughing.

Lani put his arm around my neck, pulling me close to him and kissing me on the side of the head. It was another of those overly old gestures that made me feel in the twilight zone with someone's dad disguised as a kid—someone who was trying to say, "You're okay, no matter what stupid things you do."

I found his waist under his jacket and rested my arm there. It felt surprisingly okay to grip hold of a person who wasn't my boyfriend, without any opposite-sex mini spazzes. At least, none were coming from him. He was babying me, and after a couple of minutes, it turned me kind of stony. I accused him of babying me, but he just laughed.

"Relax. Maybe you need it."

"What about you?" I thought of his life, how he could dole out something that he was probably in desperate need of himself. *Maturity thing. Even if his shaving hormones are strangely whacked, he's eighteen, at least.* "Come on. How old are you?"

"Why must we go there?"

"Because. If you don't tell me, I'm going to start believing you're one of those floating angels. Born a bazillion years ago," I joked. But after hearing even the doctor mention it, I had gotten curious enough to want to see that very old book of his. "You're just like...slightly overly wise, something. Just enough to put me on edge. I want to see that book and look at the pictures. I want to make sure you're not in it."

"There're other ways to get to know me," he said. "You can hear me ramble on about Hegel sometime. That would explain a lot. But I would say you're too keyed right now to do Hegel."

"You're right."

"You could meet some of my, uh, non-sick friends sometime, if you want."

"You got normal friends?" I asked, and almost died. One of my famous Claire statements. *Doyee.*

He just laughed. "People don't have to be desperate to want my company, you know. Wherever I've been, there were always a couple girls I got very tight with. And most of the time? They're not what you would classify as dorks. They're not the cool*est* but—"

"Like me," I said suddenly.

"Yeah. A lot like you. But last year was a very cool year."

"I thought you lived on the street last year," I said.

"Yup." He went on to say that some of the teachers at his school probably guessed he was homeless, and a lot of the kids knew, but they didn't bust on him. He had gotten accepted to an art school and just showed up every day. It was called the Creative and Performing Arts High School of Philadelphia, and it was a public school, but something called a magnet school, which they only had in big cities. He said he showed up on the last day of auditions to get in, had played the drums, and was accepted in the instrumental department.

He giggled more as we walked. "I remembered hearing about the place back from when I lived in Cheltenham. The kids there used to call the Creative and Performing Arts High School 'Homo Heaven,' which is so not accurate. Yeah, there are some gays, but in a school where people *perform* and don't just *be,* there are more intense ways to look at people. What you look like is less of an issue. Sometimes having serious problems is actually a good thing."

"What do you mean?" I asked. "In our school, you don't want to announce your serious problems. People will yack and hold it against you."

"Have you heard the expression 'You got to pay your dues to sing the blues'?"

"Yeah..." It took me a minute to remember where I'd heard that. My dad used to spew it at me when he stuck the guitar in my hand before he left for work in the mornings. I would be all *So much bullshit to make me feel better.* "So... you had friends from your school who've been through bad things?"

"Lots."

"You mean illnesses?"

"Maybe. Don't always know."

"But if you don't know, then how can you know what they've been through?"

"A lot of times it shows up in how they perform."

My glance shot up to him. He nodded. "It's almost like a cause-and-effect thing. You watch someone act a drama part extremely well...dance an awesome ballet...play a great instrument...A lot of times that horrible thing that happened to them somehow translates into talent. You wanna go to South Street? School should let out in an hour or so. I'd love to see my friend Ellen. I can call her on her cell phone. She'll come down there."

My eyeballs almost blew out of my head. I had totally forgotten about South Street—a place that was, like, art-and-music central—where my dad used to take me on days when I was feeling good. He'd said he was too old for the place anymore, but taking me there helped him remember to stay young.

We walked back down Pine Street to Fifth, then cut to South and found a café, near the corner, with outdoor tables. Lani went inside and left me sitting in one of the plastic chairs, zoning in on the strange-looking, artsy types passing by. There was the parade of black... black leather jackets, black lipstick, black eyeliner, jet black hairdos, but also blasts of color that left me staring. Bright pink and purple hair spikes. Blazing blue, penciled eyes. Most of the people looked college age, and I remembered the University of the Arts being about eight blocks over. I wondered what these people looked like when they were my age.... When in their lives had they started getting this twitch to look different?

I thought Lani had gone into the café to call his friend, but he came out with a couple of hot fudge sundaes and dropped one in front of me. I pushed on my stomach.

"Dr. Lowenstein didn't say *now,* like *today.* I just want to sit here and relax and watch the sights."

"So, watch the sights. It will help you relax, and you'll be able to eat better."

I had already eaten half that egg salad sandwich before leaving Dr. Lowenstein's office, trying to prove something to her, I wasn't sure what. I think I was trying to get her to ease up on the hot-fudge-sundae issue, which she hadn't done.

"Not to waste your money, Lani, but I'd have a much better shot at eating a whole sundae at night. Like, when it's my dinnertime and my gut is used to moving food through."

I watched him gaze at me and realized how much like an eating disorder I was making this thing sound. Plus, I had not told the whole truth to Dr. Lowenstein. The time I ate mayonnaise, I did feel sick after, like I'd eaten a whole stick of butter. And now that I'd eaten half that egg salad, my gut was busy fighting off Mayonnaise Hell. I cast a glance at the whipped cream, then Lani pressing his fingers together in front of his lips and watching me over the top of them.

He dropped them finally and said, "You keep wanting to know my age, well, I'll tell you this much. When you're homeless, people melt into each other, when you're not doing those boxes every day, like *sophomore, junior, graduated*. Everybody sort of becomes one thing. Even that line between grown-up and kid gets lost. I don't have that problem a lot of kids seem to have...I'm not immune to grown-ups. I have grown-up friends. Not that Dr. Lowenstein is exactly one of them."

I shrugged, didn't get it.

"I'm saying that the whole concept of ratting out to a grown-up is kind of lost on me. And if you can't eat that, I will have no problem calling her."

I returned his even gaze. With as much style and grace as I could muster, I made an evil face. Not a single movement stirred from the return-stare factory.

"I don't want to know your age. It doesn't matter." I swiped up the spoon, pumped my face full of whipped cream, and tried to focus on my irritation as opposed to my stomach. "Because you're just plain *old*. You remind me of my *dad*. You're an old *fart*."

"I'm an old fart," he agreed, and started eating.

"There's another reason why it would be very hard for a kid to be friendly with you." I swallowed more whipped cream. "You're, like, *invasive*."

"Yup, I'm invasive."

"And you have no shame."

"No shame. Look at this guy coming. He's rich." Lani pointed with his spoon at one of the more radical face-piercings I had seen all day. The guy had, like, nine little rings through his lip, a couple on his eyebrow, and a chain running from his ear to the middle of his cheek.

I laid the spoon down to stare. A few of these older kids looked like they'd had the kitchen drawer thrown at their faces. This seemed like the perfect place to make a huge confession. "I've always had this secret thing for black leather..."

Lani's eyes lit, like this was kind of interesting.

I thought he was missing the point. "You don't understand. Nobody on Hackett ever wears black leather anything. So...where did this love of black leather come from?"

"From *Claire*." He shrugged, and I wondered if I had to dance on the table naked to shake him up. He asked, "Well... what kind of black leather?"

My eyes scanned the people walking past, and I heard myself giggle. It was daring, trying to define my own weirdness instead of pretending it didn't exist. "I haven't seen it yet. I mean, not the type that goes with chains or black lipstick. I really couldn't see myself as a vampire type. And I don't like those black motorcycle-gang outfits. And there's those crunchy black leather jackets with the huge zippers that a lot of gay people wear. That's not it, either." I scratched my head in confusion.

"You're saying what black leather you *don't* like, but what kind *do* you like?"

"I guess a lot of people use black leather to make some kind of a statement," I said, thinking of all the groups I had just named. "I don't want to make a statement. It would have to be just 'Claire' black leather."

"When you find it, you'll know." He laid his spoon down in his empty cup and looked at mine. I hadn't yet hit ice cream. It was starting to melt down into the sides. Part of me wanted to throw something else at him. He was looking at me like *This is not working.* Yet the bigger part of me knew he was only trying to help.

Something over my shoulder caught his eye. He started to

wave and grin from ear to ear. "Classic. She's got Cooper with her. Hey, Ellen!"

I turned, grateful for a distraction. A tall girl and a shorter, skinny guy waved back, trotting across South Street. They were dressed normally, when compared to other people we'd seen on the street. In fact, the girl looked like a J. Crew model. She was as tall as I was with long, beautiful red hair. The guy was black, and despite the unusual heat, he had on a sweater that came down to his knees and a long, silky scarf knotted up near his neck. I watched them coming closer and started feeling myself wanting to become invisible. *Kids from art high school.* It was like watching actors jump out of the screen and tumble into our space.

The guy spread his hands out when he reached us, and shouted, "Lani, sweetheart, you can't just disappear and leave us all hanging. My *god*, you've really got that do working." He bounced the bottom of Lani's hair, and the J. Crew–looking girl hugged Lani.

Cooper held out a hand to me, which he sort of dropped in my hand. "Who's your girlfriend? She's *darling*." He was being completely dramatic, cracking me up, despite my sudden feeling of shyness.

"This is Claire. Claire, Cooper. Claire, Ellen."

"So, what are you doing down here?" Ellen asked Lani as she dropped into the seat beside me. "Yeah, I kept your dirty little secret. I never told anyone you were moving to *Hackett Island* for the dead of winter. What a concept. Catching any fish?" She shuddered.

Lani said, "Shh, Claire's from there."

I threw a polite smile, despite that they were studying me like *I* was something to behold, instead of them.

And to make matters worse, Lani stood up, picked up my spoon, and dropped a bomb. He got the spoon full of melting ice cream and brought it so close I went cross-eyed. "The doctor over at Franklin thinks she might have an eating disorder, but we're trying to prove her wrong."

I was nervous anyway, from wondering if I might do something awful, like hurl mayonnaise on these art school kids' laps. I could not believe he just spewed like that. I grabbed the spoon and out of my mouth came, "Do not feed me. I am not a baby. Just back the hell off."

It wasn't the way I wanted to impress these people. To my shock I heard laughter.

"Yeah, Lani, back off," Ellen said. She took the spoon out of my hand. "Hot fudge sundae. That is a very tall order for an EDO. Who'd you see at Franklin? Lowenstein?"

I nodded. "What's an 'EDO'?"

"Eating disorder. And Lowenstein? She's a witch. If you had seen Erdman, you wouldn't be here right now. He's a shrink, so he gives some leeway for the head-case elements of EDO. He would have told you something easier, like a greasy cheese sandwich. Do you heave or just starve?"

My eyes floated over to Lani, who looked like this whole conversation was perfectly normal. I threw my head back, thinking, *You sly bastard. You brought this girl here because of me, not you.* But I had already let loose once, and they were all waiting for my answer.

I stumbled, "I...never throw up food."

"Did Lowenstein even ask her?" Ellen asked Lani, waving the spoon. "This is why she refers people to Erdman so fast. She doesn't have five minutes to know what she's talking about. If you were bulimic, this would be no problem to eat. You're a starver." She turned to Lani. "There is probably no way in hell she can eat this whole thing. So just back off."

His eyebrows shot up as the whole spoonful of ice cream went into her mouth. She turned back to me and handed me the spoon. "See? You can do it eventually. I was EDO all last year. I could never have eaten this. Even now I'm not sure I could eat half."

I watched in fascination as she started pushing hot fudge off to the side, giving me some strategy on scraping up the ice cream only as it melted, eating it like soup and avoiding the chocolate.

Cooper prattled on to Lani about why they had cut their last class of the day, like this whole eating ordeal was no big thing. I took smaller spoonfuls, scraping like Ellen had done, listening as Cooper went on and on—something about their drama teacher gay bashing on him. I didn't have a whole lot of time to stay mad at Lani, because Cooper's story got too hypnotizing.

"She keeps telling me I need to round out my persona, and so, she's got me playing all these *really* masculine roles. Yesterday I was Octavius in *Julius Caesar*."

He straightened up, swung a fist in the air, and this girly little voice suddenly dropped into the black hole and out came a deep, booming, masculine one.

"*'When think you that the sword goes up again? Never, till Caesar's three and thirty wounds be well avenged, or till another Caesar have added slaughter to the sword of traitors.'*"

Lani giggled, but I sat there frozen. It was like watching magic—one person disappears and another appears.

"*'Defiance, traitors, hurl we in your teeth; If you dare fight to-day, come to the field: If not when you have stomachs.'*"

"Oh my god…how did you do that?" I stared as he plopped down again.

He waved me off. "Oh, honey, I got a million voices. Wanna hear Clinton?" He went off on a Bill Clinton fest that sounded so real you almost forgot for a minute the kid was black. "At any rate, I'm cutting drama to boycott. Dr. Sykes thinks if she keeps giving me these masculine roles, eventually she'll stop catching me painting my toenails in the back of her class. I'm a good Octavius, and that's never going to stop me from painting my toenails. Wanna see? Today they're green."

"We'll pass on your stink fest." Ellen held up her hands,

like *stop,* because he was already untying his sneaker. "I cut drama in Cooper's honor. Not that any old excuse won't do right now. Last week Erdman told me to quit making everything in life into such a serious goddamn big deal. So Friday we cut for 'therapy.'"

She giggled, like that was supreme. I watched these people laughing at their faults and weirdnesses, which were laid out in plain view of everyone. It made me freeze into my invisible-person mode, lest they call on me to be next. There was a long silence, and I decided I'd better fill it with a question.

"So...you were in therapy because you had an eating disorder?" I asked Ellen.

She shook her head and swallowed. "I was in therapy because I lost four friends in one year. All unrelated deaths, too. Very freaky. My girlfriend Cher got hit by a car and dragged about thirty yards. Broke her neck. Four days later a friend from junior high died of a heart defect no one even knew he had. That weekend, my cousin Aleese died in a diabetic coma, and no one knew she was diabetic. Three funerals in nine days. Who feels like eating, okay? I think that was the start of it. I shrunk my stomach way down, so when the real traumatic one happened, like six months later, I was prime for deciding I was too big a target for a car, a mugger, or a bolt of lightning—"

"Uhm...those first three sound very dramatic," I said.

She nodded, but then shook her head. "Me and a bunch of my friends went camping, and there were these train tracks. This guy I'd known since forever was trying to reach out and touch the moving train. He forgot that the caboose has one of those steps that sticks out. *Way out.* The last thing out of his mouth was 'Yeee-haaaa!' and this step from the caboose got him. At first we thought he'd lost his balance and was just fooling around on the ground. I was only standing about six feet from him when it happened. But when I reached him, he was so far from alive, I don't even want to describe it."

There's not too much to say after something like that. But it got me thinking about what my dad had told me once. About how somebody gets diagnosed with a potentially fatal illness, and before they die, people who were expecting to live another sixty years have died.

"We're all dying, baby," he'd said. "But we're all living, too." It made me miss my dad and wish I could visit him. But he'd know I was cutting school, and if I told him the whole truth, he'd start in on me to get some therapy.

Lani finally broke the silence. "When you take drama at CAPA, Dr. Sykes makes everyone do these sessions where they sit around and confess experiences like that to each other. It's supposed to help your acting."

"How's that?" I took a spoonful of actual ice cream, not soup, feeling braver.

"It's supposed to keep all your emotions right on the surface," Ellen said. "And when you have to act, they're, like, really available to you. I told that train story in class and started screaming as loud as I screamed when it happened. Only this time, I'd had some time to get mad about it, so I was throwing stuff, too."

I watched her, kind of rooted in horror. "What did the people do?"

She shrugged. "A lot of them had something to scream about, so it wasn't, like, out of place. It was, like, *Okay. Ellen went through four deaths. Ellen got an eating disorder.* Nobody tries to explain why bad things happen. But there's got to be something behind that theory that pain is useful. Because it got really obvious by the end of the year. People who had something to scream about were usually better actors."

Cooper raised his hand like he was in class and said, "My dad used to hang me from this hook in the closet and beat me for borrowing from my sister's hat collection. I've got this thing for ladies' hats. I can't help myself. If I see one, I have to possess it."

He said it kind of braggingly. It was hard to know whether to be more shocked at his dad's violence or his very honest confession.

I decided on: "Did he hurt you?"

"Sure. But not as bad as my mom hurt him. My daddy? He's a junkyard dog. My mama? She's a rhino. No contest between a dog and a rhino. Don't be picking on my mama's babies, man. She'd have him all down on the ground, all taking shit out on his face. I'd be hanging up there screaming, 'Mama! Don't hurt Daddy.'"

I laughed, probably as hard as Ellen and Lani. It was like laughing on a roller coaster, where something feels dangerous but too funny to pass up the laugh. Some little bad part of Hackett started peeling away from me—that part that feels the need to look and smell like everyone else, and to hide all your bullshit that doesn't fit or you're nothing. These people were not nothing. They were funny, and somehow so...relaxed, so like-me-or-ask-me-if-I-care.

Ellen pointed a long finger of judgment at Lani as she finished a sentence I hadn't caught the beginning of. "...instrumental department, yeah, right. You play decent drums, but drummers are a dime a dozen."

"And actors aren't?" Lani laughed. "I'm not meant to be an actor. I'm too...honest."

"But he can act the part of *anybody,* speaking of people who have been traumatized." Ellen turned to me. "He did a screaming three-year-old in one of our classes. At his size. You, like, totally forgot about it. And in another show? He did this sort of mean, dastardly angel, who came down to pass judgment on all the lowlifes. What kind of angel was that?"

Lani sat, absently twirling his sundae cup, like all these compliments didn't matter. But his eyes now flashed to mine, and he grinned a little.

"Floating angel," he finally said.

"You played a floating angel onstage?" I asked in surprise.

"He even had a book with pictures of them!" Ellen turned from me to him. "That book you passed off to Abby so she could make your costume. The costume was almost as authentic as the performance."

I wished I could have seen this. "What'd you do, Lani? Like, breathe fire?"

Cooper shook his finger, going, "Nuh-nuh-nuh, honey. The boy never...even...raised...his voice. You ever seen that soft-spoken character Nurse Ratched in the movie *One Flew Over the Cuckoo's Nest*? That nary-an-emotion, cold-as-ice, glaring, judgmental, hell-raising creature? All I can say is this. If you were at that performance, and you had ever knocked a crutch out from under a cripple, told a bum to get a job, bullied a skinny faggot like me, fed your sister's pet guinea pig to your brother's pet snake...you were scared. You figured you better haul your ass down to that pet store and buy your sister some new, improved guinea pig before some house landed on you. Or before you burst into flames like some accidental-but-not-really, spontaneous combustion."

Ellen shuddered. "*And* he did it in some huge, billowing, angel costume. You'd think he would walk out onstage and everyone would be all 'Too much faggotry, let me go be sick.' Not even CAPA is so above it all, okay? But he was already so in character that you just...froze. Didn't even think about it."

Lani had been watching me this whole time, kind of bored or lost in other thoughts, with his fingertips pressed together again in front of his lips. I couldn't tell whether they were hiding a grin. His eyes looked to be laughing. A chilly spot grew inside me as I watched his eyes bask with some sort of victory, like we shared a deep, dark secret. The smile got bigger and bigger until his dimples dug into his cheeks.

"I wanna see that book." I nudged Ellen, who was rambling about how this Abby still had the costume and Lani forgot to get his book back. "This is not my first conversation today about floating angels. I just want to see it . . . make sure Lani's not in it."

"Yeah, I'll get the book back from Abby," she said, "and the costume, too. Now that you have a zip code, Lani. Write down your address." She reached in her back jeans pocket and tossed him a pen.

He didn't react to her at all, just kept smiling that searing way at me. I felt kind of keyed up, like a little kid hearing about the Jersey Devil for the first time.

"He wants you to think he really *is* one of these creatures." Cooper giggled, and I thought the statement might snap Lani's eyes from me, but it didn't.

Lani turned his fingertips, all pressed together, so his indexes were pointing dead center at my chest. His voice wasn't the icy, judgmental one I expected. It was so quiet I could hardly hear it. "I was just watching what you were doing while Ellen and Cooper were talking about their problems."

I looked down. There was a major dent in the ice cream, like, two-thirds gone. I pulled my pinky out of my mouth and realized I'd been sucking whipped cream off it.

12

I lay on my bed after dinner, with my electric guitar across my chest. Now that I wasn't under the dimness of the single bulb suspended from the basement ceiling, I could see dust and dirt in the frets. *Clean it,* I thought. But my right arm was flung over the side of the mattress, while my left hand absently played along with the same Jonny Lang CD over and over again.

I stared at the ceiling, liking this image wandering through my head of me flanking my guitar pick in some black leather glove. My imagination grew to include me in black leather pants and, like, snakeskin boots, and a hat with a feather.

No, I don't think so, I thought, but smiled hazily. It was one of those fun flip-side-of-your-real-life imaginings that you could only dream about. While running through progressions with Jonny Lang, I set myself to more realistic thoughts—like what to do about this weekend.

It was Thursday, and Friday night was coming up. Half of me really wanted to be with my friends and celebrate that I was cancer free. I could relax again, so long as I could keep off the regimented eating mentality. But I couldn't stop thinking about Ellen and Cooper, how their hard times had paid off in talent. "Got to pay your dues to sing the blues" was how Lani had put it. Half of me wanted to stay holed up in this room and play around with some weird twitches.

I would remember something awful, like the first time my hair clogged the drain in my dad's shower after chemo, and then try to play along with Jonny Lang. Looking at the memories instead of trying to block them kind of froze me at first. But Jonny Lang's most noteworthy signature is his anger, a very passionate bitching that wails up and down the guitar frets. I felt like I related to it all of a sudden and started pulling into a few of his slides and reverbs—major details that I'd hardly noticed before.

It was the first time in weeks I had picked up my electric guitar and had not wanted to play my bloody basement lyrics. I hardly thought about them, except to shrug.

I had told my mom I was going to bed early, and every time the phone rang, she would shout from the living room, *"Claire. It's (fill in the blank)! Don't you want to talk?"*

It happened, like, six times, and with the seventh, I could hear her chatting on and giggling, letting me know it was Macy. Sometimes my mom thought she and Macy were best friends, instead of Macy and me. They could chatter on the phone, and usually I thought it was fine, until sometimes I'd catch them talking about *me*. Macy would recite some dorky thing I had done that day...my mom would tell her that I was my dad all over again, a social-retard musician.

I turned down Jonny Lang to listen, scared one of these days my mom would talk to Macy while too drunk and slurring. Macy was pretty sharp, but my mom was pretty careful. If she was way drunk, she wouldn't say more than "hey, hey" to my friends.

At the moment, she just sounded happy drunk. But I kept listening, hoping that Macy wouldn't mention that I wasn't in school today, thinking my mom knew. As my mom's footsteps trudged slowly up the stairs, I could hear her say, "Well, some girls just have to kiss and tell, Macy. It's their only way to feel significant."

She slurred slightly on *significant,* but I relaxed. It wasn't too bad. And obviously they were gossiping about somebody other than *moi*. I turned out the light, but Mom opened my door without knocking and said over Jonny Lang, "Claire, Macy said she really needs to talk to you, and to stop being a twit who falls asleep too early."

I took the phone.

"Are you really sleeping?" Macy demanded.

"Sort of."

"Could you have called me at least once today, dork? I didn't know what was up. I knew you split your head wide open last night, and all of a sudden you're nowhere."

"Wow...I didn't think," I breathed.

"You never think! I didn't want to ask your mom what was up, in case you cut school without her knowing."

"Thanks, Macy. That was really smart of you."

"So she thought you were in school?"

"Yeah." I sat up slowly, trying to figure out how to tell Macy what had actually happened today. Now that she wouldn't have to be freaked out over bad news, the idea of telling her seemed easier.

"The problem was a little worse than my head," I started. "In fact, I've had a problem for the past few weeks. I just didn't want to spew and scare everybody half to death. I thought, well...that I might be relapsing."

"What's 'relapsing,'" she muttered, then quickly gasped. "Oh! Claire. Jesus. I thought...you told me once...you were cured, that nothing could happen now."

I rolled my eyes, thinking I probably said that at some point, just to avoid conversations about it. I hurried on. "It turned out to be something else. I'm okay. I promise."

I could hear her breathing in the phone, like I had stunned her into remaining more calm than she usually was. She finally said, "Like, what is it? You could have told me. Why didn't you tell me?"

I shut my eyes and sighed. "I didn't want anyone flipping

out or not knowing what to say. But at any rate, I found somebody to talk to, who knows a little about stuff like this and was really helpful."

"A teacher?"

"No. Don't freak, okay? Remember Lani Garver?"

My stomach bottomed out when she said, "Oh shit, Claire."

I didn't completely bug, because her tone was not the judgmental one. There was a tremble in her voice, more like she was scared than angry. She kept starting syllables and stopping them. I had rarely heard Macy left speechless, so when she started spewing questions, I figured I'd upset her too much.

"Forget it! How are you? Are you all right? Why didn't you *tell* me?" she asked again.

I sighed. "What could you have *done*, Macy?"

There was a long silence.

"What could you have told me that would have made it any better? If I'd told you not to tell anyone, would you have been able to handle it on your own?"

"When have I ever spewed your secrets?" she demanded, despite that she'd just got caught spewing about my electric guitar the night before. I stayed politely quiet. "I could have, well, *been* there for you. What could anybody do? What did *he* do?"

I told her about the clinic and how it allowed me to get a grip on things without sending Mom into cardiac arrest. "I'm okay. It's just an eating disorder. Small one—"

"Claire, you don't have any eating disorder! That's bullshit."

"I guess there's other kinds of eating disorders besides getting by on a lettuce leaf a day, or heaving. It's not so much how much you diet, but why, they told me—"

"But you've always been skinny! They're making a big deal out of nothing."

She was giving me the facts about myself, which felt annoying. But I was freaking her out, plain and simple, and that's why she was talking like that. It made me want to say, "Yeah, you're right," even though I didn't know what I thought. She didn't give me the chance.

"So let me get this straight," she went on. "You cut school, and you went to a clinic. With Lani Garver."

"Yeah. It was an amazing day..." I started slowly, looking for some words to make her see the good in him. "It's funny. He's got that nondescript little voice, so you would never guess he can be so rock solid in a crisis—"

"Just stop. Claire, I don't know how to tell you this, but Tony Clementi almost took that kid's head off in front of the Rod 'N' Reel about half an hour ago."

I shot up and tossed the guitar on the foot of the bed. "No way."

"Yeah. I was there."

I searched my frantic memory. Getting off the bus, he only said he was going to the library. Now I wondered if I should have thought to go with him.

"I saw the whole thing. Listen, Claire. I'm really sorry you were in trouble and I'm glad you're, you know, not sick. But do yourself a huge favor. Do not repeat that story to Scott and Phil. Okay? Did I tell you that kid would be in trouble soon enough? Listen to me this time—"

"He...told me he was going to the library...," I stumbled, trying to make sense of this.

"The *library*? And you just believed him." She sighed. "I don't know how to say this, but he was bullshitting you."

"No way. Why would he lie?"

"Claire, come *on*. You can't even smell a kid who refuses to wear deodorant. How are you supposed to see a pervert coming?"

I wanted to defend myself, but she hurried on before I

could think of any defense. "Me, Phil, and Scott were in Vince's car, and we were stopping to pick up Tony in front of the Rod 'N' Reel. Bartender took his keys again, and someone had called Vince. Lani Garver was out there, having an argument with Tony, who was plowed, as usual."

She was silent for a moment, but then a huge laugh snorted out her nose, like the scandal was too much. She kept saying, "Claire, I'm sorry," like she didn't mean to be laughing.

I just shut my eyes, silently cursing at this bad luck. I had some picture in my head of Lani coming out of the library, which was a couple of blocks past the Rod. *Should have warned him not to walk past that stupid bar...*I figured it was lost on Macy that somebody would actually go to the library for fun.

"Why Tony Clementi? Why not somebody else? Did you hear Tony last night, barking about queens and all that—"

"Of course I heard it. I *caused* it, darling. *I* called him a queen. But..." She kicked in with more laughs. "Claire, I'm really glad if Lani Garver did something that helped you. What can I say? But he left his brain at that clinic or something. Can he be a little bit smarter about who he tries to pick up?"

I didn't get it at first. It took me a few seconds to remember Tony's name had come up more than any other. She was trying to say that Lani came on to Tony. I laughed, too, but for very different reasons. It's the kind of thing where if you don't laugh, you'll end up clobbering somebody for their insanity.

I finally said, "Macy, that's a lie. Lani would not do that. Tony's the type who would definitely gay bash, and so he made up the first excuse he could think of to—"

"Uh, sorry, hon. I heard it with my own ears."

"You did not."

"Are you calling me a liar?" she demanded loudly, but she still couldn't stop laughing.

I got a bad feeling about this. Macy could get mean, but it all had to do with her bluntness. *She always told the truth.* My jaw dangled as I listened, totally confused.

"We jumped right out of the car, because Tony was already in his face, loudly. Tony was kind of slurring, but he was real plain in what he was saying: 'Don't you ever try that on any guys on this island ever again. And especially don't you come on to a Clementi! Do you understand?' And Lani Garver said back to him, 'If you don't want anything, then you shouldn't be standing alone on a street corner, blowing smoke rings. Didn't you know that's a gay thing?' Tony was way drunk, but he managed to yell, 'This isn't the city, and I wouldn't know a goddamn gay thing if I fell over it.' And Tony hit him. Not hard. He had a pretty big load on. I don't think Tony hurt him, but the guy just took off."

Smoke rings...propositioning someone... I sat there frozen, remembering the funny kids from art school, eating ice cream with them on South Street, finding out I wasn't relapsing—and I got mad.

"I...don't believe you!"

"Claire? Listen to me." Her voice was sympathetic, and I could hear that condescending tone that I didn't much like, but she was trying to stay calm, for once, and for once *I* was losing it. "You know how things always go with us. I'm the one who sees someone's idiot side first. You never believe me. A week or two later, you feel stupid. I'm telling you, you've got to trust me this time and back off from him. Whatever reason he had for helping you, I don't know. But he's not all he's making himself out to be. How often am I wrong about people?"

I shut my eyes tight. She was waiting for an answer, and I found the only thing in this crazy tale that made any sense to me. "This just smells of Tony twisting something around," I stumbled. "Weren't you mad enough at him last night to practically drown him? You know he's an upstart."

"He's a lush, yeah. And obnoxious. And if Vince didn't have the car, you know we probably would not see either of them as much. But Tony did not instigate that fight. He was not gay bashing, Claire. He was defending himself. If you don't believe me, Phil and Scott were standing right there, too."

My gut was telling me something was sincerely wrong here. I couldn't imagine Macy lying any more than I could imagine Lani picking up a date on a street corner. But my imagination rarely did me right.

I commanded myself not to cry, but it didn't work. I was sniffing, and Macy was threatening to come over and "be there for me."

"Claire, I am really, really sorry to lay this on you. You've had the day from hell, the three weeks from hell. I promise I will not call you stupid for this one, okay? I'll pick you up on the way to school, okay? You think you have an eating disorder? Fine, whatever. You wanna pig out? Gain some weight? Let's go to Sydney's before school and we'll get the gooiest, nastiest doughnuts, and we'll totally mow down. I won't tell anybody about what happened to you, okay? Claire?"

I felt like I'd been hit in the face with a brick, but I couldn't think of much to say about that.

"Yeah, I'm here."

"I love you, Claire."

I just sniffed and said, "I love you, too."

13

Friday morning all my friends showed up at the corner, and we walked to Sydney's and ate doughnuts, which is so far from the usual that it could have meant only one thing. Macy couldn't help herself and had spewed the whole story. People who can't be bothered with breakfast don't turn into sudden doughnut hogs without some influence. I tried to see it from Macy's standpoint, realizing her "that's bullshit" responses last night were surely just shock. Once she hung up she probably got all worried and flipping. She would have told everyone so they would rally around and make me feel better.

And by the way they were acting, I could only think that Macy was up to the "best" of her spewing, which means dishing out a lot of orders, all "Do not be in her face. Do not upset her. If you call her stupid or naive even once, I will be all over you."

They were sweet as punch. Nobody mentioned the words *eating disorder,* but you never in your life saw girls oohing and aahing over how great doughnuts tasted. It just made it more difficult to swallow, what with the corners of everybody's eyes wandering all over me while they talked about some Spanish test.

Eating mayonnaise and hot fudge the day before must have opened the passageway somewhat. While the thing sat in my stomach like a Thanksgiving turkey, I didn't feel like heaving—at least not until we started walking to school and what happened at the Rod 'N' Reel came up.

For the hundredth time in a year, I was in awe of the power Macy had over people. My friends called me a bonehead on a regular basis until something pretty serious came up and Macy shot off her mouth at them. She had this way of making what she considered my naiveness into something sweet and endearing, as opposed to incredibly stupid.

I can't remember how the Rod 'N' Reel got brought up. But when Macy said he seemed "pretty okay and not like some pervert slut" when we talked to him out in the corridor two days ago, my eyes started filling up. Then these girls all but swarmed me, gripping my shoulders, petting my hair. Any thought of pretending Macy hadn't told them where I'd been yesterday got lost in the shuffle. Yet it was hard to be mad at Macy for giving over my secrets, when the response couldn't get nicer.

The problem was, they thought I was crying because I felt stupid. I was crying because the word *confused* had taken on some new depth of meaning. Secretly, I wasn't sure I'd been stupid. I still looked for some loophole in this story. I knew Macy would not lie to me. I knew my gut had had a way of getting me in trouble in the past. And yet, Lani had blown out a story to me yesterday about not knowing what oral sex was in eighth grade. And I'm supposed to just up and believe that he made the whole thing up because he got a twitch to make his life sound really good.

I tried to remember any look of drama or lying in his eyes, his voice. I just couldn't recall seeing any of that. And yet, a pretty big part of me just wanted to believe my friends so everything could feel "normal" again.

As we split up and I headed toward my locker, I thought about how there's a problem when you try to change what you actually believe. You can change what you say, you can change what you do, I decided, staring at my books, trying to remember what class I had first period, but you can't just change what you believe—all *Okay, today I think I'll believe this thing, even though it would have seemed crazy yesterday.* You can't change what you believe like you can change your underwear.

I sat in homeroom all frozen in my desk chair, but thinking on that even more. I guessed some people could just change what they believed. Some kids could create a relationship between two things, when really, there is none, like, *Okay, if I don't believe this, I will look like an ass, so, okay, I believe it.* I did not want to look like an ass, but I couldn't force myself to buy into this story. Especially since Lani himself was sitting three rows over, two seats in front of me, a solid reminder of my great day yesterday.

I stared into some textbook, pretending I didn't see anything or anybody. He didn't even turn around, and it looked like he hadn't seen me. But the rumor had obviously gotten around. Some of the jocks in the back were muttering things like "Blow me."

The third time some guy mumbled that, Lani turned around very calmly and sized the guy up. He just looked focused, like this big mouth was the most interesting person in the universe. And he's got those dark eyes, like a shark's. They're hard to read.

I decided one funny thing by watching this—that guys will not swap gazes for too long with someone they think is gay. And once their eyes drop, they've lost the game somehow. They can say what they want, but it no longer has half the impact.

I wondered if Lani knew that, what with everything else he seemed to know about what makes people tick. I wondered what in hell he would say to defend himself if I went traipsing over to his house after school, knocked on the door, and asked him about it to his face. My friends were practically nominating me for sainthood right now, and that tempted me to leave well enough alone. But I felt that hearing from him might be the only way to decide what was true.

After cheerleading I sneaked out of the locker room, figuring I could get away with anything at the moment, even snubbing people. When I got to Lani's house, his mother took my hand in both of hers as I passed through their front door.

"Nice to see you again," she said with a smile that could eat me alive.

"Yeah, nice to see you, too . . . Hope you're liking it here . . . How 'bout this Indian summer, huh? You must have brought it with you." I plastered a grin on my face, hoping it would distract from the horror in my widening eyes. I knew why she thought it was "nice" to see me again, and I didn't want to spew . . . *Uh, your son and I are not doing the nasty!* I blathered on, gauging how long it usually took my mom to feel satisfied that my friends had talked to *her* long enough. Then I climbed the stairs.

Lani's door was partially open, and I stood outside, sighing a few times, bracing for this. He must have heard me with his mom, because before I stuck my head in the door, I heard, "Claire?"

He was hanging up the phone as I went in.

"Friend from South Street?" I said with what smile I could muster.

"Uh . . . no." His jaw hung and his eyes worked from side to side, like he was confused about something.

"What's up?" I asked.

He just started shaking his head, pointing to a place on his mattress not covered with paperbacks and magazines, like, *Sit down.*

When I did, he recovered his normal face, though I would

say he looked tired. I hoped he might save me the embarrassment by bringing up last night himself.

"So...how is Claire?"

"Good."

"What did you eat today?"

"The usual, but add a doughnut, and Myra was, like, force-feeding me yogurt and French fries during lunch."

"That's good. How did it feel?"

"I've had about a nine-hour stomachache but didn't heave."

"Any dizzy spells?"

"Couple times, but it's not nerve-wracking, since I know it's not—" I broke off with a twitchy laugh. Now that I was here, I didn't know quite what to say. "How was *your* day?"

His eyes still worked side to side, like he was still trying to get over whatever happened on the phone. I wasn't even sure he had comprehended what I was saying. It rang again, and he rubbed his eyes.

"Uh...yeah...," he said on the pickup, and almost immediately followed up with "Uh...no...," and he hung up.

My gut tightened as a bad thought wandered through me. "Is someone giving you a hard time?"

"Uh, yeah." He looked at me this time, then shrugged absently. "Don't worry about me, I'm kind of used to this. We...were talking about you."

The phone rang again, and he picked it up and punched the off button, this time without saying anything. I just watched him, and he returned my gaze. "So. I guess we're not talking about you. I guess you want to know about last night."

I kind of flinched at his bluntness. And he sounded annoyed, like I was being nosy.

"I just heard a story about last night. And now I have to put that story together with the day I had yesterday. It's kind of a lot to believe."

"That's good, Claire. That's good that you don't believe everything you hear." His sarcasm rang out, like the world's foulest mood was pending.

"Can't you tell me? Your side of it?"

The phone rang again, and he stared at the receiver before it wandered to his ear.

"Yeah. Oh. Bless my socks. It's my great-aunt Suzie Smokes. How the hell is Aunt Suzie?" and he hung up. I got scared he was snapping. He was obviously trying to jerk somebody's chain, but it wasn't making much sense.

"So you want to know about last night," he accused me again. "Sorry, can't help you."

"Lani—" I laughed, confused. "You can't help me? I'm trying to help you—"

"I never defend the things I do."

He really looked tired, but I figured I was there to help him, not to make his life worse. "Why not?"

"Because, as Jung would say, there is no point to it."

"What does Jung have to do with it?"

"He termed a psychology phrase that I have only witnessed a gazillion times." His eyes wandered over to one of the dozen paperback books spread out on his bed. He batted it with his finger so that it slid closer to me. "It's called a convenient recollection."

I picked up the paperback and turned my eyes to the jacket. *Dictionary of Psychological Terms.*

"*Convenient recollection,*" he repeated, and I took it I was supposed to look this term up. I felt annoyed and didn't need any haughty act, not while I was only trying to be fair. But since he looked kind of ready to snap, I thumbed through until I found the term.

"*Convenient recollection.* 'A memory recalled inaccurately, to unconsciously protect against guilt, anxiety, or unwanted associations.'"

I tossed the book on the bed, going back and forth over the words in my head. They were easy enough, but I wasn't some kind of analysis genius.

"You're saying the people last night..." I couldn't figure out what he meant.

"I'm not saying anything, Claire." He lay down flat on the mattress with his legs on top of the books, pinching the bridge of his nose, his eyes shut.

I got tired of the mystery stuff and just went for a direct approach. "Okay. Macy said you came on to Tony."

"Imagine that!"

"Something about blowing smoke rings." I ignored his sarcasm. "You accused Tony of blowing smoke rings—"

His fingers moved off his nose as his head jerked to the side. He stared at me, like this was the first interesting thing I'd said yet. "Smoke rings."

"Yeah, you said blowing smoke rings was a gay thing. At least, that's what Macy thought you said." I knew Macy never missed a trick, but based on how his eyebrows went up at me before he started rubbing his nose again, I gathered I was supposed to connect her comment about smoke rings with *convenient recollection.*

"I need to sleep, Claire. So, if you're okay, and you don't need anything, and there's the remote possibility you might find something comprehensible in your Jung homework—"

The phone rang again, which prevented me from blurting the word *arrogant.* This time he didn't even say hello, just held the receiver to his ear for a minute and hung up without even opening his eyes.

"Lani. Listen to reason. People are saying awful things about you. And if *you* can't tell me anything, what choice do I have but to believe *them*?"

"Got *me*."

"Great. You're in about the finest mood I've ever seen."

"Walk a mile in my shoes."

I stood up, hauled my backpack onto my shoulder, and shook my head at him. "Okay. I'm supposing you really did brain flake like that last night, even though it doesn't make much sense to me."

"I must have brain flaked." He said it kind of singsongy, with a huge shrug.

"You came on to Tony Clementi, of all people, and asked him for sex because he blew smoke rings. Okay. I'm uhm... leaving since you're not very talkative right now." I hoped if he heard the whole thing out loud, he'd decide it was too ludicrous to let slide.

But he shrugged. "I'm just a mad rapist."

The phone rang, and the receiver was still in his hand. This time he just let the phone tumble onto the mattress. "Let my mom get it. Maybe he'll quit if he hears my mom."

"Who in hell is it?" I reached for the receiver, but he grabbed for it and swiped it around to the other side of him. "Believe me when I tell you. You don't want to hear...*that*."

It rang a third time. He cocked his head at the ceiling. "Where's my mom? Did she go out?"

"Just...give it to me!" I crawled over him on my knees, grabbing for the receiver.

When I got my hand around it, he said, "Don't accuse me of ruining your life."

I just hit the button and didn't say hello. I was expecting to hear a bunch of threats and gay bashing. All I heard at first was somebody breathing. I kept waiting to hear a voice, and when there was none, I realized there was a weird rhythm to this breathing. Then these whispered comments started to fly between breaths, and at first it sounded like a girl's voice. Then the voice came out of a whisper, and I thought it was a guy's voice. The whispering came out full of the most graphic come-on lines I had ever heard. The only comment clean enough to even put on paper was "You're *mine*, Suzie."

I clicked the off button, put my hand over my mouth, and flopped my butt down on the mattress. I'd heard *about* things like this before. As some of the fire started leaving my cheeks, my eyes wandered to Lani, who was looking directly at me this time.

"*Don't* come back and say I just ruined your life," he repeated, like somehow that could ruin my life.

"What in the hell was that?" I breathed.

"That, darling, was phone sex."

And of course, the next question from me was supposed to be, "You were having phone sex?" I suppose I looked shocked because he read my mind.

"Did I *look* like I was having phone sex when you came in here?" he blasted.

I shut my eyes and sighed. He'd been sitting with the door half open and a bunch of stupid-looking philosophy paperbacks open on the bed.

"No..." But the truth started to strike me: Somebody was seriously harassing him, and unless it was some rich old fart who didn't care how high his long-distance bill was, it would have to be somebody from Hackett.

I let out a laugh at the enormity of this scandal. It was a crime, Lani going through that mess last night and now having to put up with this so soon after. There was only one explanation if it was somebody from Hackett. And that explanation made me grab my cheeks to keep from smiling. Christ, if Macy could hear this... *Some guy in school was a closet gay—and enough of a perv to actually say this shit— who had seen Lani from afar, took a liking to him...*

I covered my mouth with my hand, but my eyes were probably laughing, and he glared. The phone rang again.

He ripped it from my fingers and hit the off button. "I'm glad you're so amused by my life."

"I'm not laughing at you, really. I'm sorry!" I defended myself, but I couldn't wipe the smile completely off my face.

I'm human, too. The question tickled my insides: *Who in the hell is the mystery lover?*

"Let's grow up and forget the toilet humor." He flopped over on his side, away from me, and I could see he was really tired of this.

"I'm sorry, I'm sorry." I lost the grin and massaged his shoulder, but I couldn't just let the conversation drop. "If you want, I'll try to find out who it is."

"I already know who it is."

"He said his name?"

"Uh-uh." He kept his back to me.

"You . . . got a love note to go with?"

After a few seconds of silence, he turned over and looked at me like I was nuts. "Claire, I can see why Macy thinks you're dense sometimes. I hit star sixty-nine."

He flopped back over, and my eyes popped. I laughed again, but silently to myself. "Whoever it is, he's a dumb ass. Wouldn't a perv think to have his line blocked? There's star sixty-nine, caller ID. . . . *Doyee.*"

"He doesn't care that I know. He *wants* me to know. For some strange people, that's part of the fun . . . the danger. He thinks I'm over here all by my lonesome, shaking in my little pink bedroom slippers." His voice sounded more annoyed than scared. I glanced down at his army boots, still on his feet, and I rocked his ankle some, trying to think.

"Can you call the cops?"

"Even if they believed it, it wouldn't be worth what would happen to me later. He knows that."

"Lani, you're making some puny little coward sound like an enormous threat. You're overreacting." I think, like everybody else, I went with a stereotype in my head of a guy who looked more like a ballerina than a fisherman. I had my first rude awakening, hitting star sixty-nine.

It was Vince and Tony Clementi's phone number. I had just

seen Vince at football practice. My eyes bugged out. I stared at the receiver, turning it over in my hand, numbly, and if there was any question in my mind about having misheard, he had caller ID right there on the back. *Clementi, Josephine...* That was the name of Tony's widowed mother, and it was followed by their number, which I knew from Macy mooching us rides places.

14

Lani's story started out like I figured. He had been walking home from the library and passed by the Rod 'N' Reel, not knowing it was a shaky place for him to be. A very loaded Tony had decided it would be a good idea to crash out in this little patch of grass on the far side of the parking lot, which was not a totally unusual sight.

Since Tony's father had died in a drunken fall from his dock, the owner of the Rod supposedly watched Tony like a hawk, and took his keys more often than not. But Tony never minded a little attention. He would fall out in the grass and start sleeping it off, which made him stand out like a sore thumb to people on the street and sidewalk. And a couple of his fishing buddies would be driving past, all "Look, there's Clementi... Guess he's looking for a ride home again."

It was, like, island legend to us natives, but he could give a good-hearted tourist a jolt sometimes—wondering if an honest, upstanding person was in cardiac arrest.

Along comes Lani.

As he told it, he squatted over Tony and said, "Are you all right?" And Tony opened his eyes, which Lani said were full of something more profound than booze—maybe ecstasy, or coke, or some injured fisherman's prescription of Percodan. There wasn't too much Tony wouldn't try. He asked Lani,

"You that new kid around here?" Lani said yeah. Tony reached up, and the rest lies between haze and the unknown, because Lani would not be specific about it. All I know is he had this little red mark on his chin I would have taken for a zit, and Lani said it came from the zipper of Tony's jeans. When Tony heard the sound of Vince's Impala coming around the corner, he didn't have enough reflex reaction working to get them both to their feet.

Yet, like I always knew, Tony starts hatching intelligence when it really matters. He made it look like he was fighting off Lani. Hence, the speech Macy heard about never, ever coming on to "no Hackett guys and especially no Clementis, if you know what's good for you."

I felt like the universe had changed shape and color. I sat on the edge of Lani's mattress, still staring at that caller ID to remind myself that this version of the story had to be true— unless the caller had been Mrs. Clementi, who was overheard at Mr. Clementi's funeral telling one of Mom's *Les Girls,* "Mother of God, at least now I don't have to worry about that gross bedroom stuff anymore." I kind of doubted her involvement.

"I don't know the first thing about smoke rings." Lani repeated it for a second time, as if to drive home his point.

"But...Macy wouldn't lie." I didn't say it to start an argument—I was just way beyond confused—but he didn't look upset.

He stuck a pillow in his lap and rested his chin on his hand with a sigh. "She didn't lie. A lie is intentional. She totally believes what she told you."

"But... *smoke rings*? How is she even supposed to come up with a concept like that? It's so out there..."

"Not really. Did she tell you there were three enormous guys there?"

"Yeah." I felt relieved that the stories agreed on some

points. "Her boyfriend, Phil Krilley; my boyfriend, Scott Dern; and Tony's brother, Vince."

"Which one of them smokes?"

"Vince," I said.

"Well, first off, she was not as close as she's letting on. These guys were, like, all over me, and there was no way she could have seen and heard it as clearly as she's remembering."

"Okay..." Maybe I could buy that much of an error out of Macy.

"I noticed her only when I turned my head because Vince blew all this smoke in my face."

"Did you say *anything* back to Tony? Or to Vince about not...blowing smoke in your face? Did you even mention the word smoke?"

"I don't remember. Probably. I probably said, 'Stop blowing smoke in my face,' or something like that."

I rubbed my forehead, hard.

"See why I don't defend myself when stuff like this happens?" he asked. "See why I didn't want to defend myself when you first came in here? If I just spouted off my side of the story, like my word was supposed to be good enough, would you have believed it?"

The thing that got me was staring at this caller ID. I would have felt torn between his word and Macy's word if it weren't for that.

"It's not as crazy as it sounds, Claire, her pulling a line like that out of her ear. It happens in courts all the time. People are under oath, swearing as good American citizens...a white killer was black, that a guy in a red hooded sweatshirt held up the 7-Eleven, when it was a girl in a black leather jacket. 'I hate Johnny Jones' turns into 'I killed Johnny Jones and dumped his body in the river.' You know how many innocent people are sitting in jail right now because they were heard or seen wrongly by somebody? People don't decide they're going to make stuff up. They see things as..."

He got off the bed, trudged to the mirror hung over his dresser, and studied his face. "They see the truth like I'm seeing my reflection. The cut on my chin from Tony's jeans looks to me like it's taking up my whole face."

I had hardly even noticed the cut until he mentioned it. I trudged up behind him to see if maybe his mirror was somehow magnifying the thing. It looked the same to me in the mirror.

"And you? Claire, you look incredibly...thin."

I grabbed a handful of fat from under one arm, then stood on tiptoes to see a roll of fat I grabbed from one hip. "No way. I've got fat all over the place."

"And you truly believe that." He walked back to the bed and flopped down on it. "The whole world is smoke and mirrors, Claire. Maybe Macy heard that fact about smoke rings in some movie and banked it away in her brain, or something. I'm not saying it isn't true about gay pickup lines. I'm just saying that I wouldn't know. Believe me, if I didn't know much about sex in eighth grade, I wouldn't know this, either."

I kept watching him, wanting to believe all this, but it was like trying to shove fifty pounds of spaghetti down my throat. The arguments kept gushing back up. I dropped down beside him, staring at the ceiling.

"But *why*? Macy always has her eyes wide open, and she doesn't like Tony much. If she saw anything to hint that Tony Clementi was hitting on boys, she wouldn't twist it around. She would laugh so hard, it might kill her. She'd be a dead woman from laughing. She'd just be sure to live long enough to spew it all over the island—"

"But she didn't see Tony force me down on him." He shook his head. "All she saw was a guy like Tony barking at someone like me. What would you think was going on?"

"Are you defending her?" I faced him in disbelief. "Cuz I'm going to call her when I get home and let her have it."

"No, don't." He put up his hands, like *Stop*. "Don't ever try to tell a person their recollections are convenient. They totally believe themselves and will never believe you."

"Macy's my best friend. She listens to me, even though she pretends she doesn't."

"Claire, people who are friends with Tony will never, ever believe that I was an innocent bystander and Tony Clementi tried to molest me. I can't believe you can't see that. It's so simple." He flopped back on the mattress, rubbing his eyes and swallowing. "I can't wait until I can get out of here again."

I couldn't blame him one bit. The thought of being mauled by some drunk...I wanted to hurl. I said, "Maybe you can graduate early."

He just laughed. "Graduate. That would be cute, wouldn't it? I don't need to graduate. It's not about graduating. It's about figuring out where to go next."

I got what he meant. "You can't just run away again. That sucks!"

He studied the ceiling for a while, and I listened to cars passing by outside. The strange heat wave still cooked, so he had the window wide open. One car seemed to stop right out front, and I got scared for a minute we were going to have some face-to-face problems. But fortunately, the car rolled on again.

He rubbed at the bridge of his nose, looking even more tired. "Claire, I know this is going to sound unbelievable to you. But...I always come out on top."

Yeah, it sounded unbelievable. Especially after what happened next.

We lay there listening to the roar of surf, getting more and more bummed out, and finally his mother came back from wherever she had been, and we heard the front door slam. Footsteps trudged up the stairs and she appeared in the doorway.

"May I speak to you in private?"

142

He blinked at her with swollen eyes. "If you really want to get me up off this bed, I'll do it, but I'm beat, and Claire won't care, whatever it is."

Her gaze wandered over to me, and something in her eyes made me want to get out of there, fast. Something like betrayal.

"Are you Lani's new *best friend*?"

I stood up slowly, wondering what gave her the right to look at me like that.

"Wherever we've lived, Lani's *always* had a best friend, you know. It's *always* a girl. I thought maybe things had changed."

My chest flashed with hurt, though I tried to think of how she could clump me in with some pattern. We hadn't exactly asked to be each other's friend. She was obviously missing the fact that we were agonizing over something. For once, no nice chatter erupted from my throat. I might have even glared.

She must have noticed, because she leaned her head into the side of the door frame. Her eyes filled up. "You look like a nice girl, and I'm sure you are. It's just that..."

She turned her teary eyes to Lani and brought from behind the door frame a magazine, which she held up, only by the very corner, with two fingers. There was a guy in what looked like a bathing suit on the cover. She tossed it on the bed, then said, "I just found this on the front porch."

Lani touched it with the same two fingers as she had, but his disgust didn't seem to register with her, either.

She wiped her eyes and asked in this trembling, pleading little voice, "Are you starting in again already?"

He gasped a little as something like snot dripped onto the floor, missing the mattress by less than an inch. He opened his fingers so the porn magazine dropped to the floor. Then he threw his head back on the pillow and said in the same singsongy voice he used on me. "Yeah, that's it, Mom...I must be starting in again..."

15

"Don't forget to tell your mom that I'm meeting you right where the bus pulls in. Let's ward off any of her mad-rapist lectures." My dad's laugh buzzed through the receiver.

I leaned against my kitchen counter, trying to laugh back. "You mean the ones about how Hackett is the only safe place in the universe? And even getting on a bus out of here is unsafe?"

"You're bringing back bad memories." My dad groaned. He was raised on Hackett, too, and didn't share our enthusiasm for the place. "At any rate, I'm glad you're coming. I've been waiting for the day when you felt like you could come back to my house."

"I'm not saying I can come all the time," I put in quickly. "I've got my job at Sydney's now, and...lots of times I have Sunday cheerleading practices."

"You're very busy," he agreed, though I sensed that he knew that was not the real problem. Certain places give you terrible flashbacks after you've had chemo. For lots of people it's the hospital. For me it had been my dad's town house. Somehow, those flashbacks didn't seem quite as important right now.

"And thanks for helping out my friend. You'll like him. He just needs somewhere to think in peace. We both kind of do."

I flinched a little, because this visit sounded like such a use-job on him and Suhar, and I suppose it was. But he didn't seem to mind.

"You're sixteen. We would expect that when you show up, it won't be alone."

"He's really, really gay, Dad," I repeated again, just because I didn't want to hear a ration of surprise once I got up there.

"Claire, I'm a session musician. If I let people's lifestyles bother me, I probably wouldn't work much."

"But don't bring it up around him, okay?"

"I wouldn't. I take it...he hasn't accepted his sexuality yet?"

I laughed and realized how much I missed my dad sometimes—probably because he asked blunt questions that made you think, instead of acting like a dad. After a minute of scratching my head, I said, "I think he's fine with who he is. He, like, takes serious offense if you try to tie him up with any adjective."

"Hm. Sounds like he's either in an identity crisis or he blew way past all of that."

"Way past. Which isn't to say he's going to have a ton of friends, you know?"

I heard the screen door opening softly behind me and saw Macy coming through. My stomach twisted up. My thought had been to get some clothes together and be out of the house in three minutes or less. *You should have had this conversation in Philly.*

"I have to go, Dad."

"*Call* your mother at work, Claire. Do not leave her a note. I'm not up for any backlash reactions over you taking a bus, and she has my cell phone number—"

"Hey. Who married her? You or me? Why am I the whipping boy?"

He sighed. I felt Macy move behind me, leaning against the

counter, as I tried to calculate how much of this conversation would make sense to her. I held my patience while knowing she was trying to get closer so she could hear my dad as well as me. Somehow, Macy having to know everything had never bothered me until this point.

"Okay, compromise," Dad said. "Leave your mom a note. I'll make sure we're at the end of the line fifteen minutes early, so I have nothing to feel guilty about. And Suhar and I will, uh, *forget* to bring my cell phone to the restaurant. Tomorrow...you and I will speak to your mom together if she reacts badly. Fair enough?"

"I don't know...," I teased him. "I think you should have to do all the talking, being that you're the grown-up and all."

"Did I ever explain to you the difference between a grown-up and a god?"

"Save it." I cast Macy a glance out of the corner of my eye. She was watching me like crazy. I avoided saying, "See you soon," before I hung up. No question, I was in a very treacherous spot, which would not be easy to get out of.

She didn't stop watching me after I hung up the phone. "What happened to you after cheerleading?"

I slithered down to the floor on my butt and spouted quickly, "I just needed to be alone. No offense or anything." I didn't want an uproar about where I had been.

"I couldn't find you anywhere! You're giving us heart attacks lately, Claire." She slithered down beside me. She threw an arm around my neck, and I slumped over until my head was on my knees.

"How's your...food thing? Are you all right?"

Food. I worked myself back up off the floor, went to the microwave and popped it opened. *Baked lasagna. Oh puke.* Mom had said she was baking lasagna for Mrs. DeGrossa's party tomorrow night, and she liked to heat it twice before she served it. Tasted better the second time around. This mega slice was from the first time around. I pulled it out, swallowing spit, reasoning that if I ate it cold, the cheese and sauce would be more chewy, less slimy.

I flinched as I realized, *You're going to miss your token appearance at Mrs. DeGrossa's party. Mom will freak. You have to make health salad. You have to ditch Macy. You have to be out of here in*—I glanced at the clock on the stove—*in fifteen minutes. Claire, even your wanting to help somebody can mess up the works.*

I swallowed more spit, shoved the lasagna into the refrigerator without bothering to cover it, hauled out the cabbage, celery, and carrots.

"Claire, what are you doing?" Macy rose slowly to her feet. "Why'd you put that lasagna away?"

"I have to make health salad for Mom's party tomorrow night. I'll eat it while I'm—"

"There is not a single calorie in that stuff!" She marched over and snapped open the refrigerator. "Okay, lasagna is fat-people food. It would make me sick, too. Look, hot dogs. I'm making you a hot dog, okay?"

I squashed my eyeballs with my palms. *Don't be this nice, please don't be this nice.*

"I'll eat lasagna." I just didn't want her doing anything nice for me.

She dumped the plate back into my hands. "Go on, sit while you eat that. You can make health salad afterward. The gang will wait for you. They're over at Sydney's, doing the usual nothing. Scott's dad is taking an overnight to the canyon. The boat won't be back until tomorrow."

I glanced at the clock on the kitchen stove. *Thirteen minutes. Screw health salad. Mom will live without it. Eat, fool.*

I trudged into the living room and sat down in my mom's TV chair, catching a fork Macy tossed at me before she plopped down on the couch.

"Please stop watching me like that. I can eat without an armed guard. But when I'm done eating, I can't go with you. I'm, uhm...going to my dad's."

"On a Friday night? *Why?*"

I took a couple of good-sized bites of lasagna, while she sat there patiently-unpatiently shifting around. According to Lani, there was no point in trying to tell someone that their ears or eyes are inaccurate—they will not buy it. I decided to maneuver things; so like him, I was starting with the facts about Tony Clementi first.

"I'll tell you something, but you have to swear you won't tell."

"Why would I tell? When have I ever told your secrets?"

I chewed a bunch of times, watching her face turn red. As if she hadn't spewed my eating problems from coast to coast as her most recent blab.

"You can't tell, Macy. Promise me."

She zipped her pinky across her heart and stuck it in the air.

"Somebody could get seriously hurt if you tell."

"I promise!" She hollered.

"I lied. I wasn't alone after cheerleading."

She hawkeyed me, and in her true fashion, fell over sideways on the couch after only a few seconds. "Oh my god. You were with *him*. Claire. Why are you doing this to yourself?"

I let it slide, biding for nerve by chewing and swallowing another huge bite. "Tonight somebody kept calling him. Somebody having fun and games on the phone. It was disgusting. Foul. Unbelievably filthy stuff being whispered at him. Like, sex stuff. Like, some guy was coming on to him. Lani kept hanging up. I heard it with my own ears and finally, I hit star sixty-nine. Guess who was calling?"

"Great." She moaned sickly. "Am I supposed to be shocked that stuff like this would be going on around him?"

"I *said,* somebody called *him.* He did nothing. He was sitting there reading a bunch of...paperbacks."

"The guy reads books because he thinks it's fun. And he flips his butt all over the place when he walks. Don't tell me he's not responsible for some homo phone calls. And since you're asking, I'm taking it this caller was somebody I know."

I swallowed. "Yeah."

Her mouth started rising on the sides as breathy laughs spilled out. Her gaze ate me alive.

"Don't hold out on me." She crawled over and stood on her knees in front of me, gripping the arms of the chair. "Was it...Larry Boogers?"

"You're way cold."

"Uh...gotta be somebody in honors..."

I dropped my fork, feeling my gut swerve—too much ricotta cheese, too fast. This was not funny; at least, it would not turn out funny. She was doing like I had been doing, thinking of all the typical male femmes. I had a bad feeling about this. I kept going, only because now I was deep into it, and she'd let me drag her halfway to Philadelphia while gripping my ankle unless I told.

I took another huge mouthful, getting more nerve while chewing and swallowing. Finally, I said, "Think fish frat."

Her smile drooped. "No. Uh-uh, no way."

"Think fish frat, but older. Somebody you kind of don't like."

I had to hand it to her. Even in this unbelievable scenario, she was sharp as a tack, though all my caution did not prepare me for her swift response.

"Tony? Is that what you're trying to say? Uh, no." She marched over to the couch, plopped down, and flipped her handbag up on her shoulder. "That would explain everything, wouldn't it? Tony can take the blame for what happened last night, instead of Lani Garver...Is that it? Claire, you've been naive and stupid before. Okay, this one's complicated, I'll give you that much. But you didn't see Tony's phone number on caller ID, darling."

"How can *you* tell me what *I* saw?" I demanded.

"I *know.* I was *there* when he got in that argument with Lani Garver."

It was impossible to swallow again, but somehow I managed. "Lani and I *both* saw that number on the caller ID. We're not both dyslexic."

Her eyes darted to the side but came back strong. "Whatever! He had it...pre-programmed in there, so it would show up! He's snowing you, Claire—"

"How is he supposed to do that!"

"I don't know; I'm not the phone man!"

"You're saying he found a way to reroute caller ID, so that Tony's phone number would show and then, what? He got some friend to keep calling? Or he was having phone sex with this number in caller ID, why? Just in case I showed up?"

"Whatever, Claire. There is no way Tony Clementi called that guy."

I slammed down my fork and stuck a fist into my gut to try and move the food around. I started out with "Macy, darling." God knows she'd said it enough times to me. "How do you know it wasn't *you* who misheard the night before, instead of some unexplainable transmutation of a caller ID?"

"Because! *I know!*" She watched me screwing my fist into my gut and tossed her hands in the air.

"I don't know what to do for you, Claire! You're hanging around with this kid, who's messing you all up. I'm writing this all off to your food problems, okay? And what is this about going to your dad's? Did this Lani talk you into leaving us? To keep you away from people who can talk sense to you?"

I watched her staring back at me with this total look of dread, and I have to say, I was tempted. *Okay, I'll forget what*

*my eyes and ears tell me. I'll just believe this other thing be-
cause...it would be so much easier. This girl cares about me
totally. And trying to change her mind is like rolling a boulder
up a cliff.*

"Macy..." I wanted to say to just forget it. I wanted to tell
her the doctor gave me some prescription and I would be
okay after taking it for twenty-four hours, or something, and
just to bear with me. But I opened my mouth, and this greasy
lasagna must have seen its chance. I flew out of the chair,
hauled up the stairs two at a time, and made it to the porce-
lain throne by not stopping to turn on the light. My knees
cracked the floor, and I was never so glad to say good-bye to
a meal in all my life.

I remembered from chemo always feeling closer to "normal" after I heaved. At this point, I felt a lot closer to normal.
It changed my mind again about what I wanted to say to
Macy. Something felt slightly more important than what's the
easiest thing to believe, though I couldn't have said what.

I flushed, wanting to sit there in peace, feeling the coolness
of the toilet seat on my arms. But Macy bolted in, switching
on the light. I slammed my eyes shut, but couldn't miss her
trembling voice.

"Jesus Christ. I'm calling your mom!"

"Oh, no, you're not! Just calm down. Give me a minute."

The water was running, and I raised my head. She had a
washcloth and was mopping my face off. She accidentally laid
into my bandage and the stitches underneath, and I screamed,
"Stop touching me! Give me ten feet!"

Then she screamed louder than I did, which I couldn't
make out the reason for, but I saw her feet jumping up and
down like a small child's. Unglued, supremely.

I got slowly to my feet, grabbed her by the shoulders, and
I rattled her around until she looked at me. "Macy. Just calm
down. Calmness. Please."

I tried to keep my own voice calm, and she quit pitching the fit, at least, but blinked at me through her tears and kept yelling. "You're losing it, Claire!"

"Whatever."

"You're going to get in some serious trouble!"

"I'm— Okay, I'm in serious trouble."

"Stop with the cool act! Your life is going down the goddamn toilet!"

I looked down at the bowl and figured it wasn't my life I'd just seen going down. "I'll tell you what's making me sick, okay? It's the thought that there are some things I cannot tell you right now. And yet, you are going to nag at me to tell you until I'm driven out of my mind. That's what's making me sick."

I wasn't sure that was the truth, but it sounded good. It worked. She held up her hands like I had a gun on her, then backed away. "Okay. Fine. Whatever. If I had something outrageously important on my mind, I sure could tell you." She turned and started walking downstairs.

She was trying to guilt me, and I could live with that. *Problem is, she's never had anything outrageously important on her mind. Except maybe this argument about someone getting in the way of her little truths.*

I came down the stairs after her, more slowly. "You promised you wouldn't tell."

"That thing about Tony? Oh, don't worry, Claire. I won't tell," she said, with fake diplomacy.

"Please. If you tell, somebody could get seriously hurt."

"Claire, how could I possibly tell? Who would believe me?"

"I never said anyone would believe it. I'm saying someone could get hurt."

"Like I'm not!" She slammed the door behind her with a shattering *bang.*

The loudness of it destroyed my toilet-flushing peace of mind, and I dropped onto the couch, burying my head under whatever cushions I could grab. I lay like that with thoughts ripping through my head. Only one seemed to stick. *Claire, if Lani's theory about smoke and mirrors is true, then there's just as much chance of smoke in front of you and Lani as that crowd down at the Rod last night. Could you have actually seen caller ID wrong? Macy loves you. She'll forget all this if you can just see it her way...*

A totally logical thought struck me. It was so intense it took a while to look at it from all sides: The way Macy recalled what happened at the Rod was the easiest thing to believe. That's why I wanted to buy into it. But I still believed my own eyes and ears. And not one thing about what I believed was convenient. Therefore, it was probably me seeing the truth, not Macy

Message from God: Do the right thing. Support him. Take him to Philly.

"Why should I?" I bawled into the pillow. "What have you ever done for me? What have you ever given me that you haven't taken away again?"

Silence. No further message from God.

I looked at my watch. I had eaten, puked, and pissed off my best friend in all of ten minutes. I still had five. I figured I was going. And it had nothing to do with any message from God that I could think of. Or from Pastor Stedman, whom my mom had let loose on me at various times in my early recovery. It had something to do with this janitor I met in isolation when I had pneumonia. He came in to mop around my bed for the hundredth time that week, and I decided to piss and moan. I had muttered how I wished people would lie and tell me I was fine. I had told him it's easier to get better when you can be at home, not facing the truth.

He had said something, and it sounded like he was quoting someone else. *"The truth will set you free, and then you shall be free indeed."*

That saying came crawling back to me every now and

again—maybe because that janitor had come into isolation in surgical garb to scrub the bed bars. And you couldn't see his face, and there was nothing to do but hear him. Or maybe it was that he truly believed he was giving me profound wisdom. I know I dropped off to sleep kind of peacefully for once, while he was still scrubbing.

I hauled my sorry ass off the couch to throw a few clothes into a bag, cursing the whole time.

16

On winter nights the rich people's summer homes glow black along Beach Drive because their huge walls of windows throw no lights from within. I studied them as I walked beside Lani, listening to the thunder of the surf, uninterrupted by the summer noises of gulls, laughter, and traffic. The unbroken echo was comforting.

My thought was to take us down Beach Drive until we got past most of the business district. We could cut back up to Hackett Boulevard right near the bus station.

"My dad and Suhar have a hot tub. We can sit in it for as long as you want."

"That'll change the universe, won't it?"

It was the first statement of mine that he hadn't answered with a groan. My fight with Macy made me feel his gloom a lot better now, and I wondered if he could turn suicidal or something. I didn't want to ask him outright how he felt, though I figured I'd better look for a more cheerful thought.

"Of all those books you've read? There's got to be something, somewhere in them, to help us laugh at a situation like this."

He was chewing gum. It spun around in his mouth a couple times. "You're probably right." He snapped his eyes shut and then opened them wide, like he was trying to set his thoughts on that. After half a block he still hadn't said anything.

"What about...*Hegel*?" I pulled out one of the few names I knew.

He chewed round and round, then flinched a little. "Problem with the big philosophers is they cared about ideas more than people. Hegel would probably have stepped over a guy trying to slit his wrists outside a bar—to get to all the people he could sit and bullshit with inside. Did you know half of philosophy was first put into words by people shot in the ass?"

"That's encouraging," I said.

"Sorry."

"What about Jung? What about Freud? They're people doctors. They've gotta care about people and situations like this."

"Yeah."

"Well? What would they say?"

He chewed his gum hard, though nothing like a smile appeared. "Freud school's one-to-ten line might be fun to lay on Tony Clementi. Some doctors say a person who has only had same-sex attractions is, like, a zero. A person who has only had opposite-sex attractions is, like, a ten. He says most people fall between one and nine."

"Hm...I'm definitely a ten."

"That's what everybody says."

I felt my eyes kind of bug, though I didn't really want to argue while he was feeling so depressed. "I wouldn't be repeating that philosophy too loudly to people."

I felt a glimmer of hope as his eyes kind of lit, like those mental cranks were turning. "Freud stole from Hegel, I think. They both believe people are not 'things,' like gay, straight, black, white, mugger, saint, but are a continually moving process. So someone who was a two as a teenager could be a five when they hit forty...People are always changing."

"What does that say about Tony?"

He sucked in a breath of air, and when he let it out again, he looked sad. "I don't know. Only that...you can't really know. Psychotherapy isn't really about knowing. It's sort of like a merry-go-round ride for little kids. You go around in circles until your insides are all tickled, and then suddenly you can cope with the world again."

"That's cheerful. So why are you addicted to it?"

"It's a fun game to try to pull apart what's true and what's bull."

"I'd rather play guitar." I sighed. "Gimme some gum."

"Last piece."

I stuck up my finger in front of him, and somehow he understood this ritual I thought only me and my friends knew about. He took half his gum, squashed it on my finger, and I stuck it in my mouth. I chewed like he did—kind of angrily. *Spearmint.*

"Remember King Solomon?" he asked. "The very wise king?"

"Yeah."

"He used to say, 'In much learning, there is much sadness.'"

"Uh...I'm looking for a subject that'll cheer us up," I hinted, but he had turned deaf, sighing in a way that made me feel gloomy to the core.

"World is all backward. Everyone who is considered really hot, really isn't. It's like...we're through the looking glass. Good is bad, bad is good. Black is white, white is black. People base their lives on convenient recollections and are considered sane. People who look too hard for truth are considered crazy. Did you know that most of the people in history whose books have lasted more than a few centuries have been either thrown into jail or murdered by angry mobs? All the prophets, the great philosophers, the disciples, people like Joan of Arc, great novelists..."

"Maybe we should be talking about something other than

your books." I stopped him. "Maybe you should just kick back. Remember what it was like to be naive. I like remembering when I was a little kid. You remember back then? Before all the bad stuff started happening? Remember...fourth grade?"

"Hm, yeah." He smiled, but it looked forced.

I chomped hard. "Don't tell me. You got beaten on for playing Barbie with the girls."

He tried to blow a bubble, which kind of exploded behind a sad smile. "Actually it was more often dress-ups."

"Oh no." I breathed, trying to decide if it was a horrible thing for a little boy to play dress-ups. In second grade this kid across the street had four huge yellow trucks. We both had fun with them. I thought about why it is that girls can do boy things but boys can't do girl things without kids beating them up.

"Well, they were just kids, Lani. Kids'll beat on each other for stupid reasons."

When I looked up, he was shaking his head. "Wasn't a kid. It was my dad."

My spirits dived to the concrete. I surrendered to this black mood. Some situations you just can't find the good side in.

After a minute he nodded. "Not only was my dad in the military, but we lived on military bases. He had me to a drill sergeant, a priest, and a shrink before I was ten."

"Because you played girl games? That sucks."

He nodded. "Because this very stupid school board implied that my parents were somehow responsible for having a kid who was...what did they call it...gender confused. My dad was trying to either change me or prove that they were fighting it and not causing it, for fear of getting a discharge, losing his job."

My jaw hung open and my gum almost fell out.

"But I have a few good memories in my life," he said.

"Hurry up and tell me before the sky falls."

We turned down Tenth Street toward Hackett Boulevard. We were halfway down the street before he came up with one.

"I have a great memory from here, on Hackett. Back when we were summer people, many moons ago. You know how people dump unwanted pets on the beach?"

"Cops finally cracked down on that a few years back."

"Before that, then. Kitten. I found it on the beach, all alone and crying on this windy, gray day. It had a disease called distemper. You're supposed to put all animals with distemper to sleep because they can't get better from it. The owners threw it out of the car, down at the dunes, instead of taking it to the vet to have it put to sleep. I took it home, hid it from my mom, and for three days I held that kitten, until it died."

I listened to the echo of the surf, which blended nicely with my sighing.

"That's...a really charged-up, great memory." I pulled him to me, by the waist. I guessed maybe we just shouldn't talk about *anything*. He threw an arm across my neck, and we crossed Hackett Boulevard like that, after looking around to make sure no familiar cars were zooming past to scope us out. The boulevard was eerily quiet for a Friday night.

"I don't really think our greatest memories are always great while they're happening," he said. "You have to wait. And afterward you have a memory of doing something way cool. I probably gave that kitten the only kindness of its life. I will always have a lot of memories like that."

I didn't want to ask him about any other memories. Considering some of the people he'd seemed to know at the clinic, I figured they only got worse, involving dying people and not just helpless animals.

"I'm paying," I said, glad to change the subject. I pulled him by the waist over to the ticket machine. "I'd rather let the ticket machine get my Sydney's money than the electric company."

It was probably more about my home than I normally would have spewed. But he was quiet as I rolled the dollars into the machine and watched two tickets roll out. As I pulled them out, I realized he wasn't even chomping gum. When I turned around, he was staring straight up into the rafters of the bus terminal.

He only had time to say, "This is bad."

Then Scott, Vince, and Phil jumped down, like three monkeys from the *Jungle Book.*

17

"Ambush! Ha-ha." Vince landed about three feet from me, laughing like crazy. "How the hell are you, Claire?"

Phil and Scott landed behind him, cracking up in a goofy way. And I laughed, too, though I never felt so spun around in my life. A part of me wanted to say, "Hey," and be glad to see them. The other half suddenly knew what it was like to be some dork, terrified instead of swooning over their sheer size.

"Going somewhere?" Vince said, like he already knew the answer.

"My dad's."

"I don't think so." Scott stepped up and grabbed me by the wrist, and since all my jerking was no contest for him, he just sounded off while he dragged me a few feet. "Your mom called Macy's cell, said she got home, and you had left her a note saying that you're going on a bus to Philadelphia. She's wigging out, and you ain't going, Claire. No girlfriend of mine is getting on a bus to Filthydelphia."

"My dad is meeting me at the other end!" I twisted my arm, but he had my wrist in a vise grip.

"Oh. Is this the same dad who sparked a doobie and got high with his daughter?"

I quit fighting him and froze.

"Macy!" My yell bounced around in the rafters. "Come out, and tell me you did not also tell my mother that secret!"

That wasn't even how the story actually went. After my fifth chemo treatment when I was totally sick, my dad brought home a joint he got off some musician and let me have a few hits. He didn't even have any himself. I was way past desperate, and he was running low on sanity, watching me suffer while nothing else helped. One of his L.A. musician friends swore marijuana stopped chemo nausea when nothing else worked. I brought it up to Macy once, when she got curious about why I waved the smell away when anyone got high around me.

"I didn't tell her, but I could, if you get on that bus." Her form followed her voice out of the ladies' room.

"We're hiding in the bathroom. *Great,*" I muttered, turning my eyes to Scott, because hypocrisy ran supreme here. "And I haven't seen *you* with any problem sparking a doobie—"

"I'm not your old man! That's disgusting, Claire! Your mom says you ain't going, and you ain't going." He turned and looked coolly over my shoulder. "Some of us care if you get yourself mugged on a bus. Some people don't."

They were all staring at Lani, who was leaning back against the ticket machine, just chewing his gum like mad and finding something on the floor to stare at.

Lani's eyes moved to watch Vince's feet come slowly toward him. He didn't meet Vince's eyes until Vince spoke up. "What are *you* doing here, sweetheart? What, you learned your lesson from us about hitting on guys, so now you're gonna try Dern's girl?"

I thought of a porno magazine tossed into the middle of Lani's bedroom floor, shaking us up enough to leave the island for a weekend. The unfairness lit me like a torch. I jerked away from Scott, but he caught my other arm and shook it. He said between his teeth, "What did I just see when you guys were coming across the street?"

Because the difference between sex and affection would

probably get lost on them I said, "Do not even go there. Anything about me and him is complete bullshit—let me go. You saw nothing resembling anything romantic."

"Yeah, fine, fat nothing, you know what I'm gonna do? I *was* just gonna take you out and try to talk to you, but if that's all you got to say? Forget your fritzed-out mom. I'm gonna take you down to the docks where my dad's making hull with his crew, and I'm gonna say, 'Pretend this is Maddie, and guess who I just found her hugging on?' You think he wouldn't smack the shit out of you and call your mom for a round of thank-yous?"

Maddie was Scott's fourteen-year-old sister. I was not afraid of Scott or his dad, because this threat was just garbage talk. But I was mad at being bullied.

"You can do whatever you want, but if you don't quit shaking me, I'm going to kick your nuts into your lungs. Back off!"

"That's great, coming from my sweet girlfriend. Don't be so goddamn crude."

He let go, and I toppled into Phil, who held me in a death grip while Macy motor-mouthed in my face. The only words I could catch were *trying to talk sense to you,* because my brain was coming apart. In spite of their caveman routine, these guys thought they were doing something right. Macy was "talking sense" in my face. My only possible way out of here would be to pull some crazed, violent routine and start swinging at people. They were completely caught up in their own insanity, yet if I did anything that would get us out from under them, who would look like the loon?

I tried to pull the same condescending act on Macy that she was pulling on me, all "Macy, back up. Macy, calm down. Macy, don't lecture me," but I finally got silent because Vince had sauntered dangerously close to Lani. I couldn't hear what he was taunting. He got within two feet, and like a snake, he shoved Lani hard enough to make me scream. Fortunately, Lani was only a few inches from the ticket machine, so his pack padded him, and only his neck snapped.

He rolled his gum into his cheek and begged, "Whatever you plan to do, just do me one favor. Don't blow any more smoke in my face. I have allergies."

My mouth formed the O shape as hoots of laughter echoed through the rafters. *Give them an irresistible invitation, why don't you...* It seemed to me that at one point, he'd said something about being able to think on his feet in situations like this. *Right.*

"You've. Got. Allergies." Vince backed up to us, laughing his side off. "Well, maybe we can help you out with that. Krilley. Gimme some fire."

Phil let go of me and slapped his pockets in pretend stupidness. "I ain't got any matches. You're the one who smokes."

"Oh, that's right. I'm the one who smokes. But I don't think I got a light. Dern. You got fire?"

Scott looked me up and down, then finally shook his head. "Vince, don't start with that bitch tonight. I wanna hear from Claire what really gives. Let's just bolt out. We know where to find Miss Garver later, if we have to."

But Vince couldn't resist and shoved Lani a second time.

"Just *don't* blow smoke in my face. I really hate that," Lani said again.

I shut my eyes, less from embarrassment this time, more from fear. He sounded bored, like maybe he was still too depressed to care if these people beat the crap out of him. *They could mess him up bad.*

Vince turned to me all innocently. "Claire. Got a light?"

I got a clear image in my head of them poking a lit cigarette all over Lani's face, and I screamed, "Leave him alone, Vince!"

"Oh! That's right! I've got fire!" He backed up to us, like he knew he could catch Lani if he decided to run. It was like some game of cat and mouse. Lani just stared at the ground as if he didn't care, didn't even try to run.

Vince pulled open the side of his jacket dramatically, and reached into the bigger, inside pocket. The lighter and a pack of Marlboros fell to the ground, because of something else that came out in his grip.

"What the—" He unfolded the rolled-up magazine until a picture of a guy in a bathing suit flashed on the cover. *The magazine Mrs. Garver had tossed at us.*

My jaw dropped all the way, and my eyes flew to Lani, who glanced with bored curiosity like he had never seen the thing before in his life. I didn't remember Lani ever touching Vince. Yet he must have planted it. I turned my back to them all, letting them think I was grossed out, because I was scared I would laugh my ass off.

Vince must have heaved it, because the thing landed beside my foot, opened to a classifieds page with several clusters of guys going at various unmentionable exercises. Then Vince did something that made no sense at all to me at first. He picked it back up, rolled it face inward, and stuck it back in his jacket pocket.

"—the hell was that?" Phil guffawed. "Clementi. Where'd you get a fag mag?"

Vince swiped up his cigarettes and lit one. I noticed his hands and the corners of his mouth were shaking as he smiled. "Somebody planted that on me."

"He didn't even touch you...You shoved him." Phil's voice trailed off into nothing. The silence was long. I had no clue how Lani had planted it, because it looked impossible. But I got seized with what was going on in Vince's head. *This magazine is familiar to him. He's seen it before. He's covering for his brother, keeping the dirty family secret...thinks his brother somehow left it in his jacket.*

He stepped up and blew smoke hard in Lani's face, and if

Lani hated smoke so much, it seemed funny he didn't even blink. He just looked over at Phil and Scott.

"Oh, somebody absolutely could have planted that." Lani nodded as he spoke, like he was on Vince's side and was somehow missing all the hatred. "I've got an uncle on the New York police force...and that's a harassment crime. Cops can find out who's harassing you really easy these days. Usually somebody sick enough to do that will leave fingerprints on it...or *something worse*...Cops can find out in a heartbeat who did that to you if they have the person's fingerprints on file. Let me use your cell phone."

He held a hand out toward Macy, who had stopped about six feet short of all the action. She glanced, confused, over at Vince, while pulling her cell slowly out of her pocket. I think she was morbidly curious to know who the pervert was or she wouldn't have touched her cell phone. But Vince shook his head slowly. Cops around here would have Tony's fingerprints on file, I realized. He'd been busted for drugs and DWIs a few times.

"I don't...want no cops," Vince stumbled in a way that made me want to turn my back again and scream, *Ha-hAAAAAAAAAAAA-ha-ha-hAAAAAAA*. I bit my lip.

"But some old schlep with a gun or a knife could be stalking you." Lani studied him, completely stumped. "Don't you even want to know who it is? Why let a pervert run loose, when he could be locked up?"

He held out his hand to Macy, who had been watching me bite my lip, soaking this whole thing up. Her cell phone dangled in her hand.

"Wait!" She pointed it at Lani as her usual sharpness struck finally. "He's just a fast little street punk! *He* planted it on you! Can't you see that?"

Lani snatched the phone from her hand with such superhuman speed, it made me see a slight possibility of how he planted that mag. "If that's what you really think, then we should call the police. Yes, let's all find out whose prints are all over that. It's completely easy—"

He hit 9-1-1. Vince came out of his shock freeze and swiped for the phone. But Lani stepped back. "Hi, I'm at the bus station? Someone's been stalking a—"

Vince swung and knocked the cell phone from his hands, and it went zipping across the floor.

"Vince, Jesus!" Macy yelled. "You don't have to break my phone! What the hell is wrong with you? A cop could prove it was *him*!" She jerked her thumb hard at Lani, but Vince seemed to know his brother's fingerprints would be all over it.

My suspicion got stronger when Vince said, "We don't need no cops. Let's get outta here. Let's just go!"

Macy chased after her cell phone, and I couldn't stand it any longer. I snorted out a laugh and cracked up totally with my hand over my mouth. I thought it would be okay because they were backing slowly toward the car, but Vince's eyes shot to me. He must have taken my laugh to mean I thought he was homo.

With a bull-elephant yell, he rushed Lani. He balled up his fist and slammed it into Lani's face, sending Lani flying into the ticket machine. He slithered down to the ground, and Vince jumped on him.

"Vince! He hit nine-one-one! Said he's at the bus station!" Phil yelled.

In his rage Vince had fallen too close to Lani's head, so he could do little more than lay meaningless little punches in his sides.

Phil and Scott dragged Macy off to the car, while she screamed, "I'm not scared of any cop! I'll talk to any damn cop!" But Vince had joints in the car, or something I couldn't make out of their mumbling.

I looked at Lani's face, half hidden by the back of Vince's

head. He had blood streaming out of one nostril, over his whole chin. Even with that, Mr. Blunt couldn't stop himself. He said off to the side, where only Vince and I could hear, "The family always knows, doesn't it? Those filthy little secrets are kept so well, aren't they? He didn't fool you last night, did he? You knew it was your brother the whole time, yet you helped him set me up for the—"

Vince found his way to his knees really fast, and he brought his fist up over the back of his head. Maybe the truth is supposed to set you free. Hearing it from Lani made me react in a way I would not have predicted in a hundred years.

Something snapped in me—something I had not seen in myself before, and yet, somehow, I knew had always been there. I grabbed a clump of Vince's hair, and with the strength of twelve years of guitar playing, I almost jerked him to his feet. I knew of no words for what he was—someone who covers a lie by inflicting pain on others. There was nothing to say. His fist whizzed the air in front of Lani when I jerked him. He glanced at me—like I was some buzzing fly, some annoyance, something that had temporarily interrupted him from getting something he wanted. I screamed, suddenly way insane, sick of people looking at me and always seeing somebody else. Behind this scream came my balled-up fists, and I whaled on Vince's face over and over, not knowing what was crunching, my knuckles or his skull. I saw blood rush from his mouth, but in the thrill of the moment, it felt good. I kept screaming, "Liar, fucking hypocrite, liar!" and someone was pulling me off from behind.

I kept swinging at the air, because swinging felt good. Vince hadn't even fought back, he'd been so stunned. He stared like he really saw me for the first time in his life. Regret already started backing up, making me feel half electrocuted, but my mouth wouldn't stop shouting horrible things, like I was possessed. I heard the echo of Macy screaming, "But he's stealing

her! He's taking her on that bus that just pulled in! Get her!"
And that's the last thing I remember before Lani tossed me
down into a bus seat and threw my bag on top of me.

He babbled about something as he climbed over me, like
did I have to roll around in the sewer, too? The bus had looked
empty, save one silver-haired lady two rows behind us. Her
arm reached up and knocked me in the shoulder with a handkerchief in it. Lani thanked her, and I flopped down in a
stunned stupor, looking back and forth between Vince's tail-
lights disappearing into the blackness of the night, and my
own bloody hands.

18

I finally shoved my hands, sticky with blood, between my legs and sat completely frozen in the dark aisle seat. Lights passed—on Hackett Boulevard, the toll bridge, the mainland—but it was all a blur. I didn't know which I was more amazed at—Lani coming through with that brilliant magazine plant, or my ability to ball up a fist and go berserk. *Claire. You got mad. You got way mad. You are going mad...*

Lani accidentally kept knocking my arm. He had started to wipe blood off his face with the lady's handkerchief until he got a better idea. Out of his pack he pulled something like those moist towelettes you get by the handful down at The Sand Bar after you've eaten a lobster or blue crabs.

Always come prepared?

I smelled lemons, though I was afraid to look. My neck would have snapped off, for one thing, but my eyes moved slightly, and it was enough to see that lacy handkerchief he'd left draped over his knee. It had a bloody splotch on it, shaped kind of like a running rabbit. It still smelled like the lady's perfume. I rolled my eyes in the other direction, but I could still hear him fussing, like he had fifty thousand of these towelettes that he kept tearing and cleaning up with.

He was trembling enough to make me seasick, so when he finally spoke up, I was surprised at how even his voice was. "Gimme your hands."

I watched him pull one hand from between my legs, and I tried to say, "Stop fussing over me," but my voice had disappeared also, and it came out, "Hhhhhhhhhhhhhh."

He wiped blood from between my fingers, like my parents used to do at the Dairy Queen a thousand years ago. I noticed my fingers would work without cracking off. But then he dug in for my other hand, and laid the towelette onto the knuckles I'd split open on the Tony Clementi ride and had just re-split on Vince.

Out of my mouth spilled something like "Gad-zuck-ta-shit-urn-ya," and my whole body started working, like a crab on its belly.

"It's just lemon juice and alcohol; it won't kill you."

"Oh my god, I just punched somebody."

"Yeah."

"A *guy*. Tell me I'm dreaming."

"You're wide-awake."

I snatched my knuckles away, my eyeballs falling out of my head as I stared at the seat in front of me. "You could lie to me once in a while. Just to ease into the facts."

He grabbed my bloody hand back, and I watched in awe as he pulled that towelette thing from each knuckle down over my fingertips. "Those first couple shots would have been nice. Defending us. But I got scared you were going to kill him."

"Tell me I didn't... actually break his nose."

"...think it was his eye more than his nose. He'll have a good shiner. You gotta work on your anger, Claire. Man. There's this charming thing called middle ground."

I got the full impact of him washing me off like a dad and lecturing me like a shrink. I guessed I wasn't through being mad, because I grabbed the towelette thing and flung it at the window. I grabbed the lace hankie off his knee, which I was sick of looking at, and flung it into his gut.

"Stop touching me! And for somebody who needs *me* to defend the both of us, you sure are high-and-mighty. Where do you get off saying that load of shit to Vince Clementi about family secrets? Did you have to tell him the truth? Sometimes a lie is a really good thing. He could have killed you!"

I jerked my back toward him and stared into the aisle. It felt good to blame somebody else, though guilt started seeping into my gut like a pile of sludge. This trip had been my idea. I'd practically forced Lani—he'd thought it was dangerous to go out on the streets. In the end he really *had* thought on his feet. Everything really had been under control...until I laughed at Vince. If I hadn't he would have kept going to his car...

I grabbed a handful of my bangs, wanting to tear them out, wanting to gouge out my stitches. I let go of a bucket of tears, instead. Lani tried to rub my shoulder as he sniffed up blood, but I pushed his hand off, squirming around to face frontward.

I eventually thought of something to say, though it was so full of hiccups I was surprised he even heard me. "Magazine plant...was outrageous."

"Call it a street trick. Good for the moment, but it'll come back to haunt us."

"Christ. Will you say something good?"

"By tomorrow, they will all have 'seen' me plant it, will swear to it, and none of them will have any interest in taking it to the cops. Because they'll 'know' that I was trying to shove perverted magazines at people, despite how that makes no sense—"

"I'd like to have one conversation with you today that doesn't completely suck."

He was wiping at his shirt with a towelette, which was pretty pointless, and moaning at the blood splotches. "Sometimes there's nothing to say. Maybe you should have brought your guitar. You could have played something till we chilled out. Does your dad have guitars?"

"My guitars don't make me feel very chill right now. In fact...they make me...nuts." I had to grip my fingers around my throat to keep from yelling the thought that whizzed through my mind: *You were wrong. You said I wasn't old enough to write music.* "Remember the, uh, bloody-poetry conversation?"

I wasn't sure he remembered until he finally mumbled, "Wednesday night when you left my house...the hidden-garbage conversation."

I shut my eyes. "Would you mind...please, not calling my lyrics garbage?"

"Sorry."

He squeezed my shoulder again, and I just pushed his hand off. "I could make Marilyn Manson sound like...like Barney. It's so...not who I want to be. So I try to ignore it, but these awful lyrics start to roll, even when I don't want them to, and I just...get obsessed with playing with them."

"Like what?" He wanted a sample.

My teary eyes shot up to his blurry face. "I've got this thing for razor blades; I don't know why. Girls chewing razor blades, parting their hair with razor blades, wearing razor-blade rings and twirling them on their fingers."

I shut my eyes. "Last night was the first night in a long time I didn't get into all that bloody stuff on my electric guitar. But you know what I was doing instead?" I blathered something about watching my hair fall out, once upon a time. "I was thinking about all this chemo shit...because of you and your friends...Paying your dues helps you play the blues or...whatever the fuck!" I was outraged again, afraid of hitting him next.

"Wow, interesting," he breathed. "Did it work?"

"You— Do I care what it sounded like!" I shoved at him, and he put up his hands up in a girly way to ward me off. "I know this whole night looks like *my* fault. Well, guess what? It's *your* fault! It has to be...My life was fine until you came along—"

"Do not hit," he said in a condescending tone.

So I shoved him once more for good measure. "Dork!"

I leaned into the aisle so I could keep pretending he was dirtying me and my life. I was going to pretend he never existed.

"Claire, your life was an enormous zit. I happened to be around when it popped."

"*My* life?" *Who gets propositioned by homo-homophobics?*

"Yes, *your* life. If my life sucks, at least I know who I am and what I'm doing. It's people reacting to me, not me reacting to everybody and everything."

"Aren't we perfect!"

"You think it's a bad thing because you're finally getting angry," he said.

"Yeah, I would say hitting Vince Clementi is a bad thing!"

"Well...me, too."

I didn't like the silence, like he was about to lay some other bombastic thought on me. He finally laid it.

"Razor-blade music and whatever...I don't really think that's so awful. I mean, it's not like you'd want to cut an album full of it and put it on display for the world. But...it's probably just using art to work out your frustrations instead of violence. You want to keep it that way. I think your biggest problem with it is *Aw,* well, what would *Macy* say!"

I did not want to laugh, so it came out like a goose honk. He didn't miss it, I guess. Must have encouraged him.

"Also, the fact that you've had a blood disease? Interesting. Who knows? Maybe it's an artistic avenue. Maybe, like, razor-blade music creates some means for you to feel control over blood."

"Don't get all bizarre on me. Please." I sniffed away a couple of tears.

"Bizarre? You know what's bizarre? Didn't you just say that last night, when you looked your sickness in the face, you didn't want to write razor-blade stuff, for once?"

I pounded my fist on the seat to keep from pounding it on

him. "I don't want to think about anything more that's bizarre!"

"Why'd you bring it up?"

"Forget it. Everything feels shitty right now, no matter what I bring up."

"Can I share something that Ellen said once?"

"No."

"She said, 'Sometimes it has to feel worse before it feels better.' I guess sometimes getting your shit together . . . it's like being on chemo."

"Just let me sit here in the quiet."

I felt him shuffling around, jostling my back. "Fine. But if I could remind you? I'm the one who got hit, not you. I'm the one who has to live in a strange body and deal with it. I think you're being way self-centered."

I felt him move away and lay his head into the window like he would go to sleep.

I felt my guilt, wishing I could punch it next. Tearfully, I dropped a hand on his shoulder. His hair was hard, caked with blood. I decided maybe I could be mature for a few minutes.

"How is it you can take the very worst things about me, like screwed-up basement lyrics, and make them into something good?"

He didn't answer. I was tired, dizzy. Then, somehow, I was lying on his chest, and he was kind of rocking me as I listened to the bus engine drone on. He looked down from above. The whites of his eyes glowed in the darkness. I could smell blood stink from his hair. Sticky strands hung over dark blotches on his T-shirt. *He's covered in blood, and yet he's working on comforting me.*

I sniffed. I wanted to say I was glad that I knew him. It came out weird. "You're too smart, you're too . . . old, you're too unselfish, and you know too much."

He chuckled. "Guess that makes me not very likable."

"I didn't mean it that way. Take out every *too*." But he stayed quiet. I knew what he meant by "not likable." I thought of my mom on the phone, how she would psycho dribble to her girlfriends—tell them every last thing that she did or thought about that day, no matter how stupid it sounded. My mom always said that people *admire* you for your strengths, but they *love* you for your faults. They love you for all your imperfections, which make them more comfortable with their own imperfect lives. My mom had been really people-smart in her better days. Sayings like that always stuck with me.

"You might seem like some obnoxious Mr. Perfect...if people are looking at you as a...as a person." I stopped, figuring I'd said and done enough crazy things for one night. But I felt he was probably right—shit *was* flying out of my life. Like basement lyrics. Like pretending I was some calm, controlled person when sometimes I wanted to scream. Like juvenile guys who played chicken and beat on guys they didn't understand.

Shit was flying, all right. And the only thing that had changed recently was this too-strange person showing up. He took me to Philly to recognize my eating problems before I train-wrecked my remission. He took me to Franklin, where people play chicken with real death, and where real doctors believe in—

I let fly with it. "But what if...you *are* an angel? Aren't you allowed to be a little better than the rest of us?" My vision was blurry, but not so much that I couldn't see his mouth widening out.

"Your neat little version of reality is crumbling, Claire." His head flopped against the backrest. I watched, waiting for him to deny being what I'd just called him. He kept quiet.

I felt six screws shy of a working piston, and I knew I would probably believe him if he told me he was from Mars. "So what are you, Lani Garver?"

"I'll tell you this much. I think it's a good thing your neat little reality is crumbling. You know what Andovenes says about floating angels?"

"Andovenes..."

"The philosopher who wrote the book Abby is sending back to me—about angels."

I nodded.

"He says you don't often find angels in places like happy homes and rich people's backyard parties. He says that angels flock to places like hospitals and homeless shelters and jails, because those people realize they need help. And so they are able to believe in strange phenomena. Funny how the world is backward. The really comfortable people don't always see much supernaturally, and to the ones who have to struggle, it's, like, breathing in their faces. The first are last... and the last are first."

My eyelids felt like concrete, but I opened them. "I feel so *last* right now. It's hard to believe that my life is actually changing for the better, when it looks to be going down the toilet."

He inhaled pretty clearly, letting the air flow out his lips. "If a life goes down the toilet, it comes out in a river and meets the sea."

I watched him smile, not buying entirely into his bullshit. "You're really enjoying this, aren't you? Avoiding the real question?"

He shifted around uncomfortably and finally spoke up. "I'm flattered. I guess. The truth is, angels are real. But so are smart kids. In every high school across the world, there are kids who read stuff like Einstein and Hegel and Freud, and who are insightful enough to pick apart attempts at truth and try putting truth in order for themselves."

"There's no one like that on Hackett," I informed him. "At least, there wasn't until you showed up."

"You're wrong. You just don't see those kids. You look

right through them. Like you look through realities in the mirror."

"Because those kids are...too weird," I concluded, maybe. "They're...*last*. For now."

"You still didn't answer my question."

He didn't open his eyes but scrunched his mouth around until a smile showed up on one side. "If I answered it, I would only be adding to your dilemma, because there's only one answer to 'Are you an angel?' If a human being were to answer that question truthfully, the answer would be no. And if a floating angel were to answer that question, the answer would still be some version of no."

"What do you mean? They don't admit to being angels?"

"Not according to Andovenes. There's this saying... 'Be kind to everyone. Because you never know when you're meeting an angel and you're just not aware of it.' If people knew who the angels were, they would be very nice when they saw one and would still do their same evil garbage when they thought none were around. Knowing who they are defeats the purpose."

I waited for him to smile, and when no smile appeared, I let out a charged-up laugh. "You tell a good story, Lani Garver. And I'm crazed enough right now to believe it."

"Congratulations. 'Crazed' precedes real sanity. You're getting somewhere."

"Do me a favor? If you're *not* one of those floating angels, don't tell me. It's the one thought I could really enjoy right now. It would prove all this insanity in my life...is happening for...some God-given reason."

I unwrapped myself from his arms and threw my head against the backrest, facing into the aisle, letting his body heat make me warm.

I started realizing that I really didn't want to know the answer to my own question of what Lani Garver was. Life is full of strange experiences, and if you're looking for explanations, you can usually find them. But explanations were making my friends out to be strange creatures—capable of violence and convenient memories and dirty little secrets at the expense of other people. Explanations were not working out. So maybe I was more in search of something mysterious—something that was about playing with the questions more than looking for the answers.

The answer might be that Lani Garver was some sweet, intelligent gay kid, and the forces behind the universe were as mundane as ever. I wanted to keep my hope for something more extravagant.

And considering I wasn't looking for answers, things happened over the weekend that were hard to reckon with. The first weird thing began right then. I lay in a weary trance, staring into the blackness of the aisle. I do not remember ever falling asleep.

The bus pulled into the station, and my eyes were wide open. I raised my head to tell Lani to wake up. The seat beside me was empty. I searched every seat, thinking he had climbed over his seat backward to stretch out. He was nowhere on the bus. His bag was nowhere, and his seat was cold. You might have thought he'd never been there.

19

I wandered zombielike over to my dad's window wall that looked out onto his balcony. In the morning light it was starting to sink in what a great job Suhar had done of sprucing up this old town house. When I was on chemo the balcony was just a concrete slab that went out about twenty feet, with a plain, stone wall around it. There was an actual garden out there now, with a bunch of fall flowers blooming and different levels of green things surrounding their hot tub.

"Wanna go sit in there?" Dad came up behind me and put his hands on my shoulders, kissing the back of my head. "I cannot believe how tall you are."

"I was already in your hot tub. Last night. A couple of times, actually—"

"Trouble sleeping?"

"Some."

"No nightmares, I hope," Suhar said. She stood across the dining room table, holding up a funny-looking little coffee pot, like, did I want some. *Espresso,* I remembered hearing her say before. I'd never tried it, but I nodded. I studied her long blond hair, trailing down to her butt, and her kind eyes as she poured, and I decided her nightmare thing had been an innocent question. I glanced down at her wedding ring, which had starred as a bloody mess in a few of my nightmares. The small diamond sparkled.

"No. No nightmares." It had been just a blank, spacey night, where I barely knocked off. "I just couldn't sleep. I can't believe how good this place looks," I added, to change the subject.

"Comes with marrying an artist," my dad whispered in my ear, then kissed it. He flung an arm over my shoulder as I giggled uncomfortably, and whispered more. "I'm surrounded by very cool women."

I flipped his arm off my shoulder, and he sighed a long one. "I see you're still affectionate, as usual."

"Part of my charm."

"I...uhm..." He handed me my espresso and stared at the saucer as I swallowed a small mouthful. Tasted scorchy. "I should have...shown you more affection when you were sick. I was afraid of hurting you if I touched you, something, I don't know...But it always bothered me, so I thought I would tell you."

I shook my head at him sleepily. I hadn't given much thought to who had touched me and who hadn't during chemo. "Why do parents always feel they're responsible for the little quirks in their kids?"

"I don't know. But I'm on this kick right now of apologizing for all the stupid things I've done to people. Bear with me."

I stepped past him, grinning, and moved toward the dining room table. "What'd you do, join a twelve-step program?"

"No. But how did you know about the steps?"

I plopped down in a chair. "Mom was in AA for about three weeks when I was in eighth grade. She kept their little book in the bathroom before she decided that wasn't her problem."

"A shame."

"Yeah, but...she's okay." I felt bad telling stories on my mom. She hadn't breathed Old Sweat Sock in my face after my chemo ended. "She only starts slobbering badly on Saturdays. And these days...she's a happy drunk, usually."

"So, why do you think you couldn't sleep?" My dad brought the subject back around. "Dream about anything when you did sleep?"

My giggles had something to do with him and Suhar both asking about dreams. I leaned my head on the table for a second and popped back up again.

"Second guess, being that it's not the twelve steps. You've had your head shrunk. By a shrink. Isn't it true what Mom says? All city people walk their dogs on leashes, pick up dog crap in little plastic bags, and see shrinks to make up for that harrowing experience?"

"I don't have a dog." My dad shrugged innocently, but I guessed that answered my question. I had vague, eighth-grade memories of my dad saying that Suhar agreed to marry him only if he found a professional counselor and figured out why his first marriage went all wrong. I didn't want to discuss their head shrinkages.

"What would you say if I told you...I actually punched somebody last night?"

My dad took a turn dipping his head to the table and popping back up. "Somebody from Hackett?"

"Well, you picked me up at the bus, and I haven't punched anybody since."

"I'd say...punching somebody from Hackett is...understandable."

"I'm a *girl*."

"I can suddenly see that." He sipped his espresso, looking me up and down. "But I don't think anger is gender specific. How bad was it?"

"He was, uhm, bleeding."

"*He?* I thought we were talking about a catfight among future fishwives. What did *he* do to you?"

I sighed really long, taking a big swallow of this disgusting espresso. "Nothing."

"Matter of principle?"

I felt better hearing it put that way. "Remember the Clementis?"

"Only the mister. Ferocious bastard. God, brings back fatal memories of high school. I was a band dweeb. Don't know how I caught your mother, especially with guys like him who wanted her, too." My dad shuddered. "You hit one of his offspring?"

"Yeah."

"Good girl. Wish I'd had the nerve to hit the mister, way back when. I understand it's too late now."

I shot a glance at Suhar, who was leaning against the buffet, listening to this story. "Are you all right, Claire?" she asked.

I nodded. "I just can't believe I did that."

I didn't know Suhar very well. She had steered pretty clear of the house when I was recovering with Dad. But the fact that she had decided not to lecture me about punching people gave me courage to go on.

"And how would you feel if I told you...my friend Lani, who was supposed to come here, actually got on the bus with me? And when I got off, he was gone? And I still can't remember ever falling asleep? Or when he could have stepped over me?"

"You must have fallen asleep," they both chimed. I hadn't said much more when I met them at the bus than that he decided not to come. I was too freaked out. *Thanks, guys, for informing me that I actually went to sleep. I was starting to think he was an angel, and he just floated off.* That would go over well.

"Yeah, you're right. I just...wish I knew where he went... and why."

"He called this morning. He's at home," Dad said.

"He called?" I dropped the cup in the saucer loudly. "Why didn't you tell me? What did he say? What happened?"

"He apologized. Said he was having a bad-hair day and couldn't make it."

My jaw dangled, and I remembered the blood caked in his hair as he fell asleep on the bus. I guessed he'd gotten second thoughts about meeting strangers while looking like that. I cracked up, though I wasn't as amused as my dad looked.

"How did he get past me? Where did he get off? How did he get home?"

"He didn't say."

The silence that followed gave me wild willies. *He floated off.* I reached across the table for the cordless phone, though I wasn't sure I was going to ask Lani about it. Some part of my gut wanted to enjoy a mystery instead of hearing some mundane explanation. *You fell asleep, and I asked the driver to pull over...*

"Why didn't you call me?" I started routing through caller ID for his number.

"I thought you were sleeping. And he didn't ask for you."

Somehow, this didn't sound good. I looked back and forth between two sets of overly innocent eyes. "He's got no phobia of adults...anything like that."

"Sounds like a college kid or even older. How old is he?" Dad asked.

"I'm not sure, to be honest. So...what did he want with you? If he's spewing my life all over the place, I'll rip his 'bad hair' out."

"No, no." Dad reached into his pocket and pulled out a scrap of paper. "He wanted me to take you somewhere. Or, at least, make sure you went there."

I looked at his chicken scratch upside down, and the only thing I could make out was a capital *E*. I laughed. "If *E* stands for Erdman, forget it. I'm not going."

I stood up to pour out the rest of this espresso. It tasted like dog doo. *All this city-people food really sucks.*

Dad followed me into the kitchen. "Claire, I really think you should go."

I guessed *E* stood for Erdman. "Forget it, Dad. All of Hackett is flipping out, and yet *I'm* elected to go to a shrink?"

"Maybe you're the lucky one."

"Yeah?" I kept laughing, dwelling on the Claire Zone of Bad Luck. "Maybe Lani should mind his own...*hair* and stay out of mine. Vince Clementi needs a shrink. Macy needs a shrink. I do not need a shrink."

He sighed. "I'm sure all the Clementis could use some therapy, but the chances of that ever happening are almost nil. Does that mean you have to fall into the stupid zone with them? Lee Erdman is a very nice guy."

"Gee. That changes everything."

"I've actually talked to him once."

"Small world, ha. You been playing musical couches while having your head shrunk?"

"Very funny. I've never been on his couch, but I've been in a pub where he lets loose with a hobby of his. He plays bass every Saturday night down at the Hollis Grill, with an amateur band. They're all shrinks. Not bad musicians, actually. The music world is pretty small in Philly—"

"And they call themselves the Shrunken Heads, right? Dad!" I gave the time-out sign in his face. "I'm not going. That's so unfair. Tell Macy to see a shrink! I'm not crazy!"

"Nobody has used that word." He stepped forward and touched my shoulder. I batted his hand off. He ignored me. "I wanted you to get some therapy when you were sick. Your life is enough to set anybody up for bad dreams and a food problem—"

He stopped, horrified at his own big mouth. I felt smoke barreling out both my ears. This was not the way I wanted to start off my first visit with Dad in a year—him seeing my "rage" side, which I just met last night. I felt scared I might throw something.

"All right, that's it." I marched into the dining room, past Suhar, who was sipping dog doo and pretending not to be listening. "I don't want to fight with you guys. I'm going to call Mr. Big Mouth and blast him. Is there privacy around here... *somewhere*?"

Suhar flitted off to their bedroom as I tracked through numbers in the caller ID, but my dad just grunted. "This isn't exactly a huge place. Go in your room, and don't banish us. But first, you ought to call Lee Erdman's office and cancel that appointment I made for you."

"DaaAAaad!" I pulled open the sliding glass door, slid it shut again behind me, closing out a lecture on how "lucky" I was that some exceptional people worked six days a week.

"Only luck I have is bad luck," I informed the cordless, finding the one number with a Hackett exchange. I hit DIAL and crashed down on my butt, with my back against the window wall. I should have felt wonderful sitting out there in this summerlike weather in my tank pajama shirt and pants. But I was fuming. Any thoughts of Lani being an angel bit the dust.

"An angel would not humiliate you before your family," I told the ring-ring. "An angel would improve your life, not make you psycho. An angel would give you help from God, not a shrink!" *Maybe he was the devil—*

"Claire?"

"Do you have to have such a big mouth!"

"Sorry. I was having a blunt moment." He sounded out of breath.

"When *don't* you have a blunt moment? Except when someone's honing in on *your* personal garbage, Mr. I-don't-like-to-talk-about-myself? Where do you get the nerve to tell that shit to somebody's parents? I am dreaming this!"

"Claire, can you do me a favor? Save it? We've got a problem down here that could get... ugly."

Our lives were down the toilet anyway, so any new problem shouldn't matter. "No, I won't save it! How could you do that to me?"

"I called to speak to you...spoke to your dad for about five minutes...I can smell a person a mile away who's had therapy. I gathered it would be no big deal to anyone except *you*. Okay? Last-minute judgment call. I wanted to take you there myself—"

"*You* were not *taking* me anywhere."

"Whatever. Please. Can you keep calling Ellen's cell phone until you get her? Remember that angel costume she mentioned having Abby mail to me the other day? From when I was the floating angel in the school show last year? I need you to find out if she actually mailed it."

"Is this important somehow?" I demanded, memorizing a phone number he kept repeating.

"My mom said there was a big box on the porch for me this morning, left by the UPS man. She didn't bring it in. When I woke up and went down, nothing was outside."

My eyes darted around the flowers, trying to figure how this was more magnanimous than a big-time betrayal. "Someone stole a package off your porch?"

"Somebody stole an *angel costume* off my porch. In a box, with my name on it."

"Angel costume..." I shut my eyes, getting a bad vibe.

"I got back here way late and had to wash all that blood out of my hair...got in bed around five o'clock. My mom woke me up around nine-thirty about the box. I went back to sleep. But I would swear about ten o'clock I heard a couple, like, high school kids coming up the street, laughing and fooling around."

"You think they got curious and stole it?"

"Maybe."

Poofy white dress in a box with his name on it. "How

poofy is it? Will the thieves think you're cross-dressing for your next trick?"

"The costume is not exactly...sexy or anything. But it came from The Cloisters. It's a really expensive store, where Abby's mom is a buyer..." He trailed off.

I pinched my tired eyes. "A ladies' dress store, I take it."

"Worse."

I couldn't imagine. I pinched my eyelids.

"It's a lady's lingerie store. Abby made the costume by layering three nightgowns."

I collapsed over sideways on the concrete. He sat there so quietly, and I finally spouted, "May I ask you a personal question?"

"Sure."

"Did you...*enjoy* dressing up in that costume?"

I could hear him breathing at the other end, then, "Why is that important?"

I felt tired of being shoved around this morning. "Because I *said* it is."

"Will you agree to go to Erdman if we talk about this?"

"*No.* But if you don't tell me, I will hang up and not help you."

He sighed a few times, in a girly way that made me want to reach through the phone and slap him. "Okay. Fine. I don't mind saying the truth. *Yes.* I liked dressing up in that costume. Not entirely because it was an angel costume, although I liked acting that part. I also like how that costume feels, yeah."

"And you...want...*me*...to go see Erdman." I could feel my zombie eyeballs bugging, and my laugh rang through the courtyard. "What is happening with my life? *I* should see a shrink?"

He sighed more, though it was pretty well buried in my laughs. "Claire, I can only apologize. Same as I've apologized to my parents, to more than one stupid school board, to my dad's friends, to that priest, to my friends of the past. I'm sorry I don't mind girl things. I'm sorry I don't stomp and hate Barbie and fart and scratch. I'm sorry I never told a makeup girl backstage at our plays to back off from my macho self. I'm sorry, I'm sorry, I'm sorry. But that's not going to change what's actually what."

I sat up, ogling between my spread-out legs at the WELCOME on Suhar's mat. "You, my friends, my dad...you're all *making* me crazy."

"I'm sorry."

I picked at the WELCOME embroidery. *Welcome to Claire's Nuthouse.* "If you don't mind, forget everything I said on the bus last night about you being...you know—"

"A floating angel."

"Yeah. It's all part of my problem. I'm...what is it called in that Jung workbook...*legally insane.* Thank you very much."

"I'm sorry."

"But I'm not going to any shrink. *All* of you down on Hackett can set up a group appointment for yourselves. And while you're at it, will you take my mom?"

"I'm really sorry."

His chronic apologies bored me to death. Some stray, normal thought rushed through my head. Probably because I was bored. "Sydney, my boss, is...*sane.* She's a retired attorney from Philadelphia, making a fortune off brainiacs who had never seen a gelato before she showed up. She can see your house from the café, *and,* since she finds us island people so amusing, she watches my friends like a hawk. Maybe she saw something. Go find out. Or maybe your mom's lying to you. She thinks you're a pervert, anyway. Maybe she got curious, opened the box, and threw the nightgowns out."

He picked up on that train of thought, like maybe this conversation about my sanity had not just taken place. "My mom swears she didn't touch it, and I believe her because she had been food shopping and had all these bags of groceries to bring in. I'm afraid to question her much further for fear she'll get suspicious that something really perverted was in that package."

"Tell her it was a school-play costume!"

"I haven't even told her yet I was in school last year."

And my *life needs head shrinkage?*

"Angel costume, wow. That's way perverse." I laughed in that way when you're laughing but not smiling. And I couldn't figure out what I was laughing at, so I laughed some more. "I'm not seeing any shrink, Lani."

"Okay."

"Hi...Lee Erdman. Nice to meet you." He motioned at a chair in front of his desk, which I just glanced at on my way past. I walked around, studying the musical instruments he had hanging all over his wall. Saxophone, clarinet, four guitars, ukulele, something that looked like an oversized violin.

The voice behind me went off. "How are you doing, doc?"

"I'm fine, Ellen. But do you people need to be in here right now?"

A shadow crossed the corner of my eye as my dad left. Ellen spoke up. "Claire called me about something else. But now she wants me to stay. She's...afraid of you."

"Why are you afraid of me, Claire?"

I ignored them, wishing Erdman's very clean Fender was my basement-encrusted Silo. I brushed my pinky across the strings. When nothing but those few *boinks* broke the silence, I felt the need to fill in.

"You're gonna turn my brain into...espresso."

A laugh snorted out Ellen's nose. I decided, *She's probably one of those Hindu city-people vegetarians who drinks lima bean espresso.* "You're gonna turn my brain into...a fucking *scone* or some city-people shit, and look at my body right now."

I whipped back my bangs, ripped the Band-Aid off my forehead, threw it in his wastebasket, made a fist with my scabby knuckles, and decided against unzipping my jeans. "I've got a bruise on my hip that looks like a bomb exploded and a better one on my ankle. I've had no sleep. I just ate a bagel with some strange orange *fish* on it, compliments of my stepmom, and before that, she tried to serve me dog doo in a coffee mug...a *coffee* mug, that came with a fucking *saucer*! Where do you people get off...giving me dog doo in a mug that comes with a saucer? I'm not *crazy*. I have been *poisoned*. My body is a mess. I had cancer once...My mind is the only thing I have left. And *you people*...can leave it...*alone*."

It sounded like somebody else. I felt like somebody else. Everyone in the world was betraying me, and I had never had any problem with anyone before in my life. Erdman picked up a pen and started writing when I said "cancer." He asked, "What kind of cancer? And why don't you come sit down now?"

I glanced in awe at Ellen, who had collapsed on his floor in a complete laughing fit over my speech. She was slapping the floor with her bony fingers. I backed away a couple of steps and almost banged into a bass guitar hanging on the wall. I turned around to look at it.

"Acute juvenile leukemia." I had always wanted to touch a bass. I ran my fingers across the strings, so thick and sturdy that no sound came out. "You play all these?"

"Just the sax and the guitar."

I glanced over the rest of them. "Wanna-be, huh?"

"You could say that. A lot of my clientele comes from the University of the Arts. It sparked a tradition of giving me gifts when more expensive replacements come in."

I wondered if that was supposed to impress me, the fact

that he had been given gifts by patients. My watch said twelve-thirty, and I wondered how long until I could sleep.

"But I understand your father's a real musician."

Since it wasn't put as a question, I didn't answer.

"You can hold one. Feel free."

He also had a twelve-string hanging on the wall, something else I had always wanted to try to play, so I pulled it down. It wasn't until I finally spilled my butt into the chair, cradling the instrument, that I realized he'd used the guitar to trick me into sitting. *He probably has those instruments hanging up there so he can trick people.* I glanced at Ellen, who had recovered from her seizure and was barely chuckling, lying on his couch. *Better her lying there than me.*

I sighed. "Promise you won't hypnotize me...or some strange shit..."

"Okay. Can you tell me why you're here?"

"She's EDO, doc. God, that *scone* thing was classic." Ellen blasted a laugh, and Erdman waved her down to shut up.

"I'm EDO? Whatever. I don't know what I am..."

Do re me fa so la ti do-o-o-o...ti la so fa me re do. Playing the twelve-string was just like playing a six-string...*do me re fa me so fa la fa la fa la-a-a-a-a-a ti do*...only you hit two strings at once.

"I know this much. I'm more sane than my friends from Hackett."

"Okay. How's that?"

I sighed. *Ti la so fa me re do.* "Do you know what a *convenient recollection* is?"

"Sure."

I still felt very wound up. But I figured I'd better talk about something or he would hypnotize me or drug me or predict my future. It helped, telling this story about Lani versus the Rod 'N' Reel, while playing the background bars to "The Wind," a very mellow, very old Cat Stevens song. By the time I got to the part in the story where I saw CLEMENTI,

JOSEPHINE on caller ID, I was talking to Erdman in a fairly normal voice, thanks to the soothing music. They had listened quietly throughout.

"So...my girlfriend Macy, she totally believes she heard Lani in front of the Rod 'N' Reel asking some guy for sex because the guy blew smoke rings. Which is so incredibly...out there...Do you *know* Lani?"

I heard Ellen snort and turned to look, despite Erdman glaring at her for interrupting. She continued, "Lani brought me and, like, three other people from my high school into this office because our lives were messed up. He knows Dr. Erdman. He's so about...helping people."

"Can you imagine him slutting? Propositioning somebody?"

She cracked up. "Seriously, this one time last year? I had to explain to him what this really meant." She flipped the bird. "He didn't know it had to do with sex."

I shook my head behind more Cat Stevens. "And people call me dense."

"People see and hear 'edited' versions of things all the time." Erdman watched me. "Something happens a certain way, and it doesn't meet what they feel could be reality, and so they 'edit' what happened."

I clapped my fingers across the guitar neck, deadening the pretty echo. "But you don't understand about Macy. She's... So. Incredibly. Sharp. We call her hawk eye. But she's also hawk ear, hawk sniffer; she's almost psychic. She can smell BO on a kid from six aisles over. I can't even smell it when the person is right beside me."

"How do you know the kid actually smells? How do you know you're wrong and she's right?"

"Because. Everyone can smell it. After a couple weeks, everyone is talking about it. Except me. Stuff like that."

He raised his eyebrows, watching me like there was something I was missing.

I shot my head back, staring at the ceiling....*ti la so fa me re do*... "And don't try to tell me all those people are hallucinating."

He shook his head. "Not all of them. Some of them are just... making it sound good. To fit in."

"They're *lying*? They don't really smell anything, but they're saying a kid smells?"

"Sure."

I thought that was a way mean thing to accuse people of. *Ti la so fa me re do*... "I don't believe that. What about the poor kid who doesn't have friends and can't figure out why not?"

"Claire, if we're talking about Lani—" Ellen giggled. "You're pretty naive yourself."

I mumbled around Cat Stevens, "I missed most of junior high school because I was sick. Is that where people, like, learn to be treacherous?"

"Have you ever heard the story about the emperor's new clothes?" Erdman asked.

"That story about the guy walking the streets in his underwear?"

He kept watching me. With a couple more pretty measures, some hazy memory flashed... people all pretended the emperor was wearing stuff—so they could fit in with the alleged cool people... Except the town idiot.

"Wait." I slapped my hand across the neck of the guitar again. Cat Stevens did not belong with these indigestion thoughts. "I'm dying here. You're telling me that my best friend, whom I trust with my life, makes this stuff up and totally believes herself, and my other friends just lie to be like her, or they totally believe themselves, too—"

Ellen cracked up again, and this time Erdman threw a pencil in her general direction.

I cast her an evil glance. "I'm sorry, I don't think that's funny. I'm not trying to be funny. I'm trying to be very serious here, so even if it sounds funny, please don't laugh when I ask. You're saying that...I cannot trust the things my own friends say."

I was met with silence, though I could sense Ellen holding her nose to keep from laughing.

"I just don't believe that. Sorry. I refuse to believe Larry Boogers is really just Larry Ivanosky, who looks like the *type* who would pick his boogers."

Erdman watched me. *Ti la so fa me re do...ti la so fa me re do...*

"But, Jesus. Who wants to tangle with Macy?" I rested my elbows on the guitar. "Okay, even if your little theory is true, it's not worth hating Macy over. This girl loves me. You would not believe how great this girl is to me."

"Why do you think she loves you?"

"I have no clue." *Ti la so fa me re do...* "It came out of nowhere last fall."

"It probably didn't come out of nowhere. Lots of times opposites attract."

*Ti la so fa me re do...ti la so fa me re do...*It was possible he was saying that he thought Macy liked how I rarely got sucked into her interesting observations about people— beyond looking where she pointed and laughing it off. But I was tired of thinking about all of this.

"I'm done. That's all I have to say."

"Still got a lot of time."

"I wanna sleep."

I started to get up, and he said, "Play something. You ever write anything?"

My eyes went from the guitar slowly up to his. *Who the hell knows what Lani told him...probably wants to psychoanalyze my razor-blade music.* "Don't pull that on me. I wouldn't play the stuff I write for my worst enemy. God. I don't hate anybody that bad."

"Then play something somebody else wrote."

I can crack the knuckles on my right hand without using my left hand. I eyed him as I cracked, actually tempted to spew some basement lyrics, for what purpose, I didn't know. Except that this was starting to seem like a place to be honest.

"Play anything you want," he said.

Truth was, I didn't want to play any basement lyrics. I didn't want to think about girls victimizing themselves. I wanted to kick somebody's foul ass. I just didn't know whose.

I broke into "Classical Gas," Dave Mason, because it kicks butt, and because the challenge of working out that classical mess on twelve strings gave my keyed-up anger something to light into. The guitar totally worked like my six-string, only it sounded like six guitars. My dad taught me to play guitar while watching the ceiling instead of my fingers. He had said that your feelings work better than your eyes, and you get good faster that way.

So I was scrunched down, and I laid my head on the back of the chair, which would partially explain why I missed all this blood splattering over the mouth of the guitar. I figured I had gotten some blister on top of my calluses that stung like a bitch. I totally forgot about running my thumb through with a plastic fork the day Lani first showed up in the cafeteria.

I finished, put my thumb to my mouth, and tasted blood. Ellen had crawled off the couch and was sitting on the floor in front of Erdman's desk, watching. Their jaws kind of hung, and their eyes went back and forth from me to the guitar. I was afraid to look down.

I just stuck my bloody thumb out to him. "I forgot to show you this cut, back when I was showing you my stitches and...everything else."

"Do you have any idea how proficient you are on that instrument?" he asked.

I looked down finally. It wasn't too bloody. The six bass

strings were shiny red, and a few drops had splattered below the mouth, creating a small stream. I licked my pinky and tried to wipe the mess up fast.

"My dad says I'm pretty good for my age."

"So, your father taught you?"

"He taught me some. But we fight too much. Too much alike."

"Then who taught you?"

I never knew what to say when people asked me that. I let the long silence speak for itself. And since we were all telling the truth today, I added, "Pretty damn scary, isn't it?"

After a minute he sat up slowly and searched through his Rolodex. Ellen broke out of her freeze, fell on her side, and started laughing again. I watched Erdman toe at her under the desk, saying, "Ellen. I think we determined you should not take life so seriously, but I'm afraid I'm creating a monster... Would you like to be in a rock 'n' roll band? One that actually finds decent-paying work around here some weekends? Some University of the Arts guys, with some older?"

I thought he was talking to Ellen. But he held this little card out to me.

20

Ellen and I walked down South Street, gazing into store windows. I would catch her reflection in the glass, watching me as much as the stuff. She was smiling.

Finally she spoke up. "So how do you feel about jamming with those University of the Arts guys?"

"I'm still in shock. Give me a few more minutes." I glanced down at the thirty dollars in my hand that my dad laid on me as we left Erdman's office a few minutes before. Ellen and I were supposed to be going shopping, but I barely even knew what I was looking at in these windows. At the moment, it was bizarre jeweled platform shoes. I shuddered.

She giggled. "You're not getting with them till tonight. So if you're going to jump for joy like a high school kid, do it beforehand. And, uhm...lose the jacket, maybe?"

I stared at a window reflection of my bright green-and-white cheerleading jacket that read ERIALC. I tied it around my waist, turning the COAST CHEERLEADING lettering in to face my butt. Fortunately, the warm weather had gotten just plain hot. I felt great in my T-shirt.

"I should look for something to wear down here. Though I didn't bring much money to add to what my dad just—"

"We can go shopping if you want, just don't look like you're trying to impress them. They won't be trying to impress you."

I stuffed the bills down in my jeans pocket, along with the twenty I had of my own, and cracked up. "I'm dreaming this whole thing. It's like, too good to be true. There's got to be a catch. D'you know these guys?"

She shook her head. "No, but if they're from the University of the Arts, they're definitely good."

"I mean, will they be, like, covered with body piercings and stuff?"

"Probably." She snorted out a laugh like I was some kind of silly. "You talked to that one on Erdman's phone. Did he sound all strung out?"

"No. Jason French." I looked at the guy's name on the card. "He was really nice. I kept getting scared he was going to ask my age. Erdman never told him that part."

"So, don't ask, don't tell."

I shook my head, sighing and laughing. "Sorry. I'm just having…brain overload, here. How do you think Erdman knows the guys in the band? I didn't even ask. Maybe half of them are, like, creatures crawling in and out of his office every week."

Her smile wandered away, and I started apologizing left and right, but it was kind of late. "Did Lani mention to you that I always have my foot in my mouth? They're called dumb-stupid-Claire remarks. I didn't mean anything by that, Ellen. I think you're really together, like, so comfortable with yourself and all. I'm just overloading."

She pulled me along down South Street, shrugging. "You have to stop thinking of people in therapy as the losers. Probably ninety percent of the population would profit by some 'tweaking.' Only about three percent either bites enough dust or swallows enough pride to get it. You're ahead of the herd."

"Brain overload…serious brain overload…"

Her cell phone rang, and she pulled it from her pocket and looked at the number. "It's Lani."

I waved my hands a little, begging.

"Hey. Wassup?...She's not here...No, she's not...Would I lie to you?...Hold on."

She put her hand over the receiver. "What's up? Are you still freaked out about the first conversation we had this morning?"

I had called her about the angel costume, like Lani had asked. She had told me, yes, Abby's mom had sent him the costume along with the book. Then I had told her about the conversation I'd had with Lani—especially the part where he said he enjoyed wearing the stupid nightgowns. We had talked for half an hour about the definition of a drag queen before Erdman and this appointment even came up.

I rolled my eyes, motioning with my hands like *magnanimous headache.*

"Your little cross-dressing episodes have given her a migraine," Ellen said into the phone, to my horror. But then she grabbed hold of my arm, shaking it a little while talking. "Hey. I can't blame her. If it weren't for my parents' divorce, I'd still be shucking clams in the summers in southern Connecticut. You don't find too many guys out that way who will go onstage in three nightgowns. Yes, darling, I know you were acting-not-cross-dressing. But I have video footage of you backstage, twirling in that thing...Yes, *twirling,* like a girl. Even Cooper was starting to bitch...So, what's up? Did you find the stupid things, or what?"

Long silence. She stopped walking. Her eyes floated over to me. "She was talking about a Macy today in the session with Erdman...Yeah, she went...It was fine."

I beckoned with my fingers for her to give me the phone. She started going, "*Ew*...the girl did *what*?...Welcome to the islands, post–Labor Day. Did I tell you to stay up here with us? Somebody's parents would have put you up—"

I snatched the phone away from her. "What did Macy do?"

I thought he might give me a ration of crap for trying to

avoid him, but he just ignored Ellen's first lie about me not being here. "I just did what you said, and went over to Sydney's once the morning crowd cleared out. She said she only saw two of your friends this morning...Macy and the one with the straight blond hair—"

"Eli."

"Yeah. They told Sydney they came to pick up your mom's doughnuts."

"My mom gets a dozen doughnuts from Sydney every Saturday, eats five or six, and throws the rest out on Sunday if no one shows up to help eat them," I explained our family ritual with a groan. "Guess my mom and Macy have been talking, as usual. *Feeding* off each other."

"Sydney had gotten your message last night about getting that guitar player from the mainland to fill in for you, so she knew you weren't around. She said Macy was trying to give her a ration of grief about you not working tonight. Macy said you weren't really sick, you were just losing it. And you were being really irresponsible to not work."

"Wow!" I felt that knife cut through my back. "She told Sydney I was irresponsible? You would not believe how many times Macy has tried to get me to blow off work. It breaks Saturday nights in half, and I can't cruise around for a couple hours."

"Sydney stuck up for you. I think she knows what's up— maybe you're outgrowing these people, and it was bound to come to a head. She told Macy to give you some breathing room—in other words, mind her own business—and maybe you just needed to get off the island for a while."

"Sydney's way cool."

"Yeah, but Macy was still mad. She told Sydney your mom is ready to kill me."

"Kill *you*? She hasn't even met you! The whole bus thing was my idea—"

"No, no, no. *You're* brainwashed, darling. I brainwashed you to do crazy things like getting on dangerous buses and leaving town."

"Dangerous buses, where silver-haired ladies give you lacy handkerchiefs? To clean up the bloody mess Vince Clementi made of you?" I groaned, remembering all of that. "I bet I know what happened to my mom on that bus the one time she supposedly got molested! I'll bet she'd had a few drinks."

"Maybe. But here's the best part. Sydney said Macy went out front with Eli, and the two of them stood on the sidewalk hollering things at my house."

"Like what?"

"I don't know. I slept right through it." He chirped a good laugh. "They didn't know I was in there. They still think I'm with you. But I asked Sydney if she saw any box on my porch while they were yelling stuff. She said she thought so. But her place had gotten kind of crowded, so she wasn't watching after that."

I shut my eyes, leaning back against a storefront, trying to decide what might have happened next. "I would not normally think of Macy taking a box off somebody's porch. When someone in our crowd gets klepto out at the mall? She gets all disgusted and tells them they're juvenile. But this is a little different . . . For one thing, she's so controlling. And she used to be able to control me so well, and I don't think she likes the fact that all of a sudden, that isn't working out."

I paced in a circle, letting myself get sidetracked on an Erdman-inspired thought. "I've loved hanging with Macy, but . . . I think it took a while for me to wake up from junior high. I feel like last year, I spent most of the time—" I broke off, looking for the words.

"In a stupor?"

"Yeah. Like that time between when you've been asleep and you're all the way awake. But if that was a stupor, what the hell am I in now? Today, I'm, like . . ."

"You finally got out of bed and cracked your head on the floor."

"Yeah. That's good, Lani."

"Least you're out of bed. Congrats."

I laughed a little. "At any rate, I really don't know what Macy would do. But you can be sure of this much. If there was a box on your porch, and Macy was out there yelling stuff, she definitely saw it. And she's so bloody curious about everything."

"I kind of got that impression when she came up to me in the school hallway and was having a coronary when I wasn't, uhm, *forthcoming* about my gender." He laughed in that high-pitched way. I guessed he'd known all along why she started talking to him that day. I felt embarrassed, but it was good to hear him laugh.

"What's the worst that can happen?" I shrugged. "She could come over to my house, all haughty, all shoving night-gowns under my nose, and I would tell her it was a costume. That would bring her down a couple notches. Where's the angel book?"

He laughed. "I'm really scared it's gone forever. It was with the costume."

"A shame. We would need that book to prove the night-gowns were meant to be a costume."

"Oh, they wouldn't want to hear that part, anyway." He blew it off, and I got the same sludgy feeling in my gut as with all his awful predictions. "They would just decide they didn't believe it. And there's one more thing, another thing Sydney said. I asked her to be really honest, because I have to know what I'm dealing with here. This place can be kind of danger-ous—if you're me. So she laid out the whole conversation for me. According to Macy I *threw* a porn magazine at Vince Clementi last night."

"'*Threw*'?"

"Yeah. Tried to shove it into his pocket, before God and

man. It was going *into* his pocket when it showed up, not *coming out*."

I paced in circles, I don't know for how long. He had predicted this on the bus last night—that by today, my friends would have seen something that hadn't happened, just so life could make sense to them. I finally stumbled out with "You really think Macy totally believes this stuff...like, she really, really thinks that's what she saw?"

"Either that or she knows she's lying."

I got a shudder that started in my ankles, went all the way up my shoulders. "Either way, she's being totally uh...*queer*! When I come home, I'm gonna sit her down and talk to her. For once, *I'm* doing the talking, not her. Just try not to worry about her big mouth in the meantime. Okay? You wanna try to get here today? Some excitement."

I told him about the band. "I get to sit in on a session with them tonight. Erdman says if it gels, I might get to do some weekend gigs with them. They call themselves Calcutta."

I pulled out the business card that gave the name, address, phone, and a little note at the bottom: NO WEDDINGS, BIRTHDAYS, BAR MITZVAHS, PLEASE.

"*Calcutta?*" He laughed like he'd heard of them, and I couldn't tell whether it was in a good or bad way.

"Don't ruin this for me," I begged him. "Tell me they don't stink."

"No." He sighed. "They're awesome. Just go. I'm going to hang out around here and see if there isn't some way I can catch any more juice on my property I've had stolen. The costume, I'm done with. That book? I'd really like to try to get that back."

"Don't do anything dangerous."

"And Claire? *Don't* be afraid to reach out and touch those guys."

I thought he was referring to my lack of affection. "I'm not half so frigid with a guitar in my hands."

"You have to meet them to know what I'm talking about. And Claire? There's another place you have to go. Trust me, okay? There's a store on South Street called RazorBacks. You must go there. You'll like the stuff a lot."

I waved under Ellen's face. She was listening to her Discman instead of honing in on our convo like Macy would have. "He says I'll like this store called RazorBacks. Can we go?"

To my surprise a laugh squirted out of her nose, and she pulled my cheerleading jacket off my butt to glance at the lettering. "I don't think you'd like that place at all. But I'm game...Guess we're about to have a close encounter with RazorBacks."

I handed back her phone, and we trotted down South Street.

21

As soon as I passed through the door to RazorBacks, I could see why Lani had said I would find something here I liked. And I could see why Ellen would not quite get it. She hadn't heard the conversation about black leather between me and Lani.

The place was a clothing boutique where, like, seventy-five percent of everything was made of leather. There were some very tiny leather outfits I wouldn't be caught dead in, along with things like candles and lotions and other South Street rages. There were also racks of leather jackets, leather pants, leather dresses. The smell of leather wafted up my nose and sunk into my gut, making me feel nervy.

Ellen followed along as I moved past the aisle of lotion and candles and went directly for the leather jackets. I spun past a few that were either longer, or belted, or covered in chains. They didn't really look like anything I would wear. I got my hand around a black one that I almost skipped past because it looked so plain. It was just simple black leather that was gathered where it ended, at the waist. There was no huge zipper, no ornaments that made it stand out—just five metal snaps on black leather. It had a leather collar. I pulled it down and checked the size. Small. I took it off the hanger wondering if it meant girl's small, or guy's small.

I asked Ellen.

"I don't think the jackets in RazorBacks are gender specific," she said, then cracked up laughing, eyeing this jacket like she was reading my thoughts. "It's plain but unique. Go for it. You'll drive the islanders crazy, looking like nobody else."

I giggled back, sending my arms into the sleeves. The leather cracked as it wrapped around my shoulders. I liked the overall effect. It was plain and genuine but didn't really make any other statement.

"Sleeves are too short," I noted in disappointment.

"Try a bigger size." A salesclerk appeared out of nowhere, leafing through the mediums. I noticed he had a pierced lip. It was just a tiny silver stud, but once I saw it, I couldn't stop looking at it.

"No medium left," he said. "Want to try a large?"

"Sure." I tore my gaze from him. I imagined myself with a ring through my lip and decided I would be picking at it constantly. *I would not want one of those face piercings if I were being totally myself,* I decided. But I liked the way it looked on him.

I took the size-large jacket from him and shot my arms through the sleeves. It hung on me. Very, very baggy. I felt disappointed.

"You could wear it with a very big sweater." Ellen giggled.

But by now I had a picture in my head. This black leather jacket, size medium, with a white tank shirt. Ribbed, really expensive tank shirt. I sighed. "You're sure there's no medium?" I asked him.

He nodded. "If it's not here, we sold it."

He looked sympathetic, but that didn't make my disappointment go away. I loved this jacket. But then I got to looking at the salesgirl's clothes as she fussed over the shelves of candles. She was dressed mostly in black—black platforms, black leather pants, black vest, black T-shirt. She was tall and thin, like me, so I got to imagining myself in that outfit. I would be six foot in those platforms and would feel like a rhino queen. The black vest looked a little like jailbait to me. But the jeans looked really good on her slender frame.

I turned slowly to look at this jacket again and wondered if my mother, miracle seamstress, could take it in. Maybe, if she wouldn't faint over my raw nerve at bringing black leather home.

"Do you see those pants on that girl?" I asked the salesclerk.

"Yeah," he said. "They're Kira's high-huggers." I guessed he was referring to how they came all the way up to her waist, which wasn't really the style around here, it seemed. On Hackett, it was still okay.

"Did she buy them here?"

He turned slowly to another rack, and I gathered Ellen thought leather pants an outrageous request, because she was giggling again. "Don't be laughing at me." I nudged her, begging. "I would never buy black leather pants. I just...I wanted to try them on and see what they feel like."

She kept laughing but said, "I'm not laughing *at* you, I'm laughing *with* you, and I hope you find a pair that fits."

The clerk held out a pair very similar to Kira's, draped over a hanger. I could see immediately that they were waist high and not hip high.

I said, "Oh my god," as Ellen stomped her foot.

"These are size five," the guy said, "and they run tight. Leather is like that."

I was a perfect size five and snatched them from him, heading toward the dressing room as he pointed.

Ellen trailed along. Her eyes popped when I got them on. "Actually? They fit perfectly...if you're into clothes fitting like a glove."

"Yeah, well...I'm not." I glanced at her J. Crew–type outfit, which was cute and expensive looking, but in no way smacked of *sexy*.

"This tightness is definitely not me. Looks horny." I stuck my head out the door and spotted the salesclerk, still going through the rack. "You got these in a seven?"

The guy shook his head. "I just looked for one, but all I have is a nine."

I took the pair from him but got a weird feeling in my gut. My perfect sizes were not there, almost like a sign of fate. *You shouldn't be trying on weird outfits, Claire. You don't need to be any bigger a laughingstock on Hackett.*

The nine was too big, but not so big that I couldn't get a good sense of what the seven would have looked like. Just big enough for a few ripples. A medium jacket and size seven pants would have been perfect. So perfect that, yeah, I probably would have bought them, despite that I'd just sworn to Ellen that I wouldn't.

Ellen noticed my disappointed look and tried to make me feel better. "I might mention that RazorBacks is way, way expensive, anyway. I can't afford to buy stuff here...but I know all the good sales at Abercrombie, J. Crew...Gap. Wanna head over to Liberty Mall?"

I checked the price tag just to be sure. My eyes popped. The pants alone were more than a hundred dollars. The jacket was almost three hundred.

I jammed my legs into my jeans, moaning to her about Lani sending me to this store. "Lani's got runaway-child syndrome. A fun afternoon for him is probably gazing at stuff he could never afford to buy and getting a charge out of just gazing. I can't do that, sorry. I can't gaze without..."

I trailed off in disappointment, but Ellen finished for me. "Without *lusting*." She giggled supremely.

"Yeah. I get shopping lust." We went out of the dressing

room as I eyed Kira's high-huggers as she set up bottles just-right on a shelf about six feet away. "Can you lust after somebody else's clothes?"

"Oh sure, you can lust after anything," Ellen said easily. "Hey, is your name Kira? Claire, here, is lusting after your pants."

My mouth fell to the O shape, but Kira only laughed along with Ellen. I guessed the word *lust* had a different meaning than down at the shore, where it meant bad biblical sex or something. She grinned, all proud of her pants. "And ours are too expensive, so you want me to cut you a cheap deal on mine, right? Ain't gonna happen. They're from my honey. He likes the way I sound in them." She walked in a circle, all swishing her butt, making squishy noises with her thighs.

I laughed hard at her response, feeling like you could say just about anything in these parts and people didn't look at you weird.

I put the pants back on the rack. "I guess I should be grateful to Lani for sending me down here," I told them. "I found the definition of Claire black leather."

"Did you say the name Lani?" Kira asked.

"Yeah, he told me to come here."

"Okay, you're *that* Claire." She smacked her forehead "Were you going to pick up your present? There's a present for you behind the counter."

I followed her in kind of a stupor. She dropped the box on the counter with an annoyed *splat,* and I kind of froze. I was expecting a bottle of perfume or something. This was an enormous box. *Something black leather,* I just knew, even before Kira nudged me. "Open it! Looked a little like some of the stuff you were trying on. Maybe you lucked out. Maybe you can exchange it for what you tried on and not owe anything."

"This guy is too nice," I said, frozen.

"He? I thought it was a she." Kira laughed.

"He's sort of...a he-she." Ellen told her.

She hooted. "I know a lot of he-she people, but usually I can guess what they are with some accuracy. Especially if I spend half an hour on the phone with he-she—who's got our catalog but insists on calling the boutique instead of the warehouse. He kept me running for half an hour."

"Where'd he get the money?" I wondered.

"Now I'm feeling my guilt." Ellen winced a little. "Last thing he said to me before he went back to his mom's to live was that his dad had left him a little money. We were all busting his stones, all 'What, you're going home so you can get the money?' He just ignored us. Never said he planned to, like, give it away buying gifts for people."

I pulled back the lid. I didn't want to exchange it, whatever it was. It was such a nice thing to do that I would keep it and wear it, even if he'd pegged me all wrong. As I pulled the two pieces out, Ellen was dead quiet for once, not giggling. I don't think I said a damn thing, either. The two of us stared and stared, trying to decide how something that seemed this impossible could even happen.

22

We trudged back up South Street toward my dad's place, and Ellen found her voice first. She tried to give me sanity-inducing statistics, which made me glad I hadn't said anything yet. She was turning out to be a good friend who had put up with a lot of my craziness back at Erdman's office. I didn't want to push my luck and say anything outlandish, like that the guy is simply not human. Or better, *He's a real floating angel.*

"Cooper and I eat together at my house lots, because both our moms work late," she said. "I can't tell you the number of times I've called to have pizza delivered, and Cooper walks in with a pizza. Same with sushi, same with gyros."

I agreed that was weird. But I didn't think friends showing up with the same food was as colossal as Lani picking out the very stuff I had tried on.

"I'm so grateful, don't get me wrong," I finally spouted. "I just feel so crazed and so...not me right now. I almost wish I didn't have to deal with an experience that seems so twilight zoney. It's not helping me feel less crazed."

"You're not crazed; you're readjusting." She tried to assure me. I'm not sure I looked any more convinced. She went on, "Besides. RazorBacks is a small, exclusive boutique. It's not like when you walk into the Gap and there's fifty million of the same thing. There were many in different sizes, but how many *styles* of black leather jackets were they selling in there?"

"Maybe...five," I mumbled.

"So, he had a one-in-five chance of picking the one you would have picked. That's not so outlandish."

I guessed it wasn't. I felt my brain relaxing a little. "And the others weren't like anything I would have ever bought."

"There you go. And the pants? They were plain, like the jacket. Logical match. You still feel like you're in the twilight zone about it?"

"I guess not." I laughed, watching her toss her red hair in a confident way. I liked her a lot, so I let the subject go without further questions, such as the big one bothering me: *How would he have guessed my perfect sizes, on top of my perfect taste? Is that just something gay guys are good at?*

The sizes were as perfect as I imagined. I modeled for Ellen back at the house, and I think she was as awestruck as I was. Then we started watching a video on my dad's couch, and I fell dead asleep. I started to have one of my recurring nightmares. In it a girl I didn't know took a guitar string and stuck the end of it up to the palm of her hand. Guitar string is very sharp, and you can cut yourself with the points. Even in the dream I could feel my stomach getting all weird, because this girl had been in other dreams. Sometimes she would thread guitar string in and out of her palm, making an X, hold it up to me, and smile. I moved toward her in the dream, and this time I tried to stop her.

"Don't," I said, reaching for her hand. "Why are you hurting yourself?"

She held up her palm. Instead of an X, she had somehow carved in this beautiful tattoo of a little bird or butterfly, something with wings in pastel colors.

She asked, "What makes you think I'm hurting myself?"

I woke up in a stupor, finding the house almost dark. Only

snow on the TV screen lit the living room. I shot up, wondering how long ago the movie had ended. Ellen was gone. I turned on the lamp and spotted a little note on the coffee table. "Call if you need anything. El." It had her cell phone number underneath. Under that was scribbled Lani's number, as if he had called, and a note from my dad that said he had left to play with his band, Suhar was with him, and she had made Japanese food, which was in the microwave. The little clock on the wall read 7:10. I was supposed to be at the Calcutta practice in twenty minutes.

I flopped back, staring at the ceiling, not freaking over the little time I had to get ready. I felt like I had two clear choices. I could take time to eat or I could try to make myself look awesome in my new black leather to go jam with these college guys. Ellen's words rang in my head: *Don't try to impress them. They won't be trying to impress you.*

I stumbled toward the kitchen, deciding I could throw on the leather pants, leave on the T-shirt I slept in. It was too hot for the jacket, anyway. I would get to wear part of my new stuff without looking like I was trying to impress anyone.

I started in on Suhar's Japanese food and plowed through half the plate before dialing Lani's number. "You are the best. I cannot believe you bought me that beautiful stuff."

"I thought you'd like it." He giggled.

" 'Like it'?" I opened my mouth to tell him I'd tried the very stuff on. But my eyes shot to my watch again. Fifteen minutes until practice, and I had to walk with two guitars.

"I'm almost late for rehearsal. We'll talk a lot more later. I just wanted to know if you found your missing nightgowns."

"I got the book back."

I almost choked on the milk I was downing furiously. "How?"

"It was in the gutter in front of the house this afternoon. Kind of like it had always been there. Guess there's no question that the package on the porch was from Abby."

"But do you think somebody took the time to dump the book back in front of your house? That's diabolical. I'll bet the book fell out in the gutter..."

He chuckled. "Claire, you're naive, but I love you, anyway."

"You actually think some rip-off artist put it back there."

"To let me know they had the nightgowns. Only they didn't have Tony's nerve, to make their delivery onto the porch. They had to leave it in the gutter, and then flee—"

"Cowards!" I blasted, pushing my plate away in frustration. "I'm calling Macy."

"She's your friend, and you can do what you want. But what would you accomplish by calling her?"

"I'll tell her off! I can't believe she knifed me in the back like that to Sydney...and then *this*? Do you really think it was Macy?" I couldn't get over this.

"I saw her this time."

"You *saw* her? Why didn't you tell me that right off?"

"I was afraid you would think I was having a convenient recollection." He laughed, but I didn't see anything funny.

"You *saw* Macy throw that book in the gutter?"

"Yeah. She opened the passenger door of Vince Clementi's car, got one foot on the ground, and heave-hoed."

I shut my eyes and swallowed spit, having a complete flashback of eighth grade. Not that Macy had ever done a mean thing to me. But back then I hadn't known about the thin lines cutting through her versions of good and evil. She could rip on and on about a fat kid pigging out on potato chips and totally terrify me that I could be her next victim.

"What did you do when you saw her leave the book?"

"Oh, I just watched." His voice picked up more happily. "But after she jumped back in Vince's car and the whole truth struck me, *I* started to laugh hysterically."

"What whole truth?"

"If they had simply gone online for ten minutes? That volume of Andovenes is worth about nine hundred dollars."

My jaw dropped. "No way. You own a book worth nine hundred dollars?"

"Check it out on eBay sometime. Instead, she could have had a decent down payment on a car. She's playing gutter games."

I laughed my side off. "Care if I tell her that?"

"Do *not* tell her that. I don't want anybody rifling my room for their next trick. And I've got a better idea than you calling her."

"What's that?"

"Go to band practice."

He wanted me to rise above it.

"I just wish I knew what she was doing with those night-gowns," I muttered, heading into the bedroom to change. "Is she going to bring them into school on Monday and, like, totally humiliate both of us?"

"Do you really care?"

All of a sudden I couldn't answer that. But I admired Lani's courage. And if that was the worst that could happen, I supposed I could live with it. I thanked him again for the black leather, and we hung up pretty quick.

I got to this upstairs empty room over a restaurant where Calcutta rehearsed, and all I noticed at first was the run of good news. First, these guys did not play any hip-hop, which thrilled me to no end. They had a horn player, and yet, they were so much about rock 'n' roll that I got to try out both the electric and acoustic guitars. Second, they were very nice, but in a professional way. No one went gaga over my guitar playing, like Erdman, but how they filled in around it said a lot.

They knew mostly eighties and nineties stuff, and I knew mostly sixties and seventies. But we discovered they and I both knew some Elton John. My dad had burned "Rocket

Man" onto one of those practice CDs back when I was sick. It starts out with just piano and a voice, and then everything comes in at the first chorus. I gripped a guitar pick, listening to their lead singer, this Jason French, laying out clean vocals to the piano, waiting for that chorus. And it occurred to me, I had never played with a backup before that wasn't on a CD or MP3.

When I hit my first chord and heard drums, synth, piano, bass, rhythm, myself . . . the rush of being surrounded by flesh-and-blood sound was like going over the straight-down part of a roller coaster. I almost lost my knees. These guys were passing through me—like we had become floating ghosts, or one giant ghost, one power.

Complete happiness can feel so much like complete terror that it's hard to tell them apart. I fought my shaking knees by jamming against the rhythm player in the parts where he had lead runs, and we made a fun game of it, like a Ping-Pong match. There's a part in the chorus that requires three-part harmony. Jason poked at me, pointed at his throat, then made a thumbs-up sign. I moved to share his mike. The music was already gel. Then this Jason and I had our lips so close to his mike I could smell toothpaste. Add to the sound three more voices, which, by some luck, nailed these harmonies. The ceiling buzzed octaves we weren't even singing.

We wandered into "Tiny Dancer," then "Levon," the only other two Elton Johns I knew. I was afraid if I made eye contact, one of these guys would eventually say, "You look young! How old are you?" Rather than risk getting kicked out, I was being way shy with my eyes. I did catch on through stray glances in the dimness of the room that these guys were old; I mean *old*. Dr. Erdman had said University of the Arts, but four of them looked like they had to be closing in on twenty-five. I probably would have noticed more things sooner if I had been staring like Macy stares.

They started talking after we ran out of Elton John tunes, and I could not believe this thing was getting better than it already was. They were arguing about putting "Rocket Man" on their album, now that they had a decent acoustic guitar player, and would Elton John's people make them pay a fortune for that? *They had an actual recording contract with Millennium, a Philly-based recording studio.*

I kept staring at the carpet for fear of drilling a happy hole in the ceiling if I opened my mouth. We got into practicing these three original songs over and over again, which were for their album.

I started to relax a little and look at these guys in that Macy way. I realized they were about the strangest conglomeration of types I would have ever put together.

The sax player and bass player were African American but were nothing like each other. The sax player had sounded way educated, and the bass player looked and talked like a street person. Jason looked like something off the cover of *Gentleman's Quarterly*. The guy who doubled on piano and synth was painfully thin, like a sixth-grade girl, and he had on a T-shirt that read: I GRADUATED **HARVARD**: THIS ISN'T JUST THE FUCKING SHIRT. The drummer and the rhythm guitar player both looked like they could have been big-time druggies. They had buzzed hair, which was thin, and you could see their scalps, which you would have put more with a diet of freebasing than milk and eggs. The rhythm player had two badly chipped teeth in the front.

Four of these guys had definitely seen better days. Jason French seemed the most normal and grounded, and I was glad he did most of the talking with me. But their talent was so hot, it made me think of Lani and Ellen: "*Got to pay your dues to sing the blues.*" The stuff had a fire to it that I'm not sure would have lit up under a bunch of middle-class garage-band lesson takers.

One song we practiced, called "Irma," was written by Jason French about some girl he had known who had gotten sick and died. It was kind of bluesy, and I provided some Jonny Lang–type runs on electric that turned out pretty good. I could not figure out an exact style for these guys, though all three original songs had something to do with AIDS. And it came out plainly near the end of the rehearsal that this recording contract involved not just Calcutta but also four other Philly-based groups who were putting together an anthology album as a fund-raiser for the local AIDS alliance.

I wasn't even disappointed to hear that, though a tour would have been nice.

"Don't talk much, do you?" the drummer said, as we were folding up rehearsal. His name was Mike. Mike went *ba-da-boom* at the end, and they all laughed.

Of course, a dumb-stupid-Claire remark followed: "I talk a lot when I'm with my friends."

"Oh! We don't rank!" Jason beat his heart like it was breaking.

Aaron, Mr. **HARVARD**, boinked out a one-hander on the piano. "Don't worry, Claire. *They* don't have any friends. *They're* obnoxious."

His finger circled around, meaning all of Calcutta, and they were all laughing and making donkey noises. I wanted to dive out the door, but I hung around long enough for one more dumb-stupid remark. Mike came toward me, drummed on my head, and I pointed at his wristband. He, the bass player, and the rhythm guitar player all wore the same type of bright orange wristband. It had handwriting on it.

"You guys trying to be twins?"

"We're all part of a certain hospice."

I couldn't remember what a hospice was. He said that on the wristband was a "buddy's" phone number. He said that many people knew that if they saw the bright orange wristband on a person in medical distress, to call that number right away.

The truth struck me finally as I remembered Lani's strange comment on the phone. *"Don't be afraid to reach out and touch those guys."* Thin-haired, buzz cuts, nicks on the scalp, not an ounce of fat in the place...

Jesus. Every one of these guys is HIV positive.

That was not exactly confirmed for me—not at that time. After my wristband comment, Jason said, "Calcutta is not just us six; it's about two dozen people that come and go... depending on who's sane, who's healthy." He laughed, and the other guys joined in, like that was some sort of funny. "Every one of us has a life-threatening illness. And since you were sent by Erdman, we're assuming you can keep our politics pure."

A small part of me wanted to throttle Erdman for setting me up with a dose of reality I'd always tried to avoid. Yet they were looking at me like this was some sort of interview question. *You're in, or you're out... Do not mess up your answer, little girl.* I felt dizzy, like my insides were on the outside, and my skin was squashed somewhere near where my stomach used to be.

"I...am in remission from leukemia. I just had a blood test that came back good, but, uhm. You just don't know, you know?"

They cheered about my blood test. They clapped me on my back. Jason kicked the drummer in the ankle and said, "See? Something just told me. This Erdman girl is gonna be really *sweet*..."

They weren't kicking me out. I'd never spent much time feeling proud of being a cancer survivor. All of a sudden I was never so proud in my life.

23

Sunday afternoon I stepped off the bus and set foot on Hackett feeling great, despite all the crap I was returning to. For one thing, my mom had chewed out my dad three times over the weekend—for letting me come on a bus, for sending me to a shrink, and for letting me walk the streets of Philadelphia by myself. She didn't know about playing in a band with a bunch of older, HIV-positive guys. She had told me to call her from the bus station and she would pick me up. But I got the thought, *I have about ten more minutes to enjoy my weekend by walking home alone and reliving it one more time. Am I entitled to a few simple pleasures before I get nagged and guilted?*

Why I would want to walk home looking like I did, I had no clue. The ungodly heat for that time of year had kept up, so I had my cheerleading jacket shoved down in a shopping bag. I had on a torn T-shirt I mooched off my dad that said BLOODY MARY on it. I don't know why I had liked the thing— it was old and faded and torn, leaving my one shoulder bare to the sun—I guess maybe I thought it fit my stage of life. Over top of it was this ratty old guitar case that worked like a backpack, sporting an electric Fender my dad had loaned me. I had been used to hiding my guitars—like, sneaking them over to Sydney's before Vince picked us up—so I would not give Macy any visual reminders that I was screwing up our Saturday nights. But now I looked like I had been nailed to a sideways cross, and it gets better.

Suhar and I had met Ellen for breakfast in the Liberty Mall, and between Suhar's artistic tastes and Ellen constantly egging me on, we went on the shopping spree from hell. I now had on my black leather pants, which I decided looked very cool with a tattered T-shirt. Ellen had planted a hat on my head called a fedora, which she said gang members wore. But it's brown and velvety, with a brim *and a feather!* It looked very cool on me, and I didn't think I looked like gang bait. It just kind of fit with Claire-black-leather. Suhar not only bought it, but she bought me a pair of snakeskin cowboy boots that I had fallen in love with, god knows why. Like I wasn't tall enough already. I thought Ellen was going to fall onto her side, laughing "with me."

I was wearing the boots and had both my jackets shoved into a huge shopping bag. The streets were pretty deserted, which is not unusual this time of year. But as I got near the corner of Hackett and Tenth, I saw a group of girls hanging there. Eighth graders, I thought hazily, because I recognized one as Eli's younger sister, Jule. She was a sweet kid. I just gave a small wave as I started past them, but Jule piped up.

"Tough hat. Where'd you get those pants?"

"Philadelphia."

Her three friends came up a little closer behind her, and their eyes crawled all over me, trying to decide if these pants were really tough. I don't think anyone from Hackett had seen a pair of black leather pants on anything but a mannequin.

I let them get their stares in, and Jule finally pointed to my Liberty Mall shopping bag and said, "You went shopping in *Philadelphia?*"

To them, anywhere west of the mainland mall was a big deal. "Yeah, my dad lives there. He's a session musician in Philly."

"Yeah, we know about your dad." Jule's eyebrows raised up, and I snorted out a laugh. My dad had a false reputation on the island of being a "famous musician," because after he left my mom, he got in this Philly band and they had cut an album. People around here didn't know the difference between an album you pay to have produced and a Columbia Records contract.

"My dad is *not* famous," I corrected them, used to their thought. "But some of the stores near him are way cool, and I've got some really generous friends, so..."

I started to move past them, locking eyes with a girl I knew as Jule's best friend, Kaitlin. She could get a Macy-type of judgmental glare going sometimes. She had her arms folded across herself, and after I passed by, her mouth went off.

"But aren't you the girl hanging out with that faggot?"

It hit me in the back of the head like a boomerang. The bag with my jacket in it left my hand, and I turned with both hands free. *Don't lose your mind again, Claire. Don't start...* My sensible thoughts rang through, but my expression must have looked like something to be reckoned with. Kaitlin jumped behind her three friends. I stopped coming, but they still took three steps back.

"If I so much as dream that word comes out of your trash mouth again, I will come find you," I said. *Shouldn't threaten people, Claire. You might have to back it up.* I didn't know if I could back up a threat, but the three sweet girls looked so scared I figured I wouldn't have to. I turned my back again, then figured I had gotten Kaitlin in the pride button. She pretended she was talking to her three friends, loud enough for me to hear.

"Oh! Okay! I guess she doesn't care that this...*Lani Garver* dressed up in nightgowns. He dressed up in nightgowns, and Macy Matlock caught him in them. *She's* been away in Philadelphia. I guess *she* missed that part."

I did another one eighty, and my sensible voice pizzled to

nothing. I reached past the three friends, grabbed Kaitlin by the collar, and pulled her through them. They all froze dead, including Kaitlin, which is a good thing, because I might have hit her. I shook her once, some version of sanity coming through in my voice.

"I know about that story. And this is important. If you have never thought of anything before in your life, you damn well better think fast and clear right now. Repeat to me exactly what Macy told you."

"Nothing! My big brother told me..." She rattled off the name of some kid I barely knew who was on the tennis team.

"Jesus Christ...," I breathed. "Then tell me what *he* said."

"Let me go!"

I just shook her out again and pulled her up closer.

She pealed off automatically, "He said Macy Matlock told him that she caught that gay kid in ladies' nightgowns!"

A box gets stolen from a porch and it mushrooms into a fashion show in less than twenty-four hours.

"So, you said, he said, she said." I shoved her into her three friends, frustrated by the idea of probably never knowing who added what.

I could hear her let out a cry of relief. I just grabbed my bag and started off before my conscience could set me on fire. She sniffed, blabbering, "She's your best friend! Why don't you ask her what happened? She's got the nightgowns! They're hanging up in her front yard! Everyone knows that story! And they're all driving by to see what that new kid was dressed in!"

I turned slowly to look, being sure I heard them right. They took off.

"Claire...there's this wonderful thing called middle ground." I tried to remember what Lani meant by "middle ground," but as I walked down my own street, my blood was on fire. I imagined my fingers wrapping around Macy's throat and her eyeballs bugging out if I found those nightgowns hanging there.

I stormed into my house, and my mom was wigging out with a million questions, from "Why in hell did you take a bus?" to "What the hell do you have on your legs?" to "Why don't you talk to me anymore?"

I kept saying, "Calm down...I'll talk to you later...later, Mom!" I finally shoved her out of my room and locked the door. At that point I realized my whole motive for being in my house was to change out of my pants, so they wouldn't get ruined if I had to kill Macy. I was shaking, scared of killing someone. I called Ellen, got her voice mail, and so I called Erdman's office and got his voice mail. I left the same message each time. "It's Claire. I think I'm going to hit someone... else. I really don't want to hit anybody else. Please call me back. I'm scared...being this mad. Call me back. Please?"

I didn't want to tell Lani this new development until I saw what was going on with my own eyes. By the time I had changed into jeans and sneakers, neither Ellen nor Erdman had called back. My mother was shouting stuff up from the living room that sounded like "Fine, go live with your airhead father if you don't care about me anymore."

I passed her again. "I care, Mom...just *don't fucking guilt me!* I'll be back."

As I walked the four blocks to Macy's, I took deep breaths and got calm enough that I decided Kaitlin had probably passed along an untrue rumor. It just was not Macy's breed of meanness Kaitlin had described—which was over in a flash, meant as an observation more than an attack, and forgotten by us ten seconds later.

I was surprised when I first caught sight of Macy's front yard, because the situation was not better than Kaitlin's gossip—it was worse. Three nightgowns were suspended by strings on hangers from the metal bar where the awning hangs in the summertime. There were three signs over the top: LANI

GARVER JR. PROM, LANI GARVER SR. PROM, LANI GARVER HONEY-MOON. The signs were not done in Macy's pretty straight up and down writing, but some choppy printing. I smelled the influence of Phil, even though I did not see him. I saw Macy and Myra lounging on the porch furniture, trying for a last-minute tan in the absence of the summer awning.

I had frozen when I first saw all this, but a car came down the street, honking at the nightgowns, and I jumped out of my skin. Macy and Myra were sitting there to get attention, not a tan, I realized. My sanity went down the drain again.

Macy sat straight up, her psychic instinct probably sensing me coming across the grass, and she had the good sense not to say anything, for once.

"Definitely not your style, Macy." I yanked two of the nightgowns, and the hangers flew across the lawn.

"Phil did it...I just left it to let you know how mad we are."

"To let *me* know? Looks to me like you're letting everybody in town know. Do you have to create a drama? There's this lovely thing called the phone. The doorbell. The e-mail, the mailbox—"

I pulled one nightgown over the top of the other. It was easy to figure out...so easy I could not believe Miss Hawk Eye had missed it—considering the third nightgown had the sleeves ripped out and an opening cut down the front. I pulled the last one over the other two like a vest.

"What does that look like? Ever see a costume before? As in...a *play*?"

For once her eyes failed her. She would not even look. Would. Not. Look. She spun her back to me and said into the garage door, "We're just trying to shock some sense into you! You're my best friend! I'm not letting you turn loon without a fight."

"How am *I* turning loon?" I should not have tried to reason with her. To let something get this dramatic, she would have had it all thought out.

"You hit Vince Clementi! *Hit* him!"

"I was supposed to let him half kill somebody?"

"You hit a guy!" She went on, deaf. "Over someone who tries to shove off his porn magazines on people—"

"Oh! Is that what happened!" I made Lani's singsongy voice.

"I was standing right there!"

"And I suppose by now that's how Phil saw it, too, right?"

She was backing away from me, looking me up and down like she expected me to jump her. Maybe that's why I grabbed her by the hair.

"Where's that magazine, Macy?"

"None of your damn business, and let me go, you maniac—"

"It *is* my business...and I'm not letting go until you tell me where it is."

"What the hell do you want with it!"

"We're going to take it to the cops. We're going to see whose fingerprints are all over it. I'm gonna prove something to you—"

"We threw it out! Vince did, or something—"

"Hey, that's convenient. Lani said you would do that." I shoved her and held up the costume. "Tell me what this looks like!"

She looked for a half a second before screaming, "Why should I care if it's a costume? Try and tell me he doesn't like wearing that shit!"

I hurled her to the lawn, probably because she had a point, and there was no way to argue it. I drove my knee into her chest, blindly. She started screaming.

"I don't care if I have to lay on you all day! You are going to tell the truth about what happened at the Rod 'N' Reel. What did you really hear?"

She was crying, but she spit out, "He told Tony...not... to blow smoke rings—"

I slapped her across the face. "Tell the truth!"

"That *is* the truth!"

I slapped her again.

"Claire, Jesus Christ! Myra, get her off of me!"

I could hear Myra on Macy's cell, to Phil I supposed, and didn't care. "Tell the goddamn truth, Macy!"

She went on wailing, and I realized there was no other truth in her brain. Lani had told Tony not to blow smoke rings on a street corner if he wasn't gay and didn't want sex. She looked really and truly scared. I was a loon, and she was telling the truth, and I was trying to force a lie out of her. That's how she saw it, how she would always see it, until she died. I had never hoped before for a Judgment Day, but I did now.

I got off her, snatched up the costume, and trudged off. She was crying the soul-filled cries of a hurt person, somebody who had sincerely lost their best friend, who had been dumped, without cause, whose best friend had turned lunatic, and there was not a blessed thing she could do about it.

24

I just hit Macy. Twice..."

"Okay, stop crying and try to chill out." It was a huge relief to hear Ellen's real voice instead of her voice mail, despite my mom banging on my door, demanding that I come out and explain my weekend to her. Before I could think, I hurled a can full of pens and put a big dent in the floor. Pens flew everywhere, and she hollered some shocked moan.

"Ellen, what the fuck am I doing? I'm losing it! Somebody's gotta come lock me up."

Her voice was intentionally calm, and I tried to focus on it instead of my mom's cursing. "Claire, are you, like, not used to being mad?"

"I'm the type who just never gets mad! All of a sudden—" I broke off because I started sniffing up tears.

"Never been mad? That's not what Erdman would say."

"What would Erdman say? Tell me!"

"Granted, stuff like this always happens on Sunday, when he ceases to exist. She sighed. "I'm not him. I can only tell you what he told me. You know how I'm always laughing these days?"

"Yeah..."

"That's so *not* how I usually am. I'm usually the opposite, stone-cold serious. When I started this thing with finding the world so funny, he said it was something I was allowing myself to feel for the first time. He said it would dominate for a while, and then eventually it would gel with my whole personality. I'd be more balanced after that."

I had my finger in one ear and the phone smacked up against my head, trying to focus on her over my mom. I slid down into a curled-up ball between my dresser and the wall, but pulled the phone away, screaming, "Shut up! And get away from my door! Fucking moron!"

Ellen's voice came through. "Claire, Erdman can show you some stuff like how to take your anger out on, like, beanbag chairs until you balance out—"

"Well, he's not here! And if she doesn't get the fuck away from me—" I could hear my mother backing away finally. "Now *she's* crying. She's gonna call Macy...I swear, they've been gossiping all weekend. She's like an overgrown child... She's gonna get drunk..." I broke into pretty big sobs.

"Okay, you can't calm down in there. Just get out of the house."

"And go where?"

"Go over to Lani's."

"I can't. I'm gonna put his head through the wall next! He started all this...It has to be his fault. He made me feel...all this stuff! I just want to be me again..."

"Sometimes? Life has to feel worse before it feels better. Did you eat today?"

I remembered Lani had quoted her on that feel-worse thing before. Not that it mattered. My sanity was sub-zero. "Just a bagel. After that, I forgot." I looked at my radio alarm: *3:20. You can remember to hit Macy, but not eat, jerk-off.*

"Just go. Get away from your mother. You won't hit him. You'll be fine."

"How do you know?" I sniffed, shaking worse now than ever.

"I'll call him. I'll tell him you're feeling whacked out and to give you food. Maybe he knows some of Erdman's tricks. He seems to know a little about everything."

"Ellen?"

She waited real patiently while I thought of what I wanted to say. "I'm not crazy. Not really...Right?"

"No. You are not crazy."

"I mean, I'm not seeing and hearing things." I drummed up an example, wiping snot off my face. "You really did say, in Erdman's office, that you had to explain to Lani about flipping sign language."

"I absolutely said it. He didn't know what the bird meant. You're not hallucinating. He's so innocent in certain ways, it's disgusting. Problem is? People put together *effeminate* with *perverse,* like they automatically go together. In reality? There's no correlation." She was laughing, too loudly. It was not that funny.

"Ellen?"

She waited again.

"Thanks."

I climbed out the bedroom window to avoid my mom. I don't remember anything about going to Lani's except that I walked between houses, dodging in and out of bushes, lest I see anyone who might by chance piss me off. I also had his nightgowns shoved under my cheerleading jacket, and the last thing I needed was for them to fall into enemy hands. I looked pregnant.

He opened the door when I was in the middle of the street, like he had been waiting for me. I walked straight into his chest, buried my face there, and started bawling all over again. He kicked the door shut behind us with his foot, his arms wrapped around me, and we walked up the stairs. Fortunately, his too-sweet mother seemed to be out and didn't accost me.

I stood in the middle of his room like a zombie, tried to suck off his calmness as he strolled over to the bed.

"Ellen called you?" I asked.

"Yeah. I saved you something."

He held the cell phone out to me, stuck it right in front of my face. CLEMENTI, JOSEPHINE stared back at me. He arrowed back, back, back, back, through about fifteen of those.

"What's the date on these?" he quizzed me.

I could barely remember my own name, so it surprised me when today's date floated through my head. "Two days ago..."

"Okay? You're not having convenient recollections of how things happened. It's not *you*."

I fell on his bed, totally tired, not feeling anything anymore.

"I made you a sandwich. Stay here; I'll be right back."

"Don't leave me alone!" I shot up, and he let me trail him downstairs, like all this was perfectly normal. I even followed on his heels up the stairs again.

"Looks like you're gaining weight. Cool." He pointed to my stomach as I chewed a mouthful of food. I put the plate beside me on his bed, getting my first hint of a smile together.

"I totally forgot." I pulled the nightgowns out—one, two, three.

His laugh sounded a little relieved. "Where?"

"You don't want to know."

We sat there in silence as I finished my sandwich.

Then I asked, "What do I do when I want to hit people? I could have broken Macy's neck. Ellen tell you?"

He tried not to laugh more but couldn't help it. "Claire, I am so tempted to tell you, go ahead, keep swinging. For one thing, you're mad about real things and real people. It's not like you're swinging at people who are trying to, like, abduct you to Saturn."

My laugh came out, "FWWWOUT." I asked for another sandwich and sat there this time, staring at the three nightgowns tossed on his bed, while he went and made it. Peanut butter and jelly...my favorite sandwich *from the old days, the better days.* I almost asked for a third but lost my nerve.

And he distracted me during the second sandwich, talking about Erdman-type stuff. "I'm not a shrink, so I don't know too many anger exercises, but I've heard of one that works, according to some people."

He took a pillow and balled it up and held it out in front of him. "Whose face do you see in the front of it?"

I guess he wanted me to imagine something on this soft pillowcase. "Macy's."

"What do you want to say to her? Anything at all."

"You...want me to hit this thing? I'll end up putting a hole through it and breaking your nose."

"No, that's made-for-TV psychology. The point isn't to get you to hit but to say things in a normal voice...find the middle ground. Just say the truth, and nothing but the truth, in a normal voice."

I explained to Macy, "Don't tell people you care about them when all you really care about is getting your own way." I called her a control freak. I apologized for hitting her, and described to her how she was too powerful, how she believed her own shit and antagonized people into believing it, too. I told her she didn't love me, she loved having a shithead for a friend who was too naive to argue with her. I told her Larry Ivanosky didn't pick his boogers.

I got pretty loud when I got to Larry Ivanosky, because I felt he had suffered a fucked-up injustice. But I didn't hit the pillow.

I told my mother she was a drunk, to get a life, and to quit trying to live through mine. I felt things about my dad I had not even been aware of before. I told him he was horny, and if Suhar didn't look so beautiful, he would have not been a distracted dad. I told Suhar to quit sucking up to me by getting me fedoras and expensive shoes; I would get to know her when I felt like it and not before. I told Lani I wanted another glass of milk, and did he have any junk food?

He went downstairs and left me alone again. I knew when he came back I should ask to see this alleged nine-hundred-dollar book and tell him that I wanted to read about angels. I wanted to tell him I thought *he* was one again, because my life was somehow getting better. Because I could feel myself getting slightly smarter, and despite how bad it hurt, I wanted to be smart. I wanted to look through that book and tell him I believed whatever it said, not because I had any proof but because that's what I wanted to believe, and if that's just convenient thinking, well then, screw everyone.

There was one problem with all of that. I didn't want to face the thought that he might say, *"I'm just an overly smart street kid, and that's the truth."*

I felt dizzy, almost rolling into a huge whirlwind—full of the souls of sad people, sick people, poor people, who were ready to believe in miracles, because what we knew with our senses just wasn't good enough. I could almost hear their wailing, and it was charged up, strangely, with hope. *First are last, and the last, first...* I took his pillow out of my lap, flopped my head onto it, and fell dead asleep. I didn't wake up until after dark. There was a glass of milk on the nightstand, a plate of chocolate-chip cookies beside them, and all the candles in his room were lit. My first thought was that I hadn't dreamed a single damn thing.

My second thought was the room looked funny...a little too clean. I saw two backpacks, stuffed in the middle of the floor. I sat up. Lani was awake, lying beside me. That's when he told me that he needed to get off Hackett, fast.

25

"When Tony did all that phone calling to me, there was one thing he didn't count on. It didn't occur to him that I would make a friend that quickly." Lani flopped down beside me on the bed.

I sat up straight and froze, remembering his prediction about Tony after those phone calls. *He thinks I'm over here alone, shaking in my little pink bedroom slippers.*

"When you and I showed up together at the bus station, that was . . . monumental." He went on. "It gets kind of twisted, how things probably went around here after we got on that bus. I'm sure Tony found out we were together, and he probably got scared you were a witness to his phone calls over here. You're a little more credible than me."

"What happened that would make you think you have to leave?" My brain rebelled against it . . . a kid feeling "run out of town" by Hackett Island. He walked me step by step through Friday night, because it would not have made entire sense otherwise.

"I only took the magazine with us because I was thinking of how mad Macy was when she left your house. I figured there was a good chance we might meet her somewhere along the way. I thought maybe I could dangle some solid evidence in front of her, threaten to have the magazine fingerprinted.

Sometimes solid evidence will snap somebody out of convenient thinking."

He shrugged, looking very tired, but went on. "It wasn't just Macy we met. It was those huge guys, too. I knew they could snatch it and destroy any evidence, no contest. I only thought to plant it on Vince about ten seconds before I did it. It's an old street trick. You can do just about anything to anyone while they're shoving you, and they'll never know. It was dangerous... but my gut instinct was banking on the idea that Vince would recognize the magazine as something of Tony's and would start acting funny before anyone would think to accuse me."

I remembered Vince repocketing the magazine like he didn't want anyone to see it.

"I figured all this already." I breathed. "It sure did feel good to torture Vince for a few minutes, trying to call the cops and have the thing fingerprinted. But your fingerprints were on it, too," I reminded him.

"Yeah, but that would have fit my true story. All that needed to be found were Tony's. Truth? The cops probably would have had no interest in fingerprinting it. I'm not even certain they can do something like that on a small island, where nothing usually happens. But I think we scared the living crap out of Vince. He thought for sure if I got a cop on the phone, the dirty little family secret would come flying out. He probably gave Tony hell when he got home. Wish I'd been there to hear that." He let out a sad laugh.

"What do you think happened?"

"Hard to say. In families covering up a secret like that, things get very tricky. The family almost always knows about something like porn, abuse, sometimes even molestation. But they don't talk about it. Not even to each other."

"Is this based on more stuff you've read?" I asked.

"Some of it." He shrugged again. "And some Saturdays I

used to hang out at the clinic until Erdman came down for his lunch burger. He'd buy me one, and we'd sit there and shoot the bull about stuff like this. He'd describe how, like, a mother and a sister can see a bunch of nine-hundred numbers on a phone bill and find out that number is for...kids or incest or strangers phone-sexing each other. They might each find their guilty relative alone, call him a pig, tell him he has to pay that bill, and yet never talk about it with each other. Both Mrs. Clementi and Vince could have pulled the same magazine out from under Tony's mattress or something. They might just...put it back or throw it out. Never say anything...to him, or to each other. In some cases it's like the whole family 'knows' but they don't even know how much the others know. Sometimes the brother doesn't even know how much he *himself* knows. There's convenient recollection, and then there's convenient forgetfulness," he rambled on. "It's called repression."

I shuddered. I would say I believed Lani about all this stuff. We'd touched on some of this in my psych class, and I believed it, then. It just becomes harder to accept when you're putting familiar names and faces with behavior that is so... screwed up. It makes you wonder. *Who could trust their own minds?*

"Who knows what went on in the Clementi house, but I'm sure that Vince went home ready to kill Tony," he said. "Probably gave him hell: How did your blankety-blank magazine get in my blankety-blank jacket? Tony knew he had left it on *my* porch, with more than his fingerprints on it. He probably wondered for about five seconds where I got the nerve to send it back. Then Vince spilled it that you and I showed up at the bus station together, all buddy-buddy. Now Tony's scared. He's sure that you know about him. He's probably even wondering if you were there when he was calling."

I hadn't had the time and didn't have the brainpower to

get scared. We were sitting there feeling safe, trying to figure out a psychology puzzle together. "I can't help but think that Macy won't eventually spill what I told her about Tony calling you. I told her at my house I had heard the whole thing. She said she wouldn't tell that part. She said no one would believe her. But she has trouble holding on to any secret. I guess the big question is..." I puzzled for only a couple of seconds. "What would somebody like Tony do to protect his reputation as a straight, tough guy? How far would he go?"

We both sat there in silence, and to ward off thoughts of the worst, I filled the air with words. "I don't care what he threatens to do. I'm telling the truth. I'll tell it to his face, and I don't care who hears it."

"I think we've told enough of the truth, Claire. Between me busting on Vince at the bus station, your little tirade today at Macy that Ellen told me about...and then, there's what I added to it while you were sleeping."

"What did you do? Did you leave the house?"

He shook his head and held up the phone to me. I saw CLEMENTI, JOSEPHINE again. "What date is on this one?"

"Today...," I said. "About an hour ago."

He tossed the phone down between us. "He threatened my life."

"He threatened your life..." My first reaction was to half shrug. Despite everything I knew about Tony being a bully, I went with the my-version-of-reality routine, which was that things like that only happen in Wyoming.

"I had done something else the night we left for Philly. I had removed the inside spreads of that magazine. The thing is old and tattered enough—I figured he knew it by heart. I thought maybe if that magazine somehow managed to circle back to Tony, he would realize some part of it was still out there. And he might think of his fingerprints, or anything else, being on it. He might get scared. If he was stupid, he might just decide I liked pornography. But if he was really, really sharp, it might occur to him why I had it, that it could be used against him somehow...taken to the cops...something, anything."

"God, you're too smart, Lani. You're too streetwise." I breathed, in shock.

"Maybe *too* is the key word. Maybe I'm too smart."

"That's what he wanted? When he called?"

"The way he put it was, 'What are you holding on to that I should have? What're you hiding in your bedroom?'"

"Jesus," I breathed. I flopped over on my back, my mouth dangling open as I stared at the ceiling. "Oh the webs we weave when..."

The rest of the line got lost in the huge, confusing plot in my head.

"Oh the webs we weave when we deal in the deceit," he finished.

"Shakespeare," I said.

"Yeah. *Julius Caesar.*"

We lay there staring, me trying to get up nerve to hear more information. "You, of course, were way too blunt when he called you, and now wish you'd kept your mouth closed," I guessed.

"I don't know what I wish. I know the truth sure feels good on the way out. I told him I had it. I told him to lay off me or I would give it to the cops—to my uncle's squad in New York, the squad I threatened Vince with. That's when Tony threatened me back. Lots of guys are blowhards. This guy I believe."

I thought of how easily Tony put Phil's lungs in jeopardy the other night over a stupid round of chicken, how he loved danger, how many drugs he had done, how his brain might have been damaged by child abuse. Still, there was this feeling of safety. All my experiences told me that people don't come barging into a house. I used that feeling to take the time to make sense out of all the bullshit.

"Lani, this has nothing to do with you and sex, or you and...a sexual preference," I stammered. "It has half to do with somebody who tried to molest *you. Tony.* And then there's Macy, who I'm fighting with. She probably decided you stole her best friend. And beyond the stupid smoke rings, she keeps imagining stuff about you to justify how that could be possible."

"Erdman calls that 'monsterizing.' It's when you erroneously make someone out to be a monster to justify your own behavior toward that person. He said spouses do that a lot to their mates, when they're trying to justify leaving or having an affair."

I listened to the sound of my breath blending with the echo of surf through the open window. I realized the wind had changed. The windows were still open, but the Indian summer warmth had turned, during my sleep, into the usual November chill.

The air was coming in cold, giving me goose bumps, filling my head with strange thoughts. "It's funny. Tony knows exactly what's going on. He knows what he is. But Macy's seeing and hearing shit. She's clueless, yet her mouth is so big."

He didn't say anything.

"Hey, Lani?"

"Hm."

"Who's scarier? Tony or Macy?"

After a moment he said, "She'll eventually screw up a lot of people, and neither they nor she will ever know. Right now we should think short-term. Tony wants that magazine spread back. We ought to prepare ourselves for whatever he might do."

"Do you think he's watching the house?" I felt the skin on my arms tighten even more, and my ears grew, like, ten sizes.

"Yeah, probably."

My eyes drifted around, and I wondered if the lit candles would show as light in this room from the outside of the house. I noticed how silent everything was. I realized I had not heard his mother all night.

I froze. "Lani? Where's your mom? Don't tell me we're alone here."

26

"The VFW? You let your mom waltz out of here to go to bingo night?" My basic fear instinct squashed my frustration down into a whisper.

"She was already gone when he called."

"Can you page her? She would at least drive you off the island to somewhere safe if you told her you were in trouble. You could stay with Ellen for a while—"

"My mom's sick of all this, Claire. That's why I ran away before, and you saw her reaction the other day. She thinks I bring this on myself. She'll give me another few choruses of how I should join a gym and take steroids, something."

He flopped back on the mattress, staring at the ceiling. He brought his hands in front of his eyes and turned them over and over, studying them. I sensed that any effort to make him feel better would go over as badly as it had the other night. In the silence the floor creaked downstairs. I couldn't help tiptoeing to the door and peering down.

His mother had left one light on in the living room that threw a small orange spotlight at the foot of the stairs. The dark gray air around it emptied into black. I listened, but only the constant whirring of a ceiling fan broke the silence. His mother had obviously forgotten to turn the fan off, despite the heat wave having suddenly turned to typical November frost. It forced a little wave of icy air that danced around my neck.

"Just the wind kicking up," I murmured, turning. He had folded his hands across his chest, and I could see his knuckles turning white. I just let him alone, hoping his mind was hatching some scheme. No question, he could hatch something when he needed to. I felt disappointed when his sigh came out quaking.

I could feel my eyes filling up. "This is all my fault."

Despite him sniffing, too, a laugh came out first. "How do you figure?"

"I should have been friends with more...dweebs." I flopped down on the mattress and tried to smile, though it wasn't working. "My friends, they're just too cool. They wouldn't know how to *help* in this case."

"Life is so ironic, isn't it?" he asked.

It's a word I hadn't used before, except maybe in a school paper to butt smooch some teacher, but I decided I would never forget it. I started repeating it.

"Ironic...ironic...irony...Life is one big *irony*...I'm turning into a dweeb. Isn't it *ironic*? Only a dweeb uses a word like *irony*..."

Someone needed to get control of this situation and be rational. Unfortunately, Lani seemed to be feeding off my mood. He stood up and peeled off his shirt, leaving his bony arms and shoulders to glow in the candlelight. He didn't seem to notice the cold as he picked up the nightgowns, dropping the first two over his head.

"Lani..." I started to tell him to not go off the deep end with me and to focus on an escape plan. But something inside me wanted to see this infamous costume. Something hollered that I might never get the chance again.

He pulled his arms into the piece that had the sleeves cut out and walked over, standing in front of his dresser mirror.

He was dangerously close to the window, and I stole over behind him, staring out at the silent street before closing it and pulling the curtains shut. I backed away toward the bed as he just stood blinking until he pointed a long, straight finger at his own reflection. His chin jutted straight out, and his posture was perfect, like the face of a clock striking a quarter to six.

My stomach twisted like I had swallowed live bugs. I got the feeling he had practiced that pose lots of times before. The walls threw off kaleidoscopes from the little rhinestones sewn into the top, paisley piece. The effect of him, the reflection, and the dancing walls took up the whole room. I could not call the overall effect girly. There was a wild strength to it, like combat in the heavens from a sci-fi story or myth.

To call this sight feminine would be like calling a girl a cat. It went bigger than humanness, bigger and stronger.

Out of my mouth spilled a whisper. "Holy shit..."

His own voice jolted me. Compared to sight, the sound was too pathetic. "What...is *that*?" he asked, staring into the reflection of his straight finger. "What *is* that? Is that a... guy? Is that a...girl? Is that a...it?"

"You pick great times to question yourself!" I moved up behind him slowly, staring over his shoulder at the reflection of his eyes in the mirror. They were so black, so wide, I could not read them. Suddenly I wasn't so sure he had been questioning himself. I could not see where he was looking. I thought maybe he was only quizzing me.

I answered, "You look like Michael."

"Michael?" His voice trembled, louder than my whispers.

"Michael. The archangel."

I had never even seen a painting of Michael the archangel. But I knew that is what a powerful and yet innocent angel would look like. Lani dropped his finger, and the two of us stood there, watching. He edged closer to the mirror, his eyes black, wide like a shark's, unreadable.

He got louder. "Is that the truth? Is that what I look like? Or is that just what you want to believe about me?"

I felt like he had been my friend since the foundation of the universe. Yet I realized the truth—I had only been with him a few times. And I could just be seeing a new, weaker side of him. *A side that didn't show so much confidence. A side that would allow him to crumble and not outsmart tough guys.* I didn't want to believe that. And I didn't want to risk hearing him say it.

"You look so strong right now. You look...beyond human, bigger than human."

I wouldn't say his response was great news. But it didn't completely shatter my hope about what he was. "What if I told you that floating angels can improve lives but they can't fight? They can't protect people from tough guys? Would I stop looking like an angel to you? If it weren't a convenient thought right now?"

The little rhinestones danced across the walls, and I sensed a strength in his rising anger that pumped up my hope, though I had no clue what layer of him I was seeing. My head shook slowly.

"Is the mirror smoking?" he quaked out.

"No," I whispered immediately. "I believe it. I really feel you are...supernaturally smart and good. So, therefore, it's true."

I could feel a new wave of energy wafting off him and hoped I was adding to his strength. So I jumped half a foot when his voice came out louder, more angry than before.

"Don't you give me that postmodern bullshit. There *is* truth. There is *a* truth. And what you want, or you feel, or you need, isn't going to change *the* truth. Any more than it's going to topple a skyscraper. There's truth, and there's belief. Don't call a mule a stallion."

"What are you saying?" I shook my head, trying to remove any "smoke" from my vision. He babbled on about fanatics totally believing they were martyrs, and martyrdom being convenient if you hate life, and convenience being irrelevant to truth. I could barely follow.

And I couldn't resist thinking on what he'd said once—floating angels do not admit to being what they are. I just couldn't jam this sight into the concept of "just a kid," not while his posture was consuming the room, eating my air. It had nothing to do with being able to magically fight off Tony. And since Lani was being so blunt, I responded to him the same way.

"I don't think my saying you're an angel is very convenient. I think it would be most convenient if you were a normal-looking guy who didn't bring this sort of shit down on us..."

He passed in front of the window, backed into the corner, and shrunk there, folding his forehead into his knees. "Touché."

"Lani...what are you doing?" I was scared he was crying.

"I'm thinking."

I couldn't tell whether he was crying or not. The wind whipped up, rattling the window. *Storm out at sea...cold, ice storm coming.* I stepped back, reaching for my jacket on the bed, then pulling it over my bazillion goose bumps.

He still had not moved. The shimmering on the walls had sucked down into him when he backed out of the candle glow, and he looked like a small child, cowering in a corner, retreating from the world.

Claire, forget about magic. This isn't the time or the place. "Would you mind, uhm, not thinking of any more philosophy right now, Lani? We need a plan to get out of here without either of us getting our heads taken off by Tony Clementi."

He didn't move, didn't answer. I jumped as a rumbling echoed up from the floor downstairs. Something cracked and broke, maybe a china figure left on a windowsill, and I commanded my imagination not to run wild. *Stupid decorating mistake made by all newcomers to this windy island...* Yet I moved to the bedroom door and stared down again. Stronger gusts of cold air blew up the stairs, yet all was silent.

I put my hand on the doorknob. Across the little hall, in the blackness of his mother's room, the silhouette of curtains danced. She'd left that window open, too, and in front of it sat some little table thing, and I could see the outline of picture frames. They would fall and the glass would break if I didn't close the window. But the air was breathing, whirling, and my willies backed up on me. I slammed the bedroom door. It was a cheap summerhouse door, no lock. Not that a lock would have kept Tony Clementi out if he wanted to come in. Just if there had been one, I would have locked it.

I picked up the phone. *Sydney.* We could trust her. I punched in the café number, praying she was working on the books or something. Lani's little clock glowed 9:11, and the café closed at six on Sunday.

Answering machine. I whispered a curse. I hit END twice and punched in 4-1-1. "Lani, snap out of it. Get dressed while you're scheming."

I asked for the home number of Sydney Shea.

"...at the customer's request this number is not listed."

I hit END again, cursing more. Lani still had not moved. "Lani! I hope your brain is in on mode! We need a respectable grown-up who would be willing to drive us off the island—"

"Claire? If those guys catch us, and this time Tony is with them...what is the most likely thing they would do to me?"

I shut my eyes, not wanting to go there. "Beat you up or pretend they're going to drown you." That was the closest I could bring myself to any graphic details. "Why waste time thinking of that?"

"Well, I can't win a fight."

No shit, Sherlock. To my amazement, he flopped on the mattress facedown. I could hear him sniffing.

"Lani, for god's sake. You did great the other night with Vince. Think of something cool like that! And get out of that damn costume." His outfit was making me way nervous, as if my gut was beginning to accept what my brain refused to believe—we could get ambushed while innocently sitting inside a house. When he didn't respond, I spoke louder. "Get up! Put your normal shirt back on—"

"Oh, stifle it, Claire! Do you really think I care what a bunch of school babies think of my stupid school-play costume? Let me think!"

That kept me quiet for half a minute, though I still thought the costume weighed into things more than he did.

I finally said more softly, "Whatever they would do, it would have a lot to do with you. Anything you showed fear over, it would egg them on. Whatever you're wearing that looks stupid or foolish, it would egg them on."

His eyes flitted around the room with a combination of desperation and sadness that really scared me. "You're starting to sound like *me*," he said, like that was oh-so-interesting an observation. It did seem like we were having some role reversal here, and as much as I didn't like it, I flew back into more of the thinking pattern that he simply was not reaching for.

"Okay, we have to take a huge, huge risk." I dialed my mom's number.

"Who's this?" Her voice sounded suspicious, like she didn't recognize the number from caller ID.

"It's me, Mom."

She let out a moan of relief. Then, "So, when'd you decide you love your fath'r more th'n me?"

I dropped the receiver, slapping my forehead in pain and frustration. "She's ripped," I muttered to Lani. *Fat chance she'll risk a DWI.* At this point the sight of Lani was making me more angry than anything else. "Would you please get the fuck dressed?"

"What*ever*." He stood up, annoyed.

"Mom, listen to me. This is *really*, really serious. If you don't want me to get myself half killed, get your car keys, get in the car, and drive to where I'm going to tell you."

"Claire, is that li'l bastard holding you captive?"

It took me a minute to realize she meant Lani and not Tony. "Mom, please! Get a reality check! Tony Clementi is threatening us. You know Tony Clementi?"

She'd known him since he was born. "S'maybe you deserve to be threatened."

"Mom! He's not just threatening to pull my hair! It's a long story! Please come and get me—"

"You're in deep trouble with y'r friends, Claire." She ignored me. "Macy thinks you've gone crazy. I know about all those people you've been hitting...and shoving. Eli's mom called here. Said Jule said you're even shoving eighth graders!"

I had only seconds to exchange glances with Lani and feel the deep pain of betrayal by a parent. He was used to it. It felt like battery acid had been thrown at my chest. I didn't have time to argue with her. Out of nowhere, footsteps clomped on the stairs. It sounded like work boots. My jaw dropped as my eyes flew to Lani. He had only gotten one piece of the outfit off. *Tony...Been in the house for some time? Listening?*

"Mom! He's coming! Mom, call the cops, please!"

The door opened with dramatic slowness, and Tony stood in the doorway. My legs collapsed, landing me on the mattress, looking straight up at him as he took the phone out of my hand.

"It's Tony. Hey, found your kid. I'll bring her home, how's that?...Mrs. McKenzie, I don't know what she's blabbering about. I would never hurt your kid. What do you take me for? Just you sit tight. I'll bring her home....No, she's just hanging out with...uh..."

He turned his gaze to Lani, who had shot up after my knees gave way. Lani's face was covered in shadows, but he backed up two steps toward the mirror, and again, the image, the reflection, the dazzling walls, his ramrod-stiff posture made him look ironically powerful again. I clamped my eyes shut, dropping my forehead into my palm, praying Tony might get scared, might see Lani like I had, if only for a minute.

"She's just hanging out with...uh...," he repeated, and there was a long enough silence that I just knew he was sufficiently freaked. I actually started to smile.

Then a laugh peeled out. "Mrs. Mac? She's hanging out with a guy, who right now as I'm standing here is dressed up in some sort of drag...Before the God I believe in...I swear... No. Don't call the police. Scott, Phil, and my brother are here, too. We will take care of this for you...You're welcome."

"Mom!" I screamed at the phone. "Don't be such a drunk! Call the cops! It's a stupid costume from a play at—"

My throat closed in some whacked-out guilt. It was the loudest, most blatant thing I'd ever said to my mom about her drinking. For a second I was glad Tony covered up my voice with loud coughing. Then I got mad. I tried to grab the phone from him. I wanted to say it over and over at her. But he had clicked the phone off and pushed me back down on the bed so hard my neck snapped.

He didn't seem too interested in the fact that Lani had kicked his backpacks into the closet and kicked the door shut with his foot. I figured maybe Lani's nine-hundred-dollar book was in one. He didn't want it to get stolen before he could sell it for runaway money. Tony was too overcome by the outfit. He stared at Lani's costume, not seeming to notice what Lani's feet were doing.

Tony finally said, "Hot outfit, darlin'. I think maybe you need to show it to the neighbors."

Lani backed into the corner beside the dresser. I could not see his face in the shadows. And I really needed to see it. I really needed to know he had thought of some way to stump Tony and that I wasn't meeting his weak side for the first time. I had no clue what Lani would do—or could do, how strong or how stupid he could be.

27

The last thing I expected Lani to do was fall on the ground and start to cry right in front of Tony. It snapped my neck back and made me suspicious he was playing some kind of brilliant game. But when he lifted his face up, real tears were spilling down. *He's not that good an actor. Nobody's that good.*

Tony went and stood over him, cat over a mouse. He had his legs kind of spread in this arrogant way that made me look around for something to hit him with. Unfortunately, the room was pretty cleared out, save some pillows and lit candles.

"Your mom told me to come here, dough boy. I just seen her." He laughed, like this was the funniest thing in the world. "She's trying really hard to make friends around here. Went to play bingo with all the locals. I watched her go down there. My mom's there, too. Your mom looked so sad, trying not to cry on your aunt's shoulders. I figured she needed a friend. One minute she tells me she's scared you're going to run away again. Next minute she says she's scared you're going to stay and ruin her life."

I flinched at the harshness of the remark, sensing the reality in it. Lani lifted his head about six inches off the floor and put it down again, not saying anything. I caught a flash of the wet shine on his cheeks, which seemed so out of character with his usual guts. Yet I had to admit . . . when even parents betray you, what happens to hope? My mom had just done it, and it cuts through you like a knife.

Tony was chattering on like we were a couple of his fishing buddies. "I told her I would talk to you, you know, as one of the nice local Joes. I told her maybe I could talk you into not running away. Maybe getting a haircut. I don't know." He hooted, finally, slapping his thigh. "I think maybe I could talk you into getting a haircut. With a little help from my friends. But I don't think I could talk you into staying here, when there's a chance you could, you know... *disappear* forever and ever."

An electric jolt almost threw me backwards as I took his meaning. Lani was mewling like a kitten. It took everything I had not to scream, "Shut *up*!" He was just egging Tony on. *This is not an orchestrated suicide. It's not.*

I reached shakily for the phone Tony had dropped on the mattress, moving it under my leg, wondering how loud it would be if I hit 9-1-1. He had his back to me and toed Lani with his work boot, and Lani tried to crawl away from him, tripping over the nightgowns like an imbecile.

"Yeah, we kind of like each other around here. We all... fit in. You know?"

"What are you going to do?" Lani still sounded like a kitten.

"Will you shut *up*," I blasted at Lani in astonishment. Tony was feeding off his fear maniacally.

"Why, I don't know what we're going to do to you! Maybe you can help us decide! Hey, maybe we can give you a choice. We can beat you within an inch of your life. We can give you a very, very close shave. All over your head! Claire can tell you about how a head wound bleeds. Or! We can throw you in a fishing net until we hear you cry 'uncle' from underwater! Did you know that Indian summer makes the air warm but that the water just keeps getting colder? It's about forty-five degrees right now. Wouldn't that be toasty?"

"But..." Lani hiccuped. I gripped the hell out of that phone, still hoping against hope he would heave up a last-minute strategy. But he opened his mouth and sealed his own fate. "But...I can hardly swim."

"Oh! You can't swim!" Tony bellowed in fake shock. "Maybe we can teach you!"

Beep...beep...beep...

I never realized how loud a phone dialed. It echoed off the walls, pointlessly. Tony spun.

"Help us!" I screamed, holding the phone out of his reach as he struggled for it. He ripped it from my grip, and I wasn't sure if the 9-1-1 call went through.

He backed away, talking as he hit DELETE, DELETE, DELETE from the caller ID. "Where's the rest of the magazine?"

Lani's eyes shot all over the room. "If I give it to you... Promise you will not throw me in any water."

Tony shrugged. "Okay. Promise."

I kicked at Lani's jeans as he lifted the outfit and reached into his jeans pocket. I accidentally kicked him hard enough to make him yelp. But if he got any stupider, we'd both wind up dead. "Will you just shut up!"

"I don't care. I don't care anymore," he cried.

"Well, if you don't care about you, could you please care about me!" I bellowed, then realized we were just tickling Tony's funny bone by arguing. He was laughing so hysterically, my anger buttons went off. I balled up my fist and came through from the side with all my strength. Despite that I knocked him pretty good in the skull, he barely staggered, grabbing hold of my throbbing knuckles and turning them to sludge.

Stupider than Lani, I just started spewing out the truth. "You know what, Clementi? There isn't even a word for someone like you. What do you call a closet gay who gay bashes? You are such a slimy concept that people don't even have a name for it!"

Before I knew what happened, I was slammed up against the wall, pinned there, choking on his tongue. I couldn't move, couldn't breathe.

I finally heaved a huge gulp of air as he breathed in my face. "I wanna hear again what you just called me. Maybe my hearing ain't right."

I just stared at him in terrified awe. I could not believe he would still deny it. He stared back at me, though I could hear Lani behind him, fussing with papers or something.

"Here! Just take it. Take it and get out and leave me alone. Just leave us alone!"

He hurled the folded pages of the magazine at Tony, but being paper, they just flitted to the floor. It looked pathetic.

Fortunately, it was a distraction, and Tony backed off from me to swoop them up. I heaved a sigh of relief, despite Lani still on his stupid spree.

"You promised. I gave it to you, so you can't throw me in the water."

Okay. He's on his own if he's that dumb.

I waited until Tony had held the pages over a candle flame and started giving Lani a lecture on how you hold your breath underwater when you're freezing. I turned and hurled myself into the hallway, jumping down the stairs six at a time. To my amazement Tony did not chase after me. I yanked open the front door and stopped.

"Scott, Phil, and my brother are here, too." Tony'd said it to my mom.

He was laughing crazily upstairs, Lani was mewling again, and I wanted nothing more than to get away from the sounds of both of them. All seemed quiet out front, but I fumbled to the back door just in case the guys were hiding. I threw myself into the night air.

I raced for the curb, trying to gauge how long it would take me to run to the police station. *Five blocks...two min-*

utes...The sky came up to meet me as I was hurled to the grass. A pile of bricks fell on me, which had the head of Phil Krilley.

"Came out the back!" he shouted.

Footsteps pounded closer. I had hoped Tony had lied to Mom. *He would have to come alone to destroy evidence.* The idea that he could dupe three huge guys to staying in the back of his truck while he went in the house...I had not conceived of that.

Phil still had too much trust. He jumped off me too quickly, and I bolted. But it was like square-dancing with three gorillas. I blindly threw punches, all my newly found anger whaling at them. One at a time I was stunning them, dodging through them. They made it a group effort. I ended up on the bottom of a football pile that somehow was not on the ground but in the back of Tony's truck, parked on the dark side street.

"Claire, we're gonna take you to the goddamn nuthouse!" It was Scott's voice. "Just calm down! Next person you hit, you're gonna get hit back!"

I couldn't tell who was on top of who. Scott sounded kind of high up. I felt one of them grab the back of my hair, tight, and Scott said, "Okay, get off her."

They started getting off, and all I needed was the sight of Vince Clementi's face in the street lamp. I could see a shiner from where I'd gotten him the other night, and I swung for it so hard, he fell over the side, roaring curses.

I was on my feet. Scott still had my hair. "Don't touch her, Vince! I don't trust you...You'd kill her or something."

Scott jerked my neck around until I was looking at him, instead. He landed a really hard slap on my face. I saw stars but went nuts again. I was swinging blindly at Scott, and he kept slapping me until I couldn't open one eye and I felt blood running down my lip. They still didn't know about this deal

Tony had cut with my mom about bringing me home and not hurting me. They ruined everything. I wanted to be delivered home with a couple of black eyes.

I was on the flatbed again, and Scott was sitting on top of me, winning this thing, but not without a fight.

"Tony! Bring him out! Let's go!" I heard Phil's voice shouting up at the window.

I spoke between gulps for air. "Scott, you know what Tony's doing up there?"

"He's bringing Princess Garver out here, so we can—"

"No, no. Uh-uh." I breathed more. "Did he tell you he didn't want you to come in with him?"

"Yeah."

"Now, why do you think that is?"

Scott's lip had curled, like he didn't trust me at all. Like I was nuts. "He wants to bring him out himself! Since the little prick came on to Tony, why shouldn't he?"

"That's not what happened! He's up there deleting his own phone-sex calls off caller ID! He's up there burning a gay porn mag that he came all over—"

"Aaaaahhhh!" The loud noise from Vince drowned me out, and he reached over the side of the flatbed for a handful of my hair. I screamed. Despite Scott hollering for him to lay off me, Vince slammed my head down onto the flatbed once, twice, and I shut my eyes as a pain in my neck turned to fire. I started seeing double, and then I saw nothing.

28

My vision floated out of black and blue haze in the freezing air. I sensed exactly where I was. I had a strong notion that I'd already come around a few times since Lani's house. I was curled up on something soft, which I already knew was a huge tangle of used, nylon fishing line that fishermen saved to repair torn nets. I was rocking gently. *Dern's Dream* was too massive to be swayed by these guys lurching around in silhouette about ten feet away from me. And from the frosty wind hitting my face, I realized the surf was rough enough to kick up this much sway.

I knew I had been brought here in the back of Tony's truck. I had come around once in the truck, and the guys had been all over Lani, who was still so ape shit that I decided I had to be dreaming. But the weather change sent cold air whipping down on my knuckles, biting my neck around my jacket, until there was nothing to do but admit this was real. I remember almost *deciding* to pass out again to escape the embarrassing, helpless sounds. The bounces as Tony gunned it helped me along with that decision.

I had come to again as the truck stopped, and found enough sense to shut my eyes.

"She's awake. She's faking it," Phil had said, and they stood there arguing about whether to leave me in the flatbed or not.

I had tried to be dead weight as one of them picked me up, though other voices were arguing that I wasn't faking it and I couldn't run. The punch I threw landed on wind, doing little more than reminding me to keep my fingers moving to avoid frostbite. They hung like weak Jell-O blobs. I thought, *Screw the whole thing,* and I passed out again.

I'd been coming in and out for a few minutes on the deck of the boat, but this time the wind seemed to wake me up more than put me back out. Hot jabs shot through my head and neck, despite the fact that I was freezing, and the sounds of laughter made me too queasy to pass out again. I finally remembered why I had decided to pass out the last time.

They had tossed Lani into Mr. Dern's huge fishing net and started to crank its huge arm out over the water, threatening to lower him under. I had thought of running, but as soon as I raised my head, the world spun on its side.

Message to God: Do something.

Despite the few splashes I could hear through the hooting and laughter, I figured maybe God had listened. They had not completely dunked Lani. I could still hear his pitiful screaming while the splashes echoed. I wanted to scream at him again to shut the hell up because obviously it was only egging them on.

The net hung over the water. Lani was curled into a little white ball, the whiteness of the costume glowing. Water dripped like a faucet, but I couldn't see if they had submerged him to his butt or to his arms. His hair blew in the raging wind, still dry.

As if right on cue from my message to God, Phil laughed and said, "That's enough. Miss Garver's had enough."

Scott agreed. "Yeah. Get him the fuck off my boat."

Vince continued to push him in the net like it was a kiddie swing. And Tony, standing back by the crank, gave it a good spin, and I heard another of those small splashes. Lani carried on like a dying cat, so I knew they hadn't dipped low enough to send his head under.

I started looking around for something to hit Tony with. It was a long shot, but if I could knock him out, Vince would try to help him, and Scott and Phil probably wouldn't do anything to Lani and me without the crazies egging them on.

The only thing I could see was a small fisherman's hatchet, lying about five feet from me. Silently I reached for it, my throbbing head realizing how crazy the odds were.

I didn't have time to get my fingers around the handle. I watched as Tony took an extra hard swing on that crank, and the net flew downward. A loud splash was followed only by whipping wind. Tony laughed hysterically, and Lani was silent... *Gone under... gonna get tangled... shock freeze.*

I jumped to my feet and staggered to the edge of the boat, screaming something in a begging voice that even I couldn't understand. The water was white with little bubbles and whitecaps. I dived for Tony and the crank, but he shoved me to the side like a rag doll, and I continued to plead with him in a voice that made me finally understand why Lani had pleaded the way he had. I never felt so completely at someone else's mercy. You've got nothing to do but grovel.

It was Phil who shoved Tony aside and grabbed for the crank. He spun it around and around saying, "Tony, let him go now. This could get too fucked up—"

The net came up, and Lani was still curled in this tight little ball, but he wasn't moving, wasn't screaming anymore.

I heard Scott say, "Bring him in! He looks dead."

Vince laughed. "He's faking it! Dead people don't shake like a leaf. Let him enjoy the breeze for a couple minutes."

"We'll make him beg!" Tony decided, getting a firmer grip on the crank. "Yo, Miss Garver! Repeat after me: Tony Clementi, you hold my life in your hands. And I would lick your boots if I was good enough."

In spite of the darkness, I could see Lani's eyes open wide. His pupils were so dark that the whites of his eyes lit neon. I actually felt relieved. *They are going to let him go... Maybe he won't get beaten up... Maybe this is it...*

He had begged for mercy well enough after Tony showed up. I braced myself to hear just the right amount of the same. When he opened his mouth, I decided monsters ruled the deep. He was some schizo. Multiple personalities. He chose this outstanding moment to return to his former blunt self.

Despite him trembling with cold almost to the point of convulsing, we could hear him real plain. "You are a closet-reading, homo-porn fanatic, scum wad, hypocrite... who dials nine-hundred numbers to get off on pretty boys. Your mother knows. Your brother knows. I will haunt you until you'll wish you were never born, if you don't—"

Tony plunged the net under. "Die, you motherfucker—"

"Are you nuts?" I screamed at the surface of the water, even though that made no sense. "What the hell is wrong with you tonight?"

Orchestrated suicide? I choked out a sob. The sobbing sounded helpless, too helpless. So my ape-shit buttons went to red again. My heel kicked the hatchet, and after watching it spin on its side, my eyes moved to Tony.

"Die, die, die!" He laughed like a crazed nine-year-old.

"Yo, pull him up!" Phil moved toward him. "Don't be messing with that bitch no more. I ain't going to jail over him—"

Scott pushed Tony toward me, and he and Phil cranked the net up. Vince watched them with his back to us. Tony cast me an unconcerned glance, like I was some discarded life jacket. I swooped for the hatchet, remembering how Vince looked at me the same way the other night. That's what sent me over the edge, people looking at me and seeing some naive wimp.

It would be the very last of my ape-shit attacks. The memory still scares the hell out of me. I decided, all in a flash, that I could commit murder, go to jail, and feel it was worth it. No decision made in a flash of ape shit is good. When I reached for that hatchet, I was looking for a way to kill Tony so I could feel great for the rest of my life.

I raised it over my head as the net broke the surface, and Tony at least had the sense to raise up a hand to ward off the blow. The hatchet came down somewhere between his first and fourth fingers. I felt flesh and cartilage and bone send tremors up the hatchet, then it clattered onto the deck. Tony let out a yell like I'd ripped his legs off. He grabbed the hand in the other, but not before I could see a black line almost to the center of his palm. Black juice sprayed from between his fingers as he fell to his knees.

I could have sworn somewhere in the background a voice was droning, "Don't, Claire."

It sent a shock of horror through me, something without words, though if words had been available, they would have been something like *Live by the sword, die by the sword.* Tony was off his knees, and the other three were moving toward me, calling me curses I had never heard of.

I realized I was in as much trouble as Lani.

29

Vince and Phil managed to stuff me in the net before I came out of shock freeze, but they didn't just plunge us under. They twirled and twisted that net like they had for Phil the other night. The only thought I could grab on to was an instinctive one—to curl up tight into a little ball like Lani was, to keep from getting too tangled in the net. But hair, fingers, sneaker tips, any little thing seemed to snag and wrap it tighter around me.

We were two balls hurling through space, smashed up against each other so that I could feel his hypothermia shaking us around like a convulsion. When I finally opened my eyes, I was a little ball looking down. Immediately below me were Lani's wide eyes. Far below was the water. They left us dangling over the water while the four of them argued below.

Tony kept screeching. "She cut off my hand...She cut off my hand..."

"She did not, and if you don't quit that baby fuckin' crying, I'm gonna cut off your head!" Vince's voice...Scott and Phil groaning in disgust...Vince's voice again. "You need a bunch of stitches, that's all. *Bunch* of stitches. Claire, you nutcase! You hurt my brother. Now we're gonna drown you—"

"You got blood all over my dad's boat!" Scott made frenzied stomping. "We are in deep shit! Get off, Tony! Go to the truck! This ends now! Get those morons out of my dad's net."

Tony backed up toward the dock and flopped one leg over the rail, trying to wrap his hand in his brother's T-shirt while holding it over the water. Vince stood with his bare back to us, too busy arguing with Phil and Scott to realize it was cold out here.

"I'll clean up the blood! I'm gonna drown that crazed bitch first—"

"Nobody's drowning!" Phil grabbed for the crank. "We got to clean up this mess, or they can prove something to the cops."

"There ain't gonna be any cops, because I'm gonna drown them!" Vince yelled.

"Nobody's dying off this boat!" Scott had a mop in his hand. He jabbed it down into the water off the side closest to us and ran it frantically across the deck. "We aren't some fucked-up Wyoming cowboys. And we aren't killing no girl."

And Vince was all "Your girlfriend fell in love with a queen!"

Scott moved right up to him, shoved the mop at his chest, and said under his breath, "Your brother *is* . . . a queen."

Despite where I was, I felt a smile forming. I suddenly didn't think we were in danger of drowning. They would pull us back in. It was fun to watch Vince break that mop in half over his knee and send the top part whizzing past Tony's whimpering head. I could feel Lani trembling ferociously and hoped he was together enough to have heard.

"They believe us . . . They believe us! You said they never would. They're just a bunch of overgrown brats," I tried explaining.

I figured he might disagree, being that he was busy slowly freezing to death while the brats finished arguing. His voice trembled so badly it sounded like a song with too much vibrato. "Never thought . . . they're totally . . . bad. Bad . . . would have . . . done a group hysteria thing . . . don't really want to kill us . . ."

I pulled my head back as far as I could, which was only about six inches from his face. Because I'd curled up in a ball, it was not hard to wiggle my fingers out of my cheerleading jacket, pull my arms in tighter and manage, in little jerks, to get the jacket over my head and shove it between us. It didn't seem to warm him much, though I wanted it to. I felt strange toward him, stunned by his charitable comment, and yet pissed at those parts of him I didn't know well at all, obviously.

"What the hell went wrong with you tonight? Acting like that in front of Tony? Why did you tell me you could always think on your feet? You're here, you know, because you might as well have begged him to drown you. Could you have lied and said you were a great swimmer?"

"No. *You're*...in this net...because you couldn't... find...middle ground—"

"Don't talk to me about what *I* did." I seethed through my teeth. "You wimped out...We looked like fools, you first, and then me. Don't lecture me! What the hell is wrong with you tonight?" I grumbled again.

He blinked at me, trembling so bad even his eyelashes shook. I thought he must be losing it, floating in and out of sanity...talking normally one minute, crazed philosophy the next. *Middle ground.* This was not the time. But it made me stare. Actually, it was too perfect a time...a perfect truth that I knew deep inside. It just shouldn't have been coming from a person in the throes of hypothermia who needed to answer the question: What the hell is wrong with *you*?

He forced himself to quit shaking for a moment when he answered. "*Noth*ing."

*Noth*ing was wrong with him....Crazy people always think they're sane. Speaking of crazies, I turned my eyes to the boat because Vince, Phil, and Scott had gotten enough of their act together to face us and deliver a speech. Tony was still whimpering off the port side.

"Do you know how ridiculous you two look?" Scott shouted. "Coupla goose eggs half upside-down. Listen up, assholes. I'm not putting no girl down under. Phil, neither. And Vince, neither. We're gonna let you go, under one condition. Nobody talks. Nobody finds out about what happened tonight. You talk, we come find you. And next time you won't be so lucky. You with me, Garver?"

"You, too, McKenzie. I'm gonna be watching you when you sleep!" Vince almost screeched. "You even *think* the wrong thing, I'm gonna drown your ass!"

I wanted to say so badly, "*Oh! Drown me like your drunk-ass father drowned!*" But my hatchet moment was still ripe.... *Middle ground.*

"Hurry up," I told them in an even voice, "before somebody dies of pneumonia."

Scott had a net pole, and he tried to drive it into the net and bring us back. His reach was short, and it slapped the water.

"Claire...are you a good swimmer?"

I glanced down at Lani, ignoring his question, all thinking, *Please, don't get morbid when we're so close to out of here.* He was looking sideways, at the deck. I followed his eyes. Tony had hauled himself onto the stern again and reached for the hatchet. He gripped it in his good hand and, with an insane screech, lay a swing into the rope that hooks the chain to the crank.

I half screamed and started answering Lani, though there was not enough time. "I've had lifesaving, but go limp, don't grab my neck!"

That's all I could share before the sea sprang up to meet us. A thousand icy teeth laid into me as the cold water swallowed us. Hitting the water made the net bounce into a little slack. Lani wrapped himself so tightly around me, I could not move my arms, could not move at all.

30

L ani became a hundred-pound snake squeezing the life out
of me in the icy blackness. The net started to unwind, loos-
ening us, but he would not ease up. I pushed off with my arms,
but he was like a rubber band. The surface light felt upside-
down as the net unraveled, then sideways, then right side up. I
kicked my legs to get away, but Lani's grip was superhuman.
He's killing us both... can't save myself, let alone him...

I also had to fight the urge to gasp or scream, the water
was so shocking. His legs were wrapped around, so I could
only kick one leg free. *Will never kick us both to the surface...* I braced myself for blacking out. My body relaxed
somewhat. Surprisingly, Lani seemed to be doing the same
thing. Without waiting to believe it, I slithered out of his loos-
ening grip and kicked. Lani's face swayed close to me one
last time. Through the murky black sea, the whites of his
eyes widened. Terrified. *Don't leave me... Don't leave me...*
My bursting lungs drove me straight up with hard kicks.

The net had become completely untangled and floated
loose. Its outline glowed in the surface spotlight, a thousand
fingers ready to choke me. I broke the surface, gulping in air
as the spotlight blinded me. The whites of his eyes still flashed
in my brain. *Terror... betrayal...*

Scott and Phil were screaming to me, but I dived under

again, eyeing what I could see of the net. The icy pins had stopped biting near the surface. I headed down for the trace of white, flailing in the lower shadows of darkness. Every instinct was telling me to get higher, away from the increasing cold, but I kicked until a flailing arm hit me in the face. I felt netting between us. *Tangled on the inside? Or had he managed to follow me up, then sink to the outside?* I charged back for the surface, for another breath.

I heaved cold air into my lungs, my eyes bulging. This time Phil's voice rang out. "Claire! We can't reel it in!"

"I'm trying to fix it!" Scott screamed.

Vince and Tony were having a loud argument that I paid no attention to. I dived again, searching through the black for the glow of white. This time it was still. A floating ghost. I kicked toward it as the instinct to break for the surface screamed. My fingers brushed the fabric, and I grabbed it and pulled.... *Still tangled.* I pulled harder, trying to stay clear of his limbs, just in case he might grab me again, but my lungs were bursting. I lurched for the surface, eyes shut tight, tears of defeat making my eyelids burst.

The icy air poured into my lungs. But a splash beside me threw me closer to the boat, and I realized one of the guys had gone down for him. Arms pulled me out of the water and into the night air. The arms gripped like giant snakes, and I screamed, coming into that wind. I squirmed in agony, but Scott was squeezing me in half. I saw a door and a huge boot kicking it in.

Scott's voice screamed louder than my own as the door gave way, banging open. "Gimme your clothes!"

"Stay away from me!"

"Do it! Phil went after him!"

In the distance I heard a truck engine starting. Scott started hurling dry clothes over my head and yelling, "Ahhhhhh!" just to keep from crying. Somehow I was in sweatpants and a sweatshirt. We stumbled out onto the deck, and Phil's screaming drew us quickly to the side. That desire to scream was overwhelming, yet I instinctively knew that something beyond the pain of the cold was making him scream.

He sputtered, "Thought I had him free, but it was only Claire's jacket! I seen him— He's outside the net! But he's all tangled! I seen that white thing, all tangled!"

Scott heaved the crank around a giant makeshift knot they must have completed too late. They would have been afraid to crank the net up once I'd said Lani might have been tangled outside. If they'd heaved it up, they might have dropped him, lost him in the strong current. At this point, they had no choice. Phil scrambled out of the way. The V-chain broke the surface, then the net. The eerie sight brought a scream out of my throat. A white nightgown hopelessly tangled in the netting, torn and inside out, hung by its lonesome...

31

I buried my face in my hands. *"But...I can't swim!"*...
*whites of his eyes...terror gaze...don't leave me down
here, Claire...*

Scott backed into me, and I ran screaming for the boat's
searchlight, moving it back and forth across the surface,
pleading with them to stop fighting and help me hunt.

But the Sophomore Show continued to wail around me.
Phil shouted up at Scott, accusing him of probably sending
the body to the bottom when he pulled up the net. Scott accused Phil of not being able to dive as deep as I had. Vince
and Tony were nowhere. As Phil dived again, Scott lost it totally. *"Oh my god... Tony fuckin' killed somebody..."*

I watched the surface of the water—front, back, and sideways—watching and praying. The wide terror in Lani's eyes
wouldn't stop replaying. *I should have been able to pull
harder, think faster...but he'd been so hopelessly tangled...*

Fishermen play chicken with each other, risk each other's
lives, but then risk their own lives to save a person they just
threw in. Strange breed. Phil Krilley dived six more times after
Scott hauled the net in, while I searched with the spotlight.
Once Phil stayed under so long, I thought he wasn't coming

up. Each time, I prayed he'd come up with an unconscious body. After the sixth time, he said, "I can't no more."

Scott threw dry clothes on Phil as quickly as he had on me, and I stumbled behind them as they ran for the truck. I thought we were running for Tony's car phone. The truck was gone. Vince stood staring at the entrance gates, pacing in zombielike circles, smoking a cigarette.

"Went to get himself fixed up," Vince said. His hands trembled almost uncontrollably. "He had to leave us. Had to. Or he would have bled to death."

Phil put a hand on his shoulder and shook him—not too hard—I couldn't tell whether it was affectionate or angry. "Vince, somebody just died. Do you understand that? Do you get what's going on here?"

"I don't understand nothing. I don't want to understand nothing. I just want...I think...I'm goin' home." He started to walk off toward the gates.

I let out some disgusted yelp, and what followed really drives home my meaning when I say fishermen are a strange breed. I got three steps into a run toward another boat when Scott grabbed my arm and slung me backward.

"Where are *you* going?"

"To call for help!"

"There *is* no help, Claire! Don't make this any worse than it is!"

I froze, stunned.

"He never broke the surface! Krilley dove for fifteen minutes! People drown in four, Claire! There is no help! Do you get that?" He shook me.

I hadn't had a chance to let any concepts sink in—alive, dead. I just knew when someone doesn't surface in the water, you call the coast guard.

"You can't just leave him." I tried to scream at him, but my words got drowned in some gluey stuff in my throat and my ears.

"He's done, Claire! It was an accident!" He shook me again. "You and Phil...you almost just lost your lives, diving for some goddamn flake in a nightgown! That's what he was, Claire! A whining, whimp-o, fucking weirdo. And nobody is going to jail over him!"

"His body is going to wash up." Phil was close to crying again.

I had turned to stone, which is the only reason I couldn't be ripped in half while trying to remember the definitions of right and wrong. If I had seen Lani do anything to try to save himself, I might not have been mad at him, too. I let go of so much to stand by him. In the end he shocked me—and only me. No one was surprised—except me. I had given up everything, and for what?

I felt betrayed. I felt terrible I couldn't save him. But I felt betrayed. I didn't want to think about living without him. But I felt betrayed.

Maybe Phil and Scott hadn't completely fallen for a group-hysteria murder. Yet they'd only come to their senses after it was too late. I felt betrayed by them, too—by everyone.

Stony, I caught bits and pieces of their argument, not quite believing what I was hearing....Something about the mysterious tides off Hackett...Phil blathered how two fishermen fell off the dock during a hurricane, and they never washed up. Yet a guy whose boat sunk a mile off the coast did wash up.

Scott said, "It's low tide. If he's gonna wash up, it'll be tonight. If not, then he ain't washing up. I'll come back at first light. I'll clean up the deck, fix the net right..."

I watched him in stunned awe. *His thinking always runs to covering up. Even now. Push it as far as you can, then cover up what goes wrong.*

I croaked out what I hoped would make them feel their guilt the most. "Do you realize...he was leaving tonight?" I thought of the two backpacks Lani had kicked into the closet, trying to hold on to his few possessions. *Like he would actually need them, now.* "How does that make you feel? If you'd just given him *fifteen more minutes* he would be gone. Never to bother you again—"

"He was leaving?" Phil grabbed me by the arm and jerked me up to him.

"He was running away!"

"Then, that's it. That's our story." He looked over the top of my head at something far off. "We'll say we heard he was planning to run away. Nobody would come down on us for keeping that one to ourselves. We don't say nothing beyond that. Even if he washes up...he ran away as far as we know... Where's that thing he was wearing?"

"Hurled it over the side," Scott muttered. "We didn't beat him...he wasn't bleeding. He was wearing jeans, right? Could look like a suicide—"

I screamed, "What the hell kind of perverts are you?"

Phil jerked me up to him hard. He clamped my arm in a death grip. "You are *so* lucky to be alive. Do you realize how lucky you are? Do you?"

He shook me and shook me. I finally caught his meaning, though his shakes and sputters sounded childish, and he was still crying. I didn't think he would be able to come through on some scheme to drown me next. *But he wasn't Tony.*

The walk home was something I can never quite remember, yet never quite forget. At one point I realized that just my head and feet were cold. I had only wool socks on my feet. Scott must have given me his football jacket, because I was wearing it. My wet clothes and Phil's wet clothes were stuffed inside a plastic garbage bag Scott was carrying. Unbelievable.

I also could not believe I was actually walking with them. I stayed focused on how weird that felt, because it was better than thinking of anything else—especially how they kept lecturing me and each other. According to Scott we would keep our mouths shut. Scott would stay up all night, make Vince drive him back at sunrise to see what had washed up, if anything. He would mop up the rest of Tony's blood, fix the rope where Tony had sliced through it, and no one would ever know. According to Phil I ought to feel damn lucky they didn't drown me along with Lani, just to keep me quiet.

They decided they would not turn on Vince Clementi's brother. They would handle him themselves, but no one would go to the cops. They figured they personally hadn't done anything so wrong, but Tony could go to jail over this— manslaughter, even attempted murder. He was already on probation for a drug bust.

Somewhere in my stunned brain I found a bit of accuracy they were missing. They could *all* go to jail if people were pissed enough. They deserved it. There was kidnapping and assault and harassment and a hate crime. I tried to think of snaking them out to the cops. But it was hard to think too deeply when I had their big shoulders and determined atti- tudes right in my face...when our cops had known their par- ents since forever, and Lani was a kid who "dressed up in nightgowns," and wouldn't Macy be happy to say so?

I didn't lose interest in the idea of snaking them out. I just didn't say squat. I ended up at Phil's, something about his par- ents were at the VFW. Scott turned a hair dryer on my head while my wet clothes went through their clothes dryer. I couldn't tell whether he was being extra nice because he was scared shitless I would snake to the cops, or because it was some strange part of the fish-frat honor code to put your vic- tims back together after you destroy them.

Vince had showed up, agreeing to drive Scott back to the wharf and help out. He said he couldn't find Tony. He lit cig- arette after cigarette off the butt of the one before. He kept commanding me to swear I would not talk. I found my middle ground this time—something between a lie of agreement and a blunt "fuck off." He seemed to take my many "Calm down, Vince" requests as a commitment to this cover-up. But every once in a while he would lose faith and threaten me with something else if I told. We went through rape, torture, fifteen ways of dying, including being dragged behind Tony's truck.

It was hard to feel like any of it was real. For one thing, it got more and more hard to hear. My eardrums felt like they'd been sliced with icy razors, all the way down to my spine. No matter how much Scott blew that hot hair dryer into them, they would not stop stinging. Just about all I could hear was my own breathing, which rattled worse and worse, as if all the salt I had swallowed was turning to glue in my windpipes. All their talking seemed like a play on some stage, and I was watching from my seat in the balcony.

As I walked back into my house, there was no thought yet of telling, just curling up in a ball and forgetting that life or death or my ears or throat existed. My mom was passed out in her TV chair. A glass filled only with melting ice sat beside her. A section of Tina's homecoming dress was in her lap, covering her like a blanket. It felt good to see something normal.

32

I realized my mother was calling my name for about the fourth time. She had stuck the phone right under my eyeballs.

"Claire! It's your father. I want you to talk to your father!"

I reached my arm out from under my bedsheet. *Wanted* me to talk to my father? *Okay. This is a dream.* But it hurt so bad to bring sounds out of my burning throat, I knew I was awake.

"Hello?"

"Your mom says you can't swallow and you wouldn't get out of bed to go to school. She says you haven't gotten out of bed all day."

"Day's it?" I asked, eyes rolling toward my radio alarm. *Three-seventeen.*

"It's Monday. Afternoon. Your mom says you've got a black eye, and she noticed a bunch of stitches in your forehead, and you won't say where they came from. I could only tell her that this weekend you had a little bandage on your forehead, and I assumed you were covering a zit. She called Macy, who said she hadn't seen you since yesterday afternoon, but that you're losing your mind and you need help."

In my fog I could only reason that Macy's words were accurate. I said, "Yeah."

"What happened?"

Something horrible...and if I stay awake I'll think of it. I started to say I was going back to sleep, but I started coughing up more salt and seaweed. Somehow the seaweed had been coming up white all day. I hocked another salt blob into a tissue my mother handed me. She was cursing and whining under her breath.

She had taken the phone again. "And if it *is* pneumonia, what the hell am I supposed to do?...I don't drive off the island, Chad. I don't do bridges...I mean exactly what I said! I don't do bridges!...Because! They make me feel like I'm going to faint!...Of course I love my child. But the bridge is icy...I just can't do it, Chad...Do you want me to kill her by driving off the bridge?"

"Gimme the goddamn phone." I stuck my razor-blade ear back to the receiver. I was on autopilot, didn't know what I was saying. "Dad, I need to leave here."

Silence. He and Suhar wouldn't want me back so soon....

He said, "Claire, you sound really sick. I think, all things considered, you should come up to Children's. I'll drive down and get you and take you to their emergency room. We'll call Dr. Haverford, just to let him know you're on your way. It's probably just a bad cold. But...we'll do the safe thing."

Thinks I'm relapsing. Maybe I am now. Maybe I don't care. From the corner of my eye, I could see Mom taking little shaky breaths. She betrayed me last night. And now she wouldn't split the driving with my father, even after watching me cough up a lung. *Last straw.*

"Dad, I told Mom I was in trouble last night. She wouldn't believe me. I almost died—"

"Oh, that's bullshit, Claire! Almost died!" She swung for the phone, but it was a weak swing. I held it to the side, then put it back to my ear again, coughing Elmer's glue.

"Yeah, I almost died. So guess what? I'm going to call

those DYFS people on Mom. I'm going to tell them to tote her off to rehab. She can quit drinking, or I'm not staying here."

I hazily recalled DYFS from school, because some kids threatened to call DYFS when their parents hit them. It was the Division of Youth and Family Services, the Gestapo around here for parents who suck. Most kids were just blowing off steam. But it felt so good to say it, I decided I would actually do it. A rush of tiredness blew off me as I listened to my dad stammer.

"Well, you know, you're always welcome with us, if, uhm," he stammered. "We'd have to look for a bigger place. That could take a month or two."

I could hear in his tone that Dad didn't have the money to move, didn't want to move.

"I don't need you and Suhar! I'll live on the street." I held the phone away from my mom for a second time, then brought it back as her hand retreated. "And I'll turn you in along with her, just because you suck, too. Why in the hell did you and Mom get married? What were you thinking?"

He was silent, Mom was a gasping lunatic, all crying and shit. She wanted to go to rehab about as much as I wanted to be out of my all-day dreamland.

He finally said, "The marriage was a mistake. But you weren't. I will come down for you, take you to Children's. Can you pack a few clothes? It'll take me about two hours to get there, what with the ice. After they look you over, if they let you go home, Suhar and I will consider..." *Blah-blah.*

I could hardly hear him over my mom's blasphemies. I muttered some thanks, hung up, and turned to her. "If you don't shut up this second, I will call DYFS, and you will go to rehab."

She didn't lunge for the phone this time but put her hand over her mouth to stifle herself. I was surprised she quit fighting that easily. *Remorse... Yeah, she feels it.*

"Get out of my room. Please."

"Well! *I* still love *you*!" she announced.

A guilt fest. *That's a real thoughtful contribution, Mom.* I only found enough voice for middle ground. "I love you, too. Stop guilting me, because I am so sick of it that I would scream if I could. Leave me alone."

She actually went out, slamming the door. I hauled myself off the bed. My chest weighed a thousand pounds. I coughed up another hill of salt into three tissues. *Claire, you probably do have pneumonia. Just take it easy.*

But my body felt lighter, just from standing up to my mom's crap for once. Next on my list—straightening out Mrs. Garver. I grew more awake, focusing on how I might screw up her life next. My mom belonged in rehab. Mrs. Garver belonged in jail.

Despite my gut instincts screaming not to think about him yet, I imagined Lani's face, with that pillow he held up in front of him yesterday. I spoke to the imaginary Mrs. Garver while I threw clothes on.

"You thought raising a kid was like having a merry Christmas. Well, guess what? You get what you get. You should have moved to the city. You don't let your kid run off and call it a solution, you trash heap."

I pulled a sweatshirt over my head. My chest felt lighter, though my black eye blinked thick and awkward. I would go tell off Mrs. Garver, because that thought gave me more strength than lying around pretending the world didn't exist. I shoved my feet into my heaviest sneakers, being that ice and snow were starting to paint a very white picture in the windy outdoors. *Indian summers, they end with a curse. This time it's an ice storm—and me. Look out, I'm a witch.* My cheerleading jacket was somewhere at the bottom of the harbor. I felt strangely glad, pulling my winter parka out of the back of the closet.

I came silently down the stairs, dizzily gripping the rail but holding my arms out from my sides so as not to make any swishing noises with the parka. But my mom was in the kitchen, anyway, cracking ice. I guessed being threatened with rehab was upsetting enough to make some people get drunk. I thought that was funny, but there was nothing to laugh about. I cracked the door in the living room and slithered outside.

Fortunately, the icy wind was at my back. It half pushed me to Lani's house. I shivered with only slight fever chills, breathing okay by stopping to hack up white seaweed every block. While I didn't feel like running a marathon, the cold air seemed to clear my head a little more, make me sharper. Thoughts started to strike me.

First, the guys' lucky streak was holding. *They were too lucky.* I realized a body could not have washed up to implicate them. It's not like the wharf is crawling with fishermen at first light, but enough people are around that even trained assassins would not try to hide or dispose of a body. Just cleaning the deck and fixing the net without being seen was risky enough for those guys. A body found by them or anybody else would have gotten around the island faster than lightning. My mom would have been in my room blathering loudly about it by eight o'clock in the morning.

So at this point, if I decided to not let Vince's threats terrify me and I went to the cops, it would be my word against a bunch of guys who would stick together until death did them part. What if the cops saw through "smoke and mirrors"? They might see what they *wanted* to see. Could our cops ever work toward bringing justice for Lani, who supposedly wore nightgowns, against a group of their own swarthy fishermen's kids?

I had no answers. I was only clear on how I'd spent my life being mad at no one, and all of a sudden, I didn't know who to kill first.

I would take Mrs. Garver by the throat and scream at her, for starters. I realized that I couldn't exactly tell her off and get the effect I wanted without spitting out the whole truth about last night. She probably noticed that Lani had not been around. But being that he'd spent two years on the streets, she probably wouldn't be thinking the worst. *She might have even thought he ran away again and felt relieved!*

But after I told her, I would *have* to tell the police. I'd have to tell them fast, because if she got to them first and got them to believe her son might be dead, I could look like an accessory to murder. The situation was growing very complicated. At this point it just made me angrier. My gut told me I was doing the right thing to go to her. I hoped my gut was right for once.

I pulled my finger off the doorbell, resisting the temptation to make it buzz endlessly. I could hear footsteps, and some *middle-ground* message blared loudly through my head.

Mrs. Garver opened the door slowly. Her eyes were very red and swollen. Her fingers shook as she wiped the bottom of her nose with a tissue. She had been crying. A lot. It shocked me, and I stood rooted, groping for the meaning. My body loosened as relief struck me. Maybe Phil or Scott had gotten too guilty a conscience and had gone to the cops. Obviously, she knew. A visit from the cops was the only explanation I could think of. While I surely wasn't up for sobbing out my grief yet, and especially not with her, I did feel a great weight lift off me. This meant I wouldn't have to worry about Vince's threats. His own friends had turned on him.

"Claire. His best friend. I'm so glad you came." She ushered me into the house, dropping her tissue without even noticing. "I guess you heard what happened."

Heard what happened? I tried to conjure up a version of last night that she might have heard that hadn't included me. Phil or Scott must have been good enough to keep me out of whatever they told the police. I still hoped they'd go to jail. But being that Mrs. Garver knew the awful truth, I lost the urge to yell at her.

"I just wanted to, uhm, make sure you were okay," I heard myself blurt out.

Her swollen eyes flashed of something like gratitude and relief. "You thought of me? Claire, you really are a nice, sweet girl." She sniffed with a trembly smile. "You are the first person on the island to show me any thoughtfulness. I've been alone here all day! My sister's coming. But with the ice and all, she won't get here until five o'clock."

She shut the door and looked at my face like she was seeing it for the first time. "Your eye . . . what happened?"

I muttered some obvious bull, like that it looked worse than it felt. But I could have said anything and it wouldn't have mattered. She realized her tissue was gone and focused on bringing another from her packet with shaky fingers, like it took all of her concentration. Then she pointed at a seat in the living room as if she had already forgotten her own question.

I plopped down on the couch, and fought to get my parka off because I was sweating Elmer's glue from head to toe. The house felt like a fiery hell. Artificial winter heat had been turned too high, too suddenly, and all the windows were closed now.

She watched me toss the coat beside me, swaying a little in her chair. It wasn't until that point—when I was seated with my coat off, and basically trapped—that I realized what I had gotten myself into.

"Claire, last time, he left a beautiful note! He must be so mad at me this time! He didn't even bother leaving a note." She twisted the tissue around as a chill shot through my sweats. "He's always written to me on holidays and birthdays. But he's never given an address where I could write back to him. There is so much I want to say! I thought this time I had more time, now that his father isn't here chronically stressing about him. I thought things would be more peaceful around the house, even if Lani got in trouble with kids at school like he used to. I thought it would...still work. Claire, if he contacts you? There's something I want you to tell him for me. Okay?"

I thought I might piss my heart into my pants as it fell. She thought he had run off again. She had no suspicion of foul play. And yet, she was this grief stricken. She *had* cared, even if she was incredibly stupid in ways. I realized I would have to be the one to tell a heartbroken parent that the news was a hundred times worse. I couldn't think of even how to begin. But she prattled on and on like she was relieving herself of some huge burden she just couldn't carry anymore.

"I know he is private, and streetwise, and very stubborn, and determined to live his life his own way. Last time, I had probably thirty people looking for him, not including the police. If he has not contacted you, I'm sure he probably will. I want you to promise me that you'll give him a message."

Shock clamped my throat shut. The pressure must have formed the tears that squirted out of my eyes. It felt like a jet stream, blinding me, but she was too blinded herself to notice, I guessed, because I heard her sob.

"Tell him I love him. Tell him I was never, ever sorry we adopted him. Tell him that when I said mean things to him... it wasn't because I hated him. It was that...I was scared. I liked him just the way he was, but other people were always hurting him, and I just wanted to prevent some of it. I was scared if he didn't change, that he would get in some very serious trouble."

I jerked my tears away as my jaw hung. *Lady, you have no idea. You have no idea, and I have pneumonia. And if I tell you, I will drop dead right here.* It was not my job to do this, I reasoned. I had walked into such a different scenario than what I had expected. I couldn't even remember what I had expected, or what had inspired me to come here. Who knew what crazy ideas sick people could come up with?

I decided to pick at my stitches, twisting them, the little pinches keeping me alert.

"If you know where he is, and he doesn't want you to tell me, I understand that, too. Tell him I won't go looking for him again. I'm the big-time loser in that battle. Now he's even older and smarter. Maybe he was right last time. Maybe in running away he was fulfilling some destiny! But Claire? I want him to visit me! I can't stand the thought of not seeing him for another two years. Or even a few months."

I felt one stitch unravel, and I pulled...pulled again. *Weird, feeling it run out your flesh...tickles.* I stared at the suture in my palm, enough sanity left to look up at Mrs. Garver, wide-eyed. She was staring blankly over my shoulder. I could have taken off all my clothes and danced naked and she wouldn't have noticed. *Interesting scenario. Two crazies in one room. Talking like they're both sane.*

On she blathered as I forced myself not to tug on any more sutures. "...agency near my husband's military base in Texas...plans adoptions of older children—children who had been orphaned or had escaped from the black market in Mexico. It was easier to get one of those children than a baby. We wanted a child so badly...I had been a schoolteacher. We figured we could handle an abused child—we would do whatever it took. And we would be doing some child a favor, who didn't have much other hope."

"That's...nice." I half listened, trying to tell myself I would have to come clean. But my gut wanted to bide for time. To get it, I thought of a question I'd really been wanting the answer to.

"So...how old was Lani?"

My heart clattered as I heard *was* instead of *is* filling the air. Fortunately she didn't notice, and just laughed a little, like some memories were managing to improve her mood temporarily. "Instead of a birth certificate, we only got a certificate of citizenship. The doctor judged by his teeth and bones he was about seven. We always celebrated his birthday on the Fourth of July! He wanted a summer birthday, so that's what we had. He loved the beach, the ocean. We would have all our relatives down for the entire day."

"You've had an unusual life." "Yeah, it's an epic saga." "I want to hear about it." "Some other time..."

There was a lot about Lani's life I would never know, I realized, and I fought to keep the overwhelming sadness from hitting me like a sledgehammer. I couldn't deal with too many thoughts on what-it-means-to-be-dead—not on top of everything else right now. I tried to focus on my gratitude for knowing a few things. I knew now that he celebrated his birthday on Independence Day. He'd been such a free spirit. *Damn, if that wasn't appropriate.*

"I just wish we could have figured out what to do with a son like Lani while living on so many military bases. Some fathers wouldn't let their sons play with him...Some tried to blame us, would ask us questions about how we'd raised him, as if they were our judge and jury, trying to figure out what we'd done to 'cause' him to turn out that way. Do you see why I wanted him to change, Claire? Do you think I'm a terrible person?"

I glanced at the small suture in my hand, noticing with satisfaction it wasn't bloody. I'd been keeping my head somewhat low, self-conscious about my black eye. I wouldn't be bleeding in front of her next. I scrunched it into my fist and shoved it into the pocket of my parka. A train of salt and seaweed rumbled up my chest, and I tried to answer. I pulled tissues out of my parka pocket and coughed into them.

"You sound like you have a terrific cold. Please, let me make you a cup of tea with lemon." She got up without waiting for me to say "no thanks." It seemed that getting this huge load off her chest had given her back some sanity.

She shoved a photo album from the coffee table at me before walking into the kitchen. *Rich Philadelphia people manners.* They have this idea that it's bad manners to leave a guest alone in a room. If they had to, they would offer you a book or the family photo album.

If I see pictures of him, I will explode. If I can't ever see his face again, I will explode.

I flipped open the album to some random page with my eyes closed, then forced them open. I withdrew my hand to my chest as he smiled up at me. Somehow it made me calmer. It was such a calm, confident smile, with almost a laugh in his eyes.

He was younger, maybe age eleven, surrounded by a bunch of blond and gray relatives who looked nothing like him. Between this sea of necks and faces was the Hackett beach in the summer. Underneath was scrawled in pretty pen, *July 4,* and the year.

He wore his hair kind of long, even back then. It dripped down over his shoulders, wet from the ocean. And maybe because I'd been used to seeing my own plastic smiles in my photo album from Macy, I got an immediate splash of the plastic in the smiles of the people surrounding him. Lani was smack in the middle of the photo, like some person had looked through the lens with military precision, to let it be known who the guest of honor was. While all the people were huddled together, only his mother had her arm around him. All the aunts and uncles were crossing their arms, or pulling in ever so slightly, like maybe they didn't want to touch him. One aunt's eyes went sideways toward him, like Macy's in that picture of us with Lyda Barone. Only Lani's smile looked sincere. *Never cared what people thought of him and his games of dress-up...even back then.*

I was so busy noticing what was going on with the other

people, I almost missed the biggest thing going on with Lani. His soaking-wet hair, shiny from seawater, dripped diamond dots onto his chest, like his dad had managed to pull him out of the water just long enough to take the picture.

I put my hand to my chest, trying to keep my heart from revving up. But his mom's statement swept through my brain again. *"He loved the beach, the ocean."*

I didn't dare think of the night before. Yet I couldn't help seeing him whimper up at Tony. *"But...I can hardly swim."*

"Claire...don't do this," I whispered, trying to prevent other memories from tumbling over one another. *"Lani, how'd you think of that magazine plant, it was outrageous..."* *"I think really well on my feet..."* *"Lani, will you get out of that outfit and help me think?"* *"Claire, I am thinking..."* *"I always land on my feet..."*

I sat forward slowly, trying to think this through like a sane person. My biggest shock the night before had not been Tony Clementi showing up or anything Tony had done. It had been Lani's reaction. A normally streetwise person playing such a cowardly victim? It hadn't made enough sense. *Was it all an act? Did he realize he couldn't fight a group of huge guys? But if he could swim—*

I shook my head hard, trying to shake the thought away. There were a million holes in a scheme like that. It was too risky, too off the wall. Other solutions would have been far easier. He could have...thought to call the cops. By law, wouldn't the cops have to take him as far as the bridge if he said he was in danger?

I didn't know. Or...he could have faked a seizure and gotten off the island in an ambulance. The hospital is on the mainland. That seemed crazy, too, but less risky than letting a bunch of huge guys try to drown you and hoping you'll get away.

But we hadn't had time to get the police or an ambulance.

Neither of us had been prepared for Tony appearing out of nowhere like he had. I'd found out the hard way, it had been too late for 9-1-1 calls.

I remembered Lani asking a question just before Tony showed up. "Claire, if those guys catch us, and this time Tony is with them...what is the most likely thing they would do to me?" I had thought he was just psyching himself out with fear. *Did he have a better reason to ask? Was he already looking for a way to beat them at their own game?*

I jumped as Mrs. Garver's shadow came over the photo album. I looked at her, looked through her.

"I didn't mean to startle you," she said, surprised at my overreaction. "Do you want honey in your tea? It's better for a cold than sugar."

"Uhm..." I couldn't think of what honey was. Somehow the question came out, but it sounded like somebody else's voice. "Did you say that...Lani was a good...swimmer?"

"I wouldn't say 'good.' He liked to frolic in the waves at the beach, but where he could still touch bottom. He didn't do too many athletic things well."

Doyee. I had been stupid to even consider a scheme like the one I'd been concocting. My disappointment almost made me slump.

"Why do you ask?"

I just pointed at the beach picture and muttered something about how I thought I remembered him from swimming lessons when I was a kid, which was bullshit. And she had asked about tea.

"Um, I'll take honey. Thanks."

So Lani was just an average swimmer. Her answer was predictable. Typical. So mundane. Life just isn't melodramatic enough to allow for a weak kid in a nightgown to outsmart a bunch of big, strong, popular people. I felt mad at myself for considering any made-for-TV hopes.

I stood up, suddenly restless. Because Mrs. Garver thought Lani ran away, I was back to my original problems. I knew I should tell her—it was a matter of honor. Then I'd have to worry about the police, and Vince seeking revenge, and all the stuff that struck me as I had walked over here. I came to the foot of the stairs and gazed up. My only hope was that some evidence of a struggle had been left in his room—something that would force the police to find the story believable.

"Mrs. Garver?" I muttered toward the kitchen. "I think I left something in his room."

"Go on up. Maybe you'll see something I missed. Something that will tell us where he went this time."

I started up the stairs, rolling my eyes to hell and back. *Mundane. Typical. Real-life answers from Mrs. Garver.* She obviously had looked in the room to notice he was gone. She probably cleaned up, too, never thinking she could be destroying evidence.

I opened the door with one finger, kind of wheezing and ripped up, not really wanting to look for anything at all. I stood there in the quiet, staring at the bed where we'd spent so much time...him picking me apart and putting me back together with a sadder but wiser perspective.

My body reacted, though my heart and most of my memories were still frozen. I reached for his blanket. I fell to my knees, brought it to my nose, and inhaled a sweet smell, more like perfume than cologne. I tried to roll my eyes, but they were filling up again, and I kept inhaling. I gripped the blanket, scared I would cry loudly and his mother would hear. I kept my spazzing throat from letting rip.

Then I saw the book. It had been under the blanket, right about where he had been sitting. I hadn't remembered it being there when I crashed out yesterday. But I hadn't been looking for it. I picked it up.

It was large and heavy, with a beautifully painted angel on

the cover and the title *Andovenes' Angéls*...with the little mark over the *e* that made me wonder if it was in English. I ran my finger over the cover before opening it. The cover was flecked with mud, and the image of Macy tossing it from the car shot through my head. *Whatever made me think she was so smart? Smart for kindergarten...*

I turned some pages, and a sweet musty smell filled my head, despite my nose being half full of snot. The pictures were colorful, strangely lifelike—almost like photographs instead of paintings. It made the angels seem even more real. There was a picture for every two or three pages of writing. The book wasn't in a foreign language, but it was in weird English, like Shakespearean English. I wasn't sure I would understand it, so I leafed through a big section about cherubs, just looking at the pictures. It was followed by another section on fighter angels. The huge angels had muscles everywhere, even in their fingers. And yet, they didn't look rough like warriors. They were a contradiction that was hypnotizing—beautiful and innocent, yet strong, with piercing eyes, leaving the impression that no beast or monster or warlord could create a problem they couldn't handle.

I leafed through until the section on floating angels cracked open. Instead of a picture of a beautiful angel on the opening page, there was a picture of what looked to be a teenager, but in old-fashioned clothing. The face and hair looked strikingly like a modern-day teenager's, and I realized part of the value of this art was its timelessness. The artist had been a kind of genius, catching all the natural best of humanity, always.

But after ogling at the healthy shine of the blond hair and the roses in the cheeks, anyone would have the same initial thought. *Wait...is this a boy or a girl?* The floating angel had Lani's same intelligent, piercing gaze, peeking out from between the branches of a tree.

The old-fashioned English was too difficult to understand, but this time I scanned through. Some lines would jump out at me, their likeness to my English being close enough to run the meaning through my brain.

> O floating angel, thou canst take upon thyself the appearance of man—or any of the angels. But possessing thy great humility, thou shalt rarely reveal thy mightier forms when in the presence of men. It behooves thy mission for men to believe thou art like them in body.

I couldn't quite get why Andovenes seemed to be talking *to* a floating angel rather than *about* one. People did weird things like that way back when. I brushed it off, remembering that Lani had said something similar: *"If people knew who the angels were, they would be very nice when they saw one and would still do their same evil garbage when they thought none were around. Knowing who they are defeats the purpose."*

I almost laughed, sensing how passionately I was going to miss his weird philosophies. My smile dwindled to nothing as my thoughts finally turned to one of the places they'd been avoiding all day. I could feel his violent trembling again, almost like convulsions, as he slowly froze beneath me in the net. The helplessness shot through me again, with the flash memory of pulling off my jacket in a vain effort to warm him. I let myself feel the burning guilt. In my own frustration I had yelled at him. *"What the hell went wrong with you tonight? Acting like that in front of Tony? Why did you tell me you could always think on your feet?"* I'd ended with a charming repeat of *"What the hell is wrong with you tonight?"* He had looked at me so oddly before responding. He'd quit trembling, as if all his energy were, for a split second, spilling into his response.

"Nothing."

Nothing was wrong with him. That had been his answer. He had everything under control. He knew what he was doing. I'd assumed he was losing his sanity.

It behooves thy mission to rely on thy superior intellect when trouble befalls thee...

I considered hurling the book into the corner, though I didn't. I could feel myself circling back to where I had been downstairs. I was back to dreaming up crazed possibilities of how Lani might have outsmarted the tough guys. Only this time, instead of hoping he was secretly an Olympic swimmer, I had hopes that he was something superhuman. I slammed the book shut to snap myself away from more insanity. But it didn't prevent the rest of that sentence from penetrating my eyeballs.

...and to refrain from thy greater forms until thy suffering is complete.

Despite feeling absurd, I couldn't resist wandering around in the difficult language until I started coming up with a translation: An angel would rely on his smarts until trouble came down, and even then, it wouldn't change out of a human form until...*until thy suffering is complete?* What did that mean? Until the suffering...became almost unbearable? *Until the freezing water starts to eat you, sinking its icicle fangs into every inch of your flesh...and your best friend kicks you and swims away from you and leaves you—*

I clamored off my throbbing knees and dropped onto the mattress, pressing my palms on my eyeballs. It's like my brain was divided in two. Half of it couldn't resist playing with myths and legends. The other half was reminding me, *Claire, you ought to be ashamed of yourself.* I decided that I liked the first half of my brain better. The crazier thoughts left me feeling more peaceful. It seemed funny. A crazy thought was probably the only thing keeping me from going crazy.

"Your neat little version of reality is crumbling, Claire." I had been looking up at Lani's face as he'd said that, rocking me in his arms on that bus ride. His smile had seemed so amused, so...*victorious*. Crumbled realities are secretly your victory. Your crumbled realities create paths to purer truth, to—

"Middle ground, Claire," I muttered, though I knew my heart wanted magic.

I opened the chapter again and took a few words at a time. I translated another section into plain English, and another, until one echoed what Marcus the medic had blathered on about.

"God informs them, you know, 'Look, there's some evil person at work down there,' and then God turns his back, cuz he can't take the violence, you know?"

The passage said the angels bring justice through natural disasters and things that wouldn't lead the average person to guess that there was a spiritual force behind them. It said people are generally unaware that these angels can call upon the sky to kill somebody with lightning, or the sea to kill somebody with a wave or a large fish.

I had laughed at Marcus. I didn't laugh now, though I realized hazily I was in the throes of convenient thinking. *Boy...wouldn't it be nice if this was truth.* I lit into thoughts of Tony Clementi being bitten in half by a shark, carried off a jetty in the jaws of a rogue wave...some tall, thin, shadowy figure standing on the rocks... *You thought it would be fun to murder gay people, hypocrite?*

I turned the next page. Lani Garver stared at me. This floating angel portrait froze me as I stared into Lani's exact eyes. I almost had to command myself to start breathing. This drawing looked like a double of Lani, the most striking thing of all being the wide eyes—wide like Lani's had been the night before, when we were buried in inky ice water. *Claire, don't leave me down here... You're kicking for the surface... You're leaving me...*

Same eyes. My chest rattled as I fought to get a breath. The more I stared at this picture, the more I realized that these eyes were wide with laughter, not fear. They shone with victory, not terror. For the first time since it happened, I let myself relive that moment, envision his eyes flashing through the black. *Had it been terror... or laughter?*

"No way," I mumbled out loud, to keep myself steady.

I shut my eyes and reopened them, and that's when my realities came crashing through. I looked over every detail in that picture, that floating angel's china-doll skin, the shiny dark hair, the beautiful features on the stocky frame that would make you wonder, *Guy or girl?*

But my doubts had to do with Ellen's friend, Abby. This must have been the picture that Abby used to make the costume. It was very close to the image in the picture. Wouldn't Abby have noticed and trumpeted about it loudly to Ellen if this painting were *really* a dead ringer for Lani? Am I seeing things conveniently? Wouldn't Ellen have said something to me about this particular picture? Told me the likeness was the weirdest coincidence she'd ever experienced?

Am I seeing through smoke and mirrors?

I snapped the book shut. But I gripped it to my chest, thinking of some scheme to get it past Mrs. Garver. I should get to keep it. Somebody else might try to sell it.

I almost turned to go downstairs when I remembered that I hadn't come up here about the book. I glanced around the room, hardly able to think. But it was obvious there was no evidence of a struggle up here that I could point out to Mrs. Garver. *Mundane. Normal room. Real life.* The candles were on the stereo shelves where they belonged... not even one had been knocked over. His mattress and box spring had not been jostled; the bed was rumpled from where I'd slept on it after eating two peanut butter and jelly sandwiches. The crumbs were still there. I looked for muddy boot prints where Tony had stood, had kicked at Lani, as Lani kicked at those backpacks.... Tony'd either wiped his boots before he sneaked in the house or we were just unlucky. *Those guys are too lucky.* The floor was clean of anything conspicuous. Even footprints, even the backpacks—

My glance passed the open closet, froze on the smooth floor, and moved slowly back to the closet. It was empty.

I laid the book on the dresser and opened every drawer, all of which were empty. Then I tiptoed silently into the other bedroom. The echo of clanking teacups wandered up, and I realized Mrs. Garver was on the telephone. Someone was keeping her busy for the moment. Gratefully, I opened her closet as silently as possible, then all her drawers, then looked under her bed. Ladies' belongings were all that I could find. I stumbled to the top of the stairs and stood there, wheezing like crazy.

I heard her hang up, and a minute later she passed by below me with a tea tray filled with two cups, a pitcher, and a plate of chocolate chip cookies.

"Mrs. Garver?" I asked, and she backed up again to look at me. "Um, the homework I left might have been in Lani's backpacks. Do you know where they are?"

Her eyebrows shot up, like her sanity had returned but mine had not. "He ran away, Claire. Obviously, his backpacks are with him. I'm sorry—"

"Never mind," I muttered, then let loose a sarcastic laugh that almost sounded angry. "I'm just...losing my grip on reality today."

I decided not to tell her anything. To tell her that Lani had died might be very misleading. It could end up being very unfair to her. That's what I reasoned on my way down the stairs, looking forward to rolling some of that tea across my stinging throat.

≈≈ 33 ≈≈

I stayed in Children's Hospital from late Monday night until Friday, having been diagnosed with pneumonia and acute bronchitis. They did some blood-bolstering thing with IVs, for people in remission who had been through a trauma. Dr. Haverford tried to tell me that sometimes a health trauma can compromise a remission and that I would have to get my blood tested every thirty days for six months. I tried not to hear that. I tried to keep my mind occupied with other things.

I called DYFS on my mom. It wasn't as hard as I thought it would be. The lady social worker was really nice when I said Mom wasn't like this before I had gotten sick. I said she had been a good mother, but now she needed some help that was way over my head. The social worker said in cases like this they usually try to talk parents into attending AA, instead of forcing them to relinquish custody of their kids and go to rehab. That was a relief. I didn't want to turn my mom's life on its head, only get her to return to her former self. I also didn't feel like leaving Hackett and staying with my dad—not after Hackett had gotten rid of Lani so easily. It was like a matter of principle for me to stay there, if I could get out from under my fear of Tony and Vince. One step at a time.

I called Ellen. She came right after school Tuesday and stayed until dinner every night, when my dad and Suhar showed up. The first night, she fired off the ever important question: "Where is Lani?"

I told her that we'd been thrown in the water and that he'd gotten away somehow, and I hadn't seen him since. I knew I could be telling a serious lie, but she might tell someone if I hinted the worst, and I wasn't ready for any full-blown police thing. Not yet. At first my wheezing and coughing was out of control, so she didn't ask endless questions. But I could sense her heartbreak...how she watched the door every time footsteps approached, like maybe it was him. It might have driven me nuts, except I figured I could tell her the whole truth when the time was right.

I asked her to share some acting lessons to pass time. She gave a couple of great performances that taught me stuff and kept my mind focused. Then Wednesday night, after my dad and Suhar went home, I used everything she'd taught me, and I called Scott.

"I just want to tell you I'm sorry for everything...It was completely my fault, and I know you could never like me now, but...I wanted to make sure you were doing all right—" I let go of a huge lungful of white stuff, but he sighed in relief so loudly I could hear it above the earthquake. I guessed it was driving him crazy that I might snake, and this phone call meant to him that I wouldn't.

He finally went on in a stony voice that said nothing. "Macy said your mom says you're in the hospital."

"I'll be out in a couple days. Got pneumonia."

The silence got way long, then some of his steel melted a little. "Claire, I never, ever meant for you to get hurt like this. It just got out of hand. Me and Phil, we're not killers. We tried to save him. You were there. Right?"

I was going to edge around to my important questions, but Scott didn't need any help.

"We went back at first light. He never washed up, but

guess what did? That white thing…that contraption he was dressed up in. Big goofball. Goddamn, that was eerie, finding that floating on a wave in a slop of seaweed. The green kind."

Bingo. I knew a body had not washed up yet. "Yeah, wow, that's awful. What did you do with it?"

"Phil and Vince and me, we—" He sniffed, not trying to hide his crying jag anymore. "We tied it around a cinder block and heaved it off the stern of the boat."

"Good thinking." I winced with guilt at my own good acting. "And…what about Tony? Where did he go after he left us?"

"To the emergency room at Port Dingo. Told them he got sliced on an outboard motor. Took twenty-some stitches."

I wanted to know if Tony had sneaked back to the Garvers' and taken Lani's backpacks, to make it look like Lani ran away. "So…he went…right home after that?"

"Uh-uh. He saw Vince's car in front of my house. He came here and crashed out, like, went totally to sleep, though the rest of us were nuts. Hospital gave him some of those pain-killers he loves so much. He says it was worth it to be stoned out on Percodan all day long."

I clamped down on my jaw, fighting my anger with a stray hope that floating angels might be real, and Tony would get what he deserved.

"Uhm…" I quickly came up with a pretty good lie to use, since he hadn't completely answered my question. "My mom said Mrs. Garver thought somebody broke into the house. She got home from the VFW that night and…some stuff was missing from their house. Two backpacks full of stuff. Tony didn't steal them when he came out of the house, did he?"

"No. He was using both hands on that moron." Scott sighed a couple of times, sounding distracted. "Like I give a flying fuck about that pervert lady and her son-slash-daughter. Whoever it was, it wasn't any of us. You can tell her that much. But, Claire, you know...me and Phil, we could go to jail...if you sound off. You know? You're still with us, right?"

They hadn't taken Lani's backpacks. I hung up without saying good-bye.

My dad somehow talked Erdman into coming around to see me—I think by promising him a banged-up old Les Paul guitar supposedly played once in Philly by Jimmy Page. He did a therapy session with me at the hospital. A session lasts a whole hour. But if Erdman suspected I had witnessed a crime, he never said, and he seemed happy enough to exchange rapid fire with me about my parents and Suhar.

During one of Suhar's visits, I asked her point-blank, to her face, "Why didn't you like to come to Dad's apartment when I was doing chemo? Were you grossed out by me?"

She told me she was very afraid of death, though she couldn't figure out why—maybe just because artists are afraid of everything. She said that seeing me back then inspired her to make anonymous donations to the American Cancer Society, though talking to me to my face had been too much on her. We ended up laughing about some of the stuff my dad does, like, Why does he sing in the shower when it sounds so horrible, and how can a guitar player sing like that?

Four guys from Calcutta came Thursday afternoon—I think Erdman tipped them off that I had been hospitalized. I ended up spewing the whole story of Lani to them—except for the potential angel stuff. I don't know why I spewed, except they seemed so cool—so genuinely concerned about me, but without making a big deal of my IVs, black eye, and general shape. I figured they were the people in the universe least likely to flip out and have a seizure about my holding back from the police.

To my shock, they were totally stubborn that I should spill my guts to the cops. I had thought, some of them being former drug addicts, that they would have had some kind of hatred for the police. But they seemed more militant than people who had never done anything wrong.

"Those guys need to pay. They *need* to pay," Jason French insisted. "You're actually ruining their lives if you *don't* turn them in."

So, finally, I talked. First to my dad, who called a lawyer. The lawyer came the next day about three minutes before a cop from Hackett—one whom I hardly knew, thank god. It was easier to look in somebody's face and snake on your friends when you can't tell if that face is liking it or hating it. At the end he asked me only one question.

"This story is five days old. Why didn't you come to the police right away?"

I couldn't think of a good answer. Yet when the lawyer cleared his throat, the officer studied my two IVs and said, "Never mind."

Despite my snaking, the guys' good luck looked to be holding just fine. The police hauled them in to the cop station to see what they had to say about any supposed drowning. They denied everything. The police sent officers to Mr. Dern's boat just to be sure. If any evidence had remained of a crime, the guys—maybe with the help of Mr. Dern—got rid of it. For whatever reason, maybe "convenient thinking," the cops decided not to call in a homicide squad to check for microscopic evidence, like blood and stuff.

They did call the coast guard to dredge the harbor for a body, probably to cover their asses. The coast guard dredged the point around Fishermen's Wharf for two days. At the conclusion, they said that either I was crazy or the tides were crazy. They mentioned the tides *had* been crazy that night, but the local police really didn't want to hear anything that might implicate islanders. They probably pretended they never heard that part. But a body never washed up.

Mrs. Garver verified my craziness to the police, telling them I had been there on Monday and had never mentioned any drowning thing to her, and besides...if her son were dead, where were all his belongings? She told them I was a nice girl, but like a lot of Lani's friends, I'd seen a little too much trouble in my life to be considered "stable."

After being released from the hospital, I spent the weekend at my father's, and he drove me home on Monday. I knew I could get a visit from Vince or Tony Clementi the first time I set foot outside my door. Fortunately, I had a week's worth of recovering to do, at least, and my mother did not leave me, despite her mood swings. She was doing Alcoholics Anonymous online until I got better. A couple of nights, she thanked me as she dialed up. And a couple nights, she looked keyed up and pissed off, like she'd much rather be blitzed on vodka.

I slept a lot, to avoid thinking that if Tony or Vince didn't destroy my future, cancer might. And I had one dream. It was one of those whacked-out sick dreams, where you're sleeping and waking so frequently, you don't know when you fell asleep. I was in bed and dreamed I rose and went to the window, looking out at the ice storm. A shadow rose on the window ledge, like someone had come up behind me. I wasn't scared, though the shadow was not the shape of my mother. Out came a man's voice and a lady's voice simultaneously, like some sci-fi movie effect. They said in unison, "Indian summers...one man's curse is another man's cause." *Weird.* I was afraid to turn and see this creature, feeling sure it would be some girl all full of razor-blade cuts. I finally turned, and nobody was there.

I knew I had been dreaming only because a second later I was in bed, opening my eyes. I shrugged it off, went to the kitchen for something to eat. If another full day had passed, I probably would have forgotten about the dream entirely. But what happened next, to Vince and Tony, has kept it in my mind and made me think about dreams, and the supernatural, and floating angels.

If I had been looking for signs of floating-angel revenge on Tony Clementi, I would have expected Tony to be dashed against the rocks of the fishing jetty in a rogue wave or something more Hollywood-ish than what actually happened.

The third night I was home, the police got a phone call that a truck had skidded off Hackett Boulevard and rammed into the post office. The police might have thought the icy force of nature caused Tony to skid off the street. But Tony told the cops a story that he insisted was true. That story forced them to test him for drunk driving and to search the vehicle. He was .02 over the legal limit, and on the floor of the passenger seat were three Ecstasy pills and an empty prescription bottle of Percodan, meant to last thirty days. It was dated ten days earlier.

Since Tony had been busted before, the drinking and possession violated his probation. He went to jail and had to serve the time from his first bust—nine months. It would be long enough for me to finish the school year without his terrorizing presence.

My first day back to school was lonely but uneventful, despite the presence of Vince, Phil, and Scott, on whom I had obviously snaked. But they seemed stirred up by the story Tony had told the cops the night he rammed the post office. The story is definitely weird. Tony said he purposely totaled his truck, and he had good reason. He told the police that he was sick of looking in his rearview mirror all the time and seeing some faggot standing in the middle of his flatbed, staring back at him.

Tony's "craziness" went into every gossip channel, probably because his mom cried on a few shoulders, and island nature took its course. People were calling me Crazy Claire for making up some wild story about a drowning gay kid who had obviously run away, and they were calling him Tanked-Out Tony. They were saying we should get married. It would have made me a little nuts, except that I had the privilege of seeing what Tony's story was doing to Phil and Scott and Vince. Talk about realities cracking open. I'm not saying they would have believed anything Tony said at this point, but his insistence that he'd been seeing spooks was eerie enough to mess with their heads. They looked like zombies my first day back at school. They had no interest in taunting me at all.

My second day of school, Vince was not there. Word seeped out that he had been found in his car—dead. His house didn't have a garage, but the one across the street did. He pulled in there after the neighbor went to work. News travels quickly around here. The police showed up around nine-thirty, after another neighbor complained about hearing an engine behind a closed garage door. It was all over school by the end of third period. I was in such a state of shock, I didn't know what to feel, except a hazy relief that he wouldn't be bothering me anymore, either.

I'm not saying I wanted people to start dying, or even that I had been looking for floating-angel revenge on Vince as well as Tony. Vince's death looked just like a basic suicide—not like he was driven into the garage by some force greater than himself who held him there. In fact, there was a note in his hand, in his handwriting. It said, "I ain't waiting around here to get haunted. I'm going after him."

Obviously, the note hinted that somebody was dead. You would think a crazy note like that might give my drowning story some credibility with the police. The most the police did was drum on Mr. Dern's head a little—we're going to get a search warrant, so be prepared. And they paid a second visit to Mrs. Garver to see if she had heard from her son yet. She hadn't, but she swore to them over and over that Lani was alive, that he'd done this before, and that she would surely contact them the minute she got her first letter from him. I smelled the stench of serious convenient thinking. Mrs. Garver *had* to believe her son was alive, or feel guilty that he stayed alive on the streets for two years and yet managed to get killed under her "safe" parental roof.

People believe what they have to, and considering the lunacy that came out of Tony and Vince, I would say it's not beyond the realm of reason to think that Mrs. Garver unpacked Lani's backpacks or destroyed any evidence of them and went about the business of telling herself they were with him in some major city somewhere. Nothing would have surprised me at that point—which isn't to say I totally believe Mrs. Garver did that. Things continued to happen that kept me asking those questions about *what* Lani Garver was.

Phil broke up with Macy about an hour after Vince Clementi's funeral. Geneva Graham hit on Scott at the funeral and managed to go out with him. I wasn't at the funeral. But later I could sit in a bathroom stall at school between my classes, pull my feet up, and hear just about anything I needed. Eli gossiped that Phil had told Macy some shit, some "You're just not right for me." Problem was, nothing was "right" for Phil. He was losing interest in everything. He quit school two weeks before the all-star football game, which he and Scott had been picked for. He kept saying school was a bore. He took a job with the city on a street-cleaning truck.

Scott quit school the first week in January, giving similar reasons, plus one other: Geneva Graham was pregnant and he needed to get a full-time job. Whatever powers Geneva has over guys still escape my comprehension. But the two of them moved into a two-room studio over someone's garage. I get the feeling Geneva keeps Scott somewhat sane. He took a job with Mr. Matlock, fixing cars. He's lost about forty pounds, looks like a shell of his former self, but he makes it to a job every day.

As for me, I became the first girl in the history of Hackett Island to quit cheerleading without being injured. Macy Matlock became the second. The reason I gave Ms. D'Angelo was that my music life was taking off and I couldn't do weekend games. Macy didn't give a reason. She refuses to speak to me, but she never gets mean. She just ignores me, though she's still pretty loud and raucous about other people. She gets that way around me, as if to show me she doesn't care, but the cheerleading thing let me know that she does. She's waiting for me to come up to her. Maybe I will someday, though the idea of having friends on this island still makes me want to puke. Other than that, my digestive track is working well these days. I've even developed a strange liking for hot fudge sundaes.

I think it's prime that Macy has no best friend right now. And I think it's prime that both Phil and Scott have fisherman parents but neither of them took a job anywhere near the boats, where the pay is a whole lot better. I think everyone who was guilty has paid, and in a somewhat just fashion.

Which isn't to say I'm going to wave a nine-hundred-dollar book all over Hackett, making wild and socially unacceptable accusations as to what Lani might have been. There's nothing in what happened that looks weirdly supernatural. We've got a suicide, three kids looking forward to living their lives in cheap, tiny apartments, two with a baby coming, and Macy Matlock hanging out by herself. The biggest weirdness has to do with Tony. Word is out that even after he got sober, he stuck to his story about why he crashed up his truck. He *still* says he kept seeing some gay kid in his rearview mirror. Because of his head injury as a kid, he qualifies for some kind of psychiatric assistance from the state. His mom is having him committed, and he could stay locked up for years.

Justice came down. Yet there wasn't much flamboyance about it. There wasn't enough to scream floating-angel revenge and have it sound completely credible.

If I add on what's happened with me—how the Claire Zone of Bad Luck seems temporarily out of service—it might add a little credibility to my story. I recorded four songs with Calcutta for P.A.R.A. (Philadelphia AIDS Relief Album), and the thing all but made us famous downtown. We got invited to play at huge halls in Philadelphia—and some in New York City—that I still can't believe. We've also been asked to do a major metro tour of eleven big cities in America, which we had to decline because people's health is not that stable, though no one has died. I have stayed in remission so far. Dr. Haverford once mentioned his theory that doing what makes you happy sometimes helps you stay healthy. For me, just being in a studio...spending Saturday nights chilling with real musicians...that was all I needed to feel on top of the world.

Jason and Mike encouraged me to help out with a support group started at Children's for people with post-traumatic stress disorder resulting from cancer. I went over there a few times and talked to the support group about how I got an eating disorder a year after chemo. I ate a hot fudge sundae in front of them, had them all laughing about Claire the klutz, dumb-stupid-Claire remarks, and my other charming talents. Sometimes I played my guitars, and they all would clap, and some would cry.

Ellen and Cooper have had the privilege of saying "I told you so" when they hear me perform. They're making reference to their belief, "You've got to pay your dues to sing the blues." My playing really has taken off again, in such a greater way than back when I was learning between chemo sessions. Back then I learned to reproduce anything I heard. Now I play my own stuff, too, and very little of it is about razor blades. I'm not afraid of my feelings, even the bad ones, and it comes out when I sing. I'm wailing sometimes, screaming, too, when it's appropriate. Nothing feels over the top.

My mom keeps going to AA, which should make me happy enough. I'd like to say she returned to being the grand, steady person she was when I was a little kid, but as Erdman has pointed out, there's no going backward in life. She's not the social butterfly she once was. She ditched *Les Girls* and has not mentioned missing my former friends. But I worry about Mom. Her mood swings are not to be reckoned with. On a good day she says, "I'll find myself, Claire." She looks like she really believes herself, especially when she adds stuff like "All good things take time. It'll be good when I know who I am, apart from parties and apart from you."

I guess that covers everybody who was touched by Lani Garver's visit to Hackett Island—except Lani himself. I think about him a lot, especially at night when the fog rolls in and I'm feeling restless. Some nights, I open Andovenes' book and stare and stare at that floating angel that looks so much like him, and I ask myself a lot of questions. Like... *Isn't it weird how so much insanity could end up improving my life?* Sometimes I get out that photo album Macy gave me, and I look at the early pictures... then I look at the ones that were taken after Lani showed up on Hackett.

There are some newspaper clippings of Calcutta, and this one really great picture of me taken by *Philadelphia Magazine*. A photographer showed up at one of our rehearsals. Jason French was dishing out orders as usual, and some of the guys were arguing with him. It's a cute photo. I'm just standing there, a couple feet off, drumming my fingers on my guitar and waiting for them to simmer. Most of my face is hidden under that fedora Suhar got me, and I look pretty stone-faced, all slouching in my black leather pants and BLOODY MARY T-shirt. The cutline reads, "McKenzie, a new Philly musical tour de force, would rather strum than argue."

There are snapshots of me and Ellen, a couple with Cooper. At the end, I put the photo of Lani on the beach, all dripping wet, which I ripped off out of his mom's photo album. It's in the very back. I watch him stare at me and laugh. I tried to copy something as pretty as Macy's backwards handwriting when I added the ident, "What happened to Lani Garver?"

Do I think he's an angel? It would be ever so convenient for *me*, wouldn't it? On the one hand, I tell myself, if he was out there somewhere, I probably would have gotten at least a postcard. On the other hand, I have a blank page in that photo album that I am saving for the day when one shows up. There's not much else I can do, except this one thing in honor of Lani that works out pretty well. I try to be nice to everyone—even on Hackett—even when people's childish naiveness is pissing me off royally. Nobody has ever asked me why I'm nice. It's a strange relationship, the one I have with the people around here. They called me Crazy Claire for a while. Then my mom started running around with newspaper clippings of me from big Philly papers, and it shut them up, but it didn't make them like me. They want to ogle at me more than they want to talk to me. And yet, all of a sudden, there are at least twenty black leather jackets wandering around the corridors of Coast Regional. Go figure.

People probably think it's strange that they can stare at me, and I smile and wave, and pick up dropped books for people in the hall, and visit kids with cancer when I have time. I wish someone would ask me why I'm like that.

I would love to say, "You're supposed to be kind to everyone, because you never know when you're meeting an angel." I could say that much and know I was speaking the truth.

Reader Chat Page

1. How does convenient recollection serve Tony and Macy?

2. Why doesn't Lani make it clear that he is a guy when Macy asks him if he is a girl? Why does it matter which gender he is?

3. Why does Vince strike out at Lani when Claire laughs about the magazine?

4. Claire says, "Complete happiness can feel so much like complete terror that it's hard to tell them apart." What does she mean?

5. Why do you think hearing the other kids' problems made it possible for Claire to eat the sundae?

6. Do you think Lani is a floating angel?

7. Claire, Tony, and Mrs. Garver all have different beliefs about what happened to Lani Garver. What do you think happened to Lani?

Chatting with Carol Plum-Ucci

Question: When did you begin writing?

Carol Plum-Ucci: When I was a kid, I lived above a funeral home—if you had cut a hole around my bed with a hacksaw, I would've dropped down onto the face of a nonbreathing visitor. Creepy, yeah, but it inspired a writer's imagination. I used to lie awake at night wondering if we had an "overnight guest" downstairs. My mom's imagination was even more bent than my own. I'd say, "Mom, there's a ghost downstairs. I can sense it." Instead of telling me to shut up and go to bed, she'd say, "Okay, we're going to catch it." She was ghostbusters central, and I went to sleep many a night with my door strung with one of her infamous booby traps. I think maybe that's why I had insomnia so much as a kid—it was more interesting to stay awake. I eventually started to write about the things I feared and the thoughts I dreamed up to comfort myself.

I wrote my first poem when I was eight. Mom was this total neat freak and usually refused to post anything on the refrigerator. But she stuck that poem up on the fridge door. It was a lousy poem (as you can imagine, since I was only eight, though I think it actually rhymed out), but the honor encouraged me.

Q: What is your writing process?

C. P.-U.: Whatever works! Normally, I write like a bricklayer: The first chapter has to work before I'll move on to the second.

But, occasionally, a manuscript emerges in stages: a stinky draft turns into a less stinky second draft, turns into a tolerable third draft.... It may take up to five—or more!—drafts. Books are like children: When they're born, you don't know which ones will be angels and which will require serious psychotherapy to reach maturity. I throw out probably two-thirds of what I write. Some of my most beautiful scenes will never see the light of day, as beautiful isn't enough when a passage is not working. I think the most important thing for writers is to keep an open mind and not be too hard on themselves during the creative process. It's all gold, for one essential reason or another.

Q: Do you work certain hours or days?

C. P.-U.: Before I published, I wrote whenever/wherever, which included the middle of the night, office lunch hours, in my car stopped at a red light, even in my bathroom using the toilet seat as a desk when we had too much company and no other rooms were available. Now I work mornings and again at night, skipping the middle passage of the day. If I write for more than four hours in a row, though, I fry my brains.

Q: Which books or writers have influenced you?

C. P.-U.: I have favorites for certain things. For strong teenage characters, I love Terry Trueman, who wrote *Stuck in Neutral* and *Inside Out*. He's got such great voices, you could read the lines over and over again. For the classics, I've probably read *To Kill a Mockingbird* fifty-five times. And it's one of those books I'll pick up in the middle of the night and I'll just start reading anywhere. Lolls me off, but in a very good way. The author I think I've learned the most from is Stephen King. He's tended to be ignored literarily because of his *ew* factor and horror motif, but he has one of the strongest voices and consistent literary sensibilities of any author I've read. I also love his potty humor. The scene in *The She* featuring the flatulent nun was probably largely inspired by his pie-eating contest scene in *The Body* (made into the movie *Stand By Me*). If you think I curse too much in my stories, it's King's fault.

Q: How do you come up with story ideas?

C. P.-U.: Usually a story starts when something happens in real life that totally burns my buns. I get on this slow simmer and suddenly my brain goes, "There's a story in this." For example, it really upsets me that very intelligent people are often dismissive of information collected by the intuition. It seems to me that modern philosophy has unwittingly crippled our ability to "know" by creating too narrow a definition for "evidence." Once, I cleared a room really fast by defending the plausibility of miracles—at a Christmas party. That and similar memories accumulated into my slow burn, and a decade later *The She* emerged.

Q: What sparked the idea for *What Happened to Lani Garver*?

C. P.-U.: I have a friend who was born in a coal-mining town. He had to leave home when he was twelve because he was so effeminate that even his parents were getting death threats from the laborers. He lived on the streets until he was nineteen. He's fine now, a college graduate with a great job. He's so sweet and happy and not bitter that I've often wondered if he is an angel. He was my impetus for Lani Garver, though he and I both marvel at how Lani emerged distinct and unique unto himself, not sharing my friend's personality when all was said and done.

Q: Do personal experiences or details ever end up in your books?

C. P.-U.: Sometimes I try to make characters out of real people, but as with Lani Garver, they quickly become autonomous and end up resembling nobody but themselves. I put many personal experiences in my work as well as things I've heard from others. My belief is that fiction is a subconscious exercise in examining reality and discovering interesting things about it. Hence, the best stories are laced with an inordinate amount of what's real.

Q: In *What Happened to Lani Garver,* Lani refers to noteworthy thinkers like Freud, Jung, and Hegel. How did you come to incorporate the philosophies of these men into Lani's character?

C. P.-U.: I wanted to created an alleged angel with a gift of intellectual precision. The whole story entertains the theme of deconstruction—the attempt to blur harsh lines we draw in the sand that are more hurtful than helpful, such as gay/straight, poor/rich, white/black, male/female. I was hoping to work a little deconstruction on the barrier erected between religion and science because the two, for all essential purposes, do not contradict each other in the least. Many people working in the sciences these days will agree with that.

Q: Convenient recollection is an important theme in *What Happened to Lani Garver.* What drives your exploration of this theme?

C. P.-U.: My initial interest in "convenient thinking," which is the mother behavior of "convenient recollection," was sparked by a statement my pastor made on a Sunday in the early nineties. He was responding to a recent act of terrorism and halted his sermon to comment, with ironic sympathy, "And, by the way, these people truly believe they're doing God a favor." It intrigued me, this concept of two people holding diametrically opposed points of view, with lives being lost in defense of each. According to the standard rules of logic, both can be wrong but only one can be right. And, therefore, in innumerable human conflicts—everything from domestic quarrels to world wars— people can become utterly convinced that folly, fiction, and even nonsense are not only entirely true, but worth killing and dying for. I've often asked myself, *How do we fall for this? And why?*

The answer I explored in *Lani Garver* lies in perception, which serves as the looking glass through which we see truth. Except perhaps in cases of divine intervention, no one sees pure truth; we see truth wrapped in perception. Acting as our friend, perception is a series of messages from the subconscious that can coat, blur, distort, and even conceal truth from us, sometimes because truth is bluntly painful or, more often, because it is inconvenient.

Q: Do you think floating angels are real?

C. P.-U.: I think the angels outlined in the Bible and in Judeo-Christian tradition are quite real (and spiritual beings from other traditions might be real also, but I'm not familiar with them). My floating angels are probably most strongly influenced by the angels who came to save Lot from Sodom and Gomorrah—beautiful enough to attract the attention of those who lusted after beautiful boys, and yet human enough to fool people as to their superhuman identities. However, I actually made the decision to create floating angels and their prophet, Andovenes (see the word *dove* in the middle?), from scratch. I felt that to trumpet from an existing doctrinal record, such as the Bible, would have been to alienate another, such as the Koran. The message is universal.

I'm not sure I developed my thesis of floating angels to such an extent that readers would actually look for them while walking down the street, etc. I'm not sure that was my point. The point was to create an alleged heavenly being who was so real, so believable, and so likable, that a reader might reflect on God and the spiritual realm as also being so real, so believable, and so likable. We go through much of our lives pondering little but what we can see, smell, touch, taste, kiss, hug, and accumulate. The things that really matter—the pursuit of truth, love for one's neighbor, the essential awareness of our eternal nature—can get lost in the shuffle.

If I've accomplished any such pondering via *Lani Garver*, I'm deeply humbled. But as my mother used to say, "Shoot for the stars and you just might hit an airplane."

The Body of Christopher Creed

Some mysteries aren't meant to be solved.

Chris Creed grew up as the class freak—the bullies' punching bag. After he vanished, the weirdness that had once surrounded him began spreading. It was as if a darkness reached out of his void to grab at the most normal, happy people—like some twisted joke or demented form of justice. It tore the town apart.

Sixteen-year-old Torey Adams's search for answers opens his eyes to the lies, the pain, and the need to blame when tragedy strikes, and his once-safe world comes crashing down around him.

A MICHAEL L. PRINTZ AWARD HONOR BOOK

AN ALA BEST BOOK FOR YOUNG ADULTS

AN IRA CHILDREN'S CHOICE

★"Plum-Ucci knows her audience and provides her readers with enough twists, turns, and suspense to keep them absorbed."
—*School Library Journal* (starred review)

Turn the page to meet Christopher Creed . . .

Dear Mr. Ames,

I have a problem getting along with people. I know that people wish I were dead, and at this moment in time I see no alternative but to accommodate them in this wish. I have a wish. Not that anybody cares, but if anybody cared over the years, it was you. Here is my wish. I wish that I had been born somebody else—Mike Healy, José DeSantos, Tommy Ide, Evan Lucenti, Torey Adams, Alex Arrington . . .

I don't understand why I get nothing and these boys get everything—athletic ability, good personalities, beautiful girlfriends. I'm sure their parents will be buying them cars next year, while I will still be riding my bicycle until my parents decide I'm old enough. Quite possibly, I'll be twenty-five. I wish to understand life and luck and liberty. But I will never do that confined to this life, the personality defects I've been cursed with, the lack of abilities, the strain. I wish no malice on anyone. I only wish to be gone. Therefore, I AM.

> Yours respectfully,
> Christopher Creed

The She

A haunting search for truth

Eight years ago, on a rainy night in November, Evan Barrett's
parents were lost at sea as a panicked Evan listened to their
frantic Mayday calls on a ship-to-shore radio. There was no
way to save them, no way to explain the deafening shrieks
behind his mother's cries for mercy. Now, Evan has returned
to his home in West Hook to search for answers to his parents' disappearance. Were they swallowed up by The She, the
angry she-devil of legend that devours ships off the New Jersey coast? Or was it something else? Something more tan-
gible but equally unthinkable?

Turn the page to hear the Barretts' last transmission . . .

All of a sudden, I hear the shrieking of The She.

I drop the shoe box so I can put my fingers in my ears, but I'm stepping all over my toy navy men and I'm heavy and my heavy arms won't reach my head. I know The She and it takes me a minute to realize this time it sounds different. It's definitely her. But she's shut up in a box or a tomb. The sound is buried, not loud and free from over the ocean. She's . . . behind me. I spin.

Looking past the dark kitchen, I suddenly don't care that it's darker back there or that I'm rushing toward her voice. The closer I get to Dad's office, the louder her shrieking gets.

I stare at my dad's empty desk chair, then the ship-to-shore radio, hearing what my intuition tells me is a dream, but I'm wide awake.

"Coast Guard, this is the vessel *Goliath*. We are approximately eighty-four miles southeast of Atlantic City. We just lost power and a valve below the waterline. We have a list. We are caught in something, a very heavy current pulling us northeast. We are being . . . sucked—Mayday, Mayday. Coast Guard, this is the vessel *Goliath*—"

I grab for the handset and push down the button, which stops the shrieking, at least while I speak. "Mom? What's wrong? Over!"

The shrieking mixes with her voice while she's talking to me, to Dad next to her, it's all mixed together. "Oh, shit, we got the baby! Evan! Tell your brother to . . . Wade! What the hell is that? Over the port stern! Look with your eyes! Mother of God!"

I want to jump through the radio to get to my mom's screaming Maydays, and I want to bolt upstairs to get my brother, Emmett. I end up backing out slowly, hearing The She until she has almost overpowered my mother's voice, which is screaming. The sound is all through me then, coming from the sky, the beach, the radio.

I'm up the stairs, throwing open the door, but Emmett isn't there. I tear down the hall to the big wooden door and the stairway that leads up and around to the widow's walk. I pass my mom's padlock, hanging open, and try the stairs that go up and up and round and round. But I'm still a thousand pounds and I can feel myself being sucked down . . . into black, deep, dizzy, swirling black. I croak, "Emmett . . . ," but I'm falling backward . . . forever and ever falling.